Sky of Swords

Other Eos Books by
Dave Duncan

THE KING'S BLADES
The Gilded Chain
Lord of the Fire Lands

THE GREAT GAME
Past Imperative
Present Tense
Future Indefinite

THE KING'S DAGGERS
Sir Stalwart
Crooked House

www.daveduncan.com

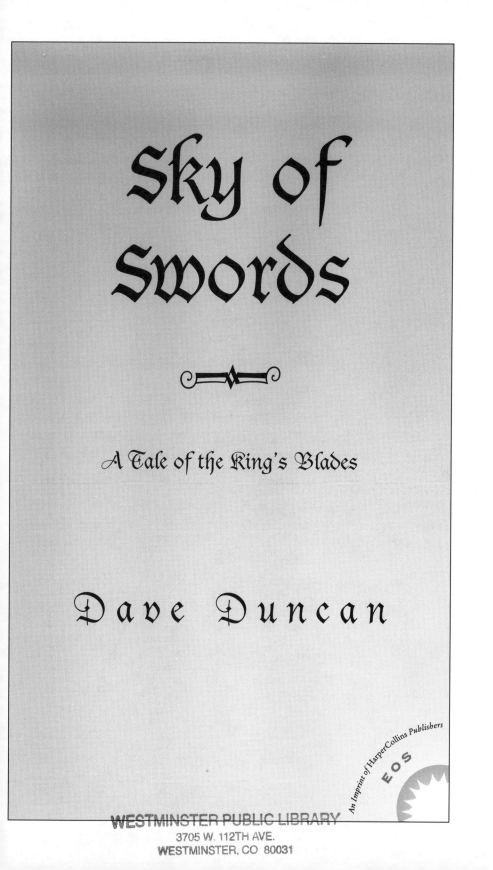

Sky of Swords

A Tale of the King's Blades

Dave Duncan

An Imprint of HarperCollins Publishers

EOS

EOS
An Imprint of HarperCollins*Publishers*
10 East 53rd Street
New York, New York 10022-5299

Library of Congress Cataloging in Publication Data
Duncan, Dave, 1933–
Sky of swords / Dave Duncan.
p. cm.
ISBN 0-380-97462-2 (alk. paper)
1. Swordplay—Fiction I. Title.
PR9199.3.D847 S58 2000
813'.54—dc21   00-037539

First Eos hardcover printing: October 2000

FIRST EDITION

RRD   10   9   8   7   6   5   4   3   2   1

www.eosbooks.com

Note

Like *The Gilded Chain* and *Lord of the Fire Lands*, this book can be read as a stand-alone novel. However, all three together tell a larger story, so if you read any two, you will discover discrepancies that can be resolved only by reading the complete set.

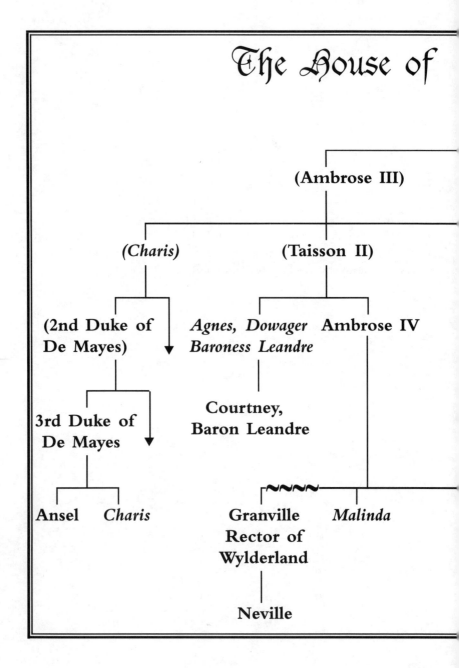

The House of

(Ambrose III)

(Charis)   (Taisson II)

(2nd Duke of De Mayes)   *Agnes, Dowager Baroness Leandre*   Ambrose IV

3rd Duke of De Mayes   Courtney, Baron Leandre

Ansel   *Charis*   Granville Rector of Wylderland   *Malinda*

Neville

Ranulf in 368

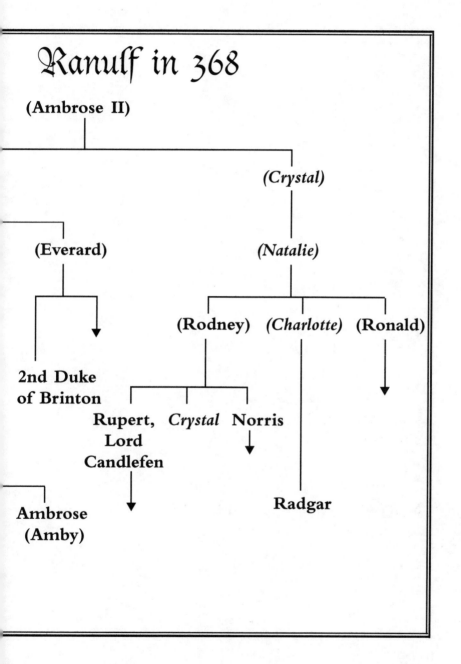

(Ambrose II)

(Crystal)

(Everard)

(Natalie)

(Rodney) (Charlotte) (Ronald)

2nd Duke
of Brinton

Rupert, Crystal Norris
Lord
Candlefen

Ambrose
(Amby)

Radgar

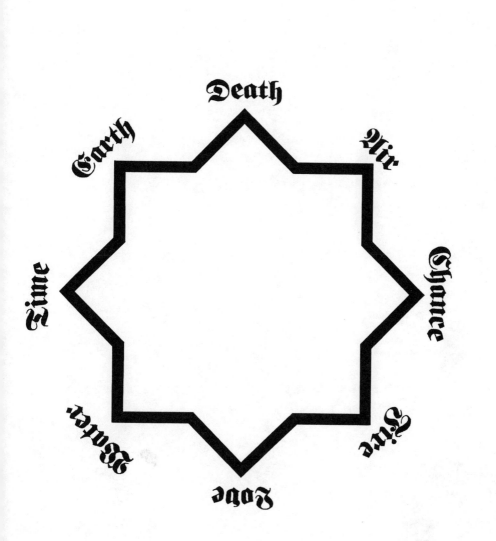

The Trial, Day One

Chin up and arms swinging, Malinda strode in through the doorway and sped along the hall, heading straight for Grand Inquisitor as if she intended to strangle him. Heels drummed on flagstones and metal clattered as her escort scrambled to keep up, for they were encumbered by their pikes and half armor, and not one of them was as tall as she.

The Hall of Banners in the Bastion was ancient and dowdy, with walls of bare stone and floor of planks, a gloomy barn at the best of times. On this squally spring day the wind was belching white clouds from the fireplace and rippling the soot-blackened tatters of ancient flags that hung from the high rafters. A hundred lanterns and candelabras barely raised a glitter from the dignitaries' finery. Behind scarlet-draped tables they sat, a row of thirteen commissioners stretching almost the whole width of the room with Grand Inquisitor in the center. A single unadorned wooden chair set in the center of the hall was presumably intended for Malinda, but she swept by it and kept on going until she came to a halt before the table, across from the horrible old man. The men-at-arms stamped to a stop behind her, and for a moment there was silence.

She had recognized him from the doorway by his height; even sitting he towered over the others at the table, the tallest man she had ever met, a human gallows. All inquisitors affected a glassy, unblinking stare as a reminder that they had a conjured ability to detect lies, but his skull-like features never revealed any expression whatsoever. Her father had appointed him to head the Dark Chamber and on her accession she had confirmed him in office, so he was one of those who had betrayed her. His treason had obviously prospered—he had been promoted. His red robes and the gold chain around his neck marked him as Lord Chancellor of Chivial; having been locked up for months, she knew nothing of recent events.

"By what right do you presume to maltreat me so?" she demanded. "Sending armed men to drag me here like a common felon!"

"Would you prefer to remain in your cell?" he murmured. Then louder—"Malinda of Ranulf, you are summoned in the King's name to—"

"The Usurper's name!"

The Chancellor's dark eyes were filmy, as if he had spilled milk in them, and hair like white cobwebs fringed his red hat, but age had not softened him. "You are indicted of high treason, numerous murders, evil and illegal conjuration, fornication, misprision, conspiracy to—"

"Considering my youth, I must have been exceedingly busy! As rightful Queen of Chivial, I do not recognize the authority of this court to try me on these or any other charges."

His name had been Horatio Lambskin on the night he swore allegiance to her. Now, as Chancellor, he would be Lord Something-or-other. He posed always as a bloodless state servant, an altruistic tool serving only the common weal. He probably believed his own lie, so he would not view his change of allegiance as a crime, just a higher loyalty. At the moment his mission was to see her condemned to death, but if he failed and she ever won back the throne that was rightfully hers, he might well turn up for work the following morning in full expectation of carrying on as before.

"I will acknowledge nothing less than a jury of my peers," she said.

They had found a way around that argument, of course. "This is not a court, mistress. A bill of attainder has been laid before Parliament, condemning you to death for high treason, divers murders, evil—"

"You sound like a parrot."

Nothing changed on the skull face. "If this bill is passed by Parliament and signed into law by His Majesty, then your head will be struck off. Parliament has therefore appointed a committee to consider the evidence against you. If you do not wish to testify, you have the right to remain silent."

Meaning she was under no duress to answer, except that she would be beheaded if she did not. If she did, she would be beheaded anyway. He was also threatening to send her back to her lonely cell, where she had languished so long without conversation or comfort or news of her friends, where every day lasted a week and a month was a year. He must know that she would do almost anything to stay here in human company for a while, even submit to the ordeal of being questioned and browbeaten.

She glanced quickly at the judges—six men to right and six to left, not one under fifty, all in furs and satins, gold and gems, a flock of kingfishers. Those closest to the chair were peers, in coronets and ermine-trimmed scarlet robes. The burghers at the outer ends were birds of lesser plumage, but even their grandiose jerkins and cloaks and plumed hats were in clear violation of the sumptuary laws. She knew all of them except two of the commoners, for they had done homage to her, swearing to be faithful and true. Amazingly, several of them were able to look her in the eye even yet. She noted the insipid Lord Candlefen, who was a distant cousin, and the Honorable Alfred Kildare still sporting the regalia of the Speaker of the Commons. . . . They had been sent here to condemn her, which they would not find difficult—two days' work, maybe three, to pretend they had tried to be fair.

So why bother? Why not just drag her out to meet the ax? Because the proprieties must be observed. Parliament must be shown evidence of some sort before it could pass the bill. Then its members could go home to the shires and towns of Chivial and report that the ex-queen had been a monster and her execution just. Nor was Chivial alone. Rulers of other lands would greet the execution of a monarch with screams of outrage. In the shadows behind the commissioners sat a hundred or so lesser folk: clerks and flunkies and certainly more inquisitors to detect falsehoods, but among them she recognized men she had seen in attendance on ambassadors and consuls. So at least part of the reason for this mock trial was to convince other lands in Eurania and perhaps to win foreign recognition of the Usurper. There would have to be some pretense of fairness, however slight.

"I protest this injustice!" She addressed the chairman, but she was speaking to the witnesses at his back. "I was given less than a full day's warning of this hearing. I have barely had time to read the charges against me, let alone prepare a defense. I have been held in solitary confinement for half a year without news or servants or even books. I am denied legal counsel, denied a jury of my peers, and yet I am expected to answer for my—"

"This is not a courtroom. Will you or will you not cooperate with the inquiry?"

"I shall happily advise the noble lords and honorable members of the truth of these matters, provided certain reasonable conditions are met. I require that I be given the royal honors due me: a chair of state, a royal title—"

"The hearings are now in session, Mistress Ranulph, and if you remain obdurate, you will be returned whence you came."

He might not be bluffing. This brief appearance might be all they needed to convince the foreign observers that she was still alive and had refused a chance to tell her side of the story.

"Let the minutes show that I testify only under extreme protest!" She spun on her heel and strode back to that lonely chair in the middle. There she would have to speak over-loudly to make her case and would be constantly aware of her isolation—all very typical of the Dark Chamber's methods.

"The committee will come to order," the chairman said. "Master Secretary, pray remind the noble lords and honorable members of the wording of Clause I."

A weedy voice began whining behind him. Malinda squirmed on the hard seat and adjusted her skirts, well aware that her dress fell far short of court standards, for although it was the best she had, carefully stowed away against the long-hoped-for date of her release, moths and mildew had taken their toll. Her jewels had all been confiscated, of course. She had been forced to dress her own hair without a mirror or even a decent comb.

Strategy . . . she must think strategy. Somewhere beyond these gruesome walls, out in the world of smiles and sunshine, her supporters would be plotting on her behalf, although of course they dare do little while she was a prisoner. The Usurper could not rest easy on his ill-gotten throne as long as the rightful Queen of Chivial lived. Assassination was what she had expected: poison or poniard or the silken noose. Every new dawn had been a surprise. She had not seriously considered the possibility of a public execution, and a public trial she had never even dreamed of before the warrant for this inquiry was thrust in her hand the previous day. Perhaps Lord Chancellor Whatever-his-name-was-now did not have Parliament quite so much under control as he would like. Had an outcry forced the Usurper to stage this farce?

Dare she consider the faint possibility that she might not be going to die of it? Alas, when hope flickered, the rage that had sustained her waned and gave way to fear, so that the skin on her arms puckered in gooseflesh and her fingers began to shake. She was on trial for her life and the deck was stacked against her.

The clerk had stopped.

One of the peers jumped in with a question. ". . . that you conspired to effect the murder of your father, His Late Majesty Ambrose IV—"

"No!" she snapped. "I deny that charge utterly."

"How would you describe your relations with your father? Warm? Loyal? Dutiful?"

"It was no secret," Malinda said deliberately. "As a child I was taught to hate him, fear him, and despise him. When I was old enough to make up my own mind, I found no reason to alter those opinions. He drove his first two wives insane and murdered the third; his fourth was to be a girl a month younger than I. I sincerely believe that he was a strong and effective king of Chivial and the realm has suffered greatly from his untimely death. In his private life he was a tyrant, and I never loved him, but his death was not something I planned or desired."

She had never intended to kill him. That had been an oversight.

1

Love can hurt: that is the last lesson of childhood.
FONATELLES

On a bright and frosty morning in Eleventhmoon, Malinda came awake with a start, remembering that this was the second day of her ninth birthweek. She jumped out of bed and opened the door to peer along the corridor at the Blade who sat at the top of the stairs near her mother's door, guarding her as he was bound to do. Blades were all built much the same, lean and nimble, and Queen Godeleva's two were so much alike that Malinda could not be certain from this angle whether she was seeing Sir de Fait or Sir Arundel. It didn't matter in the slightest. What did matter was that he was wearing forest green livery. The Queen's Blades rarely brought out those outfits now, for seven years' exile had left them patched and darned and faded. Their swords were still as sharp as ever, or so they claimed.

Sensing her eyes on him, the Blade closed his book on a finger and turned his head to smile at her. It was Sir de Fait.

"Today?" she said. "He'll come *today*?"

Yesterday there had been a grand party to celebrate her birthweek. Almost the entire population of the island had packed into the hall, bringing strong odors of sheep and other livestock—not fish, fortunately, for Ness Royal had no port. She had been given wonderful gifts: a gown of golden silk made by Mistress de Fait, a sheepskin bedcover from Lady Arabel, and *hundreds* of horn buttons, bird nets, wooden whistles, and other things made by the children of the island;

gloves and bed socks knitted by their mothers. Remembering the courtly manners Lady Arabel tried so hard to teach her, she had given thanks for every one, even if she did now have about fifty-seven wooden whistles and no use for any of them. Her mother had given her a leather-bound book of poetry she couldn't understand but would when she was older.

Other people's birthweeks were not so honored, but Malinda was Heir Presumptive—as she would happily explain to anyone who did not understand how important that made her—and every year her father the Monster sent her a gift, a very special gift. Last year, it had been a necklace of blood-red garnets; the year before, a clock with a cuckoo that came out to chirp the hours; and before that a cloak of sable, soft as smoke. The cloak was too small for her now, the cuckoo's works had rusted in the damp sea winds, and she was not allowed to wear the necklace outside of Kingstead itself, in case she forgot and went exploring caves or climbing cliffs in it, but the Monster's gift was always the most special part of her birthweek. A Blade came all the way from Greymere Palace in Grandon, three or even four days' hard riding, just to kneel to the Heir Presumptive and proffer her a package and a beautifully lettered scroll, both sealed with the royal signet. She never knew exactly which day the wonderful event would occur, because the roads could be very bad so late in the year and Kingstead's count of the moon might not be exactly the same as Grandon's. But Queen Godeleva's two Blades always knew when the day had arrived. They said it was part of the enchantment that bound them, like the sword stroke through the heart.

Sir de Fait nodded and put a finger to his lips.

"Is Mother awake yet?" Malinda spoke loudly, because she knew that nothing would happen until the Queen was up and dressed.

He frowned and shook his head.

Malinda went back inside, slamming the door. She walked across to the window to scowl out at the blue-green sea—white surf and white birds; the cliffs of the coast fading away into misty distance. She saw no whales, no seals, not even fishing boats.

How long to wait? Her mother's hours were unpredictable. She spent nights and days immersed in spiritual lore, poring over books of spells, corresponding with conjurers in both Chivial and other lands, ever seeking an enchantment to bring back the King's love. Once in a while she would emerge to lecture the world on her misfortunes, and then even Malinda was required to address her as Your Majesty or Your Grace. The price of a cuddle on her mother's knee was listening to yet another tirade on the evil deeds of the Monster. She had gradually come to realize that the price was too high. She was well aware that Mistress de Fait and Lady Arabel had effectively adopted her into their families; the Blades were her fathers, their children her siblings. She was, she supposed, grateful. She certainly could not imagine life without them around.

Deciding she would have time to dress properly later, Malinda pulled on what she had been wearing the previous day, except that she chose shoes with harder soles. Then she went in search of breakfast, skipping noisily past her mother's door.

She had a long way to go, but not because Kingstead was large as royal houses went. It wasn't—it had been put together by joining several buildings into one. She slept up on the cliff top; the hall was down in the hollow, among the trees. Lots of stairs. The moment she entered, Dian de Fait came running to hug her. Dian was Malinda's *most special* friend. They shared a love of horses, hair-raising exploration, and contempt for authority. They had differences, naturally. Dian tended to plumpness, and was ever eager to hug and cuddle; Malinda was gangling and had to watch her royal dignity. Dian kept one arm around her all the way over to the Queen's table, where Lady Arabel and Mistress de Fait sat, deep in conversation.

The two ladies were almost as hard to tell apart at a distance as their husbands were. They were both rotund, motherly, and enormously fertile. They differed in that Mistress de Fait was blond and pink and always bore a scent of fresh bread or pastry. As a native of Fishport, just along the coast, she loved Ness Royal's wild solitude, the cry of gulls, the constant rumble of surf. Lady Arabel was dark and ruddy faced and smelled of flowers; as an earl's daughter she had retained her title when she married a commoner and was the Queen's official matron companion. She sighed for the bustle and petty intrigues of court, and told endless tales of its dazzling balls and masques. The two ladies between them instructed the forsaken princess in the gentle arts of reading, dancing, and music; their husbands taught her riding and archery. Now they broke off their talk and rose to offer the Princess curtsies. That was new! Perhaps being nine made a difference. She was a lady now.

Malinda acknowledged them with a nod and squiggled onto the bench, close enough so she could eavesdrop without being too obvious. "Good morning, ladies. Is not the weather clement for so late in the season?" That was a courtly pleasantry Lady Arabel had taught her, and the ladies responded. . . . Was something wrong? Unable to put her finger on what troubled her, Malinda turned to her friend. Dian was sitting much too close, as usual. She did that to everyone, as if she had to be in contact with someone all the time, no matter who. Her mother called her the human flea.

"Your father says this is to be the day!" Malinda said offhandedly.

"Course it is. It's going to be Sir Dominic, same as last year. He is *so* handsome!"

"You don't know that!"

Dian's eyes gleamed with triumphant confidence. "Do so! He arrived yesterday. He spent the night in Widow Nan's cottage."

Malinda gaped, dreams shattering. Was *that* how the Blades knew every year? Had everyone been laughing at her all this time?

"Don't tattle scandal, Dian!" Mistress de Fait said sharply. "Widow Nan has a spare room she rents to visitors."

Not unless she slept with the pig, she didn't, but Malinda was not concerned with Widow Nan. The story was improbable anyway, because Blades did not sleep and so did not need beds. "*Did* he come yesterday?"

"Late last night," Dian's mother admitted. "He needs time to clean up after riding so far, doesn't he? You wouldn't want him stomping in here all muddy and stinking of horse, would you?"

"No," Malinda agreed, but she still felt betrayed. How many people had cooperated to deceive her? She chose an apple to eat. The apples were almost finished now, and there would be no more until she was almost *ten*! Nice to think she was in her *tenth year* now.

"Just be glad it wasn't a royal courier," said Dian, "because he would drag you out of bed no matter what hour it was. Besides, the Chamberlain does give the letter to the couriers, but the Blades deliver it for them just so they can see how my dad and Sir—"

"Dian!" her mother growled.

"It's true! Blades stick together like fish scales, Dad says."

Lady Arabel intervened. "That may be a very small part of the reason the Blades deliver the King's gift, but it's the Princess they really want to see. Remember that most Blades are only bound to a single ward, but the Blades of the Guard are sworn to defend the King *and his heirs and successors.* So Princess Malinda is sort of the Royal Guard's ward, too, because she's the heir."

Malinda considered that explanation and decided it was satisfactory. "Well, what really matters is that the Monster remembers to—"

Mistress de Fait snapped, *"Princess!"* just as Lady Arabel barked, *"Your Highness!"*

Lady Arabel was the louder. "You must stop using that word, dear. You should always refer to your royal father as His Majesty or His Grace or—"

"The Queen says—"

"Your dear mother has suffered a lot of distress in her life, and—"

"Eight miscarriages, six stillbirths, and twelve years of tyranny."

"And don't repeat that, either!" Lady Arabel rolled her eyes at Mistress de Fait.

They rarely reacted this way. Suspicious, Malinda tried again. "He thought the Blond Bitch would give him sons, but after seven years she can't even show willing with a miscarriage or two."

"Oh, spirits!" Mistress de Fait muttered. "How long have we got?"

"Not long enough, that's certain."

There *was* something wrong, and the remarks Lady Arabel now made concerning omens for a mild winter were clearly designed to change the subject.

Malinda reached for a slab of bread and the honey pot. Sir Dominic would be acceptable. He was a younger version of her mother's Blades, except he had golden eyebrows and no eyelashes. His sword was called *Bonebiter*. He could make his horse walk backward. He could also toss an apple in the air and cut it into *four* pieces before it reached the ground—although she suspected he made the first cut before he started and the two halves stuck together when he threw them up.

It seemed *years* before everyone was ready and assembled in the hall: the Queen on her chair of state, the Princess on a lesser chair beside her, Dian standing alongside as her maid of honor, Lady Arabel on the far side as matron companion, Sir Arundel on guard, and all the servants positioned along the walls as a pretend court. Queen Godeleva wore a jeweled tiara, but her dress was her usual formal scarlet, a bit shabby now, its lace trim bedraggled and limp. She was very thin; her hair was streaked with white and even a child's eye could see that it needed more care. Her ink-stained fingers fumbled continuously with a heap of letters on her lap. Once in a while she would drop one, and Dian or Lady Arabel would pick it up and return it to her. Every year the heap was larger. The Blade always took them and promised to deliver them to His Majesty. Malinda always wondered why her mother wrote to a monster.

Whatever had been bothering the other women did not seem to have affected Queen Godeleva. As a change from bouncing up and down on her chair with excitement, Malinda decided to experiment.

"It is kind of the Monster to remember my birthweek, isn't it?"

Her mother uttered a horsey snort. "He doesn't remember you even exist! When he packed you off with me, he probably told the

Lord Chamberlain to send something every year. It'll still be coming when you're a hundred years old."

Genuinely shocked, Malinda said, "But he writes, and in such a beautiful hand. . . ."

"No he doesn't. That's a scribe's hand. His own scribble is totally illegible, and he never uses words like that. The Chamberlain would have told a clerk to write something appropriate."

"Oh." Malinda subsided, not looking at Dian or anyone. Looking at the floor. Her eyes prickled. Was there to be no end to today's disappointments?

Then a hinge squeaked. It was time! Sir de Fait slipped in through the great door at the far end of the hall, not quite closing it behind him. Malinda's heart began to race.

"Your Grace!" he cried. "A messenger approaches."

"Open the door and let us see this messenger!" the Queen commanded.

Last year that order had resulted in a whirl of snowflakes, but this year the sun streamed in. A horseman was galloping furiously up the driveway. When he reached the step he reined in his horse so that it reared up on its hind legs, pawing the air with its iron hooves. The rider sprang nimbly from the saddle, pausing only to hand the reins to a waiting groom. Yes, he wore the blue and silver livery of the Royal Guard! Yes, it was Sir Dominic. He ran up the steps and came striding along the hall, clutching a package under one arm and waving his sword overhead.

"Princess Malinda!" he shouted. "Lead me to Her Grace, for I bear an urgent dispatch for the Princess Heir of Chivial. Where is the fair damsel? Woe betide any who dares hinder me in this quest!"

"Stay!" shouted Sir Arundel, drawing his sword and striding forward. "Who dares invade these halls in such warlike mien?"

A few years ago, when Malinda was just a child, she had been deliciously terrified by this charade, which happened every year. Even now, grown up as she was, she found its make-believe flattering and exciting. The real fun, though, came when it was over, when the swords were sheathed and Sir Dominic was on one knee before her, offering the scroll and the silk-wrapped package. It was too big to be a necklace this year, too small to be another cloak. She took it on her lap with trembling hands. The scroll she handed unopened to Dian. Later she would read whatever the unknown clerk had thought to write.

She fingered the seal, felt the package all over. "It's a basket! And it's heavy, so there's something in it."

"There had flaming well better be," Sir Dominic murmured. He blinked innocently when Malinda looked at him, and she smothered a snigger.

She took her time unwrapping the basket. After all, this excitement had to last her a whole year! It was a squarish hamper, beautifully gilded. There was an enameled crest on the lid, bearing her monogram in crimson and silver. Everyone was watching breathlessly. She undid the clasp and lifted the lid. She found lamb's wool packing.

"Sir Dominic!" said the Queen impatiently.

With just the faintest hint of a sigh, he rose and bowed to her. "Your Grace."

"Last year I gave you certain missives—"

"I delivered them as I promised, my lady."

Malinda's probing fingers were detecting crystal bottles, carefully stoppered. She cleared the packing away and lifted one out.

"Then why has he never replied? Not once!" Queen Godeleva held out the double handful of letters. "I have written more forcefully, perhaps even temerariously—"

"I brought a dispatch for Your Grace," Sir Dominic said quietly, producing an envelope that bore an imposing seal.

Malinda paused with her fingers on the stopper of the scent bottle. No one was watching her. Whatever it was that was *wrong* was suddenly here. Even six cut-crystal vials of the rarest and most exotic perfumes were not as important as that letter.

For a long moment Godeleva seemed shocked to stone. Then, with a piercing cry, she let her own correspondence fall higgledy-piggledy to the floor. "My recall? At last?"

"I cannot say, Your Grace."

Yet the Queen's hands hesitated above the Blade's offering as if it were a scorpion. When she took it, she held it very reluctantly, by the edges, and only long enough to read the inscription. *"This is not addressed to me!"* She tried to hurl it in Dominic's face, but it was not made for hurling. It fluttered. "There is no *Lady Godeleva* in this place! I am Queen, do you hear? *Queen!*"

Dominic had deftly snatched the letter out of the air. "A scrivener's error, I am certain, Your Grace." He offered it again.

"May I assist, Your Majesty?" Lady Arabel took the letter, broke the seal, unfolded the heavy paper, and handed it to her mistress. Malinda sat forgotten, still clutching a scent bottle, frozen like everyone else.

The document trembled and crackled in Godeleva's hands. She seemed to have trouble understanding the words, although Malinda had seen that the text was very brief.

The Queen emitted an ear-splitting scream. "No! He shall not have her! Mine! Leave me alone in this awful place?" She leaped from her chair and grabbed Malinda up into her arms. The royal gift crashed to the floor in a carillon of breaking glass. A choking fog of scent billowed up, nipping eyes and choking throats. Godeleva screamed again, even longer and louder. So did Malinda.

The women rescued Malinda. The former Queen fled howling from the hall with Sir Arundel in pursuit; Lady Arabel and Mistress de Fait trailed after them.

Sir de Fait carried Malinda outside, well away from the hysterics, confusion, and sickly stench of perfume. Sir Dominic seemed about to follow, but then changed his mind. The two of them went on alone, up the grassy hill until they stood on the crest of the cliff, staring out over the blue sea. There the Blade set her on her feet and knelt beside her. The salt wind ruffled their hair and made the weeds dance. He put an arm around her.

"That was a shame about your gift. I'm sure the King will replace it when he hears what happened."

Malinda was still sobbing too hard to argue, so she just shook her head. What need had she of perfume?

"Did you understand what was in your mother's letter?" he asked.

"I won't go!" She turned her back on him. But she didn't run away.

"You're a princess, my lady. Your destiny is to marry a prince and live in a palace. You can't rot away in this backwater pigsty any—" He broke off with a cry and leaped to his feet.

Blades were incredibly fast, but de Fait was not quite fast enough to grab Malinda and turn her away or cover her eyes. She saw her mother fly from the terrace and plunge down to the surf far, far below. And then it was de Fait's turn to scream. "Idiot! Criminal!" His curses faded as he raced for the house, leaving her alone.

Bereaved Blades had been known to run amok and slay bystanders indiscriminately, but in this case they merely went for each other. The only man who might have stopped them, Sir Dominic, reached the scene too late. Arundel died within minutes and de Fait the following day, apparently more of a broken heart than of his wounds. It was tragic, but it could have been worse.

The day after that the royal coach arrived with a six-Blade escort to conduct Princess Malinda to court.

2

The Princess is of a stature uncommon in women, but of pleasing form and in no wise unfeminine, being as graceful in the minuet as she is nimble in the galliard. Her features are illuminated by a wondrous complexion and unmarred by any unseemly asymmetry, although they denote firmness of character rather than humility, and it is said that her blushes stem more often from spirit than maidenly shyness. She is a daring equestrian, favors the falcon over the spindle and archery above the spinet, and is capable of drawing a full war bow as well as any man-at-arms, having once felled a stag at near eighty paces before several witnesses of quality. The sharpness of her wit has caused much merriment but also some offense, regarding which her royal father has seen fit to chide her betimes.

FROM A DISPATCH FILED BY THE ISILONDIAN AMBASSADOR,

FIRSTMOON, 368

Deprived at a stroke of friends, family, and the only home she knew, Malinda entered upon the most miserable year of her life. At Ness Royal she had rarely seen a stranger from one month to the next; now she was buried in an ants' nest of strangers. All eyes were on her, all ears at her door. Worse, her ogre father was everywhere, striding through his palaces at the head of his retinue, huge in his silks and furs, resplendent with gems and gold, piggy little eyes missing nothing. Great lords shivered when he frowned and guffawed in helpless merriment at his slightest quip. He regarded Malinda with distaste. Even the fact that she was tall and strong merely reminded him that she should have been a boy.

The only person she knew at court was Sir Dominic. Kind though he was, he could spare little time for the King's child, and he was too intelligent to give the court vipers cause to hiss.

If Godeleva had been a bad mother, Sian was a hundred times worse. After seven years' marriage, she remained incorrigibly barren and terrified of the King's growing displeasure. With His Majesty displaying more than usual interest in the debutantes, everyone knew which way the wind was turning.

Sian appointed Lady Millet to be the Princess's governess and assumed she had done all that was necessary. Lady Millet was about the worst possible choice—she was young and giddy, and her main interest was spicing up her diary with Blade stories. Blades were notoriously promiscuous, but Millet seemed intent on collecting the entire Guard.

Surprisingly, it was almost a year before Sian was caught trying to rectify her infertility with the aid of her own Blades, although whether just Sir Wyvern or all four of them by turns was never clearly established. Convicted of treason, she was beheaded one chilly morning in Tenthmoon. After lunch the King married Lady Haralda.

The new Queen was little older than Malinda, a dainty child of sylphlike beauty, silken manners, and iron will. Having been well coached by a regiment of harridan aunts, she tolerated no bullying from her royal master. She was reported—on very dubious authority—to have remarked that husband management was merely a question of learning to sleep with one's knees together.

Although she had the King appoint one of her many elderly aunts, Lady Wains, to be the Princess's governess, in effect she handled most of a governess's duties herself, treating Malinda like a younger sister. She brought the impoverished Lady Arabel to court as Malinda's Mistress of the Robes. She arranged for Arabel to bring Dian with her, so the Princess would have a friend—Mistress de Fait was already remarried and content to remain on Ness Royal. The Queen worked hard to bring father and daughter together, starting with their mutual interests in music, dancing, and fine horses. If her success was limited, the fault was not entirely Malinda's.

There was, notably, the spring morning when the eleven-year-old Princess was playing the spinet for the Queen and her ladies. Torn between an intense dislike of performing like a trained dog and an innate determination to master anything she attempted, Malinda made heavy work of the new piece. Having struggled through to the end, she was intensely annoyed by the applause that she knew she had not earned. At that moment, a Blade threw open the door and the King marched in. Of course the women all sprang to their feet and then curtseyed, so possibly he did not notice that his daughter was present. He raised Haralda and bussed her cheek.

"Good news, my sweet!" he boomed. "I've just betrothed that

daughter of mine to the De Mayes boy, Ansel. We must have a family dinner tonight to celebrate."

Malinda squealed, "What?" and came charging through the ladies-in-waiting to accost her father. "That little *toad*? That *pustule*?"

Stupefied by such insolence, the King roared. "You don't speak to me like that!"

Malinda was too angry to heed the danger. "I am a princess—I must marry a prince!" Recalling a scrap of conversation that had certainly not been intended for her ears, she added, "Are you skimping on my dowry?"

Predictably, the result was a disaster. She was whipped and confined to her room for several days. Ansel was actually an inoffensive lad of royal descent, her second cousin once removed. Although even the notoriously plainspoken Duchess of De Mayes never raved about her son's good qualities, he did not deserve to be classified as either amphibian or sebaceous cyst. His real defect in Malinda's eyes was that he was five years younger than she was.

Another memorable catastrophe followed a few months later, when the King learned that she had taken to riding astride again, instead of sidesaddle. That was how she had been taught to ride by Sir Arundel, but at court the practice was regarded as unladylike, fit only for peasant women on donkeys. She had been repeatedly forbidden and had repeatedly disobeyed. Ambrose exploded in a memorable tantrum.

"You brazen, self-willed brat!" he roared. "You think you can get your own way all the time. You think you can have anything you fancy!"

Alas! Malinda again forgot how to address a monarch. "Tiger's a *stallion*!" she shouted. "I'd like to see *you* try to ride him sidesaddle!"

The King almost choked. "Anyone else would be sent to the Bastion for that." He turned the royal fury on Sir Hoare, Commander of the Royal Guard. "You knew this was rank defiance! Why did you not see that our commands were obeyed?"

Of course Malinda went nowhere without a Blade or two in attendance. She got along well with them, and she especially liked Sir Hoare, who had an impish humor and treated her with the respect due the Heir Presumptive. Now he even defied the King for her.

"With respect, sire, we are spiritually bound to protect your honored daughter from peril. She has inherited your own skill and daring on horseback, and obviously riding astride is safer than—"

"She is not allowed to go steeplechasing!"

The Commander was probably the only man in the kingdom who would have dared resist the royal anger at that level. "We cannot be guardians and governesses at the same time, sire. If Her Highness thinks we are spying on her and starts distrusting us, our duties will become impossible."

Purple-faced, Ambrose swung a blow at him. Hoare evaded it nimbly. He evaded its successor also, and the King did not try a third time.

Alas! Within a week Sir Hoare was gone, replaced as Commander by a Blade Malinda had not previously met, Sir Durendal, newly returned from some mysterious mission overseas. He turned out to be one of the King's closest toadies and quite impervious to both wiles and threats from the Heir Presumptive.

When the long-awaited word came that another heir was on the way, Malinda celebrated as heartily as anyone, happy for her stepmother's happiness. The King was ecstatic and typically overreacted. His attitude to enchantment had always been unpredictable. One year he would spend fortunes on good-luck charms and prophecies, and the next he would threaten to drive every conjurer from the realm. Now he decreed that the Queen must reside until her confinement at the remote palace of Bondhill; then he cleared the countryside for leagues around of every hint of spirituality. Alas, conjuration had its uses, and healing was one of them. The Queen was delivered of a healthy boy, but all the doctors' efforts could not stop her bleeding. After days of futile efforts, they loaded her in a coach for a mad dash to the nearest remaining octogram. They were too late.

Malinda mourned far more deeply for Haralda than she had for her mother. Many times she cursed her father's stubborn folly, although never when she might be overheard.

To his credit, the King was devastated. For months he rarely appeared in public, and Lord Chancellor Montpurse ran the kingdom. It was during those months that Princess Malinda crossed the mystic bridge into womanhood. Although she was no longer heir, only her missing father and infant brother outranked her—a heady and dangerous position for a fourteen-year-old. When she entered a room, everyone rose; men stepped aside and bowed when she walked a hallway; she alone was entitled to a cloth of estate above her chair. Haralda's steadying hand had gone, but neither the distraught King nor the overworked Chancellor realized that no other had taken its place. Lady Wains, her token governess, was sliding into a contented dotage.

Already her household had grown beyond counting, like a weed-filled garden. It included lords and ladies she had never met, such as the octogenarian Earl of Dimpleshire, hereditary cupbearer to the monarch's oldest daughter. In the absence of a queen, every aristocratic wife in the country was anxious to be appointed an honorary lady-in-waiting to the Princess, although few of them ever came to court. They also wished their marriageable daughters to be maids of honor. They especially wanted their unmarriageable daughters, unwed aunts, and widowed mothers out of their way and living at the King's expense. The task of sorting out the politics and keeping Malinda's actual retinue to a manageable yet respectable three or four ladies-in-waiting and four or five maids of honor belonged to Lady Crystal, her matron companion. No one in her right mind would have taken on that job voluntarily, but Crystal's family, the Candlefens, had been out of favor for many years. Her appointment was a sort of probation for all of them, a first step in a rehabilitation that might take a generation. She was a frail, ineffectual woman, so terrified of incurring royal displeasure that Malinda found her easy to manipulate.

Lady Arabel remained Mistress of the Robes. She had distributed her numerous children around the minor gentry of the land as pages or maids of honor, but the problem of finding future dowries for the girls weighed heavily on her, making her utterly dependent on Malinda's favor. Her greatest value in Malinda's eyes was her instinct for gossip—mistress of the rumors, Malinda called her.

There was Dian de Fait. Not being of noble blood, she could rank no higher than servant, but soon after Queen Haralda's death, Malinda maneuvered her into the stewardship post of Lady of the Bedchamber. Then Dian could help support her mother, whose new husband back on Ness Royal provided little except more children.

Wains, Crystal, Arabel, and Dian—those four comprised Malinda's innermost, constant household. Around them flourished a rose garden of ladies-in-waiting and maids of honor, and beyond them stood a veritable forest of servants and officials. Courtly titles were often misleading. Her comptroller was a clerk in the office of Chancery, but her chamberlain was one of the Brintons, distant ducal cousins who must be kept happy with a few meaningless appointments. Her master of the horse was Baron Leandre, a closer cousin still, but a courtly fop who did not know a horse from a mule.

After Haralda's death, Malinda was pretty much her own mistress. She moved with the court from palace to palace throughout the year—Nocare, Oldmart, Greymere, and others—staying out of her father's way as much as possible. By now she knew most of the aristocracy of Chivial, so from time to time she would choose an interesting-sounding country house close to Grandon and invite herself and her train to visit. Lady Wains would sign anything put in front of her and Chancery would return it sealed with the King's approval. Whether or not he had seen it was immaterial. These excursions were a welcome escape from the million sharp eyes at court.

That she did not stumble into any major scandals during this period was a tribute to her native common sense. If her needle wit made enemies, they were content to bide their time.

When the King took up the scepter again, his puzzling cygnet had become an oversized swan, the cynosure of court. Like many another father before him, he was somewhat at a loss when dealing with the young woman who had unexpectedly replaced his girl child. He let her have her head as long as she behaved herself; she took care not to cross him.

Their truce prospered; by the time she turned sixteen, late in 367, he was boasting of her abilities to ambassadors and letting her act as official hostess at state banquets. He had Chancellor Montpurse swear her in as a privy councillor—while making it clear that she would not actually attend meetings. He held a very impressive state ball in honor of her birthweek, thus cuing the Lord Mayor of Grandon to offer her the keys of the city and Parliament to pass an address of congratulation.

One guest necessarily invited to the celebrations was her betrothed, Lord Ansel, now a sandy-haired sprat of eleven whose head did not reach her shoulder. At her age many ladies were already married or even mothers, while she still had at least another five years of spinsterhood to look forward to, followed by a lifetime of Ansel. He pleaded indisposition, a timely attack of chicken pox.

His mother came, though. "Very fortunate!" she barked in her customary tactless fashion. "He's even more relieved than you are. If you don't fancy the match, think how it looks to him. His wife is always going to outrank him. Even if he starts shaving early, you'll be an old woman of at least twenty-one, and probably a foot taller."

Still, that ghastly wedding day was a long time off yet. As the year 368 began, Princess Malinda was enjoying her life at court. She was unquestioned leader of the younger set, flirting mildly with young male aristocrats or Blades as she fancied, but careful never to give the old cats any scandal to whet their claws. She did not love her father, thinking of him as a sort of semidomesticated dragon, a useful guardian to be tiptoed around, never disturbed. She was even losing her fear of him, which was to prove a serious error. The terrible Night of Dogs shocked her—and a great many other people—into realizing that Ambrose IV was mortal and the country needed him. For a brief period, father and daughter were brought together by real danger.

3

Palaces always have secret doors.
SIR SNAKE

A bell tolled in the distance, punctuating the winter night with heavy, mournful strokes. Neither asleep nor quite awake, Malinda wondered fuzzily why. Then . . . women screaming, doors slamming, male voices shouting. She sat up and dragged the topmost quilt around her shivering shoulders, even as the chamber door creaked open and candlelight flickered through chinks where the bed curtains did not quite meet.

"My lady?" Dian squeaked. "My lady!"

"Who is there, Dian?" Malinda found the relative calmness of her own voice gratifying, if certainly misleading.

"Swordsmen! Blades! Not the Guard!"

"Swordsmen" might mean revolution and a squad of assassins, and Blades would be serving their ward, who might not be the King. Only the Guard was unquestionably loyal to the sovereign and his heirs. *Not* the Guard . . .

"My cloak! What do they want?"

"Emergency, Your Grace," said a baritone. "Sir Snake, knight in the Order. Remember me?" Heavy tread crossed the room. "You may be in danger. You will come with us at once, please. You and no more than two companions."

Shutters slammed. Bolts slid—*ridiculous!* This chamber was two stories above the courtyard. More boots entering . . . Dian stuffed a heavy cloak in through the draperies.

"Shoes, any shoes." Malinda pushed a leg out while she was still pulling the cloak around her; she hauled off her absurd nightcap. She felt Dian slide a shoe onto one foot, and provided the other. As she slid down off the bed and out through the curtains, her hair tumbled loose around her. The room was already full of armed men bearing lanterns, with frightened and disheveled women peering through between them. She recognized only two faces—Sir Snake and Sir Jarvis. Out in the antechamber, old Lady Wains was shrieking in confused terror above a continuo of younger hysterics.

"You come with me!" Malinda jabbed a finger at Dian, who was wearing only a nightgown. "And you, Lady Crystal. Arabel, see that the racket out there stops immediately."

"This is monstrous!" Crystal cried shrilly. "Who are these men? Summon the Guard! Her Highness will not—"

She was drowned out by shouting as the swordsmen hustled the unwanted women away. Sir Jarvis shut and bolted the chamber door behind them, leaving six men, Malinda, Crystal, and Dian inside.

Malinda's heart circled the inside of her chest like a trapped bat. Still the great bell tolled, more faintly now. At least three Blades guarded her apartment at night, so these intruders had either killed them to gain admittance—which was highly improbable—or the Blades had gone rushing off to protect their ward, the King. That implied a major threat. "What is the danger, Sir Snake? And why have you locked us in here with no—"

"Back door, my lady." Sir Snake was well named, being exceedingly lean and having a reputation for subtlety. He had been Deputy Commander before Sir Dreadnought. "This way, if you please."

Another man had tugged a section of paneling loose, making it creak open on reluctant hinges. Yet another stepped through the gap, and the light of his lantern gleamed on the damp stone walls of an extremely narrow passage. "May be easier if you carry this lantern, mistress," Snake added cheerfully. "Look out for puddles."

Malinda found her voice. *"I did not know about this way out!"* More important, she had not known about this way *in.*

"Of course not. I'll tell you when—" He took her arm.

"Let go of me!" Pushing past Crystal's protests and efforts to block her, Malinda marched forward and entered the secret passage.

At first it was only a gap between two false walls, its ceiling out of sight. It turned a couple of corners and divided, but she followed the light of her guide's lantern hurrying ahead. Her mind roiled with tales of ancestors fleeing by night, flames of rebellion licking at their heels—perhaps down this very corridor. Not revolution this time, she decided. If anything like that had been brewing, she would have heard rumors. No, the problem was undoubtedly conjuration.

Steep stone stairs led down to a low tunnel of arched brick. Her slippered feet found the puddles Snake had mentioned. The air was stale, stinking of ancient mold.

Conjuring orders had traditionally been exempt from taxation on the grounds that they performed healing and other good deeds, but there was no question that many of them sold curses and love philters, or even performed necromancy or enthrallment. For generations elementaries had been springing up all over Chivial, growing steadily richer and amassing enormous landholdings. Months ago Ambrose had demanded the authority to tax them—good economics and very dangerous politics. A prudent ruler would have proceeded more warily, but prudence was not in his bones.

Parliament, usually so susceptible to royal bribery and menace, had balked. The orders' enormous wealth could buy votes as well as he could, and the enchanters outdid him at intimidation. Chancellor Montpurse was in the fight of his life, with the Commons snarling at his ankles and the King snapping in his ears.

Of course there must be cellars under the palace, but Malinda knew nothing about them. She passed several heavy doors closed and bolted, and went through others standing open; those she heard being shut after her companions had followed. She had not known of the secret door from her room. Those were not her usual quarters in Greymere. Just before Long Night the Lord Chamberlain had asked her to move, babbling about a planned renovation. Ha! It had not happened, and in any case renovations were always done in the summer when court was elsewhere. It had been more of Durendal's scheming, obviously.

Devious Commander Durendal had foreseen the danger from the conjurers, but even he could not increase the size of the Royal Guard faster than Ironhall could turn out new swordsmen. He had improvised by re-enlisting the knights, of whom there were plenty around, because a Blade was normally released from his binding in his late twenties. In effect the Commander had created a secret and illegal private army, misappropriating state funds in the process. Having wormed the story out of both Sir Eagle and Sir Shadow, Malinda was possibly the only person outside the Order who knew about it. She had considered dropping it in her father's lap to see what would happen to Smarty Master Durendal then.

Obviously she had waited too long.

Eventually her guide led her to a low room with no other door, although shutters high on the walls must hide small windows and a rusty iron ladder in one corner led up to a trap in the roof. Icy cold, damp, and unwholesome, this crypt might reasonably be used to store wine or sea coal or even ice, but it presently held eight cots, a couple of benches, and some wicker hampers . . . probably a few rats also. The man who had led the procession was now stoking fresh logs into an iron stove in which a substantial fire was already burning. The room brightened as the rest of the party arrived with their lanterns—Dian, Lady Crystal, Sir Snake and one other man, who slammed the door and shot bolts. The rest of her escort must have remained behind to block pursuit.

The men were dressed as courtiers, but their cat's-eye swords marked them for Blades. Snake and Sir Bullwhip—a chunky, fair-faced man, whom she remembered as something of a dullard—and a pallid, blond one named . . . Victor? Yes, Sir Victor.

"I demand an explanation!" Crystal hurried over to stand in front of Malinda as if prepared to defend her against imminent rape by three swordsmen. "His Majesty shall hear of this outrage! If there is danger, then where is the Royal—"

"Hush!" Malinda said, gripping her shoulder.

Like many a chaperone, Crystal worried more about appearances than reality—how would the court react when it heard that the Princess had been abducted in the middle of the night in her nightgown? To a cellar full of swordsmen? All three women were improperly dressed, with their hair unbound. Crystal was foreseeing a scandal and the King blaming her for it. The Candlefens would be ruined yet again.

Dian, in contrast, was now smirking. "I can't see any problem. Perhaps we should huddle together for warmth?"

Lady Crystal squawked in horror and flapped her hands.

"We can blow out the lights if you prefer." Dian had no royal reputation to preserve. She had always enjoyed cuddling and lately had discovered the joys of doing so with young guardsmen.

Malinda hauled a blanket off a bed and went to stand by the stove while she wrapped it around herself. "Come here and get warm, ladies. An explanation if you please, Sir Snake."

"Monsters, my lady. Sir Bullwhip saw them better than I did."

"Dogs, Your Highness," the chunky man said earnestly. "Dogs big as bulls, some of them. Hundreds of them. They seemed to be heading for the King's quarters, my lady, but attacking anyone they saw on the way. They're climbing up the palace walls and chewing through window bars and—"

"Has he been drinking?"

"It's the truth," Snake said, frowning.

"I assume the Guard is defending my father?"

"To the last man, if necessary. Knights like us are looking after your royal brother."

"So where are you taking me?" She was not dressed for ladders.

"Nowhere, Your Grace. This is as safe as anywhere. We're under the boathouse. If the enemy finds us here, we can fight our way out and leave by river. Otherwise we wait here until the danger has passed, then return to the palace."

She eyed the swordsmen angrily. They were hiding their amusement, but only just. "This is the Old Blades' kennel, is it?"

The uncertain light made Snake's eyes twinkle, but his mouth was not smiling under his stringy mustache. "One of them. How do you know about the Old Blades?"

"How did you know about a secret back door into my bedchamber?"

He shrugged his narrow shoulders and now he did smile. "Palaces always have secret doors, Your Grace. They are a fiery-awful nuisance, because they have to be guarded all the time. I have spent many, many nights in this rat hole. And in others like it."

"But rarely alone," Victor murmured softly.

Secret doors and passages should not surprise her, for Ness Royal had several of them. Everyone was standing around, waiting for her to give them permission to sit.

Snake said, "This one may well be how your great-great-something-great grandmother Queen Estrith escaped from the rebels."

"Then it has a lot to answer for. The silly woman should have stood her ground." Malinda spoke brazenly, but apprehension of danger was making her skin prickle. Durendal's illicit private army now seemed like a very good idea indeed, burn him! His planning had been excellent. "I know what I'm going to do." She sat down on the bed closest to the stove. "Pass me another blanket, Dian. Thank you."

"Your Grace!" Crystal protested, outraged. "You can't—"

"I can try." Malinda lay down and made herself comfortable, turning her back on them all. "Guard me from my guardians if you want, or go to sleep. I don't care. Rattle your dice quietly, please, Sir Snake."

He chuckled. "Seems like a smart idea to me."

After that no one said anything more; quiet footsteps and creaks of bed webbing soon stopped, leaving only a faint, steady dripping from one corner. Malinda knew she could never sleep, but it would do no harm to pretend. She was not frightened now. Furious, yes. Furious at the insolence of open treason. Furious that busybody Durendal had been right all along. More than furious that he had manipulated her into a bedchamber with a secret entrance without confiding in her. Worried about her friends in the Guard, especially Eagle and Shadow, and Dian's Chandos, battling monsters around their ward. Worried about her father . . . Even worried about what would happen to the country if anything happened to him. These last revelations were so astonishing that she was still considering them when she fell asleep. She was probably the only resident of Greymere who did sleep that night.

Knuckles rapped on wood: thrice, twice, once. Malinda angrily pulled the blanket over her topside ear. Voices . . . sounded like Sir Felix, who had not been long released from the Guard . . . cold, damp . . . *Stink?*

She came awake with a start. She heard the door close again. Footsteps approached in the gloom.

"The emergency appears to be over, Your Grace. His Majesty and the Crown Prince are both safe and unharmed."

Blearily she sat up, keeping the blanket tight around her shivers. "How many are not?"

"The present count is twenty." Snake's voice was very unlike his usual bantering tone. "Some injured may not survive. Very nasty wounds, I heard."

"Not all in the Guard, surely?"

"Oh no. Some of them were women. Four of the Guard, my lady: Sailor, Shadow, Vance, and Heron. The Knights' count is uncertain still."

Not Eagle! Nor Chandos, who was Dian's current favorite. But Malinda had known those four and liked all of them. *"Burn them! Burn the traitors who did this horrible thing!"*

"We will certainly try, Your Grace."

Back at her suite she found not only the eight girls and women she expected but also another thirty or so and a dozen men, all slumped around in a state of nervous exhaustion—laundresses, hairdressers, dressmakers, her falconers, even her sergeant-porter. People who normally lived in servants quarters at the far end of the palace had flocked to hers in search of safety. Had she been a target for the monsters, this would have been almost the worst place they could have chosen, but fortunately not one single mutt had tried to enter. The only calm person present was Lady Wains; misled by all the chatter about dogs, she was describing a deer hunt in her youth.

"Out!" Malinda roared. "The monsters have gone. All except me, and I am more dangerous. Back to work, all of you. Lady Crystal, Lady Arabel . . . kindly make ready. We must go and wait upon my father."

She found six Blades on duty outside her door, twice as many as usual. One of them was Eagle, and it was a relief to confirm with her own eyes that he had escaped without a scratch or bruise. Sir Piers wore the officer's sash; he whipped out his sword in salute.

"To His Majesty," she said.

"He may not be in his quarters, Your Grace. They are uninhabitable now."

"Then I shall view the battlefield, and you may tell me of the battle while we walk."

She liked Piers; normally he was reticent, almost curt, but he seemed genuinely unaware that he possessed the second finest profile in the entire Guard, with eyes to drown in and the darkest complexion, smooth as oiled walnut. She had once had quite a crush on Piers. Now he formed up his squad to escort her, but they were all still bubbling like kettles. All of them except Piers himself sported one or more gigantic bloodstained teeth hung around their necks like lockets, and even Piers joined in the bragging and chatter.

It was only natural for a princess to dream of a prince of her own, even a princess betrothed to a ducal tadpole—*especially* a princess betrothed to a ducal tadpole. Malinda's paradigm of manhood had changed form several times over the years, but he almost always haunted her fancy in the livery of the Royal Guard. As a child, she had found an ever-present armed escort to be a vexing restriction. Later she had come to understand that it was a significant honor. Without accepting the Blades' conviction that they were the object of every woman's most fervent desires, one could admit that most of them had sparkle and dash. Their duty roster was determined by Commander Durendal, so she had helpfully provided him with a list of those she preferred to have attend her. He had ignored her wishes. A year or so ago she had suggested to her father that it was time for her to bind some Blades of her own. Ambrose had been agreeable until Durendal talked him out of it—a Princess's Guard would not be under his control, naturally. Small wonder that the Commander's name headed her list of enemies!

Just before Long Night, her father had ridden off to Ironhall to harvest the next crop of swordsmen. He had returned with eight new Blades, the youngest of whom was Sir Eagle. She had never seen a man who walked so like a cat; he raised goose bumps on her arms with every dark, appraising glance. At once she had known exactly what her dream prince should look like, how he should laugh and smile and handle a horse. So far she had concealed her approval from Commander Durendal, lest he clip Eagle's wings as he had clipped the others'. She could only hope that no one noticed how close she came to melting whenever he looked at her.

That morning he had discarded the smoldering eye and husky voice. He was as raucous and high-spirited as the rest of the troop, jubilant in the aftermath of a major battle. She had no chance to speak to him, or indeed much chance to say anything, as all six swordsmen jabbered about the night's struggle, of monsters invading the King's quarters, and how Leader—Durendal, of course—had locked His Grace in the garderobe at one point. Another Blade legend had been born, obviously.

The walk through the palace was a scene out of nightmare, and even in nightmares she had never imagined having to step over gobbets of raw flesh in the heart of Greymere. Workmen were collecting it and wheeling it out in barrows; floors and even walls were spattered with dried blood; everywhere reeked of disemboweled dog. Her father's suite truly was a battlefield, with empty holes where the windows had been, and head-high heaps of dog flesh. Apparently a couple of rooms had escaped the turmoil, for their doors were being guarded by Blades as the workmen hustled in and out. She knew at a glance that her father was missing.

Master Kromman, his secretary, was not. He was sitting at his desk in the anteroom, busy amid the blood and slaughterhouse stench. He rose and bowed to her. "I was about to come looking for you, Your Highness. His Majesty requests your presence at a reception scheduled for the Rose Hall one hour after noon."

Everyone detested Kromman. He had been an inquisitor in his youth and still sported inquisitorial black robes and biretta, plus the distinctive fishy stare. "Fishy" was flattering; his bloodless complexion and straggly white hair would have suited a drowned corpse. He came around the desk to her, bringing a paper.

"You will enter through the west door, probably twenty minutes later than the time I just stated. The heralds there will cue you. You are to bring your full retinue. When you greet your father's Majesty, a moderate amount of emotional display may be appropriate. I have some words here that you may find suitable, although of course you must appear to speak *extempore*." He offered the paper.

She ignored it. Obviously, this had to be one of those supposedly spontaneous functions that Ambrose liked to organize. She found the hypocrisy despicable and pointless, since nobody was deceived. "How efficient of you, Master Kromman! I had hoped you were about to impart my father's congratulations on my safe deliverance or even his inquiries after my health and well-being."

Trying to snub an inquisitor—even an ex-inquisitor—was like chewing rock. The glassy eyes stared at her for what felt like a long while before he answered. "Do you think that I would omit to deliver such a message if His Majesty had entrusted it to me?"

She shrugged. "Perhaps not. I was just hoping. Did he dictate that speech you are waving at me, or is it your own composition?"

"I formalized his instructions."

"Then I shall deformalize them. Both my words and the emotion accompanying them will be my own."

He bowed without conceding defeat. She spun around in a swirl of skirts and departed. Kromman was a snoop. He did not rank with Durendal on her list of crawly things, but he came very close behind.

4

Fear nothing except a lee shore, lightning, and blood relatives.
RADGAR ÆLEDING,
UNPUBLISHED LETTER TO HIS SONS

Inevitably, the ceremony was late in starting, so the anteroom outside the west door became packed with people waiting to make their entrance. Heralds fussed obnoxiously, as heralds always did, issuing orders, waving lists, and climbing up on the vantage to peer through spy holes at what was going on in the hall itself. Malinda joined them up there and commandeered one of the viewpoints. Nobody dared order a princess away.

Every noble within reach of Grandon had hastened to the palace to congratulate the King on his narrow escape. So had the diplomatic corps. Every guild had sent a delegation—the Ancient Brotherhood of this and the Worshipful Company of that. Ambrose stood foursquare on the dais and accepted the tributes with high good humor, although he could have had no sleep in the night. He loved pomp and adulation, especially together. In all his elaborate finery—slashed and padded jerkin, fur-trimmed cloak, plumed hat, jeweled orders, and all the rest—he looked twice the size of anyone else in the hall. Among the dignitaries at his back, only the gaunt Grand Inquisitor was taller. There seemed to be no proper order or precedence being observed, as if the entire reception was completely spontaneous, but she guessed that a dozen heralds had worked since dawn to organize it.

Some courtiers, specially favored, were being invited up to stand alongside His Majesty, so the dais was gradually filling up with the heads of the ministries and orders—Mother Superior of the White Sisters, Grand Wizard of the Royal College of Conjurers, Grand Inquisitor of course, the Lord Chancellor . . . *Lord Granville?* Still?

An overpowering odor of lilac made her look down just as a padded shoulder nudged her breast. Cousin Courtney was apparently attempting to peer out the spy hole, although he had to stand on tiptoe to do so and was using the move as an excuse to snuggle against her.

"By the seven saving spirits!" he lisped. "Just *look* at the Rector! It's easy to tell whose little darling he is!"

Malinda moved back against the rail, both to find some fresh air and to discourage further body contact. As the son of her father's sister, Courtney should by rights have been at least a duke and more properly a prince, and yet at forty he remained merely Baron Leandre, the title he had inherited from his father. He was the quintessential courtly fop, a man of lethal wit, exquisite taste, exaggerated gentility, and no importance whatsoever. He had never married, but he moved from one mistress to another with apparent ease, dalliance to liaison to affair, oblivious of all scandal. Ambrose detested him and had appointed him Malinda's Master of the Horse just to ridicule him, but not even the King could quash Courtney. He flaunted his title while bragging how he had never seen the inside of a stable in his life.

The object of his current scorn was another problem relative—the House of Ranulf must contain more black sheep than the palace had rats. The large man standing next to the King was Granville, Lord Rector of Wylderland and Malinda's unacknowledged illegitimate brother. He had turned up for Long Night festivities after not being seen at court for several years; she had thought and hoped that he had gone away again, returning to his duties of burning hovels and butchering peasants. Ambrose had been making all too much of him and apparently still was. He was a younger, harder replica of the King—not quite so tall, nor so obese, but with the same yellow eyes and fringe of bronze beard. He was deliberately wearing similar green-and-gold clothing, too, just in case any onlooker missed the resemblance.

"Magnificent!" Courtney sighed. "When the Wylds *finally* manage to put a hole in him, all we shall have to do is sit him on a bronze horse and he can be his *own* monument!"

"You have a point. There is something monumental about him."

"My spleen is my most perceptive organ, dear."

"Royal bastards are an unavoidable waste product of monarchy," Malinda said, to show that she could be malicious too—Courtney's parents' marriage had never been officially recognized. "In Chivial, unlike some other countries, they are never acknowledged."

The little man turned to look at her, having to tip his head well back. He was sweating profusely, eroding his face powder into islands. He seemed to be doing quite well for himself again, with gems glittering on his fingers; his clothes were lavish and styled to minimize his tubbiness. He smirked with painted lips. "Everything has a first time, darling. Besides, Granville has *always* been an exception."

"In what way?"

"Oh, *well!*" He beamed and edged closer conspiratorially. He was probably even more skilled at picking up gossip than Arabel, although he rarely bothered to impart any to Malinda. "It was before *my* time, of course—Granville's *several* years older than I am, you know." The Rector was actually four years younger. "It was a truly tre*men*dous scandal! The Marquise of Newport bore a son. Well, that does happen, you know, although I am sure you are too innocent to know why. But the Marquis was *gauche* enough to point out that it was *not* his and accuse his wife of *adultery!* I ask you! What else are adults *for?* He even tried to name the *Crown Prince* as the father. The problem was that your *dear* father, then the Crown Prince of course, was *several* years short of the age at which such charges are normally even considered, and the lady was three *times* as old!"

Ambrose was fifty, going on fifty-one. Granville was thirty-six. Malinda had never worked out the implications before. And here she was, an ancient virgin of sixteen! She raised her eyebrows and made encouraging *mm?* noises.

"The matter was suppressed—mostly by *rank* intimidation. The babe was *grudgingly* accepted, and there the matter rested, until just after your *dear father* succeeded, when the Marquis was dying and his own sons had predeceased him. His brothers were *very* much opposed to the title and lands passing to a royal bastard. Disloyal of them, don't you think? Your father allowed the boy to be disinherited, but Granville was old enough by then to cause trouble on his *own*! His price was an earldom *and* command of a regiment."

"And now he's Rector!"

"Oh, my dear! A very *successful* commander! He has had more success pacifying Wylderland than anyone since Goisbert II."

"Graveyards are usually peaceful."

Courtney giggled approvingly and patted her arm. "Very *droll, my dear*! I must remember that!"

Chivial had been trying to subdue Wylderland for centuries, but each new campaign just made the Wylds retreat into the bogs and hills and sharpen their swords for the next round. Granville was an efficient butcher, an expert at massacre and scorching earth, but his success would be as temporary as all his predecessors'. Nevertheless, Chivial's recent war with Isilond had ended in national shame; the conflict with Baelmark had dragged on for ten years, with Baels ravaging Chivian coasts and shipping almost at will; only the dashing Lord Granville ever produced good news.

"That is a pretty gown, dearest," Courtney said, reaching out to stroke it. "You look good in red. You look good in any color."

Malinda responded with a sharp kick to his ankle. The little man winced and withdrew his hand quickly. She wondered how one family could have produced two such dissimilar men as her half brother and her cousin—the towering, ruthless warrior, and the dumpy little voluptuary. Yet both were successful conquerors, for the curious thing about Courtney was that a man so obnoxious was enormously successful with women. She despised him, yet she could not deny his charm. Perhaps it was because his spite always seemed to be directed at other people; he invited you to share his caustic view of life.

"Ah!" he said. "Excuse me, beloved. There is my dinner at last."

He bobbed his head, minced down the three steps to the floor, and went squirming off through the crowd like a fish through reeds. He surfaced near the door to embrace a countess whom Malinda had believed to be very happily married.

She turned her attention back to the hall. It was more crowded than she could ever recall seeing it. As the air grew ever more festive, her anger waxed hotter. Why celebrate a massacre? What of all those dead people? Who was mourning them? Several of the Blades on display were bandaged. She could not see Eagle anywhere. There were more White Sisters than usual, too, although Arabel had reported that the residual taint of enchantment lingering in the palace was driving them out of their minds, so that Mother Superior was urging the King to move the court to Nocare or Oldmart.

Chancellor Montpurse had already gone, alas, because any ship of state hitting a wave this bad must drop someone overboard. Malinda was sorry about that; he was a true gentleman. She hoped he would enjoy a long and happy retirement. She was even more sorry that the golden chain had come to rest around the neck of Sir Durendal, who was Lord Roland as of this morning. He looked thoroughly glum over there on the dais, but he must have weeks of work ahead of him just to learn what he needed to do first. The Commander's silver baldric gleamed on the chest of Sir Bandit, a very surprising choice. She approved of Bandit. Everyone did. She would have expected her father to promote Sir Dreadnought.

Even the odors of people and perfume in that overcrowded hall could not completely hide the reek of dead dog. The latest estimate of deaths she had heard was twenty-two, the human tragedy lurking under all this glitter and sham. Especially she thought of Sir Shadow, who had lasted less than two months after his binding, who had been very little older than she was. He had not been able to make her heart race with a single sultry look as Eagle could, but he had been a merry soul, a genius at composing funny poems to deflate bullfrogs.

A deputation from the Commons trooped in and knelt before the King like rooks at a peacock picnic. Mr. Speaker began reading an address in a tuneless, nasal voice.

Another said at her elbow, "Now would be a good moment for Your Highness to—"

Malinda looked around with distaste and decided that Ivyn Kromman's yellowish face with its frame of lank gray hair resembled an aged fried egg, and she must share that thought with Courtney sometime.

"You would have me interrupt Mr. Speaker?"

The secretary pulled a mawkish smile. "If someone doesn't we'll be here all night. His Majesty specifically instructed me to provide a diversion about now."

She eyed him suspiciously. Was he trying to entrap her? He would not get away with it if he was, whereas it was entirely possible that Ambrose would want the Speaker muzzled.

"Very well, Master Secretary. Diversion it will be." She raised her skirts to descend to the antechamber floor. There she put herself at the head of her retinue, making sure that Crystal had Lady Wains under control, and led them into Rose Hall along the narrow aisle the heralds had managed to keep clear.

Mr. Speaker droned on, listing all the terrible misfortunes that would have befallen the country had the King's Majesty perished under the nefarious assault of the evildoers. It was not a formal address from the Commons—there had not been time for a debate. He was passing on his own ideas and sounding very I-told-you-so. Nothing would annoy her father more than that.

Studying the set of the globular face ahead, Malinda could guess that her father had had enough. His ankles troubled him and he had been standing there for well over an hour. She reached the requisite distance from the dais and sank into a full court curtsey, hearing fabric rustle behind her as all her ladies-in-waiting and maids of honor followed her.

"Malinda!" His Majesty proclaimed. "Our dearest dove!"

Mr. Speaker's voice trailed off uncertainly.

In a surprising display of affection and disregard of protocol, Ambrose lurched heavily down from the dais and advanced to raise his daughter. Caught unprepared by his tug, she almost overbalanced; only a brute-strength heave by her father prevented an embarrassing stumble. No matter—he enveloped her in an embrace. There was a lot of him inside all the vestments. There was a lot of ham there, too. He would have made a truly appalling and doubtless very successful actor. Over his shoulder she noted Dear Brother Granville frowning narrowly.

The whole court had been taken by surprise. There was a perceptible pause before someone started the cheer. Everyone duly joined in, giving Ambrose time to inspect his daughter at arm's length and then embrace her all over again. The heralds awoke to the fact that the King was now on the same level as the audience and signaled for everyone to kneel. The entire court knelt.

"They told us you were safe," Ambrose declared when the cheering faded away, "but only the witness of our own eyes can truly set our mind at rest. It enrages us that our dear children have been exposed to danger. We wonder what sort of despicable poltroons could make war on such innocents?"

Her turn. Speak up.

"Traitors, most honored Father, contemptible traitors! But my only concern at all times was for the safety of Your Majesty."

She had not bothered to prepare that speech. It was all he wanted to hear. It was also closer to sincere than it would have been the previous day—she *had* worried about him and what would happen if he died.

Beaming, Ambrose urged her to accompany him as he heaved himself up onto the dais again. "Stand beside us, my sweet." He meant *behind us and over there*. "Now, who . . . Ah, Mr. Speaker, we beg pardon for interrupting you."

The heralds gestured and the congregation rose to its feet again, all except the parliamentary delegation. The Speaker pulled a face and raised his scroll to resume reading his speech. He was the Honorable Alfred Kildare, he was a pompous attorney from Flaskbury, and he was totally bald. This detail was known because his hat had blown off on the palace steps a couple of weeks ago. In one of his pithier works, Sir Shadow had commemorated the occasion:

> Alfred Kildare,
> All air, no hair.
> The wind blows
> And so does he.

Sir Shadow would be forgotten but pompous Master Kildare would strut his way back to Parliament behind his little paunch and yatter on as before. Malinda's entry had not dampened his volubility at all. He was even repeating some of his earlier paragraphs.

"Father!" she protested, "should you be listening to this man?"

Had she ripped all her clothes off and turned cartwheels, she could not have created a greater impression. The King turned very slowly to look at her, as if disbelieving what he had heard. Everyone else just stared openmouthed.

Women did not interfere in politics. No one spoke to the King unbidden. Or insulted the Speaker. Mere slips of girls did not . . . Unmarried wenches . . . The rules she had just broken were too numerous and too potent even to list. There was no going back, so she went on, letting the angry words fly.

"He is warning that your life is too valuable to risk, which the entire country already knows. But he is hinting that you must abandon your noble struggle for fairer taxes. He may even try to dissuade you from hunting down the evildoers who assaulted you in your own palace and slew many of your defenders. What sort of ruler does he think you are? What sort of *man* does he think you are? I, too, am of the House and Line of Ranulf, and I am insulted that you should have to listen to such craven whining! Instruct him in the honor of princes, sire."

Ambrose's eyes had vanished almost completely into his blubbery cheeks; his mouth had shrunk to a pinhole. Either she had gone much farther than he expected, or he was an even better actor than she knew. Slowly he turned back to look down on the outraged Speaker.

"Our daughter speaks out of turn, Mr. Speaker. Pray forgive a damsel who has been sorely tested these last few hours, as we have all been. We are sure our loyal Commons would never counsel us to neglect our justice, our campaign for fairer taxes, or certainly our honor. Pray complete your discourse."

The Honorable Alfred opened and closed his mouth a few times. Rather than read any more, he mumbled a few loyal platitudes and humbly thanked His Majesty for his attention. He then stuffed the scroll inside his jerkin instead of handing it to the waiting page.

The Commons rose and backed away, bowing. Like earwigs. A herald bellowed out the next name: "His Worship the Lord Mayor of Grandon and the honorable aldermen . . ."

Ambrose directed a parental glare at his wayward daughter to warn her not to interfere any more. And—very, very slightly—winked. He had never done *that* before.

The reception broke up. The King departed in the midst of his Blades without a word to Malinda.

Lord Granville spared her a quizzical smile in passing. "Even a terrier may turn a bull," he muttered and was gone before she could reply. He had the gall to leave before she did!

As Malinda led her retinue down the great staircase, she beckoned Lady Arabel forward for consultation. "Cousin Courtney has paid off his creditors again?"

"Baron Leandre does seem to be well provided with funds at the moment," her mistress of the rumors said sourly, chins waggling disapprovingly.

"And who is his benefactor, do you know?"

"Lady Mildred! It happened just after the Long Night Masquerade. He's doing very well off her, they say."

"Mildred? I thought she was happily married and faithful."

"Her?" Arabel said in astonishment. "Spirits! Oh no, no! Oh, my goodness, no!"

Wrong again. It was hard to keep up with Courtney and not really worth the effort. Granville mattered more. Suppose her father never did send the warrior hero back to Wylderland? Suppose he recognized him, legitimized him, and named him Crown Prince? Whatever the traditions, after the fright everyone had received last night, Parliament would probably be very happy to let Ambrose designate a mature and competent heir. It would make no difference to Malinda, but poor little Amby would be disinherited.

5

It will take a firm hand to break yon filly to the bit.
LORD GRANVILLE, PERSONAL COMMUNICATION TO
KING AMBROSE

efore they even reached the Princess's quarters, they were accosted by a pack of distraught mothers, determined to whisk their daughters away from court before monsters ate them. Crystal became flustered; Malinda intervened with threats of royal thunderbolts to send them packing. After that, she insisted on keeping banal appointments with dressmakers and then her music teacher, to demonstrate that life would continue as before. By evening the entire palace seemed ready to make an early night of it and catch up on lost sleep.

As always, she and Dian ended their day with a private gossip while Dian brushed Malinda's hair. Her hair was long enough to sit on, although she could never understand why she should want to.

"I fail to see the point of it," she complained, seeking some topic other than the dogs. "Why must women let their hair grow long? We are never allowed to display it." Current fashion allowed exposure of no more than a finger width between forehead and bonnet.

"Men like it," Dian said dreamily. "Trail it over their naked bodies. Drives them wild."

"I thought it took a lot less than that to drive men wild." It was very annoying that her friend was so much more knowledgeable—or claimed to be. Dian sometimes mistook wishful thinking for experience.

"To start with, but they tire easily. After the first couple of—"

"I don't want to hear! You are supposed to set a good example for my household."

"I set an excellent example," Dian said. "The world would be a much happier—"

Came a tap on the door, Arabel's face unpainted and distraught under her nightcap, word of a page waiting outside . . . His Majesty requested the pleasure of his daughter's company. *Now,* of course. That was what came of having a tyrant for a father.

She could not wait upon the King without attendants, and this excursion obviously called for Arabel and Dian. With all the servants already dismissed, there was much frantic scurrying, while maids of honor attempted to pin up hair and find clothes and jewelry. Courtly garments were not designed for ease of dressing any more than Ambrose IV was noted for his patience; it seemed hours before the three of them were ready to emerge and follow the fretting page. Six Blades were guarding her door, and four of them went with her through the shadowed and silent corridors of the sleeping palace.

Normally an unexpected royal summons meant royal trouble, but Malinda's conscience was unusually clear at the moment. She had not ridden astride for months and her sense of humor had been behaving itself reasonably well. She had little time to worry, because the boy conducted her not to the King's suite but to much lesser quarters not far from her own. Two White Sisters and four Blades guarded the outer door, and there were at least a dozen Blades in the anteroom. Not Sir Eagle, though. She wondered wistfully what he did in his off-duty hours, and with whom.

Deputy Commander Dreadnought was in charge. His smile was cheery enough, but she felt as if his eyes were searching her for concealed daggers. "Just your royal self, Your Grace," he said as he tapped on the inner door for her.

She had expected that and chosen her companions accordingly. Crystal, say, would be horrified if she had to spend an hour with a platoon of Blades, but Arabel would enjoy weaseling all the latest gossip out of them. Dian would flirt outrageously and fill up any blanks on her calendar for the next month.

The little sitting room beyond was snug, with a fire crackling on the hearth and shutters closed against the winter chill. It contained two men and two chairs, one of them more than completely occupied by King Ambrose, humped over like a very weary haystack as he soaked his feet in a steaming copper basin, whose pungent herbal odor almost masked the scent of woodsmoke and beeswax. He had discarded his hat and cloak, a very rare informality—she had not seen him like that since Haralda died. He looked up blearily and yawned.

As she sank down in a full curtsey, he growled, "Up, up! Scofflaw! Where is the man? A stool, Scofflaw, a stool!"

She had not expected Granville. The Rector was on his feet, goblet in hand, leaning against the mantel. He, too, had shed his outermost garments; indeed his jerkin was half unlaced, and she had never known any man dare attend the King in that state—nor slouch against the wall in his presence, either. If they had progressed to such intimacy, this must be the latest in a whole series of informal meetings. Now she was being included in the family conference. Was it possible that the King had decided to recognize and legitimize his warrior son? It would be a popular move. Had she been summoned just to hear the news?

Granville hauled himself upright long enough to bow to her. "May I pour you some wine, Your Highness? A fortified draft, good for repelling the winter weather." His rocky face was slightly flushed, as if he had repelled several storms already.

Scofflaw, the King's elderly and dullard valet, shuffled in through another door, carrying a stool. He placed it in front of her and disappeared back where he had come without ever meeting her eye. She sat and adjusted her skirts.

"A small glass would be welcome, thank you, my lord." All grown-ups together now . . .

"You really crippled the Speaker today, girl!" Ambrose growled. "Even I can't speak to him that way." This was a blatant lie. Only a month ago he had publicly called the man a shit-house shoveler. "You trying to provoke a constitutional crisis?" He was hiding his amusement, but she knew him well enough to relax a little.

"Secretary Kromman told me you wanted a diversion, sire."

The King twisted his pudding features into a scowl. "You mean my secretary told you to speak up unbidden at an audience?"

"He did not specify means. I assumed that he was merely passing on your instructions—I certainly hope he would not presume to order me around on his own! If I misunderstood his words, I am deeply sorry to have distressed Your Majesty." Let the royal fist descend on Ivyn Kromman; she would shed no tears.

Granville held out a glass of blood-red liquid to her.

"Don't ever do it again," Ambrose grumbled. "Will not have people saying that I take orders from children! Upstart hussy!" He chuckled hoarsely. "It worked, I admit. Just this once, you hear? Burn the man! Can't stand him."

"Chop off his head, sire," Granville suggested, refilling his own goblet.

"Wish I could, Rector. *Scofflaw!* I've thrown some of those gabble merchants in the Bastion before now, but it doesn't make the Commons any more cooperative, believe me. . . . *Scofflaw!*" Ambrose sighed. "You're growing up, my lass."

"Not too soon for me, sire."

"Snake says you snore."

"He is insolent!" Malinda snapped.

"What he really said was that you slept all night."

"There was nothing else to do."

Ambrose grunted, but he was pleased. "What do you think, Lord Rector? A girl gets dragged out of bed and run through a bunch of cellars and told that the palace is under attack—so she lies down and goes back to sleep. Snake swears she wasn't faking it!"

"I am sure he has had ample experience of women pretending to be asleep, sire."

The King guffawed. "I'm sure he has. Those Blades are the greatest libertines in creation. But not many wenches have iron nerves like that, eh?"

Granville glanced thoughtfully at Malinda and took a leisurely drink of wine.

"Courage runs in the family, sire."

The King's eyes slitted. "Meaning?"

The Rector endured the glare without flinching. His solid, weathered features were Ambrose's with muscle and gristle in place of blubber. It was the face of a killer, but would she have been able to tell that just by looking at it? As the perceptive Courtney had said, the man was a human monument. She realized that he was as puzzled by her presence as she was by his.

"Just what I said, sire. The House of Ranulf has always been known for its courage." It was also known for amber eyes, and his own eyes were as gold as could be. But even the Wylderland Butcher did not dare mention that fact here.

Scofflaw shuffled in with a bucket in one hand and a steaming copper jug in the other. Kneeling before the King, he began ladling water from the basin into the bucket. No one paid any attention. Ambrose turned back to Malinda, a safer target than a hero with a national following. "Time to find you a husband, mm?"

Fortunately, hard-won experience warned her just in time that he was about to strike and she managed to conceal her shock behind a sip of wine, although it turned into a gulp. "I understood I was limited to one, sire."

Granville laughed admiringly. Ambrose scowled and then decided to join in.

"You really want to wait until that De Mayes brat is out of swaddling clothes?"

Marriage? Her mind was whirling. She thought of Eagle. He was impossible, of course, but a man *like* Eagle? Some supple young sultry-eyed ruler of a secure little principality in the warm south of Eurania? Marriage *soon*? No more the De Mayes tadpole!

Scofflaw began topping up the basin with hot water from the jug.

"Ansel is a pleasant enough young man, Father, but—"

"*Pfaw!* He's a squeaky, dimwit midget like his father."

"Apart from that."

Again Granville chuckled and again Ambrose decided to see the joke, although normally he appreciated his own humor much more than anyone else's. He was in an incredibly good mood tonight, a suspiciously good mood. There must be more skullduggery to come.

"You really still thought I was going to tie you to that herd of backwoods ruminants?" He had never hinted at anything else. "You're far too valuable to throw away on them, my girl!" He roared, lifting his feet. "That's enough, idiot! You trying to boil me alive?"

Malinda shivered. The King's idea of value and hers might have little in common. "I am flattered, Your Grace. But why . . . ?"

"You know I'm looking for another wife?"

"There has been much speculation around court, certainly."

"Well it's true. There's plenty out there to choose from. Mont-purse has been working on it for some time." He pouted. "You were the heir then. If you'd stayed the heir, you'd have had to marry a Chivian, see? De Mayes's son was the best fit and next in line after you anyway." That argument ignored Granville, Courtney, and Ansel's father. "I tied him up in case we needed him. But we don't need him now, see—now you've got a brother."

The King eyed his daughter narrowly, as if challenging her to object, but there could be no appeal against the politics of inheritance. Had she remained the heir, marriage to Ansel would have reduced the risk of a disputed succession. Conversely, with little Amby now set to inherit, both her claim and Ansel's must be weakened as far as possible. Her destiny was banishment to some faraway realm.

"May I inquire . . . You have someone in mind, Your Grace?"

"The decision will be mine, child!"

"I am aware of that, sire. I am obedient always to Your Majesty."

"Humph!" said the King. He tested the basin with one cautious fat toe. "Not so I've noticed. Self-willed minx, I'd say. *Scofflaw!* Where has the man gone now? Well, there's Prince Favon of Sandearn. Built like an ox, I understand, but stupider. There's the Czarevitch of Skyrria, but he's only seven." His voice was joking but his eyes were not. He was warning her again that she had no choice, no say. Her marriage would be an affair of state, and already Ansel did not seem such a bad idea after all.

"The decision is yours, sire." When there was no immediate response, she dared to add, "If my wishes are worthy of consideration . . . A very, very small kingdom will satisfy me, Father, if the prince is kind and healthy. Especially healthy." Not that she wanted any husband yet. Not even Sir Eagle. What did this have to do with her bastard half brother? Why was he there, witnessing her ordeal?

"Plenty of degenerates out there," Ambrose agreed. "Don't want any slobbering, lopsided grandchildren. Problem is dowry. A princess must have a dowry worthy of our honor. The Czar suggested a million crowns. He can't think you're worth much if you need that sort of subsidy! Treasury's empty. This dogs thing is going to sink us."

Puzzled, she said, "Sink us in what way, sire?"

"*Aargh!* Parliament won't let me tax the elementaries now. The King's Peace, security of the realm, and yabber-yabber. Half the members have been bought and the rest are scared spitless. And you—you can forget those extra cavalry you were dreaming about."

The Rector said, "I can only repeat what I told Your Majesty earlier: My men lack adequate winter clothing and shelter. If they do not get paid soon, they will cease to be an effective fighting force. Moreover, if you drop the loyal chieftains off your payroll, they will start going over to the Ciarán. One goes, they'll all go."

The Ciarán was either rebel chief or rightful king of Wylderland, depending on which way one was facing. The Chivial colonists were terrified of his guerrillas; he could give even the Rector lessons in savagery.

Ambrose scowled at each of them in turn. "And where's the money to come from if Parliament won't let me tax the elementaries, mm? Bah! The pickynickers won't even vote me money to build ships, yet they all scream that the Baels have cut off trade. They won't see that my revenues come from custom duties, and the filthy pirates are hurting me more than anyone! *Scofflaw! More wine!* If they won't vote me taxes to stop the Ciarán driving Granville into the sea, then they're not going to vote you much of a dowry, my girl."

Granville frowned at Malinda, then at the King. And said nothing. Then she saw . . . *No! He couldn't mean it, could he?*

"No helpful suggestions?" her father demanded. "Neither of you? Well, then. What about the Ciarán?"

Granville waited politely for Malinda to comment.

She had trouble finding breath, let alone words. If she provoked an outburst of the terrible royal temper now, anything might happen, but if she did not protest she might lose by default. She began calmly enough. "Surely Your Majesty is joking? I cannot believe that you would be cruel enough to give me away to a brute who lives in swamps and dresses in skins."

Even that hint of defiance was enough to darken the King's glare. "I'll marry you off to any man I want!"

Despite herself, her voice began to rise. "Sire, there must be a dozen realms in Eurania who could find a better husband for me than that monster—a hundred! He's a rebel! Is that how you reward treason—with your daughter's hand in marriage? You said you want no deformed grandchildren. What sort of evil spawn would the Ciarán sire on me? Wed me to a cripple if you must, or a child, or pick a plowman out of the fields, but not that murdering brute!" She was on her feet and her wineglass shattered in the fire with a gout of flame and steam. "Spirits, if you gave me to the King of the Baels himself, you could do no greater—"

"Silence!" Ambrose roared. "By the eight, you great heifer, you're not too big for me to take my belt to yet! And you wouldn't be the first princess thrown in the Bastion!"

She gasped a few times to regain control; she forced herself down on her knees. "Sire, I most humbly beg your forgiveness. My tongue ran away with me." She waited, head bowed, shivering.

"Hussy!" her father growled. "Impudent vixen! Rector, would it work?"

"Would what work, sire? Would he sign a treaty and swear an oath of allegiance? Probably—he likes variety in women. But as soon as you withdraw your army, he'll raise the tribes again, I guarantee it. Probably roast your daughter alive or give her to his men. Her Highness is quite right when she says the Ciarán makes the King of Baelmark look like a gentleman. Inside a year you'd be the laughingstock of all Eurania."

Ambrose harrumphed. That "laughingstock" would carry more weight with him than anything else that could be said. "Bah, you're as bad as she is. She wants some scented court dandy to bed with, no doubt. You want the war to go on so you can be the fighting hero."

"I am distressed if that is what Your Majesty believes. My commission is always at Your Majesty's disposal."

The King growled again. "Get up, girl! Sheath your claws! I won't marry you off to the Ciarán. We'll put that new chancellor of mine to work. Smart fellow. He'll find a husband to take you at a price I can afford. Now get out of here and keep your mouth shut."

The Trial, Day One

(CONTINUED)

"In his private life he was a tyrant," Malinda said firmly, "and I never loved him, but his death was not something I planned or desired."

Wind moaned in the chimney, wafting an especially acrid fog of smoke from the fireplace and rippling the ancient banners overhead. The elderly peer who had asked the question shifted uneasily on his stool. He was the Marquis of Midland, and King Ambrose had regarded him as a dimwit.

"The noble lord"—the chairman leaned forward and peered along the table—"may wish to reserve consideration of the witness's *feelings* until after the *facts* have been introduced. It is not what she *felt* that concerns the commission, but what she *did*."

Unwilling to meet the agate eyes set in that skull face, the unfortunate peer shrank down. Satisfied that he had established who was in charge, the old man directed his pebbly stare at the Queen again.

"Let us begin. We have prepared a list of questions for the witness. It may be simplest if we consider the crimes in the order in—"

"Crimes?" Malinda snapped. "Your terminology is overly sugges-

43

tive. Crimes there were aplenty, but I was rarely the culprit. For example, when I appointed you to my Privy Council, was I just naive or criminally negligent?"

"And were so many mysterious deaths accidents or murders?" the Chancellor rasped. "That is what we must establish. The committee will consider events in chronological order, starting with the sudden demise of Agnes, Dowager Baroness Leandre." The old man produced no notes, because inquisitors were conjured to have perfect memories. If the questions filled hundreds of pages, he would still have every one of them at his fingertips. "Pray inform the commissioners of your relationship with the deceased."

Malinda shrugged. "The facts are well known, so this is a waste of time, but time is something I have in excess. If the noble lords have nothing better to do, I am sorry for them. Agnes? My aunt Agnes. Family squabbles are an old tradition in the House of Ranulf. My father was one of five children, of whom three died in infancy. The other survivor was his eldest sister. Long before my own birth she eloped with a baron—yes, a mere baron! Not even a viscount." She had hoped to win a smile or two from the commoners, but evidently none of the commissioners was in a mood for humor. "Shocked by this lapse of good taste, my grandfather locked them both up in the Bastion. Leandre died there of sewer fever. Agnes was eventually released, but was stripped of her royal titles and her infant son, who was raised at court. Even when my father succeeded, there was no reconciliation. Not until . . . 368, I suppose. Yes, two years ago. He brought her to court. That was the only time I ever met her. She stayed a few weeks and then died quite suddenly."

"And how did she die?" asked the chairman's creaky voice.

"I was told that she went home to Castle Leandre, caught a fever, and succumbed very suddenly."

"You were told. But was that the truth?"

No it wasn't, and no one could deceive an inquisitor.

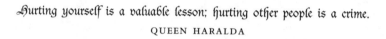

6

Hurting yourself is a valuable lesson; hurting other people is a crime.
QUEEN HARALDA

$\mathcal{A}$ week after the Night of Dogs, King Ambrose yielded to the will of Parliament and withdrew the bill to tax elementaries. But the sly fat man had not ruled Chivial for nearly twenty years without learning a trick or two. He had his new chancellor submit what he called a meringue, a trivial bill that did nothing except condemn evil enchanters. This banal measure naturally passed both houses without a murmur of dissent. The next day he dissolved Parliament and invoked that innocent-seeming act as his authority to investigate all users of conjury, to license those he deemed worthy and suppress all others, confiscating their property. Snake's Old Blade irregulars were officially chartered as "Commissioners of the Court of Conjury." They carried the war into the enemy camp and began uncovering horrors worse than anyone had ever dreamed.

The conjurers retaliated, launching what became known as the Monster War. Ambrose, who never lacked courage, increased the number of his public appearances, scorning attacks against his person. Just how many of those there were and what form they took, even Malinda could not discover. She knew that the Blades were all exceedingly jumpy and would not discuss casualties, but casualties there certainly were. Familiar faces disappeared and did not return.

Her own life was not immune. Now White Sisters were added to her household, tracking her everywhere, inspecting every room before she entered. She must not touch a single grape before a food taster had eaten half the bunch. These annoyances could be endured, she informed her father, but she absolutely refused to be shut up in a glass case like a china doll; she was of the Line of Ranulf, too, and a lot less valuable than he was. If he could defy the traitors, then so could she.

Reluctantly, but perhaps a little impressed, Ambrose agreed. Thus, in that winter of 368, Malinda enjoyed more liberty than she had known since she roamed the rocky shores of Ness Royal with Dian. She and her ladies went on numerous progresses, visiting towns she had never seen before. She launched ships, attended balls, made speeches. Civic banquets were a bloodcurdling bore, but being cheered in the streets could easily become addictive. She inspected some of the estates expropriated from condemned orders, gagging at the sight of cages where victims had been held prior to enthrallment, weeping for the mindless sex slaves created. Evidence of worse horrors was kept from her.

She got along well with the new Commander, Sir Bandit. He had the bushiest, blackest eyebrows ever seen, joined in the middle, but his mouth smiled so easily that he never seemed fierce. He was one of those rare people who could be amiable from morning till night, never grumpy or curt. When she dropped a hint that she considered younger Blades to be her most fitting defenders, he laughed and said, "They certainly think so, Your Grace!" but thereafter he assigned the juniors to attend her. She spent many an hour laughing with Eagle and his contemporaries as they rode the derelict winter roads together.

She missed Chancellor Montpurse. She was appalled when she returned from a progress and learned that he had been beheaded for treason. *Treason?* Montpurse? Unfortunate it was only minutes after she heard that news that she ran into his successor, the odious Lord Roland. Like her, he went nowhere now without an escort of Blades, not even along a palace corridor. He stepped out of her path and bowed low.

"Well!" she said. "How does it feel, my lord?"

"Feel, Your Highness?" He faked a look of extreme innocence. He was a tall man to have been a Blade, and admittedly striking in a dark-eyed, saturnine way, smooth as pond slime. Eagle and the others still worshiped him and spoke in awe of his skill with a sword—a knack whose relevancy as qualification for high office escaped her.

"To have uncovered a traitor so close to the throne? And so soon! To achieve so much so quickly must feel very good?"

He flinched. "No, Your Highness," he said hoarsely. "It does not feel good."

"Well, I expect you will get used to it." After a couple of steps she looked back. "Do keep up the good work."

Everything went well until Periwinkle Day.

Periwinkle Day was the fourteenth of Thirdmoon, around the time that spring reinvented lambs, flowers, and bright evenings. Her father and most of the Guard had disappeared; she assumed that they were taking advantage of the full moon to ride to Ironhall and harvest more Blades. The court was still resident at Nocare while Greymere was being refurbished, and just south of Nocare lay the Meald Hills, where a lady could fare forth with friends and fly a hawk or two. Malinda took an escort of four Blades, three grooms, and two falconers, but for female companionship she invited Dian and no one else. Lady Arabel frowned, Lady Crystal bleated, and Lady Wains babbled about a masque she had seen many years ago.

Malinda had never much cared for a sport that reduced pigeons to bloody feathers. She went prepared, in a divided skirt, and as soon as she was safely out of sight of the palace, she exchanged her dull little pony and sidesaddle for an eye-rolling, fire-breathing charger named Thunderbolt, who made even the grooms clench their teeth. She sent everyone home except Dian and the Blades, and just barely managed to keep Thunderbolt under control until the rest were out of sight. Then she gave him his head.

Hooves thundering on the turf, he flew off over the hills like a spring gale, leaving the other five smelling his dust. This was riding! They would catch her soon enough, of course. For all her cuddliness, Dian was a superb rider and most Blades were almost as slick with horses as they were with swords. Sir Eagle, especially, was a marvel. He soon drew out in front of the others. When he began to close the gap, Malinda "accidentally" lost her hat so her hair would blow out like a banner of depravity in the wind. It gave him a chance to show off, which he did, whipping out his sword and retrieving her hat from the grass at full gallop. That did little for the hat, but a lot for laughter, flushed faces, and sparkling eyes.

It was spring.

At noon they picnicked in a sheltered glade, complete with mossy bank and chattering stream. The Blades always knew the latest court news and more secrets than even Lady Arabel. They did not deny that Ambrose had gone to Ironhall and might be gone several days, the roads being the way they were at this time of year.

"It's shameful," Eagle remarked. "Leader's ripping the kids out of the womb to make up numbers. Fury's Prime. How old is Fury, brother?"

Sir Hector shrugged. "Doubt if he's eighteen yet."

"Ridiculous!" Eagle was all of nineteen himself, just right to squire a sixteen-year-old princess. "A Blade must be able to maintain the Legend."

"I'm sure you can handle his share for him." Intrepid shot a sly glance at Malinda.

"Not if Iris hears of it he can't," Hector countered.

They began teasing Eagle about that unknown Iris and several other trollops as well. He turned a furious red and responded with comments on their own evening activities. Blades were notorious rakes—that was part of their appeal. Dian and Chandos, totally intent on each other, were edging closer and exchanging glances that grew hotter by the minute. It was spring.

"I think," said Dian, preparing to rise, "that I shall be traditional and go pick some periwinkles." Obviously she intended to enhance Chandos's day in the woods considerably. He sprang to his feet and offered a hand.

"No you won't!" Malinda lit up her best House-of-Ranulf glare. "I need you to witness that these scoundrels behave themselves."

Pouting, Dian subsided. Chandos sighed piteously. Hector and Intrepid leered.

"Why do we have to behave ourselves?" Eagle asked innocently, giving her one of his skin-tingling looks.

Malinda smote him with an even better glare. "Because."

Intrepid said, "Hector and I will chaperone you."

"No you won't! If the court harpies hear about this outing, they'll have quite enough to feed on without that. Dian can't lie to the inquisitors and you can."

"Can we? I didn't know that." Intrepid turned to Chandos, who had a reputation among the Blades as an intellectual. (Courtney would say he must have been caught reading a book once at Ironhall.)

Chandos shrugged. "Maybe. I probably could if my ward was in danger. It would be my conjurement against theirs, though, and the inquisitors' is pretty strong."

"I am not your ward," Malinda said, "and Dian is not going to let me out of her sight while you lechers are around."

With that they all had to be content.

But it *was* spring.

Tired and happy, they returned to the palace at twilight, with Eagle riding Thunderbolt and Malinda demurely sidesaddle on his horse. They went right to the stables. The hands were all at their evening meal.

It was stupid, it was crazy, it was madness . . .

It was spring.

Malinda cornered Eagle in a tack room, closing the door behind her. When he tried to escape she blocked him.

He dropped his normal air of banter and backed away. "Please, my lady!"

"It's been a wonderful, marvelous day. It needs a kiss to complete it."

"You want to get me beheaded?"

"I won't tell—if you do it, that is. If you won't, then I will scream that you tried to rape me at least a dozen times in the hills."

He muttered angrily, grabbed her shoulders, pecked her cheek, then tried to get past her.

She clung. "A real kiss!"

"That was a real kiss! Please!"

"No it wasn't. Show me how you kiss Iris."

"*Your Grace!* You are not that sort of girl!"

"Pretend I am and kiss me. One real, lingering kiss. Show me."

"Death and fire!" he muttered.

She was almost as tall as he was, but his strength astonished her. She had not expected to be crushed so tight, or the pressure of his mouth on hers, or the way his tongue prized her lips apart . . . or the sudden flare of lantern light as the door creaked open. They sprang apart. She screamed. Eagle moaned.

There were two of them there, barely more than faces in the dark because of their black inquisitor's robes and birettas. One of them was Secretary Kromman. Another man pushed his way between them— Sir Dominic, who was Acting Commander during Bandit's absence. His always-fair face shone like chalk in the gloom. For what seemed an hour, nobody spoke. Horses clumped hooves and crunched hay out in the stalls. Malinda felt her world collapsing around her. She could not imagine what her father was going to say. Spirits knew what she had done to Eagle.

"It was entirely my fault, Sir Dominic. I ordered him—"

"Give me your sword, guardsman. You are confined to quarters."

Eagle drew his sword and handed it over in a silence that hurt like a scream of pain.

Kromman said, "Sir Dominic and I will escort you to your apartment, Your Highness."

"I don't take orders from you!" she yelled. How *could* she have been such a fool?

"Then I must refer the matter to the Lord Chancellor," the nasty little toad sneered. "I trust you recognize his authority in the absence of His Majesty?"

Roland! Of course this must be all Lord Roland's doing. When he had been Commander Durendal, he'd spied on her all the time, so that she had only had to say one kind word to a Blade and he would be snatched away from her service and assigned elsewhere. Now Roland had trapped her.

"Stand aside!" she roared and elbowed her way out of the tack room.

She had barely bathed before a page delivered a note from Chancery: Lord Roland begged the favor of a brief audience concerning the marriage negotiations.

He was coming to gloat!

She was tempted to refuse on the grounds that the hour was inappropriate, but that would feel like cowardice; her pride would not allow it. She replied that she would be honored to receive his lordship. She did so in her presence chamber, which in Nocare was spacious. She brought Wains, Crystal, and Arabel for support, but Lord Roland came alone. Even in his scarlet chancellor's robes and gold chain of office, he still moved as gracefully as a fencer, floating across the floor, bowing low, kissing her fingers. His dark eyes revealed none of the triumph he must be feeling.

"I most humbly beg Your Grace's pardon for intruding so close to the dinner hour."

"My time is always at your lordship's disposal."

He produced a paper. "A brief list of names here. If Your Highness would be so kind . . ." His minuscule smile to her companions was enough to convey the message that this matter was so enormously confidential that they should all withdraw at once to the far end of the hall, which they did, instantly, and without a single word from her. The mere name of Lord Roland was enough to make them all run in circles like rabbits—idiots!

The paper, when she unfolded it, was totally blank.

"I have given strict orders," Lord Roland said softly, "that none of the persons involved is to mention the incident to anyone whatsoever, not even Grand Inquisitor. I should much prefer that it remain that way, but Kromman is a worm."

She blinked in astonishment, and then her fury redoubled. If the Secretary was a worm, what did that make the worm's master?

"He revels in creating trouble, so your father will certainly hear of the matter when he returns. Until that time, nothing must change. Sir Eagle will be allowed to fulfill his duties as if nothing at all happened, and I most strongly urge, my lady, that you do the same. Just be sure that you are properly accompanied at every moment."

His hypocrisy was unbelievable! Not trusting herself to speak, she thrust the paper back at him.

He took it and bowed. "I shall do my best to persuade your honored father to overlook the incident. Most important of all, Your Grace, I pray you not to speak with any of the people involved." He retreated a pace and raised his voice. "I shall arrange for the artist to wait upon Your Grace's matron companion to arrange a sitting at Your Grace's convenience."

Bowing again, Lord Roland withdrew. He paused at the door for a word with her companions, and they all twittered like sparrows.

Slimy, sneaky, despicable rodent!

Whatever orders Lord Roland claimed to have given, the news was all over the palace within an hour. Crystal went whimpering to bed with a headache. Arabel tried to berate Malinda as if she were still a child. Dian called her a witless numbskull. Even Lady Wains caught the prevailing mood and wept in bewildered misery. Worst of all were the Blades. When she went for her regular evening visit with Amby, Dominic himself was there to lead her escort, but neither he nor any of the others would speak to her. They stared right through her in silence. There was no sign of Sir Eagle.

Rumors grew faster than toadstools. By morning she had been discovered naked in the straw with at least one Blade and probably several. Just like Queen Sian, of course . . . Her case was not at all like Queen Sian's, but she could not fight faceless lies. To run through the palace shouting, "It was only one kiss!" would do no good at all.

She knew that her only hope—a very faint one—was to get to her father before Roland did. Alas, the King returned late at night, and the first she knew of it was when the Healer General himself arrived the following morning to inform her that she was running a slight fever and needed bed rest. The mythical ailment required strict quarantine, so all her maids and ladies and servants were removed and replaced by grim-faced nurses. She was under house arrest.

★   ★   ★

Her room contained a bed, a few pieces of furniture, and a garde-robe, but nothing to read and no one to help her with her hair or the devilishly inaccessible laces on her clothes.

The next day, having been granted time to meditate upon her failings, she had to submit to examination by a team of healers and midwives, whose only concern was to establish whether she was still a virgin. She had not yet recovered her temper after that degradation when she was called out to her own presence chamber to face a panel of inquisitors, two men and one woman. *They* had the audacity to sit behind a table and expect *her* to stand in front of it. When she protested, they showed her their warrant with the royal seal. If she tried to lie to them, or refused to answer any question they cared to ask her—fully and to their satisfaction—they were commanded to have her removed to the Bastion. The implication was that it contained equipment capable of making her answer.

One kiss!

So she stood and fumed before their glassy eyes and answered a thousand questions: impertinent, personal, irrelevant, and humiliating. How many men had she kissed? How many men had touched her breasts? Had she ever fondled a man's groin, either inside or outside his breeches? They asked about things that had never even occurred to her. "Why should I want to do that?" she demanded more than once, and each time the fish-eyed horrors replied that she must answer the question. The kiss was not the real problem, though. Did she recall the King's Majesty forbidding her to ride a horse astride? How many times had His Grace told her this and when? How many times had she deliberately defied that royal command and when? How many other royal orders or wishes had she flouted? Was she aware that this was treason? Who else had known she was disobeying? And so on and on. If she shaded the truth by even a hairsbreadth, they accused her of lying. The kiss did not matter.

The next day the whole process was repeated, with a new team of doctors and midwives, a new team of inquisitors.

On the third day she rebelled. She hurled her dinner tray out the window and announced she would starve to death before she would answer one more question. She fully expected to be carted off in chains, but instead they locked her in and left her alone.

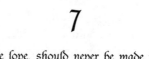

7

War, like love, should never be made in public.
BARON LEANDRE

By the second day of her fast, it took every scrap of willpower she possessed to continue throwing the trays out the window, the savory odor of roast swan being undoubtedly the cruelest torment ever invented. On the brighter side, she noted that the rose garden below was now closed off, but that spectators gathered behind the barricades at mealtimes. The word was definitely out, and dear Father would not like that.

She was so shaky by the third day that she needed several hours to dress herself, but dress she did—if she must be dragged off to the Bastion, it would not be in her nightgown. Once dressed, though, she just lay on the bed and did nothing, other than think about food. And once in a while think of poor Eagle, whom she had so terribly wronged, or Aunt Agnes, who had borne a child in the Bastion and been stripped of all her royal titles.

The rattle of the bolt was her only warning. She heaved herself up as the door opened. Commander Bandit looked in, glanced around without meeting her eyes, and then withdrew. She had just time to put her feet on the floor before Ambrose's bulk filled the entrance. The room swam giddily. She dropped to her knees, more heavily than she'd intended.

The door thumped shut. Someone else had entered, but she kept her eyes on the King's great calves, bulging his white silk hose into meal sacks.

After a while he said, "We will hear your appeal for mercy now."

"I am truly sorry to have caused Your Majesty distress."

"*Hrrumph!* That is not adequate, not nearly adequate."

"I kissed a boy. I confess that it was forward of me, but the difference in our ranks prevented him from making the first move.

He obeyed my command reluctantly—as your spies must have told you—and neither of us had any intention of letting the matter—"

"Wanton! Here I am negotiating with the kings and princes of half Eurania to find a suitable match for you, and I discover I may be peddling spoiled goods!"

Then she did not care any more. He had made his decision. Whatever it was, nothing she could say would change it. "That is not true, as your troupe of performing seals must have reported."

"You defied my express orders about riding sidesaddle!"

"Only when sidesaddle would have been suicidally dangerous."

He growled low in his throat. "I have told you before that you are a woman, not a Yeoman Lancer. Get up!"

She rose and waited, hands clasped, eyes downcast. His belly was a great mountain of cloth of gold; his pudding fists rested on his hips. At the extreme edge of her vision were his eyes, glittering in a face like a bucket of butter. The other visitor, the witness to her shame, was a woman in a dark gown. Malinda could make out no further details, but the King turned to her.

"Princess, your niece Malinda."

Shock! Malinda looked full at the woman. She was ample, clad in black, much like a sack of roots, leaning on a cane she clutched in a weathered claw hand. Her hat was years out of date, with unsightly wisps of white hair showing under it; her gown was shabby and ill-fitting; her complexion dark and earthy, as if she had not washed her face in years; her nose protruded as an ugly blob amid the wrinkles.

"Well?" the King barked. "Greet your aunt, child!"

Had she been stripped of her titles? A reigning monarch's daughters should take precedence over his sisters. Malinda sank in a curtsey, which sufficed to conceal her confusion for a moment. Before she rose she had her features under control. "I am delighted to meet Your Highness at last!"

"Humph!" said Princess Agnes, sounding very much like her brother. "Well, that won't last long!"

The King chuckled. What had he cooked up with this ugly hag? "Her *Royal* Highness Princess Agnes."

Malinda bobbed a slighter curtsey. "I beg Your *Royal* Highness's pardon." There was hope yet. If Auntie had been elevated so high, it was so she would outrank a mere *Highness,* and thus Malinda was a princess still.

"Agnes has graciously agreed to act as your governess," Ambrose announced, "until we get you safely married off. Obviously I kept you on too slack a rein, but that will now cease. Need I say more?"

"I understand, sire."

"Then I'll leave you two to get to know each other. There will be a state dinner tomorrow, welcoming my sister back to court, and I expect you to behave yourself perfectly—then and in future. Know that you escaped the dungeons by the skin of your teeth."

Pompous fat oaf! The ladies curtseyed as he turned his back, although Agnes's move was barely more than a nod. As soon as the door closed, she hobbled stiffly to the nearest chair, thumping her cane all the way. She sat down as if every joint hurt.

Courtney's mother! They were roughly the same rotund shape, but she was taller, as big as Arabel. And this sour old crone was to be Malinda's jailer from now on? Her royal honors had been restored as her reward, and could doubtless be un-restored very quickly if she let her niece get away with anything at all. King Ambrose must think he was being very clever.

"Congratulations!"

Princess Agnes continued to fuss with her skirts for a moment before she acknowledged the comment with a frown. "And what is that supposed to mean?"

Chuckling, Malinda strode over to the window to inspect the weather. The empty ache in her insides had been swept away by excitement and had not yet returned.

"Exactly what it says. Whatever happened between you and my grandfather, your return to court is at least nineteen years too late. I am delighted to see justice done at last, and happy to have been the means, even if my part was unintentional." She swept across to the chair and pecked the old woman's cheek. "Welcome!"

Her kiss was rewarded with a scowl that the old tyrant himself might have admired. "You needn't try your charms on me, young miss! I won't fall for sly tricks. From now on you won't be out of my sight for one minute. There'll be no more romping in the hay with Blades, I promise you!"

"Aunt— You don't mind my calling you 'aunt,' do you? I swear I have not romped in hay since I was about eight. I kissed a young man in a tack room, and that is as wicked as I have ever been or want to be. Yes, I went riding astride, but where's the harm in that? You have no need to treat me like a willful child."

"We'll see about that! 'Very tight rein,' your father says!" The crone settled her wrinkles into an expression of crabby satisfaction.

Malinda grinned long enough to bring back the scowl. "My father does not understand women and never did! 'Royal Highness?' You drove a hard bargain, I'm glad to see! Courtney must be pleased?"

"Courtney? Tenth Baron Leandre, now Prince Courtney, shortly to become first Duke of Mayshire?" Agnes bared yellowed stumps of teeth. "Oh, they made a mess of him, didn't they! His father would have wept with shame to have fathered that poltroon!" Her teeth clicked shut; she had a mouth like a rattrap.

"But . . . I don't understand!"

"You think your father's hard on you, child? You don't know what the word means. Mine took my baby from me. Snipped him loose and carried him away before I ever set eyes on him. They reared him at court. For his own good, they said. Wanted to keep an eye on him, they said, but they were holding him hostage so I would do as I was told. So I did. I behaved myself, just for his sake, moldering away in the ruins of a castle; and now I find they turned him into that stool bucket! Courtney? Don't talk to me of Courtney!"

Compared to that, Ambrose would not be breaking the family mold if he did marry his daughter off to the leader of the Wylder rebels. After a moment, Malinda tried again. "Have you met little Amby, yet? Your nephew?"

"Why should I want to? One smelly brat is much like another."

She was a sour, embittered, thoroughly untrustworthy old crone. But she was also a woman who had been treated most ill by her father and brother. From the look of her garments she had been poor; from the look of her hands she might even have dug her own roots or scrubbed her own floors. Victory should taste very sweet after a lifetime in exile, and yet court must seem intimidating now, even to a lioness tough enough to have wrung a dukedom out of Bullyboy Ambrose.

Malinda went over and knelt beside her. "Because he's the only really nice person in our entire family! He's adorable! I have missed him sorely these last few days and I expect he has missed me. He's talking now and . . . well, you'll see. Let me show you around the palace, dear Aunt—how exciting this must be for you! We'll go and visit Amby and then—"

"No, we won't! The state dinner is tomorrow and tailors are coming to measure me for—"

"Phooey!" Malinda clutched at the clawlike hand. "Tailors wait on princesses, not the other way 'round. Let me pull that bell rope, Aunt, and if my maids have not all been beheaded, I'll have you dressed up in no time. One of Lady Arabel's gowns will fit you well enough for now. They'll do your hair, primp and titivate you, and inside an hour you and I can saunter forth to astonish and amaze the entire court!" Somewhere in that hour there ought to be time for Malinda to tuck away a couple of pastries or a lightly grilled ox. . . .

Princess Agnes glared—suspicious, but tempted now. "What are you up to?"

"Aunt, Aunt! Nothing, I swear! Whose side do you think I am on? I have no quarrel with you, but my father has treated me very badly—not as badly as yours treated you, but badly enough. All I did was steal a kiss! He thinks he's been very clever, setting you up as my guard dog, but we have far more in common that he realizes, you and I. I intend to be on my very best possible behavior, honestly! I want you and me to parade past dear Ambrose IV arm in arm, noses in the air, bosom friends. Then what will he think? Now may I pull that bell rope?"

Her aunt scowled darkly, and then—very slowly, like a snowman melting in a Secondmoon sun—nodded her permission.

8

His Majesty has granted the following noble personages his gracious leave to withdraw from court . . .
COURT *GAZETTE*

Malinda's scandal was totally eclipsed by the sensation of her aunt's return to court after a forty-year absence. No one ever supplied grist to the palace gossip mills like Princess Agnes. She did restrain herself for a few days, just long enough for Courtney to be formally proclaimed a prince of the realm and Duke of Mayshire. Then she let rip on morals, manners, fashions, and whatever else caught her jaundiced eye, slashing everyone in sight, for she had the same razor tongue as her son, although she totally lacked his humor. Ambrose and she had never gotten along; time had healed nothing between them. She called him a fat despot to his face and said he had never grown up; he was heard shouting that he should have left the old sow in her mire. She was a sore trial to Malinda—crabby, suspicious, and stubborn as a granite barbican; but she did need a friend and guide in the palace, as Malinda had guessed, and the two of them combined in a reluctant and shaky alliance against Ambrose's tyranny.

Courtney, who had cadged off women all his life, was suddenly rich, moaning that he did not know what to do with himself anymore. Ambrose had been generous, and could well afford to be, for rivers of wealth were already flowing into his treasury from the confiscated elementaries. Free of the constraints of Parliament as no king of Chivial had been in centuries, he wallowed in his good fortune. He showered lands on his favorites, reinforced the Rector's army in Wylderland, began planning massive renovations to all his palaces, and built up coastal defenses against the savage Baelish raiders. He even talked of creating a navy that could carry the war to Baelmark itself, although no one took that idea very seriously while the Baels' blockade was strangling every port in Chivial.

Now, if he wished, he could provide his daughter with a truly royal dowry. Malinda was required to sit for several artists, but where the portraits were sent was kept secret even from her. Chancellor Montpurse would have confided in her. The odious Lord Roland would not admit that the sun usually rose in the east.

Sir Eagle was seen no more and no one knew what had happened to him. The Blades had not forgiven Malinda.

Although Lady Wains was sent back to her family, the rest of Malinda's household survived the crisis. Agnes made halfhearted efforts to recruit her own ladies-in-waiting, with a not-surprising lack of success, but since she insisted on keeping Malinda right under her eye, the two of them must necessarily share a single establishment. That was one source of friction between them. Their widely divergent interests were another.

Agnes did nothing and went nowhere. She suffered greatly from pains in her joints, which the Healer General attributed to an imbalance of humors, and specifically an excess of choler and black bile—a diagnosis her son described as self-evident. The skilled palace enchanters could provide some relief, so a visit to an octogram became part of the old lady's daily routine and perforce of her niece's routine also. Apart from that, Agnes had no interests, no friends, and certainly no intention of exerting herself. After a lifetime of lonely poverty in a tumbledown castle, she enjoyed the luxuries of court—meaning fine food, music, and just sitting around. Malinda sat beside her and endured excruciating boredom. However bad marriage might prove to be, it could never be worse than this.

Her penance ended, without warning, one summery sunny morn-

ing in Fourthmoon. The court had just moved to Oldmart, and the
two princesses were sitting with their ladies in a shady corner of the
terrace, listening to a group of lutists. The players were quite skilled,
but Malinda was surfeited with culture and sorely in need of some
physical activity. She fretted and fidgeted. In the pause between two
pieces, while the lutes were being retuned, a gawky page approached
her, bowed clumsily, and offered a letter on a silver tray. She did not
recognize the arms on the seal nor the handwriting nor yet the heavy
floral scent. Intrigued, she was just starting to slide a finger under the
edge when the paper was snatched from her hand.

"I'll read that first!" her aunt announced.

Malinda pealed like thunder, blasted half the oaks in the deer park,
flooded the arable lands of Dimpleshire . . . not quite. Somehow she
kept hold of her temper. "It really does not concern you, Aunt," she
said sweetly. "It's just some Blades wanting to know if I can meet
them in the stable again tonight."

Agnes had less humor than a cockroach. With a sniff, she broke
the seal and unfolded the paper. And died.

The King was not in the palace; both the Chancellor and Sir
Bandit were with him, wherever he had gone. The meeting convened
an hour later in the Princesses' presence chamber was addressed by
the Deputy Commander, who looked haggard far beyond his years.
A dozen other grim-faced Blades stood by the door. The Guard had
rounded up all the witnesses, including the three footmen who had
come running when the cry went up, the healers who had been
summoned, even the page. He was in tears. Most of the women were
still pale and shaking, including the two White Sisters whose job it
was to detect such lethal enchantments. Prince Courtney of Mayshire
was the calmest person present, looking more amused than distressed;
but then Courtney was a cynic, never a hypocrite. During the month
he had known his mother, the two of them had avoided each other
as much as possible.

Malinda had taken the chair with cloth of estate that Agnes had
installed only the previous week, but everyone else had to stand. She
was grinding her teeth in fury at the crime while simultaneously de-
spising herself for not being as upset by her aunt's death as she ought
to be. But she had narrowly escaped death and the nervous reaction
might be still to come.

"It seems likely," Sir Dreadnought said, "that the traitors intended
to kill Her Highness, and only accidentally slew Her Royal Highness instead."

"A brilliant formulation of the obvious!" Courtney was leaning against the side of Malinda's chair as if unable to straighten under the weight of his finery.

"Was this the first attempt on my life?" she asked.

Reluctantly Dreadnought said, "No, Your Grace."

"Indeed? When Commander Bandit returns, inform him that I wish to see him at his earliest convenience!" *How dare he!*

"Yes, my lady. Rolf?" The page looked up, red-eyed. "You bear no blame, lad. You were only doing your duty. We shall find out how the letter was delivered to the palace, but I doubt if that will lead us any closer to the killers. Er, Sisters . . ."

"Yes, we failed!" snapped Sister Ember. "But we will make our report to Mother Superior."

Dreadnought thrust out his jaw as if he were about to argue. Malinda forestalled him.

"When you do, pray mention that I am also partly to blame."

The room erupted in hubbub.

"Quiet!" Dreadnought barked. When he had silence he asked, "How so, Your Grace?"

"Because Agnes went to see the healers every morning. I noticed that the Sisters tended to stay well back from her for several hours afterward—not just Ember and Willow, here, but any Sister assigned to us. I assume that the taint of conjuration distressed them. I was amused and said nothing, whereas I should have recognized the danger and spoken up." As she certainly would have done if the idiots had informed her of the earlier attempts. "It was foolish of me. Had you been closer, you would have sensed the conjuration—wouldn't you?"

The Sisters exchanged worried glances. "We should have been able to detect the trap from where we were," said Willow, the tall one.

"Not necessarily!" Dreadnought took control of the meeting again. "The traitor enchanters are developing an ability to smuggle conjurements past the Sisters. We don't know how they are doing it, but you can see how dangerous this will be for us. From now on, you will have to stay much closer to your wards, Sisters. Leader will discuss this with Mother Superior. . . . The villains are getting better, and we must stop them from finding out how good they are, how close they came to success today. So I am going to keep the Princess's death a secret. Do you understand?" He glanced around the big room and the score or so of shocked faces, then uncertainly at Courtney. "Your Grace, of course, we all offer you our deepest sympathy in your sad—"

"Please don't."

Dreadnought bit his lip. He was very good with a sword, but a poison-tongued prince was an unfair opponent for anyone. "I hope to have the *Gazette* announce that you and your mother have withdrawn from court to visit your new estates."

"Announce *anything* you like, dear boy. Who ever reads it?"

"Then Your Highness will cooperate?"

"No." Courtney yawned, quite indifferent.

Malinda intervened. "Do you think you can actually do this and keep it secret, Sir Dreadnought? I mean, smuggle my aunt's body out of the palace? And I suppose she will have to die officially somewhere else in a week or two? Can you possibly keep so many people from talking?"

He nodded earnestly. "I think it can be done, Your Grace. Obviously His Majesty will have the final say when he returns, but in the meantime I should like to take an oath of secrecy from everyone now present." Dreadnought was not capable of working all this out by himself, certainly not in an hour. He was following a pattern, which probably meant that this could not be the first such deceit.

"Then I give my consent," she said. "I will be the first to swear."

"I really *must* dash," Courtney said. "I am auditioning musicians for my new orchestra and I'm *hours* late already. Your courage uplifts us all, darling." He bowed and pranced off toward the door.

Malinda waited until he had reached the center of the room. "You have my permission to take him into custody, Sir Dreadnought."

"I am most grateful to Your Highness."

The Blades at the door smirked as Courtney stopped and looked all around him. Then he regarded his cousin under the cloth of estate.

"You can't arrest *me*, darling!"

Malinda smiled and decided that was answer enough.

The fat little prince scanned the room again. Perhaps he was eager to spread the juicy story of murder and attempted murder. Perhaps he just enjoyed being a bur under any available saddle. But he knew when he was beaten. "Oh, *very* well. I'll give you my word."

"I'm afraid that is no longer enough," Malinda said before Dreadnought could speak. "Since you refused your parole before, you may later claim that you give it now only under duress. The Guard will take you in custody until my father returns to judge the matter. You officially left court an hour ago, remember?"

Ambrose would certainly approve. He would laugh his head off.

Courtney spluttered. "This is tyranny!"

"Yes," Malinda said. "I had no idea it was so enjoyable. Do carry on, Sir Dreadnought."

The Trial,
Day One
(CONCLUDED)

⟨━◆━⟩

"The witness has admitted," the chairman rasped, "that Princess Agnes had been set in unwelcome authority over her, that public announcements concerning the death of Her Royal Highness were deliberately falsified, that she was in fact assassinated by a murderous conjuration, and that she received this poison from the witness's hand. The inquiry is adjourned until the morrow at the same hour."

"Wait!" Malinda yelled.

She was hoarse and battered by hours of interrogation, but she had forgotten how fast a day could go, after months when they did not go at all. The windows were black now, with the flames of lanterns and candelabras standing as leaves of gold in darkness and faces as pale moons with eyes. The inquiry had taken only one break, during which she had been conducted back to her cell to dine alone on foul-smelling water and sour gruel while the commissioners were entertained in the Governor's quarters. They had been entertained so well that half of them had put their heads down on the table and snored all afternoon.

The chairman rose to his incredible height. "The inquiry is adjourned. Remove the witness."

"I was telling the truth!" Malinda shouted, as loud as her abused throat could manage. "You have inquisitors. Let them testify that I was speaking the—"

A hand like a wolf's jaw closed on her arm. She jumped, not having realized that there was anyone so near. The squad of men-at-arms was clanking toward her from the door, but two black-robed inquisitors were right beside her and might have been standing behind her chair for hours.

"Tell them I was telling the truth!" she yelled, and was roughly jerked around. The other man caught her other wrist and doubled her over in an arm lock. He was shorter than she but infinitely stronger.

"You will be silent or be hurt," the first man said. "Walk!"

It was unfair! If she lied, they would know and denounce her, but they would not confirm it when she spoke the truth. The chairman had deliberately left the commissioners with the impression that she had knowingly killed Agnes.

She had to stagger several paces in a crouch before the inquisitors released her and let her straighten up. The men-at-arms closed in around her and marched her back to her cell.

The door clanged shut behind her and locks grated. Down on the floor a single candle flickered beside her evening meal—a bowl of gruel, a slab of black bread, an earthenware pitcher of stinking water. The candle was a special luxury, because most days she was fed at sunset and left in the dark till morning. The winter nights had been very long.

It could have been much worse, of course. There were dungeons in the Bastion where the sewage rose and fell with the tide, where prisoners were chained upside down or subjected to unthinkable torments. At least she was aboveground.

"I'm back!" she said cheerily. "Horatio? Winter? Moment? I'm back. They didn't cut my head off, just asked a lot of silly questions."

She, who had owned a dozen palaces, lived in one room now. It was square and barren—rough stone, rough planks. A window tunneled through the wall offered a restricted view of the river, and she spent many hours just staring between the bars at the boats and ships going by and at the tiny-seeming houses on the far bank. Her world was furnished with a straw mattress, a threadbare blanket, a couple of bags to hold clothes, a rickety chair, and a bucket, which her jailers might omit to empty for days on end if she annoyed them. Little else, not even a table. A second door led out to a walkway, where she could exercise to her heart's content.

Her jailers were two square, solid women with the unwinking fishy stare of inquisitors. Although both were shorter and older than she, they knew a thousand ways to hurt and hold people, and in the first few days of her captivity they had quickly trained her to obey—twisting fingers, pinching ears, applying pressure to the sides of her neck and other places she had never known were so susceptible to pain. Singlehandedly, either one of them could crumple her up and make her howl for mercy. They rarely spoke. They had never revealed their names, so she called them Pestilence and Nightmare. Theirs had been the only faces she had seen in months, until the hearing that morning.

She removed her dress and folded it away in a bag. "Have to look nice tomorrow, don't I?" Shivering, she put on her other one and sat down on her mattress to eat the mess in the bowl. "I hope you all had a nice quiet day without me bothering you? Guess what, Horatio? Your namesake was here, in the Bastion! He talked at me all day!"

Horatio lived above the door. He had very long legs. Winter was the clever one who had chosen the best hunting ground, skulking in a safe crack in the masonry and spinning his web between the window bars. Moment was very tiny, like Malinda's friend Sister Moment, and she lived in a crack in the floorboards. After the first week of her captivity, Malinda had decided she must hear a voice, even if it was her own voice; and talking to spiders would be no worse than talking to nothing—as long as they did not answer back, of course, and so far they never had. On really bad days she would break a thread in a web just to watch the owner repair it, which might pass a whole hour or so. It seemed so unkind that she did not do it very often.

"They wanted to break me, you know!" Talking while she ate helped to keep her mind off the food. "And since they're going ahead with the trial now, they probably think I'm mad enough to suit their evil purposes. But they're wrong! They haven't broken me. I got through the whole day without weeping or screaming or begging. I didn't confess to anything. I expect tomorrow they'll get to Father's death and try to make me seem guilty of treason. Well, they won't succeed!"

When she had scraped the bowl and choked down some water, she undressed and curled up small in her blanket. "Good night, all! Good night, Moment. Good night, Horatio. Good night, Winter."

How long could she spin it out? How long before the commissioners went away and left her alone again with the spiders?

9

The said monarchs do hereby pledge and agree . . .
PREAMBLE, TREATY OF DRACHVELD

Ambrose was first stunned and then infuriated by the news of his sister's death—and uncharacteristically maudlin in his celebration of Malinda's narrow escape. He heartily approved of what she had done to Courtney. "Can't think why I've put up with the toad for so long," he grumbled. "He might have been dangerous when his mother was my heir, but he couldn't stir up trouble in a henhouse now. Wasted a good dukedom on him." So the Prince was packed off to his new estates to arrange for his mother's funeral now and her official death later. He probably enjoyed the irony of that, except that he had no one to share it with.

The assassination did not persuade the King to abandon his campaign against the enchanters. Nor did he change his mind a week later, when it became Malinda's turn to congratulate him on a very close call. Hawking in the Great Forest, he was cornered by a monstrous thing, half man and half giant cat; it disemboweled Sir Knollys and broke Intrepid's neck before Dreadnought killed it. Even then, Ambrose never considered surrender.

Around midsummer strange rumors began to fly. As usual, Arabel was the first to hear, and one breathless hot afternoon at Hilburgh Palace she came hurrying over the grass to tell Malinda, who was attempting to play ball on the great lawn with Amby and a reluctant

65

Dian. No one over the age of three could consider such torture to be fun when everyone else was sprawled on couches under the trees, being plied with cool drinks by sweating pages. Only an especially spicy tale would make the Mistress of the Robes move at all.

"They say His Majesty is about to announce his betrothal to Princess Dierda of Gevily."

"I hope the lady is of stoical disposition."

"Probably not, in view of her youth." Arabel's eyes gleamed. "Her Highness is a month younger than you."

Malinda missed an easy catch, causing the Crown Prince to shriek in derision. "Then you had better start looking out for my trousseau," she said. Her father would never tolerate the ridicule that must follow a wife younger than his daughter. It would be daughter out before queen in.

Marriage might be a release from a court that increasingly felt like a prison. The nobility found excuses to stay away, because court now seemed a dangerous place. There had been no more talk of governesses, but security alone curtailed Malinda's freedom almost as much as Agnes had. The Blades and White Sisters were stretched to their limits, so she rarely ventured outside whichever palace was the current residence. Throwing balls for Amby was entertaining in small doses, but it did pall. Looking at his flushed face and dumpy figure, she tried to imagine him a year from now with a baby brother or sister—and herself holding his baby niece or nephew.

"And whose blushing bride will I be?"

Arabel shrugged her bulging shoulders. "Still the same two favorites—Prince Hesse of Fitain or—"

"I thought he was dying of the coughing sickness?"

"They think he'll last a few years yet. But the Duke of Anciers is leading the pack now."

Malinda sighed. "I know—he's the one whose last three wives died under mysterious circumstances."

"Not just wives, either," Dian said. "I heard he has a strong preference for virgins."

"Someone should tell him we're reusable. Is the 'For Sale' sign still hung on my back?"

"Inscribed in fire."

Other news was mostly good that summer. In Wylderland the Rector won a great battle, capturing the Ciarán himself and sending him to Grandon in chains. The Baels maintained their blockade but seemed to have stopped raiding, and there were persistent rumors of a treaty in the offing. More elementaries were raided, more horrors uncovered, more orders suppressed. Familiar faces among the Blades and White Sisters disappeared and were replaced by disconcertingly young ones. Sir Snake and his Old Blades claimed to have destroyed a nest of traitor conjurers somewhere in the marshes of Eastfare.

Court was at Nocare and the Meald Hills were gilded and bronzed by fall when a page brought word that Lord Chancellor Roland craved audience with Her Highness concerning her marriage.

She should have received him privately, of course, in her withdrawing room with only Blades as witnesses. For some perverse reason she decided on a public audience in the presence chamber, with Arabel and Crystal for support and the ladies-in-waiting and maids of honor at the far end, just out of earshot. They were all dying of curiosity, but they could do so and cremate themselves for all she cared—this would be the most critical news of her entire life. Regiments of butterflies cruised her insides.

Roland was punctual to the first chime of the tower clock. He left his guards at the door and swept forward with that distinctive grace, carrying a slim folder. Watching him approach in his rich robes, she realized that she could not expect a husband any handsomer than the Chancellor himself and should be prepared for much less—a child or a grandfather or some ghastly inbred degenerate. . . . He bowed, came forward, bowed again, and knelt on the cushion to kiss her fingers. His hand was warmer than hers.

She wasted no breath on pleasantries. "How may I assist you, my lord?"

She had not told him to rise. His eyes stared up at her, darkly inscrutable yet somehow suggesting that two could play tricks like that.

"I bring joyful news for Your Grace." He opened the folder and handed her a paper.

It trembled in her grasp. She stared at a skillful drawing in silverpoint, the head of a youngish man gazing into the distance. He wore a close-cropped fringe of beard and hair much longer than a Chivian's, both of which the artist represented as light in color; the eyes even more so. The features were strong rather than handsome, but they had the leanness of an active man. No indolent fop, this . . . likely intelligent. A soldier, perhaps, or even a poet—there seemed to be a gentleness about the eyes. . . . Would she see this face every night and morning for the rest of her days? Not nearly so terrible as her nightmares had prophesied . . . and somehow—maddeningly, vaguely—familiar.

"A widower," Roland said. "He has no legitimate children, and none at all that I know of. His wife was an invalid for more than ten years and he could have put her aside, but never did."

All very comforting! The sketch trembled in her grasp. She thrust it at Arabel and had to swallow a few times before she could speak. "Appearances can be deceptive, my lord. Has he a name?"

"I believe his appearance is less deceptive than his reputation, mistress. He—"

"Who is he?"

Roland drew a deep breath. "Radgar Æleding, Your Grace."

"The *pirate*?"

"The King of Baelmark."

Her hand flew up to strike him. Roland braced himself for the impact, but made no other move than that. She stayed the blow.

"Is that the best you can find? Or the worst you can find? That *slaver* . . . murderer . . . that *monstrous* . . ." Her voice cracked. "You insolent upstart! You would sell me to a fiend? Chain me to those barren rocks? My father will hear of—" She ran to the door.

She *tried* to run to the door. Roland was on his feet and holding her wrist before she had taken two steps. She had never known a man to move so fast.

"Unhand me!"

"Your father is not in the palace, Your Grace," he said quietly.

"Take your disgusting hand off me!"

He released her, but he was between her and the exit. "His Majesty is inspecting coastal defenses and will not return for two days. Will you hear me out, my lady?"

The Chancellor had chosen his moment well. Or else her father was not man enough to face her tears. At that realization her anger burned up hotter than ever, drying away any hint of tears. *Sold! Booty!* She spoke through clenched teeth, for Roland's ears alone. "I will kill myself before I go to that man's bed!" Untold thousands of Chivians had been taken by the brute, enthralled into mindless tools, sold at the far ends of the world by Baelish traders. Dozens of cities he had burned, towns sacked, ships seized. Now the King's daughter . . .

"My lady," the Chancellor said softly, "please hear me out. The peace treaty is already agreed and sealed. Your betrothal is the key to end this terrible war, which has dragged on for ten whole years now and caused so much suffering. But there is a clause in there that King Radgar himself insisted on. You must testify that you accept this marriage voluntarily, of your own free will and—"

"My own free *won't*! If that is the case you can rip your precious

treaty into strips right now and hang it in the privy." She was shaking
with fury now, shouting at him, oblivious to the scandal her words
must cause. "I don't believe a word of it! If that ghoul—"

Roland did not raise his voice, but its deep tones rolled irresistibly
over her protests. "King Radgar's own mother was carried off from
Chivial by force on her very wedding day. He is adamant that he will
not—"

He was gone.

Malinda turned. Again displaying astonishing agility, the Chancellor had jumped past her just in time to catch Lady Crystal as she
toppled over in a dead faint. Half a dozen Blades sprinted across the
room to help, and only then did Malinda recall that the woman Roland had been discussing had been Lady Charlotte Candlefen, Crystal's
aunt. That was why there had been a vague familiarity about the face
in the sketch! King Radgar was Crystal's first cousin, and through that
slight connection, he was also a distant relative of Malinda herself.

The Baelmark branch of the family was rarely mentioned.

Later she went for a walk in the park with Dian, holding hands
and kicking the fallen leaves, as they had done when they were children. Blades tracked them at a distance, half-seen figures moving under
the great beeches.

Dian was trying hard to be supportive. "You will appeal to your
father, of course?"

"If he's signed a treaty it's too late."

"Baelmark will be an interesting experience. I've never tried any
red-headed lovers. I wonder if their . . . yes, of course, it will be."

Malinda shot her an astonished look to see if she was serious.
"You're not coming!"

"Oh, of course I'll come with you! You'll need someone and
frankly it's not going to be easy to—"

"You are *not* coming to Baelmark with me and that is *final*!"

"So what else can I do?" Dian argued, but weakly. Obviously—
and understandably—she was relieved not to be facing exile to the
Fire Lands.

"Get married. Or are you lying when you say Chandos proposes
every time you go to bed?"

"Who's Chandos?"

"There's another? Tell me! I know he hasn't got red hair, but
what else has he got?"

Dian sniggered. "The usual." She began going into details.

★   ★   ★

Four days passed before Malinda was allowed in to see her father, and even then he received her in his bedchamber, far from any public spaces. She could scream tantrums there and no one else would hear, except Scofflaw and the two young Blades standing rigidly by the door, Sir Orvil and Sir Rufus. The King was in his shirtsleeves and doublet, overflowing a bench, while Scofflaw brushed what was left of the royal hair.

"Never mind kneeling and groveling. If you've come to whine, it won't do any good. You told me once you wanted a healthy man, and Radgar Æleding is built like an oak keel. Nothing unhealthy about him. Virile as they come, I'd think."

"He's a monster!"

Her father's face was ideally designed for pouting. "No he isn't! I have it on excellent authority that he is a very personable man, even charming. The way he treated his first wife shows that."

Ambrose IV was an expert on the treatment of wives.

"A slaver!"

"Bah!" The King clenched his fat fists on his knees. "He's a very ruthless fighter, that's all. How do you think the Wylds regard me, hmm? Am I personally responsible for every rape or theft my armies commit in Wylderland or Isilond? War is war and what a soldier does in it has little to do with his private life. Don't believe all that nonsense about poverty, either! The Baels may have started with a cluster of bare rocks, but they're rich enough now to pave every inch of them with gold. Radgar Æleding could buy half of Chivial out of one pocket."

"Was this abomination his idea or Roland's?"

"Doesn't matter whose idea it was." He was growing impatient, hinting that she should now withdraw. "What matters is that now we have a peace treaty after eleven years of bloody war. If his price is one willful wench in honorable marriage, then who are you to say that the killing and slaving must go on? Do you rate yourself so high, hmm?"

There was the pit of spikes. There was the dungeon that she could never escape.

"How do you rate your honor, sire?"

He stared at her as if unable to credit his ears. "You don't speak to me like that!"

"I do now! Any decent father would have had the grace to break the news to me himself. Or even told me the terms demanded and asked my consent." She saw Scofflaw gaping at her, Scofflaw who normally noticed nothing.

"Vixen! Ungrateful wretch!"

"Oh, yes, go ahead and roar! Huff and puff! Throw me in the Bastion. Then hand me over to the Baels in chains and tell Monster Radgar that I freely consent to this marriage."

Ambrose heaved himself to his feet so he could glare down at her, and now his voice was dangerously quiet. "You have a choice, miss. You can agree to this marriage of your own free will or you can face a charge of high treason. Months it took Roland to negotiate that treaty and you're going to throw it all away? You'll condemn more thousands to death or slavery? More years of slaughter?"

"Why didn't you just ask me?" she whispered.

His eyes seemed to shrink even smaller as he appraised her, wondering if he had won. "What would you have said?"

There was no choice. "I'd have agreed of course." As she said those words, all the anger drained away. Not even hate was left. Only contempt: he could have told her himself.

"Then why trouble you any sooner than necessary? It might have all fallen through in the end, like all the others." He stumped forward and clasped her in his great pillow arms. That way he didn't have to look at her. "I know how frightening this must be for you. You've always had the courage of our great ancestors. Show it now. The Thergian ambassador will act as Baelish consul for the present. He'll have to approve the wedding arrangements, but I'll leave them all up to you. Lord Chamberlain will do whatever you want. Spare no expense, put on a great spectacle! I have my own wedding to organize. Let's see which of us can stage the finer display, hmm?"

She would be gone across the rolling seas before the future Queen Dierda arrived, so she would never see that other wedding.

Ambrose released her. "Well?"

"Most generous of you, sire! Every girl dreams of a showy wedding."

Incredibly, he believed her. Beaming, he patted her shoulder and told her to run along and get started.

The most extraordinary rumors churned through the court—that she had struck the Lord Chancellor, that she had screamed at her father in public. She did not bother to deny any of them, and it would have made no difference if she had.

Lady Crystal had fallen into a decline. In tears she begged leave to withdraw from court, and Malinda gave her consent, which she had no authority to do. Then all her ladies-in-waiting and maids of honor wanted to go, too, just in case they got packed off to Baelmark, so she gave every one of them permission and was left with only Dian and Arabel and some servants. The Lord Chamberlain duly published the departures in the *Gazette* and she realized that she now had power, because Ambrose needed her. She had escaped from her father's rule and was not yet confined by her husband's.

She almost choked during the formal betrothal ceremony, when she had to make public declaration before the diplomatic corps that she welcomed the match and freely consented. She got the words out somehow, and later signed an equally false letter to Monster Radgar himself. His reply, when it came, she burned unread.

But there was the wedding to plan, and the chance of a small revenge.

The Astronomer Royal had designated 368 a thirteen-moon year, but the season was already late. Although Baels sometimes sailed in winter, no one else ever did, and Princess Dierda must travel by sea also. . . . Adding it all up, it was obvious that there was simply no time to organize the two weddings. The King sulked mightily but eventually agreed to put them both off until spring.

Malinda cared for few of the ambassadors, but mijnheer Nikolai Reinken of Thergy was an exception, a silver-haired, grandfatherly man with twinkling blue eyes. He had been the first person to present her with a betrothal present, a pair of gold earrings which he swore had been enchanted to ward off seasickness. More significantly, he clasped her hand warmly in both of his and said in a voice both heavily accented and conspiratorial, "I have met your future husband several times!"

"You have been to Baelmark?" She was surprised. Few who went to Baelmark ever returned.

"No, no, but I hear is a very beautiful land. King Radgar comes to Thergy quite often. Incognito, of course. But he is goot friend of King Johan! Most charming man! Most courteous."

Her mind boggled at the thought of a charming pirate, a courteous slaver. She wondered if mijnheer Reinken was her father's "excellent authority."

His Excellency kissed her hand and released it. "He will not off course to Chivial come for the wedding. Is not the way kings are married."

"Just as well, or I might find myself trying to reassemble my husband for the wedding night."

His Excellency laughed diplomatically. "Certainly Radgar is not the most popular bridegroom you could have chosen, my lady. Chivial has a bad view of him, yes?"

No worse than his bride's.

One nippy Tenthmoon morning, Ambassador Reinken came to Greymere with several clerks to begin discussing the wedding plans. Lord Whitney, the Chamberlain, was there also, a desiccated, permanently worried old man; he had scribes with him, too. Malinda brought only her Blades, confident that the sword was mightier than the pen, no matter what anyone said.

Lord Whitney welcomed the acting Baelish consul. Ten nibs dipped in inkwells and began to scratch. Mijnheer Reinken responded. More scratching. Eventually the talk became relevant.

"King Radgar especially asked," Reinken said, "that you not attempt to become goot in Baelish before the wedding. He feels Baelish conjuration will be superior at imparting this language."

"And Chivian is his mother tongue anyway?" Malinda asked, causing the Lord Chamberlain to wince and the Ambassador to smile tactfully.

Kings were usually married by proxy. The surrogate groom would then escort the bride to her husband's realm for another marriage ceremony and all necessary et ceteras. "Worry you need not!" His Excellency proclaimed. "Radgar will send a bark or caravel. He will not make you cross the ocean in open boat!"

"I want a dragon ship," Malinda said firmly. It was, she felt, a tradition in the family.

The old man shook his head dismissively. "No, no, my lady! A longship has no cabins! You will be exposed to the elements. Days of wind and spray! Storms!"

"I want a dragon ship—shields, red sail, monster beak, and all! I want real pirates at the oars. It will give the guests something to remember."

"It will indeet!"

The Lord Chamberlain shuddered. "Memo," he dictated. "Have Yeoman Cavalry standing by."

She had won her first point. She then proceeded to argue her second. Forget tradition: she would not be married at Greymere. Mobs would riot in the streets of Grandon—her father had just been forced to prorogue Parliament after the shortest session in history because the members were enraged that the second in line to the throne was to marry the Baelish pirate. No, her wedding would be at Wetshore, which was a few miles downstream and handy for the longship. She quashed Lord Whitney's protests easily. The King had given her a free hand, had he not?

With Wetshore accepted, she had won all the points she needed. The rest could come later, when there was less chance of her father finding out what she was up to in time to stop her. Although she did not realize it, she had already opened the door to disaster.

10

Do you, Radgar, take this woman . . .
CHIVIAN MARRIAGE SERVICE

*H*er wedding day dawned, sort of. She had been lying awake for hours, listening to the steady drum of rain, the syncopated beat of the drips from the eaves, the trickling of gutters. A confused, uncertain daylight was creeping slowly in through clouds, casements, bed curtains. This was the day. The tides had determined it, but it happened to be Periwinkle Day. Poor Eagle!

So far everything had gone according to plan. Incredibly, it had been less than a month ago that her father had lifted his head from his own grandiose plans for balls, masques, banquets, parades, and triumphal arches to look and see what his daughter had arranged for her wedding. He had then come very close to an apoplectic fit. "Spare no expense," he had told her, and she had spared every expense she could find. No balls, no banquets, no parades, not even a buffet lunch. The Palace of Wetshore was a decayed and ramshackle dump, long due to be torn down, and capable of holding only a fraction of the notables who expected to attend a royal wedding. She had been able to omit many people she did not like—about four fifths of the aristocracy, three quarters of the diplomatic corps, and most of the King's ministers. Unfortunately, Lord Roland, who had contrived her sacrifice, had duties that required him to be present. She had also included many people she liked and the King did not—Courtney, for instance, and all the Candlefens, who would have preferred not to come because they were relatives of the groom.

To the world it would seem that her father had not merely sold her to a slaver but had even denied her a decent wedding. How wonderfully he had screamed when he found out! Petty? Certainly it was, but she would get no other satisfaction. Why should she want pomp and display? What did she have to celebrate? Soon would come the month-long celebrations of His Majesty's marriage to Princess Dierda, and his daughter's trivial fit of pique would be altogether forgotten.

A clock chimed somewhere. She counted the strokes. Still too early to rise. She would embark at noon to catch the tide, sold and delivered. At least three days to Baelmark, perhaps three weeks if the winds were contrary.

The loudest of Ambrose's bellows had come when he realized that she was planning to depart without any entourage at all. Her household by then had been down to two, not counting servants. Arabel's trunks were packed, and as soon as she had seen her princess dressed for the wedding, she would be off to a post Malinda had found for her as lady companion to a certain crotchety dowager. Dian, also, would be around to help this morning, but she slept now in the matrimonial bed of Sir Bandit, after a swift and surprising courtship. Her husband had no need for a bed or time to waste in one, but he did visit her there at quite frequent intervals. Sir Chandos had borne his loss with commendable courage and the help of friends.

The invitations had been sent out, Baelmark had approved the arrangements, and the wedding itself could not be changed. Ambrose could do something about her train, though, and thus avert the scandal of a princess traveling unattended. Although no family wanted its daughters to endure such a journey or be prisoner in a faraway barbarous realm, he had found her two maids of honor, Lady Dove and Lady Ruby. How much they cost him in lands and appointments and royal favors no one knew, but Arabel insisted that the price had been enormous. Ruby was just a mouse who could not resist the bullying of avaricious parents. Dove was so stupid that she seemed to class Baelmark with Appleshire. Given half a chance, Malinda would leave them both behind on the beach.

The next thing she knew was the bed curtains being thrown open with unnecessary vigor.

"Terrible morning!" Dian said brightly. "Rained all night; roads will be rivers, but no wind, so the sea should be calm. I brought you some breakfast."

Malinda shuddered and pulled the quilt over her face. "No breakfast, thank you. I'll stay here. I feel like a day in bed."

"No, that comes later," Dian said. "That *is* the fun part, believe me."

She had only two events scheduled that day, and the first one was to go and spend an hour with Amby. He had a slight fever, was coughing a lot, feeling very sorry for himself. He did not know yet that he would never see her again, and in the end she did not have the heart to tell him. She stayed so long that Dian had to come and fetch her.

Later, being dressed by Arabel and a team of helpers, Malinda watched the procedure in the mirror with a curious detachment. What would the slaver think of his prize when he ripped her clothes off for the first time? Her hair was her best feature, dark brown with bronze highlights, like old oak. Clean skin, but Baelish lice, fleas, and bedbugs would probably take care of that. Her breasts were still high and not nearly as heavy as those broad shoulders warranted—men were very interested in breasts, Dian said. Dian would naturally like to think so. If Malinda's husband-to-be wanted her for childbearing he would approve of the wide hips; she ought to be a good for a dozen or so before she wore out. If he preferred sylphs for bed wrestling, he could send her off to work in the fields. Would King Rat consider that hefty young body worth ending a profitable war? Or would he just take her and laugh and let the war go on?

She had chosen a simple blue woolen dress, suitable for ocean voyages in open boats. Its open skirt revealed a gold kirtle to match her eyes. Over it she would wear a sable cloak that Father had given her, which had belonged to some of his wives, and on her head a gable hood with lappets to keep the worst of the weather off her face. No jewelry at all, she had decided. All the best jewels in Chivial had ended up in Baelmark long ago.

"Ripped all his clothes off," Arabel said.

"What?"

"The Countess. She practically ripped all his clothes off then and there." The mistress of rumors was regaling the team with scandal while braiding Malinda's hair.

"Whose clothes off?"

"Thegn Leofric's. But Lady Violet got between them . . ."

Leofric was King Radgar's proxy for the wedding. He had arrived the previous day, the first Bael Malinda had ever seen, other than corpses rotting on gallows. His longship and its two escorts now awaited her, at anchor in the estuary not a mile from the palace. She had first set eyes on him when he had presented his credentials to the King. She had been required to stand on the dais beside her father and recite a set speech, which she delivered in a singsong to show what she thought of it.

"Your Excellency is as welcome as the first swallows of spring, being a sign that my long winter of loneliness is over. Seeing the substitute, I am now doubly eager to meet the original."

If Thegn Leofric was not truly a welcome sight, he was certainly an unusual one by Chivian standards. His right eye socket was hidden behind a silver patch inset with what she had at first sight assumed to be a chunk of green glass; after a glance over the rest of him, she had realized that it must be an emerald. He was far from young, with jagged white scars on his ropy forearms and craggy, weathered face, but although his hair had receded and faded to a yellowish gray, he still had enough of it to dangle a ponytail halfway down his back. His clothes were equally bizarre but superbly made—a short-sleeved, knee-length sea-green smock, richly embroidered with coiling serpents in silver thread and bright stones; below that, ornate cross-gartered leggings and soft buskins. Like a servant, he wore no hat or cloak, and yet jewels glittered on his hands, belt, and dagger, while around his neck hung a triple string of glorious pearls as big as thumbnails.

He spoke perfect Chivian, probably spiritually imparted. "My lord is as impatient for that meeting as your exquisite self, Your Highness, although the reports he was given have utterly failed to prepare him for the joy awaiting him. As you can see, we Baels have no horns, no fangs."

Humor was a game that two could play. "It is well known that you eat babies, though. Do you have any special instructions for the cooks?"

The audience drew breath in shock.

Leofric laughed easily. "No, Your Grace. Whatever way you normally prepare them will be agreeable to me."

Ambrose chuckled. The court exploded in applause. So she had lost the first round. When she could be heard, she tried again.

"King Radgar has been Lord of the Fire Lands for almost twelve years, I'm told. I understand that few kings rule in Baelmark so long." With luck she would be widowed soon and free to return home.

The thegn shrugged. "He's good for many years yet, my lady. I'm sure he can hold on to the throne long enough."

"Long enough for what?"

"For one of his sons to succeed him."

"I didn't know he had—" Then she understood and felt herself blush crimson, while her father led the court in communal guffawing. The idea that Baels could have a sense of humor like ordinary people was a considerable surprise, almost annoying.

She had angered her father by inviting Courtney to the wedding; she decided to set him on Thegn Leofric at the earliest opportunity.

Even unarmed, the Bael raised the hackles of every Blade who set eyes on him. They skulked in corners and slunk in shadows, stalking the invader with suspicious scowls. While lowering their eyebrows, he raised the ladies', yet he seemed curiously indifferent to their attention. Despite that, he had been a considerable sensation at the party in the evening, and apparently even more of one after Malinda left. Several ladies of the court notoriously carved notches in their bedposts, and a genuine Baelish raider would be the catch of the year in the promiscuity stakes. . . .

"And who won?" asked Lady Ruby, shocked pink by the story.

"Violet did," Arabel said. "She practically dragged him upstairs by his topknot." She would not have been there, but her information was usually correct.

"I do hope he was worth her efforts," Malinda said icily.

"It seems likely." Dian entered the conversation. "According to the Guard, he left Lady Violet's chamber a couple of hours later and was admitted to the Countess's."

Upstaged, Arabel snorted disbelief. "At *his* age?"

"I think he could afford the very best in conjuration, don't you?"

Arabel said, "Hmm?" thoughtfully. "Well, I can find out how Lady Violet made out, anyway."

It seemed only seconds before Malinda was standing in a very crowded room between her father and that same Leofric, facing Lord Chancellor Roland, who was asking, "Do you, Malinda, take the man Radgar, here represented, to be your wedded . . . honor . . . obey . . . cherish . . ." She wondered what vows the Baelish wedding ceremony demanded, or if it was just a series of threats. She did not recall answering the question.

"Do you, Radgar, take . . . ?"

She pressed her signet into the wax and watched Thegn Leofric do the same.

★　　★　　★

She sat at his side in the coach, chaperoned by the blank-faced Lady Dove and the tensely suspicious Sir Dreadnought. A flashy troop of lancers from the Household Yeomen cantered alongside. Rain streamed down the windows. The park at Wetshore was a wide expanse of grassland, grazed close by sheep and used for events such as horse racing and archery that could be either sporting or military. It seemed very green under a dull pewter sky and skeleton trees, while off to the south stretched the leaden expanse of the Gran estuary. On the edge of the bank a gaudy canopy fluttered, and beyond that swayed the mast of a Baelish longship, red sail furled along its yard. Even a king would wait on a bride, and Ambrose was already in place, backed by the blue blur of the Royal Guard. Landward trailed a long serpent of umbrellas, hundreds of important guests waiting under the watchful eyes of heralds until they could advance to say their farewells. Lesser dignitaries were being kept in the background by lancers and men-at-arms. The Lord Chamberlain's office had estimated this part of the ceremony would last two hours, but the tide had already turned and the ship must sail by noon.

She should make conversation, but if she asked whether the hospitality had been satisfactory, Leofric might tell her in embarrassing detail. "What is your ship called, my lord?"

Baels were all supposed to have red hair and green eyes, but his eye was a faded blue. "She is not really mine, Your Grace. I borrowed her. She is *Wæternædre,* which means 'water snake.' I think one of the others has come to fetch us, though."

Two more longships were just visible in the rainy distance. "And what are their names?"

"*Wæl* and *Wracu,* mistress."

"Meaning?"

He hesitated an instant. " 'Slaughter' and 'revenge.' "

"Oh. Well, I did ask for a real dragon ship. I should not expect it to be called *Duckling* or *Custard.*"

Just then the coach creaked, squeaked, and finally shuddered to a stop. As a herald opened the door, buglers played a fanfare—which she did not recall being in the program—and onlookers cheered. She was supposed to step out onto the platform directly in front of her father and curtsey, but he was not visible and the space under the little canopy was packed solid with senior nobility anxious to stay dry. They squeezed back to let her in. The rain had ruined all the plans, she was running late, and now there was shouting and men running. She registered Thegn Leofric emerging behind her, the hateful, fishy stare of Secretary Kromman—how did that slime ever get into her wedding?—and the cynical smirk of tubby little Courtney, whose wedding present had been the largest diamond she had ever seen. Amid all the clamor and confusion, she heard Amby cough.

With his fever? Out in this damp? Forgetting protocol, she thrust people aside—"Let me through! Out of my way! Let me through!"—until she reached him, down at knee level, clinging to his nurse's finger, little face blue with cold. She grabbed him up and hugged him, glaring at the *imbecile* governess, Countess Napham, who would have brought him simply because she lacked the sense or courage to question a royal order. Malinda peered around. "Father? Your Majesty!" But she still could not see him, who was normally so visible in a crowd, and the shouting and bugle blowing was louder. Lancers cantered by, shaking the ground.

"Trouble, Your Highness?" inquired the steel-cold voice of Lord Roland at her elbow. He must have followed her.

"He's sick!" she said. "He should be home in bed. Healers—"

"Of course. Allow me. Sir Bloodfang!" That resonant voice could slash out commands that oak trees would jump to obey.

"Excellency?" Bloodfang was not the sharpest of the Blades, which was why he so often found himself guarding a three-year-old.

"Escort the Prince and his attendants back to the palace and have a healer look at him."

"Good-bye, Amby!" she whispered, passing him to the Blade.

"Your Highness," said Thegn Leofric at her other elbow, "your royal father has summoned us."

"What?" She looked around at the seething multitude of barons, viscounts, earls, marquises, dukes, government officials, military officers, consuls and ambassadors—and all their grand ladies, of course—all entitled and determined to kiss her fingers and wish her good chance in interminable detail. Dove and Ruby must be in there somewhere, saying their farewells. Good riddance! She laid a hand on the thegn's arm. "Then let us respond."

They stepped down onto the grass and into the rain. Pages came running to hold umbrellas over them. They squelched toward the river and the King, who stood on the edge of the bank within a solid phalanx of glowering Blades, incandescently furious. Someone must suffer when Ambrose looked like that.

"Thegn! It was agreed that no man except yourself was to come ashore."

Leofric scanned the scene below with his solitary eye. "Well, sire, that would depend on how you defined 'ashore,' now wouldn't it?"

Few large coastal buildings in Chivial had not been sacked by the

Baels in the last decade. Wetshore had survived because it was protected by wide mud flats—black, sticky, smelly, and impassable—covered only briefly at high tide. Lord Whitney had produced plans for a grandiose memorial pier, which Malinda had rejected in favor of the simplest possible dock, just a stair down the grassy bank and a jetty running out from it. *Slaughter*—or possibly *Revenge*—was now tied up alongside this, with her dragon's head prow staring balefully at the spectators. She was only an open box with a mast, tapering bow and stern, flaring wide amidships, menacing yet beautiful. Along either side hung shields, round and gaily painted.

What was enraging the King was that her crew had disembarked and formed up along the jetty in a double line, like an honor guard—a whole shipload of armed Baelish raiders. Helmets and weapons shone even under the pewter sky. Perhaps technically the pirates were not ashore, but they were uncomfortably close to the assembled elite of Chivial, and everyone knew what had happened at Candlefen Park, thirty years ago. That had been a wedding, too.

Spirits! Malinda's heart had begun hammering very hard, wanting out. Here, within the Royal Guard and beside her father, she was still in his realm. Safe. Down there, at the bottom of the steps, she would enter the savage domain of her raider husband. Some part of her wanted to turn and flee in terror. Another—much smaller—part was whispering that the adventure had begun. Although Thegn Leofric might not be typical and might not stay on his best behavior very long at a time, he had at least shown her that Baels, at least some Baels, were capable of acting like civilized human beings, at least sometimes; so there might, just possibly, be a tiny, very faint chance that Radgar Æleding was not the terrifying child-eating rapist and sadist he was always made out to be.

"I say they're ashore!" Ambrose snarled. "Get them out of there!"

"As you wish, sire. Ready, Your Grace?"

She heard her voice say, "Ready. Good-bye, Father." And with her hand on the thegn's arm, she began to descend the wooden steps that led down to the dock, leaving all the hundreds of guests with no bride to kiss good-bye. She had just contrived the largest mass snub in the history of Chivial.

"You know how to review an honor guard, of course?"

"I think I am capable." Her knees trembled, her mouth was dry—the only dry part of her, because no umbrella-wielding page was going to venture close to those monsters. The treads were awkward, too short for two strides, too wide for one. Had anyone thought to tell

Dove and Ruby that she had gone? She had never seen a *naked* honor guard before. "Aren't they cold?" Her teeth were close to chattering.

The thegn chuckled. "Probably all freezing their buns off but not about to admit it. If they'd come ashore to do mischief, they wouldn't have left their bucklers behind and they'd be wearing even less."

Less than leather britches, boots, and steel helmets? Or perhaps he meant their adornments, for now she could see that every man in the crew was a glittering wonder of gold and silver, pearls and precious stones—arm rings, earrings, necklaces, boots, belts, and baldrics. There was more wealth on these brute sailors than there was on all the guests up in the park.

She reached the jetty and the thegn removed his arm. Raising her chin, she marched forward between the two lines, swords erect on one side, ferocious axes on the other. Young men, older men, green eyes staring fixedly ahead and never meeting hers. The Household Yeomen were no better disciplined and the Blades would not come close. Light shone on jewels and steel and wet skin. She had never dreamed that men could be so hairy, and in the Baels' case hair was invariably red—ginger, auburn, copper—braids or loose tresses, beards and mustaches, often chests, arms, and shoulders too. But they were human beings, just men—some grizzled, some little more than boys. No horns, no fangs. Not even rickets or rashes or fleabites.

She had arrived at the end of the honor guard, the end of the jetty, the stern of the ship. One man had remained aboard. He was decently—if bizarrely—dressed in smock and cross-gartered leggings without a gem in sight. He held up a hand for her as she stepped over the side and descended a set of steps to the grated floor, feeling the ship rock very slightly underfoot. She had left her homeland, never to return.

She turned and surveyed the longship, full of oars, storage chests, confusing ropes and cloth bundles. Unexpectedly, it smelled of beeswax and faintly of pitch. Ruby and Dove were descending the staircase, escorted by a Blade. Above them, the crest of the bank was packed with neck-craning courtiers, interspersed with mounted lancers, all bleating like goats at their first sight of a dragon ship and real pirates. Thegn Leofric had boarded beside her. Suddenly he bellowed an order, and Malinda jumped.

A wave of Baels hurtled over the array of shields, their boots hitting the gratings almost simultaneously. *Revenge,* or else *Slaughter,* lurched and tipped. A moment later a second wave followed the first. She staggered. The man who had helped her aboard caught her elbow and spoke a greeting.

"Good chance to you," she said, shrugging him off. "Thegn Leo-fric, you need not wait for those two women. Go without them. Depart at once, please."

Again the thegn yelled an order. Ropes were flipped loose, oars run out, and the ship slid away from the jetty and began to turn as the wind caught her. Then something registered. . . .

Malinda spun around. *"What did you just say?"*

The man smiled. "I said, 'My lady, I am Radgar Æleding.'"

11

J have known Radgar since we were children, yet he can still astonish me. He owes much of his success to being completely unpredictable.
SIR WASP, PERSONAL COMMUNICATION TO LORD ROLAND

The drawing had not done him justice. She had never seen eyes of such intense color, green enamel, and there was no silver in the fringe of copper beard. He had cut his hair shorter . . . certainly did not look thirty . . . did not look a monster.

"Your Grace!" She began a curtsey.

"No!" His hands flashed out and caught her elbows. "You don't kneel to me!" Their eyes met. She looked away. If he had expected some delicate courtly flower, he now knew he had bought a great hulking wench. But he had lifted her as if she were Amby, so he was no runt himself. He must have the muscles of a woodcutter.

Oh, spirits! If the Blades or the Yeomen guessed that Monster Radgar was there, within reach, she would be a virgin widow. She looked to see how far the ship was from the jetty. Not far at all, drifting aimlessly on the rain-pocked water. The oars were spread out like wings, motionless.

He said, "My pardon if I startled you. Did not your father tell you I was here?"

She shook her head. He could not have known . . .

The King of—*her husband*—frowned. "Did he even tell you that we knew each other of old?"

"Why . . . no, Your Grace." Ruby and Dove and the Blade had

stopped, uncertain whether or not to continue. Up on the bank, her father was peering over the heads of his cordon of Guards, and the fury on his fat face was clearly visible. He had *recognized* Radgar? How could he? But—

"He assured me, Your Majesty, that he had good reason to believe that you were gracious in your person and of gentle manner."

"How kind of him!" Radgar said angrily. "Such was not his opinion when we met twelve years ago. It seems he came very close to lying to you about our acquaintance. Would you agree that he was trying to deceive you?"

Why discuss her father? Couldn't he even offer to kiss her cheek? Her fingers?

The pirate raised his eyebrows. "An honest answer, my lady! Did your father deliberately hide from you the fact that he and I know each other personally?"

Bewildered, she said, "Perhaps he forgot a brief—"

"I am sure he did not. What other tricks did he use on you? What threats did he make to force you into this marriage?"

She did not understand. "Your Majesty, I wrote to you! I testified before the—"

"Yes, you did, because I would not sign the treaty until I was given assurances that you were not being forced into a union you found distasteful. I must still hear it from your own lips."

"Your Grace . . ." The multitude onshore had fallen silent, staring at the longship.

"Why did you not wait for your two ladies to board?"

"My lord husband, why don't we sail?"

"Later!" he said angrily. "Because you knew they did not want to come? Because they had been forced into accompanying you? So what about you? You are happy at the prospect of spending the rest of your life in Baelmark bearing my children?"

"I am honored to wed so fine a king!"

"Oh, rubbish! You may be terrified or disgusted or shivering with excitement. You cannot possibly feel *honored*. I'm a slaver and a killer of thousands. But my mother was forced into her marriage, and I will not take you as my wife unless I am convinced that you are truly happy at the prospect. I think you were bludgeoned into it. Speak! Persuade me otherwise."

He was bullying her, just like her father. "Unfair, my lord! I have told you already and you refuse to believe me. You call me liar?"

"I call your father worse than that. Did you not accuse him of slaving?"

She flinched under the accusing green stare. She had said lots of things, but not everything that had been reported. "I may have used intemperate words in the shock of . . . I mean . . . The news was sprung on me . . . I promise most faithfully, Your Grace, that I will never presume to speak that way to you."

He scowled.

She tried to assert herself. "I am of the blood, so I will marry whom I am told to marry. I have always known this was my purpose, and I presume to say, my lord, on first sight you seem much less offensive than other suitors whose names have been bandied around me in the past. . . ."

He sniffed. "I am flattered, but I did not mean Radgar Æleding as a two-legged male animal. All men are much the same in the dark. Most women close their eyes in the action, anyway. Kings also marry sight unseen, lady, and it is not your appearance that makes me reluctant—far from it! No, I mean any king of Baelmark. My name in Chivial is held in low esteem."

Fire and death! Was he seriously offering to release her? A wild surge of hope almost stopped her heart, but such a solution was unthinkable and must be resisted. Her duty forbade it. So came anger: "You will force me to beg? A royal marriage is often a bridge between former combatants. What of the treaty? If you refuse me, must not the war continue?"

The longship floated slowly downstream and farther out over the rain-speckled water. The crowds on the bank continued to buzz with puzzled comment. Everyone must have guessed by now who alone could be holding up proceedings like this.

Radgar shook his head sadly. "I could have ended it any time in the last ten years, my lady. I did not want to retract my youthful boasting, and that is a foolish reason, mere pride. As it happens, there are legends of heroes who swore blood feuds but then became entangled in coils of love and so were forced to recant their oaths—I am sure you can fill in the details for yourself. Thus marriage to you would provide a face-saving excuse for me. Strange that it was your father and not I who thought to roll you up in the treaty scroll."

She opened her mouth and then closed it quickly.

"Aha!" he said. "You thought the match was my idea?"

"That was what I was told, but I thought it was Lord Roland's."

"Durendal? No. He has too much honor to sell a lady himself, but he fetches when his master throws. It was all your father's idea. He was desperate to end the war, and evidently he lied to you yet again. Well, I will end it without you, I promise."

"Oh!" Temptation! Freedom, a chance to waken from the long nightmare! "You swear that?"

"I swear that. You are free to go."

"You shame me!" She tried to meet the steady green stare, cold and deadly as oceans.

"I honor you, mistress. My father carried off my mother by force, but I refuse to abuse a woman so."

Rubbish! What game was he playing with her? There was more to this than met the eye. "Indeed? What of the thousands you carry off into slavery?"

"Except that. That is war, and I hate it. I do truly intend to end it now, Princess, and you need not be sold into slavery. I give you back your freedom."

Still she wavered. "You shame me!"

"I shame your father. Having shown the world how low he will sink, I am content. Go in peace. You need not breed pirate babies for a living."

Anger and suspicion that she was somehow being deceived . . . joy and hope that the weight of half a year would be lifted from her . . . shame at being rejected . . . worry what her father would do . . .

Hope won.

"I will obey Your Majesty's command."

Radgar raised her hand to his lips. "My loss, Princess. This was not a pleasant nor an easy task. Take us in, helmsman."

The ship seemed to move itself on his command, like a circus horse, until the stern nudged the end of the jetty. He moved the steps for her and offered his hand. As if in a dream, she mounted to the dock and looked down at those incredibly green eyes gazing up at her. They seemed almost wistful, not the eyes of a monster. He said something flowery that she did not bother to hear.

She turned away and began to walk *home*. It was over. She was free. Fates knew what her father was going to say. He had offered his daughter to a pirate and the pirate had spurned her.

Ruby and Dove had already gone, but they no longer mattered. Some adventuresome pages and younger courtiers who had ventured partway down the slope of the bank were hastily scrambling back up in case the pirates came chasing them. As she neared the steps she glanced back and saw that the ship—whatever its name—had still not departed, but was again drifting aimlessly. Ahead of her the Guard had cleared the stair and the way was open right up to her father, who stood at the top, fists on hips, glaring at her. Would he throw her in the Bastion and put her on trial for treason? He must be sorely puzzled to know what the pirate king had been up to. So was she.

Unless . . . She spun around for another look at the longship, and at that exact instant a crossbow cracked.

In her nightmares long after, she heard the whistle of the bolt going over her head, and perhaps she did in reality. When she looked landward, her father had vanished. The howl that followed raised the hair on her neck. She had heard that same howl once before, long ago, when she was a child—when her mother died. It was the sound of bereaved Blades. Only this time it was much louder.

12

Seconds matter more than years do. One instant can change your whole life forever.

SIR DOG

Screaming in fury, Malinda raced back along the jetty until she stood at the end of the rain-soaked planks, facing the cold, gray waste of water and shaking her fist at the longship as it vanished into the mist, borne on the rhythmic beat of great fir wings. Its job was done. King Radgar had plumbed new depths of treachery. She had never been a bride, only bait. Why had her father been such a fool as ever to trust that monster?

She turned to survey the horrors. The notorious Blade Riot after the death of Goisbert IV had involved only a dozen or so Blades. Here almost the entire Guard had seen Ambrose struck down under the worst of all possible circumstances—death by deliberate violence, and not even from ambush but by an enemy they had already identified and failed to balk. The secular troops nearby would restrain the violence, but they would need time to react and Blades were deadly fast.

A human tide was flowing over the lip of the bank as people tried to escape the slaughter, but few of them could keep their balance on the slope. Gaudily dressed men and women were rolling down like raindrops on a window, some of them already trailing blood. Among them went uniformed Blades and men-at-arms, even a few mounted lancers, and at the bottom they all splashed into the mud and water. Judging by the noise, there was worse bloodshed under way up in the park. The Blades, she supposed, were either trying to catch the departing pirate or punishing one another for what had happened or perhaps just lashing out in unbearable fury. She saw a couple of them manage to stop their own descent halfway and cling there, striking at anyone going past. A horse skidded down on its haunches, screaming in terror, with a lancer on its back and a Blade on top of him, sawing through his throat. The crowd in the water grew ever larger, boiling the mud to red foam. Some of the survivors were trying to reach the jetty, arms flailing as they fought their way through the ooze.

Too many people and horsemen converged on the staircase, turning it into a sluice, but then it collapsed altogether and slid down into a charnel heap, which at least blocked the end of the jetty from the demented Blades trying to catch the departed dragon ship. They might well attack Malinda herself—after all, the bolt had come from her direction and their madness did not need a reason.

So far the only other occupants of the jetty were some wounded courtiers, who had extricated themselves from the carnage at the bottom of the steps, but that was not going to last. Several men were scrambling up onto the boards from the water, and some of them were certainly Blades, still armed and crazy. How long until they stopped screaming and came to their senses?

All Blades were struck from the same die and hard to tell apart at a distance, but the first one to make it up looked like Foulweather. Fortunately he headed landward to slaughter other refugees. Sir Huntley scrambled up out of the river and went for him, both of them screaming.

But they were only the first. At the far end, where she was, the water was deeper and the man trying to climb up was having trouble doing so while holding his sword. He had both arms on the boards, supporting his weight while his feet sought a foothold in the pilings. She ran forward and barely recognized Sir Falcon, so much had rage distorted his face. She slammed a foot down on the sword. "The King is dead!" she shouted. "Long live the King!" That was the recipe, the only thing that might bring rampaging Blades to their senses, because they were bound to defend both the King and his heirs.

"Long live the King! Long live the King!"

His Majesty King Ambrose V, aged three years and a few months.

Falcon screamed back up at her and tried to beat on her foot with his free hand. Then he found enough wits to grab her ankle and haul on it, so she swung a savage kick on his nose with her other foot and promptly fell flat on her back. Her ankle came free, though; he had gone, leaving his sword behind. She was up on her feet in an instant, grabbing it up hungrily. When his bloody face emerged from the water, his screaming sounded very different. Again he heaved himself partway up, and this time even got one foot on the deck, so she swung the sword down two-handed across his neck.

When she opened her eyes, there were only red bubbles. . . . She had probably just killed a Blade and had certainly disarmed one, which was even rarer. Two more of them were fighting a duel halfway between her and whatever was happening at the landward end. She ran to them, still clutching Falcon's bloody sword.

"Long live the King!"

Alas, Screwsley and Orvil were far too busy battling and screaming to pay any heed to her as she stood there yelling her mantra, "Long live the King! Long live the King!" Then Sir Huntley ran Orvil through from behind. Before he could pull his sword free, he was struck down by Screwsley, who promptly swung around to deal with Malinda. She howled in terror and half jumped, half fell off the jetty.

The water was shockingly cold and black as midnight. For a few choking moments she could not tell which way was up, but here it was no more than waist deep. Spluttering and coughing, she struggled to her feet, sinking into the ooze as if trying to take root. There, right in front of her, was the bedraggled but still obviously crazy Sir Screwsley, who must have followed her down. Mad eyes gleaming, mouth wide open in his unending scream, he swung his sword.

A great wave swept her over and submerged her again in blackness. It slammed her against something very solid, probably pilings. Again she fought her way back to air and daylight. The cause of the current was a plunging, struggling horse. As the water cleared from her ears, she heard its rider shouting.

"Malinda! Quick! Malinda!" Incredibly, it was Lord Roland in his chain of office and crimson robes, although he had lost his hat. He sheathed his sword and held out a hand for her, keeping his horse under control with the other. She grabbed, and he hauled her up behind him—astride of course. Her waterlogged dress crawled right up her, leaving her legs exposed, and spirits knew where her bonnet had gone. Perforce she threw both arms around her savior to stay on. The body floating there must be Sir Screwsley.

The horse went plunging and splashing landward.

"What in death's name are you doing here?" she yelled.

"Rescuing you, of course."

This was a cavalry horse. How had he got hold of that? Had he ridden it down the bank? To save her?

"Thank you!"

"Thank me when you're safely home!" he shouted. "Thank the spirits you sent the Prince away, though."

Oh, Amby! "Will he be all right?"

"He should be—he's the heir. And he's only a baby . . . We must get to him before his guards hear the news, though. Hold on!"

They had reached the shore, and the rump on which she was so precariously perched tilted almost vertical. "You can't ride a horse up this cliff!" she howled.

Yes he could.

The deluge of bodies had stopped; a few people were clambering back up on hands and knees. Hoof by hoof, the poor horse struggled to be a mountain goat. In grave danger of sliding off, she clung tight to Roland, her face hard against his bony back.

Her father was *dead!* That enormity had not penetrated yet. The giant presence that had dominated her life and the whole country for so many years was suddenly missing. She might not come to terms with that for weeks, or months. Amby was only a baby, a sickly child who seemed to need a healing every few days for coughs or fevers. So who would rule his realm until he grew up?

What happened if he *didn't* grow up? She tried to thrust the thought away—spirits, her father wasn't even cold yet—but the question kept slithering back. Princess Dierda was not going to provide any answers now. Malinda was heir presumptive again, and an heir much closer to the throne than was healthy. Life expectancy in royal families usually dropped significantly during regencies.

"What did Radgar say to you?" Lord Roland had his head in his horse's mane.

"He said Father cheated . . . that Father must have known who he was."

"He recognized him. They met in Ironhall, years ago. Radgar trained there."

"No!"

"Yes. A clever, clever man! He distracted us all with that honor guard just now—it made us all think of swords and axes and forget about archery. We forgot that the war was a personal quarrel that needed only one arrow."

Not far to go now, but she could feel her knees and hands weakening with the effort of hanging on. "Why didn't Father tell me he knew him?" *Why quote an "excellent authority"?*

"Because . . . because Baelish kingship isn't like ours, but twelve years ago your father pretty much had the heir to the Baelish throne in his hands. What he planned to do with him I don't know, but Radgar made a fool of him—he escaped, went home, seized the throne by murdering his uncle, and then declared war on your father. Not on Chivial, on its king. I should have seen . . . Bandit . . . Death and fire! We should have all seen!"

Lord Roland would not enjoy being outwitted; it would be a salutary experience for him.

The gasping, shivering horse reached level ground and tilted the world back to its normal position. Roland patted its neck and gave it a few moments to breathe. The park looked like a battlefield, with bodies everywhere—men, horses, women, even a pathetic page lying stiff in his own blood. Not many of the dead were Blades. The canopy had collapsed. Here and there, survivors were sitting up, nursing wounds or wandering in shock, and there were lancers riding in the distance—they seemed to be chasing Blades and cutting them down. The only screaming she could hear now was the sound of the wounded.

Roland growled something she did not ask him to repeat. Then he urged the horse forward. If he went any faster than a walk, she was going to fly off. Her hair had fallen into a great lopsided knot over one ear and her skirts were bunched up around her hips.

"Those poor people!" she shouted. "We should help them!"

"No, my lady!" he shouted back. "You have duties to perform that no one else can."

A broken neck would not improve her performance, but he urged the horse into a canter and she did not fall off. At least it was not a trot. They raced past small groups of survivors straggling back to the palace; she heard some angry shouts behind her, but could not tell whether they were directed at her or the Lord Chancellor.

Her father was dead. The history of Chivial had just changed direction. She was not married to a foreign pirate king. She was still here, not there. But nothing was the same and never would be.

13

J do swear upon my soul that J will be faithful and bear true allegiance to His Majesty Ambrose V as lawful sovereign of the realm of Chivial and Nostrimia, and Prince of Nythia, and J will defend him to the utmost of my power against all traitorous conspiracies or attempts whatever which shall be made against his person, crown, and dignity; and that J will do my utmost endeavor to disclose and make known to His Majesty, his heirs and successors, all treasons and traitorous conspiracies and attempts which J shall know to be against him or any of them; and all this J swear without any equivocation, mental evasion, or secret reservation, and renouncing all pardons and dispensations from any person or persons whatsoever to the contrary.

THE OATH OF ALLEGIANCE

Roland rode right up the steps to the arch, where two men-at-arms and three dismounted lancers stood guard. Strong hands helped her down, and she realized that she had left her shoes in the mud flats. Roland's heels hit the flags; he passed his reins to one of the Yeomen. "Any trouble, Ensign?"

"No, my lord." The officer was a willow sapling with a cotton-fluff mustache and a very worried expression.

"It should be about over. If they can speak the oath of allegiance, they're all right and you may admit them."

"And if they can't, my lord?"

"I told you what to do. Good luck. My lady?" Roland escorted Malinda into Wetshore Palace at a near run. "You need a change of clothes, Your Grace. Will there be anything in your quarters?"

"Probably." She had left a few things for Dian to distribute among the servants. "But the doors may be locked."

He went up the stairs two at a time, wet robes flapping around his ankles. She raised her sodden skirts and kept pace in her stocking feet.

"We'll try the door first," he said.

That meant he knew of a way in that she did not, just like in Greymere on the Night of Dogs. She made another mark against Lord

Roland on her mental charge sheet. True, he had come to save her at no small risk to himself, but what were his motives? He was obviously trying to use her for some purpose of his own. Regencies bred their own especially foul brand of politics, and no doubt he would be one of the leading experts in this one. He was probably scheming to be regent himself.

The door was unlocked. They went into the anteroom, dim and cool and silent.

"Please be as quick as you possibly can, my lady."

"Why? What do you want me to do?"

"Sorry!" His smile flashed and was gone. "Your brother is being guarded by four Blades. I ordered his quarters cordoned off, but I need your help in breaking the news to them. Please?"

The coldness in his eyes implied danger not mentioned. The horrors might not be over yet, and even Amby might be at risk.

"Of course!" she said, and ran. Her presence chamber was barren, stripped of furniture. She had no servants. She would need a whole new household, a new wardrobe. . . .

She crossed her withdrawing room to her dressing room and at least that was still furnished. She went straight to the curtains and hauled them back to see what she was doing, then turned to the wardrobes, wondering where to start. If Lord Roland had arranged her father's death . . .

"There she is now." Sir Fox emerged from the closet.

Malinda's scream froze in her throat.

"So she is," agreed Sir Fitzroy, stepping out from behind the fourposter.

They both held swords. Fitzroy's was bloodstained. Fox's livery was splattered with mud and blood. Their smiles were mawkish, frozen, meaningless; and their eyes seemed horribly wrong—staring past her or through her, not at her. They converged on her, and she backed away until she met the wall. She knew she should scream, but she couldn't even draw breath. Lord Roland would come running, but he was three rooms away and those swords were only inches. . . .

"Stop!" she croaked, almost inaudibly. "What have I done?"

"Done?" Fox said, smiling at her left ear. "What has she done, brother?"

"She killed our ward, brother," Fitzroy told the wall.

"Yes, she told the pirate to kill our ward."

"She will have to die, brother."

"Have to bleed."

"No, it wasn't her." Lord Roland was leaning nonchalantly against the doorjamb with his arms crossed. "If you want the traitor who killed your ward, it isn't her."

He was still too far away to rescue her if the madmen lunged, but his words distracted them. They rotated so their crazy eyes and frozen smiles were directed at him. Very gently, very slowly, Malinda began to edge crabwise along the wall.

"Who was the traitor, Brother Durendal?" asked Fox.

"Yes, Leader, tell us."

"Who must we kill? We hurt. We must kill the traitor."

"Mm?" Roland still seemed supremely bored. "Remember Sir Wolfbiter? Classmate of yours."

"He died!" Fox said sharply. "He was your Blade and he died."

"Did you kill our brother?" Fox began walking toward Roland.

Fitzroy followed. Malinda wondered if she should dive into the closet and try to hold the door against them. Or where she might find a weapon to help Lord Roland . . .

"I didn't kill him," the Chancellor said casually. "It was Master Secretary Kromman who killed Wolfbiter. Kromman killed your ward, too. It was his idea. He talked your ward into inviting the pirate to come in his ship so the pirate could shoot him. It's Kromman you must kill, brothers."

"Where is Kromman?" Fox whispered. The point of his sword was at Roland's throat.

"He's downstairs in my office, rummaging through the files. You'll find him there, brothers. Go and kill him because he killed Wolfbiter." He stepped casually aside and listened as the running footsteps died away. "All right, my lady?"

The room was swaying. She nodded uncertainly. *Of course! I defy death every fifteen minutes just to keep on my toes.*

He turned his back. "Then please hurry. It's even more urgent now. They must be getting in the windows."

She opened a wardrobe, then another, found some dresses. "Why did you follow me to this room?"

"Because I discovered the secret door ajar." Lord Roland still had his back to her.

"What if they do catch Kromman? What if he really is where you said?"

"He probably is. He loves to snoop, and he never misses any chances."

"Did he really betray my father?"

"I have no idea. I suspect the Baelish marriage was his idea. I know he'd developed a curious interest in the epic poetry of Baelmark. Can't prove anything."

"But they'll kill him!"

"*Tsk!*" said the Lord Chancellor. "So they will. Are you nearly ready yet?"

"You could help me with these laces."

In a dry dress and shoes and a bonnet pulled over the sodden bush of her hair, she hurried along the corridor beside him. "Will they remember? The mad Blades—when they come to their senses, will they know what they've done?"

He sighed. "Yes, we remember." That was an odd way to put it. He would have been only a child when King Taisson died, and there had been no riot then anyway.

"Then why did you send those two after Master Kromman?"

He glanced at her with eyes like chips of frozen basalt. "I had to get rid of them somehow. My office *ought* to be locked."

"But why Kromman?"

"Because today I am free of a promise." He increased the pace and did not explain.

He must suppose that she was too far in his debt now—doubly in his debt—to reveal his part in the murder, if it happened. But what if he was the traitor and Kromman had gone looking for evidence to expose him? And how many other people would presume, as Fox and Fitzroy had, that she herself was the traitor? The assassination would probably have been impossible in Grandon, and holding the wedding at Wetshore had been entirely her idea.

They went up one more stair and along a gallery. Looking down, she could see people standing around in the entrance hall, and more streaming in through the main door. They were weeping, comforting one another, gabbling out tales of horror. It was still not long since her father died, and the survivors were only just returning to the palace. The death toll might not be known for days.

Except for that, Your Grace, did you have a nice wedding?

The gallery was blocked by a dozen or so people, some of them lancers. The ensign in charge was even more chinless and worried than the one on the front door. He almost wept with relief as he reported to the Chancellor.

"No one's gone in, my lord, as you said. These healers wanted to and I refused. Those two women came out, looking for them." He swallowed. "I've been expecting a Blade to come looking to see—"

"Who's left in there?"

"The Prince . . ." Another swallow. "I mean His *Majesty* and two attendants and the four Blades, my lord."

"Not Lady Napham?" Malinda demanded angrily.

"No, Your Grace."

So Amby's governess had stayed at the farewell ceremonies, had she? Serve her right if she'd been chopped up by mad Blades!

Roland nodded inquiringly at Malinda. "Ready?"

Swallowing was contagious, suddenly. "What do I have to do?"

"I'll try to get the women out of the room and the Blades in, all together. If I can't, I can't. When I nod, you pick up the child and break the news. It should work. Keep holding him and you should be safe."

She nodded, and he opened the door. *No more killing, please!* In the antechamber, Sir Marlon and Sir Fury were playing dice, but they were on their feet in a flash. "Lord Chan—" Marlon began and then his smile vanished. "*My lady?* What—"

"Quick!" Roland strode past them. "There may be trouble brewing. Where's His Highness?"

All four of them moved together, but only their hero, the great Durendal, could have won his way past the Royal Guard without an explanation. They sped through another room and into Amby's bedroom. He was sitting on the floor, grumpily playing at wooden blocks with one of the nursemaids. The other stupid wench was snickering on a couch with Sir Hawkney. Sir Bloodfang was resignedly sharpening his sword with the glazed expression of a cow chewing cud.

"Lindy!" Amby said, brightening and holding up his arms to her.

She swept him up and hugged him. He seemed less feverish than before. "You feeling better now, big fellow?" Behind her, Bloodfang was grunting out questions; Roland was chivvying the two women out.

Closing the door, Roland nodded to her. The Blades were growing suspicious.

"The King is dead!" Malinda forced her brother around to face them, although he wanted to snuggle into her shoulder. "Long live the King! The King is dead. Long live King Ambrose V!"

"Long live the King!" Roland strode forward and knelt to the child she held. She joined in, and they chanted together: "Long live Ambrose V!"

For a terror-filled moment she thought it would not work. The four Blades had gone white with shock. Bloodfang's eyes were taking on the same unfocused look she had seen on Fox and Fitzroy. Hands crept toward sword hilts. Then young Fury cried, "Long live the King!" and fell on his knees beside Roland.

Marlon followed . . . Hawkney . . . and Bloodfang. Done! She gasped with relief.

Roland rose. "Swear! Swear allegiance to Ambrose V."

"What happened, my lord?" Hawkney groaned, and the others took up the refrain: "Oh spirits!" "What happened?" "Tell us!"

Only when they had sworn did Roland begin to answer, and he was interrupted by Fox and Fitzroy bursting into the room with Oak and Brock and Dominic right on their heels. All of them were bedraggled and blood-spotted, but it was the horror in their faces that Malinda noticed most, as if they had been tortured into insanity by expert tormenters. Moaning and babbling, they knelt to their new ward. In the distance, others were shouting out the oath to win admittance—under normal circumstances Blades would walk right over any Yeomen who dared to question them.

Still clutching her brother and king, Malinda grudgingly nodded approval to Lord Roland. Whatever his ultimate motives, this had been well done. "What next, my lord?"

He shook his head wearily. "That was only the Guard. Now comes the court, and after that the whole country. If you please, my lady, bring him down to the throne room when I send word? Sir Dominic!"

"Brother?" Dominic staggered to his feet. From the look of him, he'd been in the river, but there was dried blood on his sword hand. His lack of eyelashes accentuated his horror-stricken stare. "My lord, I mean."

"I'm appointing you Acting Commander until Leader or Dreadnought turns up. Keep the Pr—keep the King safe. And Her Highness, also, of course. *And get this filthy rabble cleaned up!*"

At the moment Roland was no exemplar of elegance himself, but the deliberate brutality worked. Dominic stiffened as if he had been slapped.

"Yes, my lord." He squared his shoulders and unleashed a bellow of his own: "You! On your feet, you despicable lot! Clear a path for His Excellency."

Soon Malinda found herself standing beside the empty throne, still holding Amby, who kept drifting in and out of sleep. He was small for his age, but growing heavier every second. Perhaps she was feeling the weight of his troubles, poor little orphaned king. If he was king. They had all been assuming that he was, but that was still not certain.

Never adequate, the presence room at Wetshore was now so packed with the great of the kingdom that even the old and the wounded had to stand. Courtiers' finery had been reduced to rags—torn, mud-soaked, and in some cases bloody. The stench of sweat and river mud seemed to mingle with a nauseating miasma of rage directed at Dominic and the dozen or so other Blades clustered behind the baby king. They were all clean and smart now, but ivory-faced, stark as corpses.

No one knew the toll yet. She had invited four dukes to her wedding and only two were present now, three ambassadors out of eight. Grand Inquisitor was there, and the Lord High Admiral, and Courtney beside her, but what of the Lord Mayor of Grandon, Ambassador Reinken, the Earl Marshal, the Lord Chamberlain, Mother Superior? Why had Dominic not yet yielded his command to Bandit—was Dian a widow so soon?

"Ready to assume your *duties,* Your Grace?" Fat little Courtney in his scrumptious apparel was nuzzling close. "I understand that the Act of Succession assigns the regency to the next in line." Today's scent was musk.

"Not the next *man?*" She could not recall, although she knew that past queens had served as regents while their husbands went off to war—her own mother for one. It was not impossible that she would find herself ruling Chivial in a few minutes.

Not very likely, of course, since she was legally still a minor. On the other hand, the standard rules of inheritance did not always apply to royalty. There was no certain age of majority for kings of Chivial, as several regents had discovered at extreme cost to themselves. She knew this because for years it had been her business to know this. No matter what the law said or how much hair grew on his chin, nor even how sturdy his sword arm, a Chivian king who had succeeded as a minor began to rule on the day the Royal Guard started taking his orders. Goisbert II had been twenty, Ambrose I a mere fifteen, to the astonishment and ruin of his wicked uncle. There were no such precedents for queens regnant, unless one counted the case of Queen Adela, whose Blades had suddenly decided that she was insane and *stopped* taking her orders.

"I can't imagine your *dear* father letting *me* get the job, darling," Courtney lamented. "But a regent has to be of the blood, and I think Brinton's too remote. Besides, is he *here?* You can see better than I can. Did he run into some Blade trouble, do you suppose?"

"Yes, Brinton's here." But De Mayes was not. The Duchess was, comforting young Ansel, who was weeping.

"Go to bed now," Amby mumbled.

"Soon." If she became regent, she swore, she would be that rarest of gems, an honest one, dedicated to bringing her brother safely to a secure throne.

"Pray silence for His Excellency the Earl Roland!" bellowed a herald, and the grumbling subsided reluctantly.

The Chancellor was the calmest person present, and his deep voice took command of the room. "Your Graces, Your Excellencies, my lords, ladies, gentlemen. As your worships all know, the succession is determined by statute, the Succession Act of 242, which codifies the ancient customs of the realm—that only the sovereign's lawful issue are eligible to succeed; that the crown shall pass first to his sons in order of age, then his daughters; and failing direct issue, then to his brothers and their issue *per stirpes,* and so on. However, that same act then acknowledges that the monarch may exclude particular persons for especial reasons. In practice, this means that the succession lies within the royal prerogative and is dictated by the deceased king's will, within limits."

He could have added that those ill-defined "limits" had provoked not a few civil wars. Half brother Granville, for example—if Ambrose had dared to name his bastard as his successor, would the country take up arms to give little Amby his rights? Or would the Lords and Commons agree that the Rector was the better choice in this instance?

Roland held up an envelope. "Some months ago, I presumed to advise His Late Majesty that his forthcoming marriage and that of his daughter, the Lady Malinda, might make a review of his current will timely. I stress, my lords, that I did not know then what that existing will contained, nor do I know now what changes he thereupon chose to make. A king's testament is the most secret of documents. A few weeks later, he called me aside after a meeting of the Council, together with the Lord High Admiral, the Lord Chamberlain, and the Earl Marshal, and commanded us to witness his signature. The text was not revealed to us. We duly did so and I placed copies of the will in the vaults of Chancery. Master Kromman?"

Evidently the Secretary had survived the Chancellor's attempted murder, because there he was, in his usual black robes, sour-faced and sour-voiced as always. "My lords, I testify that the package Lord Roland is holding is one I sealed on that occasion."

When the seal had been shown to the senior notables, including Malinda, and all had agreed that it was genuine and unbroken, the package was opened; Roland and the Lord High Admiral testified to their signatures. Then Eagle King of Arms was commanded to read out the will. The bent little man was very pretty in his ornate tabard, but he had worn it for thirty years and no longer saw or spoke clearly. A younger, louder herald took over and the room hushed for him.

As he droned through the preamble, Amby stirred again on Malinda's shoulder. Did he sense that his life was at a critical moment? He was very hot; he weighed as much as a teenage blacksmith. She was not quite close enough to read the text over the herald's shoulder, although she could recognize her father's crabbed hand.

The beginning was unimportant—bequests to Scofflaw, to grooms, cadgers, huntsmen, falconers, and dozens more, on and on. She had trouble visualizing her father going to so much trouble, writing all that out personally in several copies; it was a touching and surprising view of him. Then suddenly: " 'To Granville, first Earl of Thencaster and currently our loyal Rector of Wylderland, in recognition of his superlative services to our realm . . .' "

The audience came alert.

" '. . . we grant the right to style himself and his line "Fitzambrose" and we do bequeath to him the honor of Stonemoss, together with all lands, styles and honors that have historically pertained thereto . . .' "

"But he's *still* a bastard," Courtney muttered cheerfully.

Spectators glared at him. The herald paused. Amby coughed weakly and went back to sleep.

" 'And finally, our crown and right of Chivial . . .' "

Here it came . . .

" '. . . we do thus designate our beloved son Ambrose Taisson Everard as our true and lawful successor, as set forth in the Act of Succession, but should he die before us or without lawful issue, we ordain the succession to such lawful male issue as the spirits may grant us within future marriages, and failing such further lawful male issue, we designate our lawful daughter Malinda, followed in order of age by such lawful daughters as the spirits may grant us within future marriages, provided that no such daughter shall succeed who is married at that time to any man not a subject of the crown of Chivial.' "

Malinda had not been dispossessed in favor of the hypothetical daughters of the now-hypothetical Queen Dierda—she was a little touched by that, the first hint of sorrow she had yet felt for her father. There had just not been time to mourn him yet.

She was the heir again, first in line!

" '. . . failing succession of the heirs of our body, we decree that the crown shall pass to our beloved nephew . . .' "

"That has to be a misprint," Courtney said loudly. This time a few people laughed at the Prince's wit.

So long as Malinda remained heir presumptive, she was going to have Cousin Courtney at her back. She would have to trust the Blades to keep an eye on his dagger hand. The audience shuffled uneasily, waiting for the important part: Which of those two would be regent?

" 'We furthermore decree that in the event of our designated heir succeeding while a minor, we bestow governance of the realm and exercise of royal powers upon a Council of Regency of twelve persons, including and presided over by a Lord Protector; and we hereby appoint as Lord Protector . . .' " With sadistic stagecraft the herald took a moment to turn the page. " '. . . the aforementioned Lord Granville Fitzambrose, first Earl of Thencaster and Stonemoss. We appoint as members of the said Council . . .' " The herald's steady whine was drowned out by a belated shout of *Long live the King!* which was taken up by everyone. The King whimpered crossly at the noise and burrowed deeper into his heir's shoulder.

Malinda and Courtney had both been passed over. She could see Lord Roland through the forest of heads around her, but his face was as unreadable as she hoped hers was. Had he expected to be named Lord Protector? Would he survive as chancellor under Granville? Who was going to be conspiring with whom to do what?

Courtney had much the same thought. "Fascinating!" he said. "Now the *intrigue* can begin. Who do you suppose will *die* first?"

The Trial,
Day Two

The midday meal was usually the better of the two because it varied, so there was always a surprise to look forward to—roots or fish soup, rarely even meat. Today the overpowering smell of fish in the cell should have made Malinda's mouth water, but she was far too upset to think of eating. Even as the main door was being barred behind her she stormed across the room and hauled on the other. It creaked open. As long as she behaved herself, it was left unlocked during daylight hours. She marched out into the rain.

The walkway was straight, about four feet wide, and led nowhere; fifteen paces brought her to the end, a permanently locked door into the next tower. She wheeled around and strode back. On one side flowed the Gran and on the other lay the great bailey of the Bastion, where Yeomen drilled, horses trotted by, sometimes a band played, and rarely children laughed at their play. Directly under her feet as she walked was the Rivergate, so she often heard boats arriving and leaving: splashes, men's voices, sometimes women's, sailors cursing when they thought no one could hear. She could *hear* all these things but never *see* them, because the walls were higher than her head and roofed near their upper edges with a ladder of iron bars. She had tried climbing on her chair and then pulling herself up, but she could not poke even her head through, let alone climb out.

Sometimes birds came to keep her company—pompous pigeons or sinister ravens. Today a gray and white gull stood on the landward wall, peering down at her with a beady yellow eye.

"It's not fair, do you hear?" she shouted at it. "He cheats! Cheats all the time!" She put on the Chancellor's croaky rasp: " 'Did the pirate make any promises to you?' 'No,' I say. Then one of the inquisitors behind my chair blurts out, 'The witness is lying!' How am I supposed to concentrate knowing those two creepy horrors are lurking at my back all the time, where I can't see them? And I think *they're* cheating, too. Don't inquisitors have to see your face to tell when you're not speaking the truth? They can't see mine. I think Lambskin himself signals them when he wants them to speak up."

The gull did not comment. Queen Malinda turned again and marched back.

"So, 'Well,' I admit, 'he did promise me he could end the war without marrying me.' 'By killing your father, he meant,' he says. 'I didn't know what he meant,' I say, or try to say, but I'm not allowed to get the words out; he cuts me off or one of those ghouls behind me slaps his hand over my mouth. 'The witness will be gagged if she speaks out of turn and interrupts the work of the inquiry.' He cheats, cheats, cheats! I've been questioned on all this before, so he has the records and knows what to ask and what not to ask."

She realized that her bonnet and dress were getting wet, so she left the gull scratching its back and went into her cell. She could pace just as well in there, although only four paces, not fifteen. Four steps this way and four steps that way and four steps . . .

"Of course," she told the spiders, "he went after Lord Roland, trying to make him out to be a traitor. 'The witness is aware that Lord Roland did later confess to treason?' 'Yes, but—' I say, meaning, 'Yes but nothing to do with that,' but I'm not allowed to say so! Not fair! 'The witness is aware that Lord Roland directed the team that negotiated the marriage treaty?' 'Yes, but—' 'Was it not that treaty that brought your father to a place and time where Radgar Æleding could be sure of finding him?' 'Yes, but—' 'And Lord Roland reacted to the unexpected murder of his king and the consequent outbreak of mayhem and murder all around him by arrogating a troop of lancers that should have been attempting to control the slaughter, issuing them detailed instructions to the contrary, and sending them off to do his bidding, while also commandeering a horse and going to rescue you under dramatic circumstances—all this with no hesitation when he supposedly had no foreknowledge of what was about to happen?' He was the greatest fencer of his day, so of course he had lightning reflexes, but do you think I was allowed to say so? Not fair!"

Four steps this way and four steps back . . .

She paused suddenly at the window. "Winter! You've caught a fly! How clever you are!" Watched her eight-legged friend feeding, she decided she might as well swallow whatever was in that bowl and stop it stinking up her bedroom. She sat on the chair with the clumsy bowl on her lap. She had plenty of time. The commissioners would be packing away a dozen courses and as many wines over the next two or three hours.

"He cheats. Horatio Lambskin cheats! That's why he sat me so far from the foreign observers. They're the ones he really wants to convince, and he's put me a long way away so they can't tell whether I'm telling the truth, because some of them must have had inquisitor-type training too." She tried a spoonful of the fish and gagged.

"And it isn't going to get easier, you know," she whispered, looking down at the crack in the floor where Moment lived. She always thought of Moment, like her namesake, as being the most sympathetic of her tiny listeners. "He's tied me in all sorts of knots over things I had nothing to do with. He's tricked me and distorted what I said and refused me chances to explain what I really meant . . . and I'm innocent!"

Whereas there were things coming soon that she would find a little harder to explain at the best of times. Charges of misprision, grand larceny, complicity . . . the death of Kromman . . . other deaths that were certainly due to self-defense when properly explained but might not look that way by the time Horatio Lambskin had finished twisting the facts around. . . .

Suddenly she leaped to her feet, sending the food flying. "Blades!" she howled. The crock hit the floor and shattered, spilling fish gruel in all directions. "My Blades! Where are you? Why have you deserted me? I need you!"

14

Readings are camel drippings.
AMBROSE IV

$\mathfrak{M}$aster Kromman was about the last person Malinda would ever choose as a traveling companion, but he was waiting for her beside her coach—bowing, smiling his death's-head leer, and "most humbly" craving the indulgence of a ride into Grandon with Her Grace so that he might bring certain important matters to Her Grace's attention on the journey. She could not recall ever seeing him in sunlight or even outdoors before; he was something she associated with candlelight and shadows, like cockroaches.

"We shall be delighted to have the pleasure of your company, Master Secretary," she said, and if his inquisitor's skills told him that she was lying in her teeth, the problem was his. The trip should take no more than an hour, unless the rain had washed out the roads. She accepted a hand from Sir Piers to mount the steps. Her father had been dead for two days; court was moving back to Greymere for the state funeral. As soon as her train cleared the gates, another would start assembling, and the wagons would still be rolling at sunset.

The yard was a swarm of men and horses. Dominic had divided the surviving Blades in two—half under himself to protect the infant King, and the rest under Sir Piers for the Princess—but the Guard here was seriously outnumbered by lancers of the Household Yeomen. She could think of several reasons why she might have been assigned so large an escort, and none of them appealed. She assumed it must be Lord Roland's doing.

She settled on the rear bench, opposite Kromman and next to Dian, pale-cheeked and subdued in her mourning.

"Leaving this place," she said as Piers closed the door on her, "feels like the best thing I have ever done. I shall never return." As if the wedding, massacre, and funerals were not enough, a mass departure of servants had turned Wetshore into a free-for-all. Even a princess had been forced to scrounge meals in the kitchens. She had taken it on herself to appoint Arabel to the office of King's Governess. She had designated Dian as her matron companion, commoner or not. Dominic continued to run the Guard and Roland seemed to be running the entire country single-handed, but everything would depend on Granville. Until he arrived and took charge, nothing could be settled.

As the carriage began to move, she said, "When shall we see the Lord Protector?"

Kromman pursed his bloodless lips. He seemed even more gaunt than usual, red-eyed from long nights at his desk. "The Council's first act was to send a courier north, of course, but it will take him at least four days, perhaps a week, to ride to Wylderland. The roads are very bad just now. A copy of the dispatch was sent by ship."

"That will be faster?"

"Unless the Baels intercept it, which is very likely. Allow as long for His Excellency to make the return journey."

"And how many vacancies are there on the Council?"

"Six. His Excellency will undoubtedly wish to name replacements as soon as possible."

Was that what this slimy inkworm was hunting—a seat on the Council?

Sad fingers of smoke showed where another day's funeral pyres were being lit, the sun rising mistily over a waterlogged landscape. The carriage and its fifty-horse escort went boiling through Wetshore village in a storm of mud, heading for a highway that would be even muddier. Kromman sat in silence, clutching a dispatch case and staring steadily at Malinda, waiting for her to ask his business. Dian just gazed fixedly down at her clasped hands. She had hardly spoken in the two days since Bandit bled to death in her arms.

"Have you a final count on the death toll, Master Secretary?" Whose secretary was Kromman now—the Council's?

He pulled his mawkish smile. "Fifty-four, Your Highness."

"What? Oh, that's ridiculous! The Guard alone lost more men than that. Three hundred? Four?"

"The Council's official bulletin specifies fifty-four, Your Grace, including eight men in the Royal Guard."

"Eight?" Dian cried, waking from her nightmare and looking as if she wanted to use his gullet for fish bait. "Bandit, Dreadnought, Flint, Mallory, Panther, Chandos, Raven, Herrick, Fairtrue, Huntley, Dragon—"

"Stop, stop!" Malinda said.

Dian did not stop, she changed direction. "They did it to themselves! The other people panicked and were trampled or fell down the bank and drowned in a foot of water. The Blades were all together around the King and when they rampaged, they turned on one another. The lancers rode them down like animals! Even after they'd come to their senses, the Yeomen rode them down. Blades were slaughtered as they begged for mercy or lay on the ground wounded. And then the medics and healers ignored them. Walked right past to find—"

"Stop!"

"The bulletin does admit that there was some panic," Kromman agreed primly, "but it attributes most of the deaths to the Baelish archers. The Council considered the wording with much care."

"And you stop, too!" Malinda was sickened by the hypocrisy. The truth lay somewhere in the gulf between Dian's distortion and Kromman's outright lies, yet obviously the Council version would do less damage to the country. Better to blame such carnage on the Baels than the Blades.

The three of them sat in silence for a while—or, to be exact, they bounced on the benches without speaking. The carriage was growing dim as mud painted the windows. Hooves and wheels together sounded like a river in spate.

"What was the matter you wished to discuss, Master Secretary?" If he was going to start angling for a job in her household, he had better bait his hook well.

"The matter, my lady, touches on the security of the realm and yet is so near to Your Grace's person that I hesitate to lay it before the Lord Protector without Your Grace's permission to do so."

"You may proceed. I keep no secrets from Lady Bandit."

"Thank you, Your Grace. Have you ever heard of *readings,* my lady?"

She had certainly not expected that question. "Fortune-telling? Chicanery or superstition, I always thought."

He showed yellow teeth in his awful smile. "In most cases, certainly. Sir Snake has exposed many instances of . . . No matter. On the other hand, the Office of General Inquiry has developed certain methods that have, on occasion, yielded results of some merit and value." He used words like an angler used feathers.

"The Dark Chamber can foresee the future?"

"Grand Inquisitor would not put it so baldly. Just say that certain information can be obtained concerning a person's fate or future behavior, and often without that person's knowledge. Indeed, I believe that the subject's presence makes the reading impossible."

"Go on. How is this done?" Malinda noticed that Dian was taking an interest in the conversation, and that could only be good for her.

"I am no conjurer, Your Grace."

She gave the expected response. "But you can outline the principle?"

He sighed. "As far my limited understanding goes, the conjuration is a form of reverse necromancy. Your Highness is doubtless aware that skilled enchanters can reassemble the spirit of a dead person under the right circumstances. Again, most such claims are 'chicanery and superstition,' as Your Grace so aptly put it, but not all are. Of course, the essential key is what is vulgarly referred to as 'bait,' some item very closely associated with the deceased—such as his corpse or some bones . . . it was to prevent such tampering with the dead that cremation was instituted during the reign . . . I beg Your Grace's pardon. Thoughtless of me. A lock of hair works well or a significant possession—a wedding ring, for example, worn constantly for many years. Given this, a good team of conjurers can often reassemble the spirit of the departed."

"But can you trust what the spirit tells you?"

"Provided you trust those who conjured it, Your Grace. Now the readings I mentioned work on similar principles, except that they call back the elements of the spirit that has not yet been disassembled by death. In effect, they are communication with the future dead. Obviously the element of time must be revoked with care, and there can be no repeat; it only works once. Yes, the results are often ambiguous or fragmentary, but they have proven valuable in many instances. The Dark Chamber is rarely gullible."

But often manipulative, she suspected. "For instance?"

"For instance, the inquisitors have known for more than fifteen years that Lord Roland was destined to kill your father."

Was she now to hear the other side of the feud? "King Radgar killed my father."

"But Lord Roland directed the commissioners who negotiated that treaty, Your Grace, and thus provided the opportunity. In the moment of crisis, did he not take charge with truly remarkable presence of mind, almost as if—"

"My father was aware of this reading?"

"Certainly, but he was a skeptic on the matter, I fear."

She knew how Ambrose had heaped scorn on opinions he did not share. "Then I think I am, too, since he had much more experience than I have."

The Secretary sighed. "He did not have access to all the information, Your Highness."

Sneak! Now he would start negotiating terms of employment, no doubt, in return for the rest of the story. Unless . . . No! "Are you implying that you did a reading on my *father* without his knowledge?" There must be a law against that.

The windows were now so caked with mud that the Secretary's features were hard to make out. "Whether or not the previous Grand Inquisitor obtained His Late Majesty's permission I cannot say, but the report I have read indicates that his reading confirmed the one made later on Sir Durendal, as he was then. It accused him of regicide."

"And what reading have you obtained on me?"

Again she expected him to sidestep the question until she crossed his palm with silver, but again he answered without hesitation. She was still underestimating nasty Master Kromman.

"The reading is that you will be Queen of Chivial, Your Grace, although not for very long."

Dian gasped. Malinda nursed her anger for a moment before she spoke, choosing her words with care. She knew very well that her value had increased, now that only one tiny heart beat between her and the throne. She knew that this ink-slobbering slug would be only the first of many trying to ingratiate themselves with her. Lord Roland had begun doing so within minutes of her father's death. She knew Amby was a sickly child and what Kromman said was not an unreasonable guess. Above all, she must do nothing, say nothing, make no alliance that would encourage anyone to shorten Amby's life and reign.

"There are laws against imagining the King's death!" The coach was rocking and bouncing over gravel and she had to shout above the racket.

"With deepest respect, Your Grace, although I did not mention His Majesty your brother, I see I have given offence and humbly beg pardon." The secretary shut up like a strongbox.

Slime! "What reading did you get on my brother?"

After a suitable pause . . . "I may speak without prejudice, Your Grace?"

"Yes. All right. You have my word."

"They could get no reading from your royal brother. Nothing coherent. Only weeping. The conjurers speculated that he dies very young."

She wanted to choke him and tear his corpse to pieces. She felt tears in her eyes. She knew that she was strongly inclined to believe him.

Believe him in this. Not in everything.

"If you wish to lay this bizarre tale before the Lord Protector, then I have no objections."

"Thank you, Your Grace. It would be best to draw his attention to Lord Roland's treason."

"Suspected treason. By the way, Master Secretary, have you ever heard of a man named Wolfbiter?"

"No, Your Grace."

"*Sir* Wolfbiter—a Blade."

He chuckled. "I assumed so. Ironhall lets those boys pick the most bizarre names for themselves: Wyvern, Snake, Bloodfang . . ."

"Or Bandit?" Dian snapped.

"Never mind!" Malinda said hastily. "Listen! What is that noise? Dian, can you open the window a crack?"

Dian could, and they all peered out. They were in Grandon already, and Malinda realized with a lurch of dismay that the people lining the street were booing. Their jeers and yells were loud enough to be audible even over the rumble of the coach and thunder of hooves. Booing her? Probably not, because they could not tell who was inside the mud-splattered coach. They were shouting *Killers!* and throwing things at the King's Blades.

15

*The Princess is looking for ladies' maids and if you were in her service
we could see each other every day.*

UNIDENTIFIED BLADE

State funerals were distilled torment for the participants. Malinda
could remember enduring Haralda's: bands and speeches, torchlight
procession, flames leaping skyward in the night, her shock at seeing
her father weep in public. She had played only a minor role in that
one. This time she would be chief mourner, with no one to back her
up except Cousin Courtney. She had been tempted to delay the ceremony until the Lord Protector arrived. Had she screamed loud
enough, she could probably have had her way, but five days was long
enough to store a corpse, even in an icehouse. Let the new order
arrive in celebration, a week or so from now, with loyal addresses and
triumphal arches.

It was close to sunset and she was seated at her dressing table in
her ugly black mourning gown, with Dian demonstrating to three
newly acquired ladies' maids how Her Highness liked her hair pinned
up. The cortege would be lining up in the courtyard; the pyre stood
ready on Great Common. This would be a long night even if the
rain held off.

The worst of it all was the feeling of hypocrisy. Five days was
long enough to come out of shock—even Dian had started smiling
again, once in a while—and after shock came realization. She could
not honestly mourn a father who had given her so little cause to love
him. Although his absence was a gigantic hole in her world, it did
not ache and she suspected her life might be easier in future. She
regretted his death, yes, for it would bring great troubles to the land.
She also felt guilt over it. Had she reacted faster when King Radgar
rejected her, she would have realized that he was tearing up the peace
treaty. She could have run along the jetty, shouting warnings. Useless
to tell herself that security was the Blades' job, not hers.

"He's had his nap!" Arabel declaimed, rolling in with all her chins smiling. "He seems much better. I do think he could come along for the first part. You know how he likes bands!"

Malinda swung around on the stool, causing her almost-completed coiffure to collapse in an avalanche of pins, combs, and braids and Dian to yell an unladylike word at her. Being faultlessly trained, the maids did not need to be told they were not wanted; they bobbed curtseys and disappeared, closing the door quietly.

Arabel watched them go with the annoyed expression that meant she sensed a story not yet heard. "Half the dowagers in court are up in arms because you stole their favorite maids. How did you find them all so quickly?"

"I called in a team of experts to help," Malinda said cryptically. It had given them something to think about. "Amby is *not* coming and that's the end of it!"

Arabel pouted. She fancied herself on the reviewing stand, holding up the King to watch his troops march past. "But Lord Chancellor Roland—"

"Lord Chancellor Roland will never overrule me on this, because if Amby were to catch the merest snivel of a cold at the funeral, then Lord Fancypants Roland would get his head chopped off for treason! Understand?"

"Yes, Your Grace. Of course, Your Grace." Arabel shrugged, then smiled as she did when she had a gem to share, which was likely the real reason she had come. "You've heard the news?"

Malinda's sour mood had little use for gossip. "What news?"

"Murder!" Lady Arabel's eyes gleamed.

Dian squeaked. "What? Who?"

"Master Secretary Kromman. Yes, indeed! They found him about an hour ago, down in the rose garden with a sword beside him and a hole through his heart. Can you imagine a mousy little man like him fighting a *duel?*"

He would have had no choice, and no chance either. Malinda caught Dian's horrified eyes and looked away hastily.

"Hmm . . . no."

"But why?" Arabel demanded, for once missing the undercurrents. "That's the question! I know he used to be an inquisitor, so he's probably had some training with a sword, but what *gentleman* would call out a mere *clerk?*"

"Well, I daresay we shall find out in time. My hair, please, Dian."

They would never find out, and it had not been a gentleman; Ironhall enrolled refuse from gutters and ditches, not scions of the nobility. No doubt Lord Roland had an excellent alibi. He would not have needed to dirty his own hands, because any Blade would be happy to do a favor for the great Durendal, no questions asked.

Master Kromman would not be laying any charges of treason before the Lord Protector.

Malinda was still pondering the crime as she paraded downstairs with a dozen Blades around her. There was no use trying to denounce Lord Roland while Lord Roland was the government. By the time she reached the entrance hall, she had decided she must wait and see what the Lord Protector did. If Roland was confirmed as chancellor, then she would have to reveal her suspicions, but if he was thrown out to sink back into the cesspool, she would leave well alone.

Once upon a time every Blade escort had been a pack of hounds eager for the chase, but now they plodded like footsore beagles. Only time could heal their ghastly memories. Piers was even more solemn than usual, almost old. She tried to remember how he had looked when she was thirteen and she had swooned unto death a dozen times a day for secret love of him.

Down many stairs and across the great entrance hall, with her train rustling on the tiles and spectators kneeling to the chief mourner. Out to the torches in the courtyard and the coach and four. When Piers opened the door, she stopped abruptly. That was not the right man inside.

"I understood I would be riding with Prince Courtney."

"There's been a slight mix-up, Your Grace," Piers said quickly.

And how did he know that, when he had been upstairs with her? "A mix-up on purpose?"

"Hmm, sort of, Your Grace."

Angrily she climbed inside and sat down opposite the murderer. He was wearing a black hat, and a black cloak covered his scarlet robes. Just by the way he sat, he conveyed exhaustion. The door closed; hooves clattered as the Blades swung into their saddles; the coachman cracked his whip. The coach began to move.

"Your Highness," the sonorous voice began, "I am deeply sorry to intrude on so private a moment. The matter is very simple, but it will not wait."

Would he threaten her or beg for understanding? "This moment will serve as well as any other, Lord Chancellor. You have heard about Master Kromman, of course?"

"Of course."

"And who do you think did that terrible thing?"

They were out in the dark street already, so she could not see his face. Just because he was charming did not mean he was an honest man.

"I have no idea. I expect they drew lots."

She gasped. "You admit it?"

"I admit to saying what you heard me say to Fox and Fitzroy, Your Grace. I admit nothing more, and not even that much to anyone else. For seven years I kept the secret of Kromman's crime, as I had promised your father I would. When I needed to get those swords away from your throat, that was the first means that came into my head. I am sure that neither Fox nor Fitzroy did the actual killing, because I got to them as soon as they were rational and made them give me their parole, but by that time they'd already told some others." His tone sharpened. "I cannot mourn Ivyn Kromman, my lady. He was a despicable murderer, who betrayed one of the finest men it has ever been my good fortune to know. I rejoice at his death. Denounce me if you wish."

Burn the man! Denounce him for saving her life? Was that really what had happened? He was as slippery as an eel in an oil barrel.

"I shall think about it. We are almost at the Common." She heard him smother a yawn. "Was there some other matter you wished to discuss, then?"

"Blades, Your Grace, still Blades. Ironhall has been stripped bare, as I am sure you know. Your father went there only a month ago, but since then the Guard has been almost wiped out. It is down to thirty-eight instead of about a hundred. Three of those men are crippled and there is no one to release them from their binding. Nothing we can do about that, but I am sure Grand Master could spare a few more seniors in such dire circumstances."

She smelled a trap. "Surely this matter can wait for the Lord Protector's arrival?"

"Certainly it can." The Chancellor sounded patient, as if she were being tiresome. "But then his will be the hand that holds the sword that binds those boys."

"You are suggesting that I go to Ironhall and bind some Blades of my own? To me? Princess Malinda's Blades?"

"Yes, my lady, that is exactly what I am suggesting."

The coach had slowed to a crawl. She could hear a band playing a dirge somewhere close.

"But that would require royal or viceregal authority. Who would sign the warrants?"

"I would, my lady."

"That would be stealing . . . er, misprision." Was that the right word?

"Yes, it would. My authority to give away Blades is questionable at best, and the Lord Protector may be very wroth. But that is exactly what I am suggesting."

"Why?"

"Your Grace!" he said with open exasperation. "There are only thirty-five Blades left—fifteen currently guarding you, sixteen your brother, and four me. What will happen if we have another Night of Dogs?"

"I expect they will all rush to save Amby, because he's their primary ward. But another Night of Dogs is very unlikely. Not likely at all. The traitor conjurers will wait to see whether the Lord Protector intends to continue the policy of suppressing the elementaries."

The Chancellor sighed. "You don't *know* that!"

"And if he does persevere, then he will need the new Blades more than I do now." She could hear singing. The coach was barely moving. Any minute now they would halt and someone would open the door.

"I'm not sure about that either," Lord Roland said, even more wearily.

What *was* he up to? Snaring her in conspiracy to commit misprision, whatever that was exactly? "You would never let me have Blades of my own before! You always talked my father out of letting me bind my own Blades."

"Yes, I did, my lady. But circumstances have changed."

"Oh, really? You no longer worry that I might jump into bed with one of them?"

"You are older and hopefully wiser. Your father no longer holds your leash, and since you are the heir and will be for at least another fifteen years, you are not going to be married off to any foreign prince. Jump into bed with anyone you like."

"Insolence!"

He grunted. "Sorry. I am very tired."

"And I am very angry. You have always picked on me, Durendal-Lord-Roland. Even when you were only Commander of the Guard, you used to watch and spy and see which Blades I was friendly with and then deliberately assign them elsewhere so I would never see them again."

He chuckled. *Chuckled!*

"How *dare* you!"

"Your Grace . . . I am sorry. It was that 'only' I was laughing at . . . *Only* Commander of the Guard? My feet didn't touch the ground for a week after your father appointed me Leader."

"No! You were laughing at me. Why were you laughing at me?"

The coach stopped, rocking gently.

Roland peered out at the torches. "I never picked on you, Your Grace. I warned the lads that princesses were off limits, that's all. And once in a while one of them would come to me and say something like, 'It's my turn now. She's breathing steam at me.' Then I would post him to a safer berth. As soon as you started giving them sultry looks, Your Highness, they wanted out, and fast! You've heard of the Legend? It's real. It works. It's a side effect of the binding and princesses are as susceptible as other women. Why should any Blade want to lose his head—literally lose his head, I mean—stealing kisses from a child when he could safely bed any woman who caught his fancy and take all night to do it?"

After that, the silence seemed to tighten like the ropes of the rack.

She wanted to die. Why didn't Piers open the door and let her escape? She heard her voice say, "What did you do to Sir Eagle?"

"What did *you* do to Eagle? He was expelled from the Order. They struck him off the rolls, dropped his sword down the drain, and impressed him as a deckhand on a square-rigger trading to the Fever Shores."

For one kiss? The brutal injustice of it turned her shame to rage. "A notoriously dangerous voyage! With orders that he was to be one of those who do not return, I suppose?"

"My office gave no such orders, my lady."

"But isn't that how they would interpret the King's will?"

"Most likely." A sigh. "As it happened, the captain had instructions to let the lad escape at the first foreign port they reached."

"Your orders? You defied my father by giving those orders?"

"Your father often repented at leisure of edicts he issued in the heat of—"

"I don't believe you."

"I am sorry."

There was nothing more to say, nothing at all.

Sir Piers opened the coach door for her. Moving as if in a dream, she stepped down and went to stand beside other family members: Prince Courtney, the Duke and Duchess of Brinton, and young Ansel, who was the new Duke of De Mayes, and one or two other, even more distant, relatives, such as Lady Crystal's dimwit brother, Lord Candlefen.

★　　★　　★

The funeral itself was not as bad as she had feared it would be. A surprising number of the inhabitants of Grandon turned out to watch the torchlight parade and listen to the bands. The rain did not stay away altogether, but there was a convenient dry spell just when she had to walk over to the pyre and put the torch to it. She sat under a canopy during the speeches, watching golden flames dance in the darkness as they returned the remains of Ambrose IV to the elements from which they came. Not long after midnight the pyre began to collapse and a sudden downpour was excuse enough to declare the ritual over and head for home.

Sir Piers and his men escorted her back to her carriage, and this time her companion was Courtney. Tonight he reeked of rose water.

The coach had barely started moving when he said, "*Gorgeous* funeral!"

"It is late and I'm tired."

"We *need* to have a talk, darling."

"Can't it wait until tomorrow?" Or next year. Or never.

"I don't want those gossipy Blades of yours listening."

Was *that* why everyone wanted to talk in coaches? Her head ached. "Talk about what?"

"*Granville,* dearest. He's going to make a try for the throne."

"If Father had wanted—"

"Your father is *dead,* girl. Dead people don't count. He made a very stupid compromise—he acknowledged Granville but didn't legitimize him. Then he blundered again, naming him Lord Protector. The Rector is not the man to settle for second best."

"The Council will control him."

"No, dear. That's what Dear Uncle wanted, but the Blades spoiled it, don't you see? Your father named the Council, but he named offices, not people—Grand This and Lord High That. Whenever he died and that will was needed, those places would be filled by people he had appointed to his own Council. The hand of the dead would still rule."

"Yes," she said. "But—"

Courtney chuckled. "Think, darling! He also said that the Lord Protector could not dismiss any member without a majority vote, so he needed six supporters to create a vacancy. However, he can appoint a replacement on his own—a very *reasonable* provision, because you don't want a clique on the Council keeping it below strength."

"And the Blades . . . Oh, spirits!" The rampaging Blades had killed six of the men who should have been on the Council. Granville could start his reign by packing it with his own supporters. Then he could use his majority to oust the others, men like Lord Roland, and quash any hope of dissent or opposition.

She had never heard her effete cousin show any interest in politics before. All her life the only question to ask about Courtney had been whose bosom was he clasped to now. From the barely nubile to the barely mobile, they had all been alike to him, so long as they had been female and had money.

"It won't," her cousin remarked slyly, "take much to convince Parliament that an experienced soldier with a grown son is better than a sickly infant with a juvenile sister next in line."

"He is not sickly! He is the lawful heir."

"He may be *very* sickly if Granville meets with any resistance. Have you picked out drapes for your cell, yet, sweetheart?"

"Your humor escapes me."

"Then think harder. The Lord Protector has to summon Parliament. That's one thing he *must* do, but he may put the cart before the horse and seize the throne first. If he does that, then you and baby Ambrose are going to be breathing through the tops of your necks very shortly."

It was brutal, but there were precedents. "The Blades—"

"The Blades," Courtney sneered, "are the *only* reason Granville just *may* choose to work through Parliament, to save another massacre. Since the Blades are sworn to defend Uncle's heirs and successors, they will defend our smelly-bottom liege against outright force, yes. But if Parliament accepts Granville as your father's successor, then *they* will too. Their bindings will, no matter what their personal feelings are. So nobody will get hurt—except you and your brother, of course. *You* may just get married off to the Great Hoohong of Thud, perhaps, but the kid will certainly catch a bad case of pillow on the face."

"No!" Yes. It was all horribly logical. She had been resisting such thoughts for days.

Courtney sighed. "Darling, *don't* you see? Granville has a dozen ways to proceed. He can start by taking you out of play. It's easy enough to make out a treason case against you, Cousin. King Radgar came to marry you, but after you explained things he changed his mind and killed your father instead. *Whatever* did you promise him? That's all the argument your dear brother Granville needs to lock you up and chop you up."

"That is not true! I can defend myself before inquisitors."

"If you ever get the chance. Even if you do, inquisitors know which end of a boot to lick. Unhealthy place, the Bastion. When you pick out your summer gowns stick to a nice red that won't show the bloodstains, mm?"

"The Blades won't let him arrest me."

Courtney snorted in derision. "They're the brat's Blades, dear, because he's the heir. You're only their second-best ward. The indictment for treason will bear his seal and be perfectly legal."

No! No! No!

Maybe, maybe, maybe!

Was this what Lord Roland had been hinting?

"What are you suggesting?" The coach was almost back at the palace.

"My dear, I've been bored to death these last few months. Mayshire is dull as a grave, but on balance, I believe it's preferable, although narrowly so. 'Out of sight, out of mind' will be my motto from now on, but if I do get noticed, then I'm afraid it will be 'Long live King Granville!' as loud as I can shout. I hope you understand my problem. Just want to say good-bye, Malinda darling. I'm sorry you have to end this way."

There might be a hint of real regret under the sarcasm, but no one could ever imagine the dumpy, dandyish Courtney donning shining armor to defend his infant cousin's life or rights. He was a hedgehog, never a badger. The wheels' rumble became a roar as they passed through the palace archway.

"Farewell, Courtney dear," she said. "I hope you prosper in your rural retreat. Good luck with the carrot crop. I never credited you with political acumen before."

"Great spirits, girl! That just shows how good at it I am. I have spent a lifetime scuttling around wainscots."

"So you have. Can you give me any farewell advice?"

"Advice is never worth more than it costs. What happened to that trinket I gave you?"

"The diamond? It was so gorgeous! It must have cost you a fortune."

"No, it was an heirloom. I found it in among Mother's things. Can you imagine? Stupid old trollop hung on to it all those years when she didn't have enough blankets to keep her bed warm. Where is it?"

"It was with the rest of my jewels and clothes. They were loaded on one of the Bael longships."

The carriage had stopped; a Blade opened the door.

"Then I suggest," Courtney said, easing his bulk along the bench, "that your *safest* course now, Princess, is to go to Baelmark and ask for it back. And stay there as long as you can. Good chance to you."

He clambered down the steps and minced off into the palace.

Malinda accepted Piers's hand to descend, feeling shakier than she could ever remember. The entrance hall was almost deserted and dark, with few lanterns glimmering. The Blades' tread rang very loud on the tiles. Halfway across the wide floor, she said, "Sir Piers?"

"Your Grace?"

"Will you please inform Lord Roland that I was wrong, and that I have changed my mind? I will very gratefully accept his offer."

"*Yes, my lady!* Sir Fury, convey that message to his lordship."

The relief in Piers's voice rang like bugles. Fury disappeared into the darkness in a clatter of boots. She had been a blind fool not to admit the dangers that lurked in her path, but if she had Blades of her own, then no one was going to serve warrants on her—not without a fight, at least. The worst that could happen would be having to testify to the inquisitors, and she had nothing to hide. Only a cynic like Courtney would suspect the Dark Chamber of trimming to the political wind. Perhaps cynics lived longer.

"If I may suggest, my lady?"

"Your advice is always welcome, Sir Piers. Please remember that."

"Thank you, Your Grace. My lady, I think there's no time to waste. That's what Durendal says. Let's go now."

16

182: Sir Bandit who, on 14 Tenthmoon 285, while riding in escort on his ward in the Great Forest and having observed archers contesting their path, did charge them and was shot down, but his ward lived.

183: Sir Boare who, on 1 Thirdmoon 292, disputed a royal warrant for the arrest of his ward and single-handedly slew three men-at-arms before dying of his wounds.

IRONHALL, *THE LITANY OF HEROES*

As the gibbous moon faded in the dawn, nineteen horses cantered along the Great West Road. Malinda had never foregone a whole night's sleep before and felt strange, almost light-headed, but some of that strangeness was pure excitement. With her were Dian and fifteen

young swordsmen in civilian dress. At first glance they were just a
party of gentlemen escorting two ladies who chose not to ride sidesaddle, but a closer look would have detected their cat's-eye swords.
Gradually the sun climbed into the clearest sky Thirdmoon had offered
yet, raising mist from waterlogged fields. The day offered lambs, daffo-
dils, periwinkles. It provided thrushes, skylarks, and violets if you had
time to look for them. For the first time since Ambrose's death, Blades
were laughing. It was escape. They all felt it, as if the court of Chivial
had been shrouded in some dread miasma and they had broken free.
Even Dian was smiling and doing a little of her old flirting. Grief and
guilt and fear would catch up, but for a few brief hours they could
be outrun.

Roosters were still crowing when the company crossed the Gran
at Abshurst and stopped to change horses. Finding so many fresh,
decent mounts was not easy, but easier then than it would be later in
the day. By law the Blades, like royal couriers, could take their pick
at any posting house in the land.

"All right, my lady?" Piers asked solicitously.

"I'm fine," Malinda said. "When will we reach Ironhall?"

"Even on these roads we should make it for the evening meal,
Your Grace." Suddenly he revealed a glimpse of the old Piers, the
one she had known before the Wetshore Massacre—a grave mien
with hints of mischief twinkling underneath. "If you're man enough
to hold the pace, that is."

"*Man* enough? I'll make you a wager." She thought quickly,
seeing the grins spreading. "If I once ask you to slow down, I'll carry
you into Ironhall in my arms. Otherwise you carry me!" She was as
tall as he was and probably weighed much the same.

Piers looked shocked. "That would be beneath a princess's dignity,
Your Highness!"

"The Royal Door!" Oak and Alandale said together. The other
onlookers hooted.

"The Royal Door is private," Piers conceded. "But then there's
a staircase up to Grand Master's study."

"It's a bet!" Malinda said. "In and upstairs, too!"

"I feel faint," Dian muttered. "Leave me here, please."

The chill between Malinda and the Blades that had persisted since
the Eagle affair was melting at last. As they cantered down the long
hill to New Cinderwich, she said, "You know, Sir Piers, I had a
terrible crush on you when I was young."

"I am most flattered to hear it."

"Did you notice?"

Staring at the road ahead, he said, "Sort of, my lady."

"I wasn't very subtle?"

"Um . . . not very, my lady."

"Did you ask Durendal to transfer you to other duties?"

"Don't remember."

"Answer me."

"Yes, I did. It was a bit embarrassing, my lady." His face was beet red.

"Thank you for being honest." She had been a terrible fool. The quarrel she had been waging with Lord Roland had been entirely her own invention. "I'm afraid I blamed him."

That remark provoked a half-hour lecture on the virtues of the former commander. She had heard it all before, but this time she believed it, or most of it. Nobody could be *that* good.

"Who killed Kromman?"

"I have no idea, Your Grace."

"Why—did you draw lots?"

Angry glare. "Only those of us who knew Wolfbiter."

They trusted Lord Roland's word enough to do murder on it.

Third horse, fourth, fifth. She was raw from knee to knee; she would not sit down for a month; not yet past noon and she could barely keep her eyes open. Dian kept yawning, although she had enjoyed half a night in bed. At Flaskbury both posting inns together could not muster enough decent horses for them.

"We'll have to leave some of the men behind, Your Grace," Piers said, "or else take a break. That's a good inn, my lady. You could lie down for a while and—"

"Get the blasted horses saddled and let's go!"

"There can't be all that much hurry, my lady! I wasn't serious about the wager."

"I was. Let's go."

They left seven men to follow more slowly, and rode on as hard as ever.

Fields and pastures, orchards and forests—it was all new country to her; she had never journeyed so far to the west before. She was amused to realize that Ironhall lay on the way to Mayshire, so Cousin Courtney would be following her along the Great West Road later today—considerably later. Noon would be an early start for him.

She rode beside, and talked with, each of the men in turn, asking about Ironhall, filling in details of the strange monastic life that had shaped them, its peculiar traditions, and the bizarre and potentially deadly ritual of binding. As the day progressed, she noticed the joyful mood turning sour again. The Blades could not be suffering from lack of sleep, as she was, and they were all too fit and tough to be seriously fatigued. She found the answer when she asked young Alandale if this was his first trip back since his binding.

"Yes, my lady. It's usually a big event—swaggering before the juniors, bragging about women, part of the tradition." His face said that there would be no bragging this time. It was guilt that had caught up with them.

"They'll have heard about the massacre already, though."

"Not the details."

"Must they hear the details?" she asked, thinking of the Council's fairy tale. "Why not give them the official version and let the Baels do the killing?"

"Can't." That one word held enough pain to fill a dungeon, but clearly brother could not lie to brother.

This was not a good time to be recruiting new Blades. Again and again she mulled over her problems and Courtney's warnings. Yes, it would be odd if Granville did *not* make a try for the throne when he was so close already. He was the firstborn. Her father had shut the door in his face and left the key in the lock. Why? Of course, Ambrose had not anticipated exactly this situation. He had not expected the will to be needed so soon, or Malinda herself to be still available, the Dierda union of no effect. He had been too vain, perhaps, to be the first king of Chivial who disinherited a lawful son in favor of a bastard.

They changed mounts again in Holmgarth, where Sir Marlon pointed out the house where he was born. Blades almost never mentioned their childhood, because enrollment in Ironhall wiped the slate clean—and by all accounts some of the young demons had acquired quite messy slates even at that tender age. It was Marlon, an hour or so later, who diffidently asked Malinda if she had heard of the sky of swords.

"Yes . . . all the cat's-eye swords ever issued. A Blade's sword always goes back to the hall?"

"And they're hung above the tables. Um, just thought I'd mention, my lady . . ." He grinned shyly. "If you haven't seen it before, it can be quite scary. Of course, the new kids are told stories of chains breaking on windy days and so on, but that's not true. They swing a bit and jingle, is all. I expect you'll be eating in the hall, and it's a sort of joke. . . . Visitors tend to stare . . . keep looking up, you know?" He craned his head back in demonstration.

"Thank you," she said. "I appreciate that. No gawking! I'll try to keep my eyes on my food."

"Oh, you won't want to do *that,* Your Grace! Not Ironhall food."

It was Piers himself who raised the subject of Grand Master, and he obviously chose a moment when no one else could overhear.

"His name was Sir Saxon. Did your royal father ever mention him, Your Grace?"

"Not that I recall."

"Well, he's not popular. Even the knights grumble behind his back. Bandit threatened to slit his nose for him, and that's not like . . . Bandit wasn't that type at all!"

"What does he do wrong?"

"He's sort of . . . *small,* my lady. Mean, I mean. He natters. One day he treats the seniors like bosom friends and the next as if they're still kids. Either way will do, but you can't mix them."

"And how does he treat the younger boys?"

"Well, begging your pardon, my lady—like dirt."

"Why are you telling me this?"

Piers pulled a face. "I suppose so you won't be surprised if I slit his nose. I haven't had much practice at this."

From Holmgarth on to Blackwater, a depressing little mining community on the edge of Starkmoor, and then up into the wild lands . . . wind rose, sky grew gloomy. The bleak tors were clothed in shadow and the tarns leaden. Malinda conversed no more, needing all her attention just to stay in the saddle and not fall asleep. Spirits, but she'd won her wager! And she was going to collect every step of the stakes, too. She could not imagine climbing stairs under her own power except perhaps on all fours.

"There it is," Hawkney said, pointing. "And we've been seen, see?"

Constrained between moor floor and a felted cloud roof, the setting sun blazed straight in her eyes, but she could discern the forbidding cluster of black stone buildings under a rugged hill. Less easily, she made out other riders heading that way—four of them, well strung out, going as fast as they could to carry word of visitors.

"It's not easy to sneak up on Ironhall," Marlon said approvingly.

"Except at mealtimes," Sir Oak countered.

17

242: Sir Havoc who, on 15 Seventhmoon 337, being in attendance on his ward at a wedding in Candlefen Park when it was assaulted by Baelish raiders, did slay five of them before being himself cut down, but his ward lived.

243: Sir Rhys who at the same wedding was slain by a crossbow bolt, but his ward lived.

IRONHALL, *THE LITANY OF HEROES*

The Royal Door was an inconspicuous postern at the base of a circular tower. Malinda tried not to wince as she dismounted, although screams of mortal agony would have been quite in order. Oak had opened the door. Hawkney and Marlon were holding reins. Everyone looked expectantly at Piers.

"You're really going to force me to do this, Your Grace?"

Regretfully Malinda regarded the windows; she could see no faces watching, but she dare not risk a scandal now.

"Maybe next time."

Piers moved closer. "When we're inside?" he asked throatily, giving her a glance as sultry as a laundry.

"No!" she said firmly. "I'm a big girl now."

She regretted that decision right away, for the stair was steep, but she clambered gamely on, coming at last to a solid-seeming door. Piers rapped once and entered. The room was small for its furnishings, old and shabby, and yet welcoming enough with a newly-lit fire crackling on the hearth. It held a table, three wooden chairs, one deep leather chair, and a settle beside the fireplace, some bookshelves, a very threadbare rug. . . .

"Sir Piers! It is true about Leader, then?" Grand Master was younger than Malinda had expected, perhaps not yet forty. His eyes had surveyed the two mud-caked women, flicking from one to the other, and his expression was guarded.

"Leader and many others, I fear," Piers said. "Your Highness, may I present Grand Master?"

He bowed low. Malinda removed a mud-caked glove and offered her fingers to be kissed. "It is an honor to visit Ironhall and to meet you, Grand Master."

"Your Grace is most kind. May I offer a chair, some refreshment?" His sneer was probably just a habitual expression, not a greeting or comment. His clothes, like his room, were shabby or even threadbare. Although he was of middle size, like all Blades, she saw what Piers had meant about his being small, as if he were trying to seem larger than he really was. Or perhaps she was just prejudiced.

"No chair, thank you. I am enjoying standing. I shall accept a share of your fire, though."

She moved closer to the hearth, aware that the chill in her bones stemmed more from lack of sleep than cold. The men adjusted their positions accordingly. Tension flickered between them like summer lightning.

"And a quaff of ale would be very welcome," she added in case the subject got overlooked. "You too, Dian? Two, please, Grand Master."

"Three," said Piers.

Grand Master went to the other door and spoke instructions to whoever was outside it. He returned, was presented to Mistress Bandit, said some maudlin things about the former Commander, inquired politely after Malinda's journey. Then he remarked, "I am saddened to see the Guard frightened to travel in uniform."

Piers raised hackles. "A common precaution when we are not escorting the sovereign, as you well know."

"I cannot recall hearing of it."

The summer lightning flickered again. Fortunately, the ale was then passed in by an aged servant. That first swallow was one of the great experiences of Malinda's life.

Piers said, "You can guess why Her Highness has come to Ironhall, Grand Master. How many can you spare?"

"You obviously have not read my reports."

"Dominic didn't find Leader's keys until yesterday and has had no time to read anything."

"Dominic is Leader now? I have not been officially informed."

"Acting Leader. The Lord Protector will make the appointment."

"How many casualties?"

Piers glanced to Malinda for permission.

"Go ahead, Sir Piers," she said, fighting a need to yawn. If this meeting lasted more than a few minutes, she would fall asleep standing up and fall in the fire.

"Three wounded beyond repair," Piers said, "sixty-two dead."

"No!" Grand Master closed his eyes in pain. "Never has the Order taken casualties on that scale! Never!" His dramatics were overdone.

"It has now. Plus, as near as we can tell, about two hundred civilians and Yeomen. The Council won't reveal its tally."

"No, no!"

"Yes, yes! The Guard is down to thirty-five, Grand Master, the smallest it has ever been. We're also into a regency and you know what those can do to us. We'll have both His Majesty and the Lord Protector to cover, plus Her Highness—and the Monster War may still be on for all I know. Politically, the Order will be fighting for its very life. So, Grand Master, how many Blades can you spare for Her Highness?"

Saxon's mouth settled deeper into its usual pout. "Deeply distressed as I am by the need to refuse Her Grace, the answer must be, 'None!' "

"Think a little harder," Piers said coldly, bringing his sword around within easier reach.

"Blustering won't create warm bodies." Grand Master turned a disagreeable smile on Malinda. "Your honored father absolutely cleaned us out a month ago. Ever since the Night of Dogs, my lady, we have been rushing boys through training much faster than normal. Our standard course is five years, but many candidates need longer and none of the present enrollment have been here even four years. We just cannot go any lower. The boys are not ready: physically, mentally, or emotionally. Their swordsmanship is totally inadequate."

"How many seniors?" Piers demanded. He seemed to have grown taller. If he was faking his anger, he was doing it very well.

Grand Master continued to smile at Malinda. "Only six. Until yesterday we had four, but even they are barely fuzzies, and the two I just promoted hardly qualify as beardless grade. We need twenty or more seniors to partner the younger candidates in fencing. The standards have slipped much too far already, and I cannot in good conscience—"

"Sewage!" Piers shouted. "Describe these four seniors. Pretend you're still reporting to King Ambrose."

The old man rounded on him. "But I'm not, am I? Whose warrants did you bring, Sir Piers? Are they signed by the Lord Protector? Has the Lord Protector even taken the oath of office?"

"They are signed by Durendal as acting chairman of the Council of Regency and they bear the Council's seal. The Council is *de facto* ruler of the land until the Lord Protector takes office."

"Bah, housekeeping duties—milking the cows and emptying slops. Only the Lord Protector has authority to deed Blades. Suppose the time comes that he wants some Blades and discovers I have given away all I had on an inadequate warrant? What happens to me then, mm?"

"Less than may happen to you now, you croaking incompetent! Report on these four seniors!"

Grand Master shrugged. "Prime is Candidate Audley. He's very handsome, will look marvelous in uniform, but he fences like a tortoise. Second . . . Your Grace does not want Second. He is crazy. In normal times he'd have been expelled long ago, but we keep him around to tutor the juniors. I would certainly not trust him at court with a sword."

"His name?" Piers snapped.

"I forget what we wrote in the rolls. He won't answer to anything but 'Dog.' Your late father used to become quite irate at such foolish names, Your Grace, but sometimes we have to accept them. Third is Winter. He's probably the best swordsman of the bunch, which is saying very little, but he's immature, highly strung. Bites his nails to the wrist."

"I wet the bed!" Piers snapped.

Grand Master blinked, thrown off stride.

Piers's face was pale under the mud. "Many seniors grow nervous as their binding approaches. They can't sleep, they twitch, and bedwetting is not all that rare. In the name of mercy, we don't talk about it, Saxon! And if it was true in my day, six years ago, think what it's like for these kids, with Blades being eaten by monsters and chopped up by their own brethren? Monster War, Wetshore, and now a regency! Well, carry on. Who's fourth?"

"Abel. He's just a silly kid. Makes obscure jokes, plays pranks. He'll be all right in a couple of years." Grand Master offered Malinda a quarter of a bow. "I am deeply sorry, my lady, but the barrel is empty."

"We'll see about that!"

"*Quiet!* Quiet both of you!" Malinda was gratified to see both men flinch before her anger. Piers's obvious hatred of Grand Master was not helping her cause, and the older man could balk her completely. "Stop behaving like children! Shouting solves nothing. When is the evening meal, Grand Master?"

"Imminently, Your Grace. Of course the Order will be deeply honored if—"

"Then, please have us shown to our quarters. Since Sir Piers is so distrusting, he may wish to test the four seniors' swordsmanship. When the meal is over, we can continue this discussion in the presence of the men themselves."

"Men . . . ?"

"The four senior candidates."

"That is not how we traditionally—"

"*But,*" Malinda smote him with her best House of Ranulf glower, "it is how we will do it this time. You say they are not ready, and you may well be right. Sir Piers suspects you of lying, while you question his authority. I say that protecting me from the dangers ahead may be beyond a dozen Durendals. I will not ask these boys to throw away their lives for me unless they are both adequately trained and properly informed about the situation."

Piers rolled his eyes as if he wished she would not interfere.

Grand Master bowed. "I know the masters will be deeply honored if Your Grace would care to take a glass of wine with them before the meal. . . ."

The hall was longer and wider than Malinda had expected. When she entered on Grand Master's arm, followed by the rest of the masters and the Blades who had brought her, all the boys rose from their benches and began a rhythmic cheer, a sort of *"Hup! Hup! Hup!"* They probably cheered any guest, but her identity would be known to them. Very few women ever saw the inside of Ironhall—although her mother had—and she wasn't seeing a great deal of it now, for the only light came from candlesticks on the tables . . . and also, she suddenly realized, from a mist of flickering stars just overhead. The famous sky of swords dipped to not much more than twice head height above the center aisle, curving upward toward the sides, and every restless blade reflected the many dancing flames beneath. *No gawking!* she reminded herself, and kept her chin down as she paraded along the aisle.

At plank tables stretching out on either hand stood the students, or candidates, as the Order called them. First the youngest boys, cheering shrilly, pushing and jostling one another; then progressively older and taller, but also progressively fewer. The first two tables were crowded to discomfort, while at the far end stood only six solemn young seniors, proudly wearing swords. Last was the vacant high table and Grand Master's throne.

"The solitary blade on the end wall," Grand Master remarked, "is *Nightfall,* Durendal's sword." He meant the legendary founder, not Lord Roland. "As you can see, it is broken. He died in his sleep, in bed, and his sword was found like that beside him. A mystery never solved."

"Perhaps it had been broken for years and he'd carried it around in its scabbard like that without telling anyone."

"Perhaps," her host conceded sullenly.

He brought her to the high table and the cushioned throne, for royalty had its privileges and one of them was always the best seat in the house. She sat down gently and tried not to think of the long ride home awaiting her in a couple of days. On her left sat Sir Lothaire, Master of Rituals, a scholarly, vaguely absentminded man with glasses. Piers and Dian were at high table also, and the rest of her escort had joined the half-dozen seniors. Alandale could try his bragging on his former friends now, but he had better stick to women as a topic.

A stray draft jangled its way through the sky of swords, setting five thousand steel teeth softly gnashing, flashing a million stars. Each blade hung through a link, and there were dozens of chains . . . she pulled her chin down again.

The masters had taken their seats, which was the signal for the boys to resume their places on the benches—with renewed squabbling and punching at the soprano tables—and servants appeared with carts. She was ravenous but halfway through the meal she was going to fall flat on her face, asleep.

"Wine, Your Highness?" asked Grand Master.

She declined another glass of wine. She studied the six at the seniors' table, chattering with the visiting guardsmen. Whatever their actual ages, they were three young men and three tall boys—the distinction was perhaps unfair, but real enough. Only one of them could be described as handsome.

Since Grand Master was cross-examining Dian about Wetshore, she turned to Master of Rituals.

"Sir Lothaire, pray name the seniors for me. That dark-haired charmer must be Candidate Audley? He is going to pop every female eye in the palace." Just wait until Lady Violet set eyes on *that* one!

"Oh, we all do," the conjurer said, so smoothly that she was not sure how serious he was. "Opposite him is Winter."

Winter she was always going to think of as the nail biter, and he did look a little jumpy. Who wouldn't be jumpy in his shoes? Abel was one of the three kids. He was showing off, telling stories and laughing. The other two, Crenshaw and Hunter, looked more frightened even than Winter, but then they had been moved into the front line only the previous day and now here was a potential ward come harvesting Blades. Even if they were not called out themselves, they might be left behind as the only seniors in Ironhall. They were having trouble managing their swords, threatening to trip up passing servants.

That left Dog, who was the largest, probably the oldest, distinguished by coarse, unattractive features and untidy tow-colored hair protruding from under his hat like straw. He was eating stolidly, ignoring conversations on either side of him.

"He's big for a Blade, isn't he?"

"Wide, certainly," agreed Lothaire, who believed strongly in his own ability to talk while chewing. "He was already over our height limit when he was admitted, so we applied . . . necessary ritual to stop him growing . . . didn't work as well as usual. He may have been too young . . . grew no taller but spread out sideways and forward. You should see the chest on him . . . expect you will, won't you? The others call him Ox or Horse sometimes. He doesn't like that, which seems odd when he named himself Dog . . . hasn't affected his agility much. Can whip a broadsword around like a rapier, quite incredible . . ."

There was no shortage of appetites in the hall. The fare was simple but ample and tasty enough. Everyone ate heartily, even the older knights, and the servants rushed around refilling platters as if they were shoveling dirt in a hole. Malinda herself ate more than she had in years and felt better for it. Tomorrow she would be required to fast in preparation for the ritual. She made trivial conversation with her two companions, well aware that they were trying to eavesdrop on Dian and Piers, who were being brutally cross-examined about the Wetshore Massacre. The seniors were interrogating the Blades in the same fashion, and only her rank was protecting her from similar treatment.

The eating ended, Grand Master rose and waited for silence. "Brothers, candidates, as you can see, we are honored by the presence of a royal guest tonight. Before I make the introductions, we shall have our traditional reading from *The Litany of Heroes*."

With a harsh scrape of boots and benches, everyone rose, Malinda and Dian just a fraction behind the rest. A servant had pushed a wheeled lectern to Grand Master's side, and now he turned to the great book resting on it.

" 'Number 275: Sir Intrepid who, on the fourth of Fifthmoon 368, was escorting his ward on a hunt when a conjured monster in the form of a giant manlike cat emerged from the bushes and attacked his ward; he interposed and wounded it in the leg before it broke his neck with a blow of its paw, but his ward survived.' " After a moment's silence, Grand Master closed the book. "Let us remember and honor our fallen brother."

Malinda had known Intrepid! Two hundred and seventy-five? Her mind balked like a horse at a fence. She turned again to Master of Rituals. "The boys hear a story like that every night?"

He nodded, blinking through his spectacles. "There are other readings, too . . . when a new boy takes a hero's name, when new names are added. Lots of those recently!"

Grand Master had begun introducing her. If Intrepid had been 275, what was the total now? Did the Wetshore casualties qualify? "Who gets listed?" she whispered.

"Whoever saves his ward from peril or dies trying."

No, the Wetshore sixty-two would not be added to the litany.

" . . . and welcome Her Highness," Grand Master concluded.

Big cheer.

"Lady Bandit, widow of the most recent Leader."

Huge, prolonged cheer, tribute to the Commander everyone had liked. It went on and on, until Grand Master cut it off. Dian stared down at her lap, blinking rapidly.

"Sir Piers, unofficially acting deputy commander of the Royal Guard."

Piers took a bow, but the cheering was restrained. It grew steadily fainter as each additional visitor was announced, and ended with some jocular booing at the naming of Sir Alandale.

"These are sad times," Grand Master conceded. "Our beloved sovereign, head of our Order, was treacherously slain less than a week ago. The toll of our brethren was far greater than we at first heard. Sir Piers was there and will say a few words."

In the days when Malinda had dreamed of being the love slave of Sir Piers, she had not appreciated his ruthless streak. He had revealed it today in his casual dismissal of Kromman's murder and perhaps even in the way he had manipulated her into riding posthaste all the way to Ironhall. Now he showed it again when he described the Wetshore Massacre for his brethren. He spared no horrors: the Baels had shot only one arrow, the Blades had rioted, sixty-two had died, perhaps two hundred others. Each new revelation was greeted with gasps and moans. He did offer a few rays of light—most of the civilian casualties had been caused by the panic; they had been crushed or had fallen down the bank. Most of the Blade casualties, so far as the Guard could determine, had not been caused by Blades. The mounted Yeomen had taken fearful toll of their old rivals.

"None of our dead can be honored in the Litany," he said, "but perhaps they did not die entirely in vain. When the answers are known, brothers, their loss may count in our favor." The youngsters at the far end of the hall would not understand; the older boys might not; the knights certainly would. Questions were going to be asked and the Order's very existence might be in jeopardy.

"It has been no joy to tell you these things, brothers, and yet I have even sadder tidings, perhaps the worst news ever reported in Ironhall. You have heard that the bolt that killed our liege was fired by the King of the Baels himself, Radgar Æleding. I saw him on his ship a few minutes earlier. I recognized him. I guessed who he must be. I knew him under the name of Raider, although I had not known until then what he had become. I knew him here, when he was a candidate in Ironhall."

Uproar! Even the masters joined in the shouts of denial.

Piers stood mute until the hall stilled. "Our greatest foe was once one of us, brothers. He was a senior when I was the Brat. He refused binding when the time came, of course, and fled from Chivial back to his fiery lair, where he seized the throne and declared war on the land that had given him refuge. This fact King Ambrose managed to suppress. The rest of us were led to believe that Raider and another candidate had been bound by the King for some secret service outside the Royal Guard. To add to our shame, brothers, Radgar Æleding must have known what would happen to the Blades present at Wetshore when he slew our ward. We were betrayed by one of our own." Piers sank back on his stool.

Grand Master let the horrified silence drag on for several minutes before he whispered. "Your Highness?"

Malinda nodded. Her eyes would not stay open, but she had been making speeches for years and there was grave need of one now. He introduced her again. She heaved herself to her feet and sent her voice to the far end of the hall.

"Grand Master, masters, knights, companions, candidates . . . I have long wanted to come here and visit the Order which has served my family so well for so long. I am honored to meet all of you who dwell under the sky of swords. Alas, these are dark times, both for your order and for my family. Yes, and for our homeland of Chivial, which is now ruled in the name of a child. Regencies are never easy. In the long years ahead before my brother can come into his inheritance, I swear to you that I will dedicate my life to his welfare, his service, his—"

"*I will die for you, Princess!*"

The voice was harsh and discordant. Dog was on his feet. At once his neighbor on either side jumped up and tried to drag him down. Staggering but still upright, he yelled again, "*I will die for you!*" Angry murmurs swelled all around. "Ask whatever you want and I will obey—" Oak and Marlon went to add their weight to the heap, and four men together forced Dog down onto the bench.

Grand Master did not say a word, but Malinda could hear him anyway: *I told you so!* Dog was crazy.

"Honor and courage and service," she said, "have been for centuries the hallmark of your brotherhood. I should like to believe that they have also distinguished the House of Ranulf. It is in the darkest of times that honor and courage and service shine most brightly. So let us make this our pledge together, you and I, here under the sky of swords, that we shall always hold true to our ways, our laws, and our traditions. Then centuries as yet unborn will look back on us and see, not our darkest times, but our most glorious."

She sat down to enjoy the ovation.

She had naively hoped to have a reasoned discussion with the four available seniors, outlining the political situation and the dangers she foresaw, but the hour was late and she was exhausted. It was Piers who took control of the meeting that assembled back in Grand Master's study. She did not dare sit down lest she fall asleep, and when royalty stood everybody stood—the four candidates in an uneasy line in front of the window; Malinda, Dian, Piers, and Grand Master opposite. There were not enough candles and the fire had collapsed into ashes. It was bedtime. The world trembled with weariness.

"They're not as bad as Grand Master said," Piers told her. "They need much more practice and instruction, which is what we've been seeing in all recruits lately, and they won't get any better if you leave them here because they're spending all their time on the juniors. So are the instructors who should be helping them. A couple of months at court and the Guard will lick them into shape for you."

"And what do we do, here in Ironhall?" Grand Master snapped.

"You cope as best you can, which is what we're all doing."

Now was the moment for Malinda to open that discussion she had wanted. Already she realized that her noble talk of ignoring traditional ways and giving the boys the right to refuse had been folly. Dare she mention her doubts about the Lord Protector? His scheming would be much harder if she had four Blades around her, but the four would be crazy to volunteer if she told them how grim her prospects really were. She looked uncertainly at them. Audley was instantly impressive—stunningly good-looking and apparently confident. Dog was only slightly taller but much burlier. He was frowning; there was something odd about his eyes, but she did not want to stare. Winter looked terrified, ready to vomit. Abel was grinning nervily; he was only a boy. Where to begin?

While she hesitated, Piers spoke again. "I expect you're all shaking in your socks. I know I was when I got to this stage, but all you have to worry about is the binding, and thousands of men have gone through that unscathed. Once you're bound, you never lack for courage. The binding will provide it when you need it." He probably meant those words especially for Winter, and certainly Winter raised his chin. Abel's brave grin widened. Dog scowled harder.

"You all know," Malinda began, "that our new king is too young even to understand what 'king' means, but we do, and we know what honor and loyalty mean. I give you my most solemn oath that I have no designs on the throne. I want my brother to grow safely into manhood and come into his inheritance. If the spirits of chance decree otherwise, then I hope to inherit in my turn. But you know the dangers of minorities. It is my—"

"I will die for you, Princess!" Dog rasped, stepping forward.

"Wait!" Grand Master yelled, moving to block him.

It seemed that Dog merely made an idle gesture, but the impact of his arm sent the older man flying; he would have sprawled flat on his back had he not collided with the table. Taking no notice of him, Dog dropped on his knees at Malinda's feet and grabbed her hand in two huge, horny paws.

"I don't want you to—" She tried to pull free, but her hand stayed firmly where it was.

Dog kissed it. "I'll be your man, Princess."

"And I, also!" said Audley, coming to kneel beside Dog. As Prime he should have been first, but he smiled easily, taking no offense. Abel and Winter almost collided in their haste to join the line.

"Well done!" Piers cried. "You've gotten yourself a fine Princess's Guard there, my lady! Shut up, Grand Master."

18

189: Sir Valorous who, in Thirdmoon 302, was captured by Isilondian soldiers and died under torture without betraying his ward.

IRONHALL, *THE LITANY OF HEROES*

"Ah, you killed him," Sir Lothaire said sadly. "You must try not to twist it on the way out. Try again." He made another mark with his charcoal.

Fortunately, the victim was only a dressed pig's carcase on a chopping block in the Ironhall kitchens. Two smirking varlets were holding it upright while Malinda attempted to bind it to her Guard. She was not happy. The morning was too young, the kitchen reeked of tainted meat as butchers' premises always did, the carcase crawled with big black flies, and yesterday's ride was still a painful subject. She steadied the sword, keeping it level as she had been instructed, and pushed, hard. The blade slid in and struck a bone on the far side, making the holders stagger.

"And *out* again!" Master of Rituals said cheerily. "Yes! Much better! Don't worry about hitting a rib or shoulder blade. It looks more dramatic if you stick 'em all the way through, and the lads like to have two scars to impress the ladies, but as long as you're into his heart, he's bound. Provided you don't carve him up on the way out, that is. Then he's dead. Again? Well done. Try it with this."

The sword he now offered her was a notched and rusty horror, almost as long as she was tall. She gasped at the weight.

"I can't use this! I could swing it maybe . . ." She raised it, using both hands, and the kitchen helpers leaped backward.

Lothaire guffawed. "It does have to be his heart. Cutting his head off won't work." Conjurers often had a strange sense of humor.

"What's wrong with the other one?"

"You must bind a man with his own sword, and I know they've made a broadsword for Dog. Try on this gauntlet. If you hold the blade with your left hand, you should be able to manage. This one isn't sharp, but tonight's will be like a razor. . . ."

136

★   ★   ★

They emerged into the courtyard, where the visiting guardsmen were ferociously clattering steel with candidates, bellowing comments and instructions. Dian had waited out there, in the fresh air.

Beside her stood a hefty, flaxen-haired young man, who growled, "Will you spit me clean through tonight, Princess?"

She wondered if that hoarse rumble was Dog's natural voice or if he had learned to fake it to fit his chosen name. In sunlight, she could understand the strangeness she had glimpsed in his eyes the previous night—the irises were so pale as to be almost white. So were his lashes. He looked blind.

"You do not address Her Highness that way!" Master of Rituals snapped.

"She can tell me if she doesn't like it." No smile, no smile at all.

"I prefer," she said, "that you stay with formal forms of address."

"As Your Grace wishes," Dog rasped, bowing. "If you want to practice your sword work on a real body, Your Highness, I don't mind going first tonight."

"Oh, Dog, do behave yourself!" Master of Rituals snapped. "This is typical of him, Your Grace. He's been warned a thousand times, so if you want to leave him out, then—"

"No!" Dog roared. He fell on his knees and raised clasped hands in supplication. "I am only trying to be helpful, Your Highness! Just offering to go first in case you botch the first attempt."

Sir Lothaire shook his head. "I am deeply sorry, Your Grace. He means well. He just can't help it. We've tried every punishment in the book and they make no difference. I'm afraid one either takes Dog as he is or not at all."

"Is he safe?"

"Oh, yes. He's never hurt anyone, although he could break most of us in half if he exerted himself. I'd worry more that he would refuse to hurt a real enemy. . . . It's just what he says and when and how he says it. The decision must be yours, Your Highness."

Dog doubled over as if to kiss the ground. "Please, please! I try. I keep trying, all the time."

"Do so and we'll see," Malinda said weakly.

Sir Lothaire sighed. "It's just the way he is. Let us go to the Forge, Your Grace."

At first the Forge seemed to be only a low, moss-covered dome with small peaked windows, but there was more of it underground, a crypt reached by a flight of stairs. Spring water brimmed over eight stone troughs around the perimeter and ran in gutters to a drain in the rock floor. Five raised hearths bore crackling fires and three others had been banked so they merely glowed. The array of tongs, pincers, and hammers hung on the walls; the bins of ore, miscellaneous bars and ingots; the eight huge anvils—all were reminders that this was a working smithy, the place where the famous cat's-eye swords were made. It was on the ninth anvil, an iron slab in the center, that youths were wrought into living Blades. An octogram of white tiles inset in the rock floor around it formed Ironhall's elementary, rife with all eight elements.

"Now you have to meditate," Master of Rituals said cheerfully.

Malinda shivered in the dank air. "Meditate on what?"

"Anything . . . the books don't say." His glasses slashed firelight. He lowered his voice. "I think it's just so the candidates can't complain that they didn't have time to think about it." Chuckling, he bowed and strode off to the stairs.

Malinda headed for the hottest-looking fire. Winter, Abel, and Audley separated and made themselves as comfortable as possible beside a hearth apiece. Dog stood where he was, staring across at her.

"Do you need me?" Dian asked with distaste. "Because if not, Your Almighty Highness, I'm going to sneak back to bed . . . er . . . alone," she added with a hint of her old grin. "Really."

"Bring me my cloak and I'll allow that."

What was there to meditate about except the future, about which she could predict nothing whatsoever?

Soon after that, Master Armorer came to ask each candidate in turn what name he wanted on his sword. He went away and the excitement was over. After about an hour, Malinda decided she could stand no more boredom. She walked around to the nearest candidate, who happened to be young Abel. He looked up with wide eyes and began to rise.

"No, sit," she said, and joined him on the floor. "If we must meditate, then let's have something to meditate about. Tell me how you chose your name."

He hesitated. "Well, Your Grace . . . It sounds good. *Able* to do things, capable. And there have been five Abels in the Order, far back as the archives go, but the name never appears in *The Litany of Heroes*."

"You want to be the first?"

A juvenile grin flashed. "I thought it must be lucky."

"Makes sense! And what are you going to call your sword?"

"*Willing*. That's a joke, see—Abel and *Willing*?"

"A good one. I shall need a commander for my Guard. Tell me why I should appoint you rather than one of the others."

He gaped. "Me, Your Grace? Oh. Um. I'm the second best swordsman, after Winter. Commander Bandit was a very good Leader, wasn't he, because everyone liked him? I think I'm pretty popular, Your Grace." His cheeky grin returned and stayed.

She was not impressed by his reasoning, but she admired quick wits. "And if I decide to appoint one of the others, which one should it be?"

"Dog!"

"Everyone says Dog is crazy."

"Oh, he is, but he's clever, too."

Puzzled, she asked, "Just why do you think he'd make a good commander?"

Abel chewed his lip for a moment, not looking at her. "Because he's been Second for the last month, and Second is responsible for discipline, you know, keeping the juniors in line. It's tricky and a lot of Seconds fail and have to call on Grand Master for help. Everyone thought Dog was too soft, and Hawthorn lipped him the very first day. Hawthorn's no lightweight, but Dog held him out the window by one ankle—upside down, see, one-handed, and two floors up— and made him count to forty-nine." Abel sniggered. "He, er, wet his shirt, Your Grace! And Dog said the next man would have to go to a hundred and fifteen. Since then Dog just has to look at them with those eyes of his and they crap their— Beg your pardon, Your Grace. Scares them, I mean. I think Dog could keep us in line for you."

"I'll keep that formula in mind," she said, rising. Grand Master had not been overharsh in summing up Master Abel as a silly kid.

The next one around the octogram was Winter, ferociously chewing his nails. She asked the same question she had asked Abel.

"There are s-six Winters in the Litany. It's a g-g-great heroes' name to live up to."

"And what have you named your sword?" *Icicle? Frost?*

"Fear."

"Fear? Why?"

"Because fear is the . . . Because I hope to strike *Fear* into the hearts of your foes, my lady."

"I hope you do. Give me some reasons why I ought to appoint you commander."

He flinched, thought for a moment. "I'm the best swordsman of the four of us, although Sir Piers didn't think much . . . I wouldn't be a very good commander. I'm a fire-time person."

"What's a fire-time person?"

He blinked owlishly at her. "Everyone has two dominant elements, one virtual and one manifest. My manifest element is fire—I'm restless, inquisitive, jumpy—and my virtual is time. It's a bad combination for a leader. Good mix for a swordsman, though."

"Interesting! I thought I knew more conjuration lore than most, but I've never heard that theory before. What about your friends?"

Winter brightened at the chance to lecture. "You really should ask a White Sister, my lady. She could sense the elementals directly and know for sure. I'm only guessing, but I do know them pretty well, so I'll say that Abel is air-love. He's flighty, erratic, but everyone likes him. Or maybe air-time, since he's so nimble. Audley's water. That's obvious, because he's so smooth, always fitting in. Plus, um, I'd guess *love* for him too, my lady. Dog . . . Dog's a puzzle. Earth, certainly, because of his strength. I think his virtual element is chance. . . . Odd things happen to Dog. One day one of the old knights lost the cat's-eye out of his sword. The setting was worn, see? Grand Master offered a reward and Dog walked out across the moor and found the stone right away—and he hadn't been out there for days, so he hadn't seen it fall or cheated or anything!"

"He's lucky?"

"Sort of." Winter chuckled nervously. "On the way back an adder bit his ankle. That's typical of him, my lady. If any man's going to be struck by lightning, it'll be Dog."

Malinda was impressed, sensing a quick mind. If Winter was more apprehensive than the others, it might be because he had too much imagination.

"Thank you, Winter. You've given me something to meditate on. Getting back to the original question, if I don't appoint you commander, who's the best of the other three?"

"Oh, Audley, Your Grace! Nothing ever rattles him."

Audley was next—slim, dark, toothsome. He smiled at her as if she were just a pretty girl, not a princess. If he was as good with a sword as he was with those eyelashes, he would conquer the world.

Why had he chosen that name, she asked.

"I just liked the sound of it, Your Grace, oddly enough."

And his sword?

"You saw Durendal's sword hanging in the hall? Well that's *Nightfall,* and no one would ever use that name again, but I'm going to call mine *Evening.*"

She gave him the royal stare until he flinched, which took longer than she had expected. "Two is too much. Don't you know that making terrible puns near the heir to the throne is a capital offense?"

"Puns?" He wafted the lashes again. "*Me,* Your Grace?"

"Yes, even you, oddly! Can you think of any reason why I should appoint you the commander?"

"Other than as a *puni*shment?" he murmured, glancing around the Forge. "Just by default, my lady. I'm not nearly qualified to be a commander yet, but I'm closer than any of the others."

"And if my distaste for puns drove me to choose one of them, which should it be?"

Again Audley studied the other three. "Winter. He's smart and conscientious; if Sir Piers was right about binding giving him more confidence, then he'll make an excellent Blade. Abel's an airhead and a smartass. Dog's . . . unpredictable. Talks like a madman."

"So he says odd things, but what does he *do?* Can I trust him?"

"Oh, yes. Don't listen to what he says. He absolutely refuses to fence unless his opponent wears a mask and padding—seniors usually don't, you see. It's not that he's not good with a sword. He's just stubborn as this anvil on that, won't take the chance of hurting anyone."

"What about young Hawthorn?"

Audley shot her a surprised glance. "Even Grand Master approved, and he never has a good word for Dog usually. He has a sense of humor. It doesn't show very often."

"He's always been like this?"

"Long as I can remember. He had a very hard time of it when he was the Brat. He was so big, even then, and we . . . the sopranos discovered he wouldn't defend himself. . . . Sailor was Prime and eventually he had to step in and put a stop to it. Two boys were expelled for sadism."

"Why was he put in Ironhall? What had he done?"

"We don't know." Audley hesitated. "He cries out in his sleep."

"Saying what?"

"Nothing we can ever make out, except he seems to want someone called Ed. If we say there was a lot of dog howling last night, he just shrugs those mountain shoulders of his and goes away, walks out by himself. In an hour or so he'll come back, and that's all. He'll be all right, Your Grace, I'm sure. We'll need him if we ever have any real fighting to do; Dog's strong as a bull. They've probably made a broadsword for him." He thought for a moment. "He's no slouch with an ordinary saber, though."

She went to sit beside the problem Dog. He stared at her with no expression on a memorably ugly face. In the dim light of the Forge his bizarre white irises were less noticeable, but his nose was twisted, his mouth and jaw lopsided, and one ear was puffed out like a puffball.

"Why did you choose the name Dog?"

After several seconds came his grinding growl: "A dog is a loyal and fierce defender."

"But to call someone a dog means they are of little worth, low repute."

Eventually she realized that he was not going to answer, because she had not asked a direct question. She tried a smile and it was refused.

"What are you going to name your sword?"

"Why should a sword need a name? It won't come when I call."

"You weren't paying attention when they did the bit on manners, were you? Tell me why I ought to appoint you commander of my Guard."

"You mustn't. I won't be commander."

"Then who should be?"

He stared at her, perhaps thinking, perhaps not. Finally he growled, "I don't care. Any of them." He shrugged what Audley had called his mountain shoulders. His insolence irked her, although it seemed more indifference than deliberate offense.

"Don't you ever smile?"

"When a dog shows his teeth it is not amused."

"Laugh, then? Do you ever laugh?"

He thought for a while. "Long time ago I did," he said, and turned his back on her.

The day dragged by in boredom and hunger. She meditated mostly on her two brothers—the infant king and the ruthless warrior—but she found no new insights. As the high windows began to darken, a couple of armorer apprentices came and poked up the fires into cheerful blazes. Master of Rituals shuffled in, accompanied by Dian with a pile of laundry, followed by some juniors carrying what seemed to be tabletops.

"Bath time, Your Highness," he explained cheerfully. "I'll just run through the ritual with you quickly if you would be so gracious as to come over to the octogram. . . . Your part is very small, but vital, of course, and you spend most of your time standing here, which is love point. Directly across from you, the candidate will be at death. The Brat is always chance. . . . With only four to bind, we won't need to reform the octogram between bindings, just reaffirm the dedi-

cation, and I shall chant Dispenser. . . ." He babbled off into technical-
ities, as conjurers were wont to do.

She listened, trying not to be distracted by the juniors, who were
chuckling and smirking and whispering obviously lewd remarks, while
busily linking their wooden panels together to make a sort of unroofed
shed. What was the joke? Abel was grinning, Audley making a brave
effort not to, and Winter's face had been locked into a sickly smirk
since noon. Only Dog remained serious.

". . . you and the candidates have to bathe at water, death, chance,
and finally love. That order is very important. There . . . there . . .
there . . . and finally over here." Lothaire smiled, spectacles shining
gold. "Complete immersion."

Dian was obviously more amused by the prospect than by anything
that had happened since Bandit's death. "Towels, Your Wetness, and
a very slinky sort of monk's robe with cowl. Court will go wild over
it when you set the next season's fashions."

Master of Rituals awoke to the nuances of the situation. "It might
be best if the candidates went first? Boys, bring the screens over here
please. Then you can go. Quickly now! We had to find this in the
cellars, Your Grace. Master of Archives says you are the first lady to
bind a Blade since the late Queen Sian. . . ."

Soon after that, Dian and Malinda were sitting by the fire at air
point, completely enclosed in the head-high fence, hearing a succession of splashing noises and yowls of agony outside as the four would-
be Blades performed their ritual cleansing. That was all Malinda did,
anyway. Dian found a knothole that gave her a one-eyed view of the
trough at death point. She seemed quite impressed by someone.

When the four thoroughly-chilled young men had dried and
dressed themselves, they helpfully moved the screens and set them up
around the trough at water point so the Princess could begin her own
ordeal. The water felt as if it should have ice on it. She wondered if
all this hardship was really necessary for the ritual or merely another
sadistic test of dedication.

Darkness had fallen and only firelight lit the Forge. Just before
midnight the knights, masters, and candidates came trooping in; and
suddenly time, which had dragged endlessly all day, leaped forward in
a blur. She was standing at her place in the octogram, with Grand
Master, Master of Rituals, a frightened boy who must be the Brat,
and her four future Blades. Eight in all, of course. There was
singing. . . . Some elements were invoked, others revoked. There
were arcane rituals with handfuls of grain and gold coins. . . . Malinda

was not sensitive to spirituality, but the sepulchral echoes alone were enough to make her scalp prickle. And then the Brat was squeaking out his lines, laying a sword on that great metal slab in the center . . . Dog helping Audley off with his shirt . . . Winter marking his chest with charcoal to show where she must strike. . . .

A half-naked young man was standing on the central anvil, holding his sword aloft in salute to her while he spoke the words of the oath in a shaky voice:

"Princess Malinda, upon my soul, I, Candidate Audley of the Loyal and Ancient Order of the King's Blades, do irrevocably swear in the presence of these my brethren that I will evermore defend you against all foes, setting my own life as nothing to shield you from peril, reserving only my fealty to our lord the King. To bind me to this oath, I bid you plunge this my sword into my heart that I may die if I swear falsely or, being true, may live by the power of the spirits here assembled to serve you until in time I die again."

She had never seen real fear before. His eyes showed white all around the irises and his sword hand trembled; but he spoke the ancient words without a fault and jumped down without stumbling. He moved gracefully, sinking on one knee to proffer the sword to her, then backing away to sit on the anvil. Winter and Dog clasped his arms to steady him. The rest was up to her. Even Audley's lips looked white, for he must wonder if a woman who had never touched a sword before today was now about to kill him. "Don't look at his face," Master of Rituals had told her, "watch the sword." She looked down at the sword she held no more steadily than Audley had.

Oh, spirits! *It was curved!* At her practice session this morning, Lothaire had never mentioned curved blades, but this sword they had made for Audley had a slight but unmistakable curve to it.

She *must* get it right first time. This ritual had worked thousands of times in the past. Her mother had bound Blades; it could not be very difficult. She had only three words to speak. She lined the point up with that mark on the boy's chest, desperately trying to stop it trembling, saw him wince as she pricked him and drew blood.

"Serve or die!" She *pushed* as hard as she could, trying to turn the hilt to keep the wound as small as possible. It slid in so easily she almost stumbled; it struck bone. Audley made a horrible hoarse noise that she assumed was a death rattle and screwed up his face in a rictus of agony, wrenched against his holders; she pulled . . . *try not to twist it on the way out* . . . but she must twist it to follow that arc. . . .

The sword was free in her hands, dripping blood, but the wound healed before her eyes. Dog and Winter released their grip, leaving white pits on Audley's arms. The Forge rocked with cheers. Then Audley was standing, beaming at her, holding out his hand for the sword—his own sword, *Evening*. She wiped sweat from her forehead and returned his smile.

The participants shuffled places, there was more chanting, but briefer this time. Dog spoke the oath in his animal growl, which must be his natural voice. The second binding should be easy. But one glance at the huge broadsword he was holding without visible effort told her that it would weigh more than a horse. As he sprang down from the anvil, she bent to snatch up the steel gauntlet Sir Lothaire had given her for just this purpose. She gripped the monstrous thing by hilt and midpoint; its blade was a handsbreadth wide. But then Dog's chest and shoulders were giant-size to match. Could Winter and Abel possibly hold him still for her? And how hard must she push to penetrate all that muscle?

Don't look at his face. . . . She did, of course, and was amazed to see him gazing back at her with no indication of fear at all. He was flushed, not pale, and his strange eyes were staring at the approaching sword with a sort of hunger, or eagerness. She had stopped—he scowled at her, and she told herself she must not prolong the ordeal just because he was managing to hide his suffering. She put the distant point of the sword at the black smudge and pushed as hard as she could. "Serve or die!" This time she missed bone completely and ran two feet of steel out his back before she realized. A torrent of blood flowed down to soak his britches. His spasm of pain sent Abel and Winter flying, but she hauled the sword out cleanly, steadying it again with her gauntleted hand.

The cheering rolled as loud for him as it had for Audley. It was curious that a character as odd as Dog should be so respected. Even when she returned his huge, dragon-slaying sword, he did not smile. Anyone would think he died every day.

Now she was gaining confidence. But Winter was next, and when she had thought Audley looked frightened, she had not known what real terror looked like. He whispered the oath almost inaudibly, stumbling twice, starting over. Even innocent-seeming breaks like that in a ritual could invalidate it, and she saw Master of Rituals open his mouth to order a fresh start. But Winter got through the oath correctly on the third attempt and stepped down from the anvil. He approached her slowly and flopped down on both knees as if his legs had given way. When he held up the sword to her, she saw the sweat dripping off his chin. Who was she to torture a boy like this? She tried to answer that desperate appeal in his eyes with a smile of comfort and wondered if it would look like blood lust to him.

The sword was a rapier, very light, slender as a needle. *Fear* he had named it. Audley and Dog held him for her. He closed his eyes and she struck *Fear* into his heart. There was almost no blood.

As the cheering died away and she returned the sword to him, she saw that he was grinning through tears of relief. She wanted to tell him that courage was not lack of fear, it was overcoming fear, and he was probably the bravest man in Ironhall that night—but she would not shame him by saying so in front of the others, and he must know it anyway.

Young Abel looked scared, but he would be glad to get it over with. *Willing* was a light, straight sword, nothing fancy. It slid in and out of its owner's heart with no fuss . . . *willingly,* perhaps.

All done.

Screaming with excitement, the juniors swarmed into the octogram, chattering like starlings, demanding to inspect scars and bloody swords. Knights and masters crowded close to offer congratulations. But the four new-forged Blades had eyes only for their ward.

"Sir Audley," she said, "I appoint you Commander of the Princess's Guard."

He bowed, but his smile said that was only to be expected. "I am deeply honored. Your orders, Your Grace?"

"For now, just get me to the food," she said.

Tomorrow she would lead forth her tiny army to do battle for their sovereign lord the King.

19

These monstrous killers, these bloodthirsty, murdering beasts who are loosed against us.

THE HONORABLE ALFRED KILDARE, M.P.

For the first week or two after his binding, a Blade was notoriously reluctant to let his ward out of his sight. Malinda had to insist that she did not need four guards standing over her while she undressed, no matter how sincerely they promised to keep their backs turned.

They inspected her bedroom as if counting spiders—all four of them peering under the bed and in every drawer. She assumed that they all stood guard outside the door till morning.

Sir Piers and his men had ridden away before the binding began, but he had left a fat purse with Dian to cover homeward expenses. Malinda had never touched money in her life, so next morning she handed it to Sir Audley and told him he would have to account for it all; he swelled up like a puffball at being given this responsibility. They ate a leisurely breakfast and set off on the Blackwater road. Winter was the only man she saw look back even once.

Audley was good company: respectful, poised, and witty without being too addicted to puns. He tended to pull rank and ride on her right, leaving space on her left for someone else only if the trail was wide enough. In farmland it was usually just a wide expanse of mud across unfenced fields, but in the forests it could narrow to little more than a bridle path, and then Malinda was preoccupied with low branches and her Blades worried about ambush. Since Ironhall's political instruction had not yet caught up with the new reign, she outlined for each man in turn her concern for her infant brother's safety, her distrust of the Lord Protector, and the various strategies she thought he might try. They should know their enemy. They were shocked to realize that the Royal Guard itself would not necessarily remain on her side.

She soon learned that the only political thinker among them was Winter, who went swiftly to the heart of the problem, and stopped chewing his nails long enough to ask, "If the Lord Protector can persuade Parliament to legitimize him, then he would be the lawful heir? Would you try to contest that?"

"I would not expect you four to fight the entire country, no. I hope my brother and I would be decently treated, as minor royalty. I strongly suspect we would not be, though. We and our descendants would remain a threat to the Granville line."

Winter gnawed a pinkie for a moment. "But we already have a king. When you start deposing rulers you create precedents, don't you? Next time Parliament doesn't like the sovereign it can change the laws again. Pretty soon you'll have an elective monarchy like Baelmark's."

"I thought the Baels did it with swords, but that's still a very astute argument. Thank you!"

"The Baels' way is quite complicated," Winter said earnestly and proceeded to give her a lecture on Baelish government. After enduring that, she felt justified in asking him how he was going to hold his sword when he had eaten his fingers off completely. He looked hurt.

*   *   *

Dog's reaction could not have been more different. He kept his blind, white eyes on her as she outlined the problem, then he growled, "I will deal with him for you, Princess."

"Deal with who, er, whom? How?"

"This Lord Protector. It is easy to kill someone if you don't mind being caught. I will kill the Rector for you."

"You will most certainly do no such—"

"I am your Blade. I will do anything you want, Princess. That is what I am for. They told us at Ironhall that a Blade is born to die."

"Well, I am telling you—"

"I will obey any order you give me, even if I must die doing so. You can destroy me if you want."

"I do *not* want, you great"—Malinda restrained her vocabulary—"man. You are not going to kill anyone, you hear? Not unless I am in danger. Or you are, of course."

If she had been scraping the bottom of the Ironhall barrel, she had done very well, she decided. They were naive and undertrained, but they all showed promise. Audley was personable, Winter clever, and Abel just needed time to grow up. Dog would probably be a good solid guardian once she learned to ignore his bizarre remarks. Their origins were humble and they would not be mistaken for nobility, but part of the Ironhall miracle was that they could now behave as the nobility expected its retainers to behave, fit to serve in its palaces and mansions.

On the rare occasions when she got one of them alone, she pried gently into his past, which was absolutely none of her business. The tales she heard were standard—boys abused, orphaned, or abandoned. Abel had been a vagrant, dumped in Ironhall by a sheriff who did not fancy sending a child to the mines; Audley had fled his home village after beating up a drunken and violent stepfather; Winter had been tossed from foster home to foster home until he was so wild that no one could tolerate him. Dog, inevitably, was different. He rasped, "I don't have to tell you that," and reined in his horse so that she rode on without him.

The weather was perfect. She saw no urgent need to cripple herself with another marathon ride. A leisurely journey would be a valuable chance to get to know her Blades before she put her life in their hands.

"Where shall we overnight, Your Grace?" her Commander inquired as the western sky began to redden.

"At the King's Head in New Cinderwich." She had noted it on the way to Ironhall, amused that the picture on the sign looked so unlike Amby. She was being perverse, because there were several royal hunting lodges within reach, and so was Bondhill Palace, all of which would have caretaker staff. Any rural gentlefolk would be ecstatic to grant her hospitality. But an inn would be a novel adventure for her.

Audley frowned. "As you wish, my lady." Then he laid down conditions. She must not reveal her identity, her rings and bracelets must be put away out of sight, she would be addressed as Mistress Ward, cat's-eye pommels would be kept hidden under cloaks, and so on. She hid her amusement and agreed to her guardian's terms. He chose a room at the end of the corridor for her and Dian, plus the one opposite, from which his team could watch her door without standing in the passage all night.

Only Dian did not enter cheerfully into the game. "I'll take the fleas if you'll feed the bedbugs!" she said grumpily. "Have you smelled the dining room yet?"

True, the food was a nasty shock, but the stink in the dining room was mainly that of old ale. It was large and dim, busy and rowdy. Soon all six of them gathered around a plank table to fight with the grease soup and roast gristle. After the novelty wore off, Malinda noticed she was no longer the sole object of interest in her companions' universe. Conversation had died; eyes roamed, mouths forgot to chew. There were *girls* present—wenches! They swaggered and flounced; they flirted with the male customers; they had certainly noticed the four Blades. Only gentlemen wore swords, and all gentlemen were rich by their standards. Innocent though Malinda was in the ways of the world, she knew what was being offered. She knew that the King's Head was very different from the King's palace. She exchanged grins with Dian.

"Master Audley?"

"Er . . . Mistress?"

"You may issue each man one crown apiece as an advance on wages."

Eight eyes stretched very wide, then three young men grinned wildly and even Dog brightened. Abel turned an astonishing shade of excited pink.

"Beg pardon, er, mistress," Winter said, "but how much will you be paying us?"

"I have no idea. What's the going rate?"

"Room, board, and livery are standard," Audley said glumly. "Some wards don't give their Blades money at all. The Guard pays one crown a month."

"Is that what it's always paid or has it been raised since the Monster War started?"

"It hasn't changed in a hundred years."

"Then I think two would be about right for a smaller, elite force."

At that they were ready to roll on their backs for her or let her scratch their ears. The Commander of the Royal Guard might have words to say, but if Treasury disallowed her extravagance she could make up the difference from her privy purse.

Bugs or not, Malinda slept well, undisturbed by whatever exciting events might be occurring next door. In the morning Dian, self-proclaimed expert and self-appointed snoop, reported seeing an altogether different swagger to the Princess's Guard. "Any man has to check it out at least once before he's quite sure of it," she explained. "Look at Abel! He's two inches taller! He's got a chest!"

Malinda could see no difference at all. "How about Dog?"

"Dog," Dian said in an awed whisper, "spent *all* of it."

They reached Grandon about noon. The capital was by far the largest city in Chivial, with more than a hundred thousand inhabitants; and that day at least half of them seemed to be hurrying through its narrow, shadowed streets, dodging wagons, pushing carts, jostling, and shouting. The racket of wheels and hooves on the cobbles was almost drowned out by the bellowing of livestock and the shouts of hucksters. None of Malinda's Blades had ever seen real crowds before, and they closed in around her like human armor—Dog out in front, Audley and Abel flanking her, Winter as rearguard. Poor Dian was left forgotten at the back, in spite of all Malinda's protests.

They came at last to Sycamore Square, which should have been an easy open space, but this was market day and the other half of the population had packed itself into a single teeming mass studded with stalls and barrows. Shouts to clear the way were ignored; people were jostled by the horses; someone recognized the distinctive arrogance of those young swordsmen and then spotted the cat's-eye hilts. A yell of "Blades!" was rapidly followed by a shower of missiles—vegetables, fish, filth from the cobbles. Hands reached up to grab reins or bridle.

The Princess's Guard reacted with superhuman reflexes, impeccable training, and a complete lack of preparatory instruction from their ward. Audley yelled orders and grabbed Malinda's reins; Abel slapped

the rump of her horse with the flat of his sword and the entire troop
plunged forward, abandoning Dian, who was of no importance in
their world at that moment. In perfect formation, five horses plowed
through a turmoil of fury and terror. People screamed; swords flashed
and slashed. Across the great square went the Blades and off down
the most convenient street, emerging from the spreading riot without
taking casualties or suffering damage to anything except their dignity.

Even then they did not slow down. Malinda, of course, yelled
that they must go back and find Dian. Audley did not refuse; he just
kept demanding, "Which way? Which way?" Ironhall would have
been proud of him. He brought her safely home to the gates of
Greymere, where the Yeomen men-at-arms gates swung down their
pikes at the sight of this unruly troop of plunging, lathered horses.

"Her Highness and escort!" he roared, fighting a rearing, panicky
mount. The Yeomen gaped at these shabbily clad youths flaunting
cat's-eye swords.

"We did it!" Abel screamed. "Our second day and we blooded
our swords! Most Blades never do that in their entire—"

"Shut up, you idiot!" Winter shouted, just as Malinda said something much less polite.

In escaping from Sycamore Market, the Princess's Guard had ridden down everyone who'd gotten in their way and slashed at anyone
within reach. Undoubtedly they had rescued their ward from a hostile
crowd as they had been taught to do, but they had also caused the
second Blade massacre in less than a week, and this time within the
heart of the capital.

20

You have to learn your way around the palace.
SIR DOMINIC

From the main door, Malinda ran all the way to Chancery with her
Blades at her heels, leaving a trail of gawking, scandalized courtiers.
The Lord Chancellor, she was informed, had ridden north that morn-
ing with the rest of the Council to meet the Lord Protector. She ran

then to the King's quarters and there, as she had hoped, found Acting Commander Dominic. He was playing dice with some others in the antechamber—the King being engaged in having his nap. As he was rising to greet her, she gasped out the bad tidings and he flopped back on his stool. She had never seen a Blade turn chalky white before.

"First you must send men to look for Dian!" she finished.

Sir Dominic shook his head and went on shaking it while he spoke. "I have none to send. We can ask the Chamberlain's office if they can spare any Yeomen. But almost everyone's gone north. Oh, spirits, Your Highness, how bad was it?"

She glanced around at her four crestfallen guardsmen. "Did any of you *not* hit anyone?" Four heads shook. "It was my fault, Commander. I heard Blades being booed when I was on my way back from Wetshore. I did not warn Sir Audley. I gave him no instructions."

"I'd better alert the Yeomen. There may be a mob at the gates pretty soon."

"Your Grace?" Winter asked, without taking the finger out of his teeth. "On whose authority did you bind us?"

"Durendal's," she said.

"But if the Lord Protector hasn't even—"

"I don't think we need discuss that now, Sir Winter. Sir Dominic, I'd like to introduce my guards to you, but I think I'd better go and tell the Chamberlain's men about this trouble right away. You are not really concerned."

But the Lord Protector would be.

Dian turned up unharmed very soon after and located Malinda in her quarters, where Lady Ruby and Lady Dove were watching in alarm as the four Blades trotted around like excited dogs, sniffing every corner. Seething with anger, Dian gave Malinda a generous piece of her mind. Dozens of casualties, she said—mostly women and children crushed in the panic, but some sword cuts, many injuries, blood on the cobblestones. There was a mob on the way.

Sir Audley drew his sword and sank to his knees to offer it to her. "Your Grace, I have failed. My errors have exposed you to—"

"Idiot!" Dog grabbed him with a mighty hand and hoisted him bodily out of the way. Flushed with anger, he thrust his blind marble eyes close to Malinda's. "What did he do wrong? Was he supposed to let them kill you or hurt you? We were just going through. They attacked us. *What did he do wrong?*"

Astonished, she fell back a step before his fury. "Nothing! The fault was mine." The last time she had ridden through Sycamore

Square she had been cheered. That had been before the Wetshore Massacre. "You did right, Commander."

And even Dian had to admit that anything Malinda tried to do now would only make things worse. She had no authority. The minor clerks who had been left to run the palace and the country would neither make their own decisions nor take orders from her. Everything must wait for the Lord Protector.

Awakening to the fact that her Blades were not merely downcast but also bedraggled and dung-spattered, Malinda sent for the court tailor. He arrived in a very few minutes—a dumpy, breathless little man whose life was one long despair because aristocratic clients expected instant service and indefinitely delayed payment. At his heels shuffled an army of underfed apprentices, bearing samples and swatches and tapes. He must have been hoping he would be engaged to replace the entire wardrobe Her Grace had lost to the Baels, for he made a poor job of hiding his disappointment when he learned she merely wanted four liveries in record time. He sent away half his minions and all the lace, velvets, and brocades they had brought with them.

The matter was far from routine to the Blades, though. They preened as the remaining flunkies surrounded them and began measuring and scribbling notes.

"My blazon, of course, is a lozenge vert, a lion rampant argent," she said. "You are familiar with the green I prefer?"

"Indeed yes, Your Highness. The deep forest tone? Accessories and minor garments—hose, shirts, footwear . . . ?"

"Whatever the Royal Guard gets."

"Then silk for the Commander?"

Wrinkled woolen hose were a common sight on guardsmen. There were only eight legs in her troop and their owners were feeling very hangdog since the debacle in the market. "Silk for all of them. The best."

Avarice brightened the tailor's eyes. "Then shirts and undergarments too . . . silver buckles . . . embossed calfskin . . . pearl buttons? Velvet for the cloaks? Even the Deputy Commander—"

"I said the *best!* Spare no expense."

He bowed lower than she would have believed his girth permitted and began to make tactful inquiries about Her Highness's personal needs.

Shortly after that, while the disbelieving tailor was double-checking the measurements his apprentices had made on Sir Dog, in pranced a surprise visitor who was himself a dazzling sartorial spectacle.

"Malinda, *darling!*" Arms wide, Prince Courtney advanced to embrace her, only to find himself blocked, looking up into the dark and stormy eyes of Sir Audley.

"It's all right, Commander. This is my cousin."

Audley stepped back out of the way and bowed. "My most humble apologies, Your Highness."

"Mm!" The little man looked him up and down with approval. "I know some persons who would be *most* interested to meet you, Commander."

"Your Highness is gracious!" But Audley's manner belied the words, biting them off, making them sound like an insult.

Courtney regarded the others. He minced around two tailors for a closer look at Abel. "And this handsome young lad?"

"Not him either!"

"Audley?" Malinda muttered, surprised at the sudden tension in the room. *Nobody* could consider Courtney a menace! A fop, yes, but harmless.

"Well, *do* think about it," her cousin said obscurely. "I can guide you away from some gentlefolk who have extreme tastes." He eyed Dog thoughtfully. "Or to them. *Malinda,* darling! You did yourself proud at Ironhall, I see."

She allowed him to buss her cheek. Today he reeked of lavender. "I thought you were going back to Mayshire?"

He waved his hands vaguely. "Well, you know how it is, my dear. One simply cannot *tear* oneself away from one's old friends so easily." If he was implying that he had been making the rounds of all the beds he had graced in the last quarter century, then the mind must reel. "And *dear* Granville might be offended if one was not here to welcome him."

She doubted that. She suspected Granville's taste for Courtney would be much the same as her father's—little and seldom.

"I hear your brave guardians already proved their worth," he said, and in a dramatic whisper, "Who is the one with the shoulders?"

"Sir Dog. We did have some trouble. It was a tragic misunderstanding and I blame myself for—"

"Oh, don't *ever* do that, child! There will always be others willing to do that for you. Besides, peasants assaulting a princess of the blood? They got no more than they deserved. Your father would have had the Lord Mayor crawling into the palace on his knees offering cart loads of gold in recompense. Don't worry about it."

"That's very kind of you to say so."

"They got their comeuppance now, anyway," her cousin said with a smirk. His eyes kept wandering toward her Blades. "The slender one?"

"Sir Abel. What do you mean by comeuppance?"

"A mob, darling. Shouting rude things outside the gates. The cavalry has just dispersed them and I fancy this time they got a lesson they will remember. Well, I must fly."

Courtney swept off into the palace labyrinth. Malinda wandered over to the window and stared out at stable rooftops, wondering what faceless flunky in the Household Yeomen or the Chamberlain's office had ordered out the cavalry, how many more people had been hurt. She would probably be blamed for this disaster also, and she certainly blamed herself. Blades were dangerous weapons; she had acquired four of them by dubious means and failed to keep them under control.

"Sir Audley?" she said without turning, and when he reached her side, "you took offense at something Prince Courtney said."

"I humbly beg pardon, Your Grace. I will attempt in future—"

"No, I want to know why. His words seemed innocent enough. I thought he was offering to introduce you to rich ladies, and I suppose you prefer to make your own friends, but . . . No?"

Audley muttered, "Not *ladies,* Your Grace."

She continued to scan those roofs industriously. "Sorry, but you'll have to explain."

"Er . . . They warned us at Ironhall that there were ways a Blade could make extra money at court, Your Grace. Ladies, obviously, but . . . other persons, too. Your cousin was mentioned."

"You were warned against *Courtney?*"

"Specifically, Your Grace."

"I thought he was a . . . a ladies' man."

"That too, Your Grace. He has friends who aren't—all sorts of friends, they said."

She sighed. "I have a lot to learn."

"So do we," Audley growled, "but none of us four wants lessons of that sort. If we did, we could have had them at Ironhall."

Spirits! The world grew stranger every day.

The first forest-green-and-white liveries were delivered before nightfall, with cloaks and footwear promised for the next day. They effected a very dramatic improvement in her Blades' appearance. Dian faked a swoon into Sir Audley's arms. Malinda was tempted to try that move herself. Four swoons, in fact. Well, three. Dog still had a rumpled look, like a dressed-up bear, but Dog would not shine in polished armor. He had been much more impressive just sitting on the anvil with his shirt off.

Later Sir Dominic came calling and Malinda proudly presented the members of her Guard, all of whom had been long after his time in Ironhall, of course. If he thought her taste in livery extravagant, he was too polite to say so. "Looks like you did much better than I feared you would, my lady, because Grand Master's reports read like a postmortem. Now, any swordsman needs regular practice, so I propose that we spell off your guardsmen during the night. My men will pledge solemn oaths to defend you as if you were their own ward . . . which you practically are. And of course we can take them two at a time so that you will never be without—"

"No!" Audley looked appalled. So did Abel and Winter, while Dog just glowered and fingered his sword hilt.

Dominic grinned. "You also have to learn your way around the palace, Commander, and learn more about court in general."

Although visibly flattered at being given his title, Audley still hesitated. "Perhaps in a month or two."

"I think the matter is urgent," Malinda said. "I do not wish to be defended by second-rate swordsmen. Besides, everyone needs recreation. Commander Dominic, you will see they have some time to enjoy themselves?"

"We can show them around. Do you suppose they prefer girls tall or short, lithe or chubby, shy or passionate, willing, eager, fond, frantic, or feverish?"

The Princess's Blades exchanged glances. Then Audley said, "If Her Highness issues a direct order . . ."

A couple of days later, she asked him if he had been shown around the palace yet and was both amused and annoyed by the guarded way in which he said, "Yes, my lady."

"Greymere is a very old building."

"Indeed it is. Bewildering."

"And riddled with secret passages."

"Oh?"

These were not the quarters from which Snake had abducted her on the Night of Dogs. "Is there a secret way into my bedchamber?"

"Um . . . I promised . . ." The bold Sir Audley cringed like a child caught stealing muffins.

"You also swore on your soul to shield me from peril. Suppose assassins come in that way?"

"No one could possibly enter that way. It leads to rooms reserved for the Royal Guard."

"Then suppose the murderers come for me through the front door, slaughtering the Blades on duty there, how can I flee through an exit I cannot locate?"

Audley by now was scarlet-faced, yet he had his heels well dug in. "The Guard hoards these secrets because the fewer people who know about them the better, Your Grace. Greymere was built by Ambrose the First a hundred years ago, and this suite was his personal apartment. He had a private staircase down to what was then more sleeping quarters, and the heraldry displayed in the cornices is that of Countess Blanche, his famous—"

"Notorious."

"Notorious, um . . ."

"Mistress."

"Friend. But now the chamber is a dressing room off the Guard's fencing gymnasium."

"Fascinating! Good memory!" When she drew herself up, she was as tall as he was. "Show me."

He followed her into the bedroom, but by then he had found another excuse. "I promised Leader, Your Grace. If he learns that I broke my word, he'll never trust me again. I can't carry out my duties without the cooperation of the Guard."

"That's fair enough," she conceded. There was no use driving the man into open rebellion. "You show me how it opens at this end, and I will never tell anyone else, nor will I let the Guard find out I know about it."

Reluctantly accepting this compromise, Audley went to a pilaster between the fireplace and the window. "What they said was . . ." He gave the fake pillar a hard shove to the left. When nothing happened he tried it the other way and then it moved just far enough to reveal a handhold in the wall. A tug on that made a section of the paneling swing out, exposing steps leading downward. "There!"

"Thank you, Commander." She walked away. He was beautiful when he was mad.

Another result of the midnight study sessions showed up the following morning, as she was preparing to leave her apartment. She overheard Dian saying, "Ooh, isn't that gorgeous!"

Malinda looked around. Young Sir Abel had his hands behind his back and was in the process of turning scarlet.

"Isn't what gorgeous?"

Audley glared at his subordinate. "A bauble, my lady. The Guard allows them, but if you find personal display offensive, I can forbid it while he's on duty."

"That depends what he's displaying. Show us, Sir Abel."

With a grimace worthy of a well-used torture victim, Abel held out his hand to show a ring bearing a spectacular pearl. It was an unusual pink shade, and must be worth more than he would earn in a lifetime. Malinda wondered if any of Cousin Courtney's friends were involved.

"Gorgeous!" she said. "What an unusual color!"

"Exactly matches his ears," Dian remarked.

"He must have worked very hard to earn that!" said Dog.

"The lady is generous," said Winter.

"Not necessarily," Audley suggested. "She may be quite stingy. Depends how good he is."

Abel, needless to say, was now ready to die of mortification.

"If he wants to wear it, Commander," Malinda said, "then I certainly have no objection." All her life she had seen Blades flaunting such trinkets; they had even joked about them in her presence as if she would not guess what they meant.

"He should not display it near you, Your Grace," Audley said, heading for the door.

"Why not?"

"Because he swore to shield you from pearl."

"Please let me kill him," Dog growled.

Malinda led out her private army, well pleased with its progress to date.

21

Only the unloved sleep alone.
BARONESS DECHAISE (LADY VIOLET)

As a bubble-thin crescent in the sunset proclaimed the first day of Fourthmoon, the Lord Protector, Granville Fitzambrose, Earl of Thencaster, rode into Grandon behind the mounted band of the Household Yeomen. He was escorted by a battalion of cavalry from his army of Wylderland, because the detachment of the Royal Guard that had ridden north to meet him he had immediately sent home again. Behind him rode members of the Council, including Lord Chancellor Roland. The hero was welcomed at the city limits by the Lord Mayor, the aldermen, and many senior peers of the realm. The inhabitants of the capital roared their hearts out, strewing flowers, blowing trumpets, beating drums.

Malinda had been advised that she would head the reception committee at the palace. Amby was kept indoors to watch the bands through a window, but the heralds placed her in full view at the top of the steps. This was undoubtedly intended to signify that she waived her right to be regent as set out in the Act of Succession. No one had yet suggested that she should do otherwise.

The heralds had reluctantly allowed space at her back for two Blades. One of them had to be Audley, and she had let the others draw lots. Dog had won, which was a pity, because no amount of primping could ever make him look elegant and putting him next to the stunningly handsome Audley just drew attention to his incorrigible ugliness. His flaxen hair appeared soiled against the snowy lace at his neck and the osprey plumes fringing his bonnet; the plumes themselves seemed to have wilted in despair. But who was she to criticize appearances? She was flanked on one side by Courtney and on the other by the ancient Baron Dechaise, First Lord of the Treasury, and she was a foot taller than either of them.

When the Lord Protector came striding up the steps, she sank into a full curtsey. He went right by the entire reception party, spurs jingling. The Council necessarily followed.

She rose, feeling her face flame at the snub. The reception committee buzzed with angry whispers. Even Courtney straightened out of his bow looking furious, and she could not recall ever seeing him reveal his true feelings before.

"The politics have started," she said.

"They never stopped, darling. I think I shall interpret *that* incident as permission to leave court."

She went to call on Amby and was refused entry because the Lord Protector was within, paying his respects to the King. She returned to her suite to wait for his summons.

Since her journey to Ironhall she had assembled a new household. She was still attended by the rabbity Ruby and the bovine Dove, but she had sent invitations to others and had now acquired two maids of honor whom she knew of old and whose company she enjoyed, Alys and Laraine. Both of them were about her own age, and skilled players on the spinet. She had persuaded Mother Superior to assign Sister Moment to her household—Moment was tiny, vivacious, and a superb lutist. Thus singing and dancing were available without bringing in outsiders. Add Dian and four dapper Blades and evenings in her suite could become entertaining to the brink of hysteria. What happened after curfew she preferred not to know, but Dove made cow eyes at Winter from dawn till dusk. It would not be like a Blade to refuse such an appeal.

That night her household was edgy, being well aware that snubs that would be mere rudeness elsewhere could be deadly at court. Lady Malinda was now a leper until the Lord Protector indicated otherwise. Dog again offered to kill Granville, causing Audley to rant at him and Lady Ruby to shriek in horror. As the hours passed it became obvious that no summons was coming. Eventually Malinda declared the day over, but she snarled at Dian during their regular bedtime chat.

She dozed for an hour or so, then came awake with a start. What was Granville planning? Why cut her in public like that? Was she to be charged with treason for her father's death? Embezzlement for stealing four Blades? Murder in Sycamore Square? In the gloom of the night her worries multiplied like ants in a pantry.

Eventually she rose. Donning slippers and a fleecy robe, she went to stare out the window at the stars above the darkened city. She was tempted to pace, except that the old floors might squeak . . . and that thought reminded her of the secret stair. The temptation was too great to resist. She had no lantern, but she did not need light to slide the pilaster aside and pull on the panel. How many of her forebears had opened this door in breathless eagerness, hurrying to visit a paramour? Shivering in the night chill, she faced nothing but blackness.

Remembering having seen a handrail on the fireplace side, she groped for it and then let one slipper explore the edge of the first step. Four steps brought her to a corner; the rail turned to the left. Her toes established that the stair continued along the back of the chimney. Eight or ten more steps brought her to another sharp corner to the left, meaning she had gone halfway around the chimney column and was now facing her bedroom again, albeit below floor level. One of the curses of Greymere was the rooms could never be properly warmed in winter because the ceilings were thirty feet high, so obviously this stair must go down a long way. She had come far enough. Suppose she twisted an ankle?

Suppose that faint thread of light down there was real? It refused to go away when she blinked, but her hand could block it. She edged forward and knelt to explore the wall by touch, eventually concluding that there was a hatch there, about waist height, and it had not been perfectly closed the last time it was opened, which might have been a century ago. Possibly no one else in the world knew it existed, because only a lunatic would venture up or down this secret stair without a lantern, by night or day; and with any other light at all the tiny glow would be invisible. Even she had seen it only when her eyes were in exactly the right line.

She found raised moldings and pulled . . . pushed . . . shoved until she felt the panel slide and the crack of light widened. She restrained a strong desire to snigger. Had her ardent ancestor, Ambrose I, been aware that his Blades were spying on him when he called on Lady Blanche? This was certainly a vantage designed to overlook the royal antics. If Audley had told the truth about a dressing room off the gym, she should be able to turn the tables now and pry into the private lives of the Royal Guard. Of course a princess would never dream of spying on a bunch of scantily clad, sweaty young men, would she?

Unfortunately, yes.

She put an eye to the slit, but made out only a misty trellis of light and dark. When she pushed the panel wider she caught a whiff of sickly scents—beeswax, wine, perfume, people. She was trying to peer through one of the complex cornices that decorated the tops of the walls in this wing of the palace, but the plaster trellis was draped in a gauze of ancient cobwebs, loaded with dirt, dead insects, and candle smoke. Grimacing, she removed her nightcap and used it to wipe away some of the filth.

Then she could see down into the room that underlay her bed-chamber. It was dim, lit by five or six candles on a chandelier and the flicker of a hearth almost directly below her. The original space had been divided by a later wall of plainer paneling; and what remained was crowded by a couch in front of the fireplace, a bed against the new wall opposite, and a table and stools in the center. This chamber was not how she would have expected a dressing room to look, but it explained Audley's reluctance to show her the secret passage. The bed curtains were open, revealing bedclothes presently unoccupied but well rumpled. A least a dozen wine bottles were scattered around the room, although Blades were abstemious drinkers . . . and there was a man lying on the couch, reading.

He had let down the chandelier until it was not far above his head; it hung directly in her line of sight so she could see little more than his legs. That was extremely annoying. White hose and shiny-buckled shoes were almost universal on men at court; calves like those were not. The sword lying on the floor within instant reach was a full-sized two-handed broadsword, and she knew only one man who lugged one of those around.

She had never imagined Dog as a reader, but then he was a constant source of surprises, from his rare flashes of humor to his crazy outbursts. And here he was, whiling away half the night guarding the back door to her apartment! With a silent whisper of gratitude she slid the hatch shut and crept back up the stairs to her room.

Yet sleep eluded her for a long time. She kept thinking of the guardian downstairs, wondering what he read—poetry? Law? Some Blades had unusual fields of interest. And she also remembered Dog sitting on the anvil at Ironhall with his shirt off, the only one of the four who had faced death at her hands without a trace of fear.

Radgar Æleding raised the crossbow to his shoulder and laughed at her. She tried to scream but her breath would not come. She tried to run and her feet would not move. He fired and the bolt hissed past her ear. She turned in time to see—

In time to wake up, sweating and shaking. How often must she endure that dream? Some nights she saw her father with the bolt lodged in his eye. Some nights she did cry out a warning and it was he who laughed at her and all the Blades joined in. Some nights it was Sir Eagle on the longship, aiming the bow at her.

Dawn was not far off, the sky a paleness behind the chimneys.

Granville. Poor little Amby and his persistent cough.

Dog reading in the room downstairs. She smiled.

Wait! Something wrong? She thought back. Her nightcap . . . She had used it as a duster, and when she returned to her room she had tossed the filthy thing on the floor without a thought. How could a princess explain a nightcap covered with soot and grease and cobwebs? If the chambermaids noticed anything at all amiss, the Blades would hear the news through the pores in their skin. She scrambled out of bed and saw the deadly thing just lying there on the rug, smirking at her. Toss it out the window? It had her monogram on it. She had no fire to burn it. She would have to hide it, and there was only one safe hiding place. She slid the pilaster aside, opened the panel. . . .

And again succumbed to temptation. The Blades would have changed watch at least once in the night, so who was guarding her now? What did he do to pass the time? She crept downstairs, trying to ignore the voice of conscience whispering that the bed was what really intrigued her. She had trouble finding the right molding without the telltale crack of light as a guide, but then the panel slid as silently as before.

The scene had changed. The couch was empty and the chandelier had been hauled up to a more normal height. Clothes lay scattered on the floor beside the bed, and its curtains were so nearly closed that she could not see inside. She thought they were moving, as if in a draft, but she could not be sure. The chandelier hung motionless on its rope, candle flames burning steadily.

Well! Innocent she might be, but she could guess what was happening or had been happening. Some of the strewn garments were certainly feminine, and although she could not tell color in the gloom, the man's doublet and jerkin were too dark to be the Royal Guard's blue. It might be her green, but other private Blades in the palace wore dark livery. Why argue, why be surprised? She had agreed that her Blades needed recreation and everyone knew what that meant to a Blade. Whichever one he was, he would surely have the outer door bolted and Blades never slept, so he was guarding the secret passage just as effectively as Dog had done. He probably had some kitchen drudge or chambermaid in there with him. No lady would come to a den like this.

The bed curtains promptly parted. A boy slid down off the mattress and straightened up in shameless nudity. He stretched luxuriously, arms overhead, looking utterly content with his lot. Slim, boyish, and almost hairless—it was Abel.

Malinda recoiled. It took her a moment to catch her breath and persuade her conscience to let her steal another look. By that time he had strutted over to the table to inspect the bottles. Was this where the decadent young scoundrel earned his pearl ring? And who had provided it? As if he could hear her silent questioning, he slopped wine into a goblet, strolled back to the bed with it, and flung the drapery aside. The occupant rose on one elbow to accept the glass. It was Lady Violet. The *infamous* Lady Violet! Naked, of course, with her great fat breasts flopping loose. She was at least twice Abel's age. Slumming, evidently, because she owned a mansion near the palace and a huge suite of rooms within it—well, her husband did, but everyone knew they slept apart. *He* slept apart; she slept with any man who asked her and quite a few that hadn't. Cradle robbing! Corrupting innocent boys with precious gifts!

Malinda closed the hatch, only just refraining from slamming it. She stumbled up the stairs, almost weeping. After all that she had done for them—overpaying them, dressing them in the best clothes money could buy, agreeing to give them time off—now they were betraying her like this! And with that trollop! She had not been so upset in . . . Well, not since she had been caught kissing Sir Eagle a year ago.

22

Princess Malinda is a strumpet who sells her maids of honor, orgies with her Blades all night long, and buries babies at midnight.
LORD PROTECTOR GRANVILLE

Next morning Sir Abel was the same peach-faced dewy youth as always, but Malinda could not look at him without remembering the naked libertine doing his catlike stretch after whatever he had been doing to, with, or for Lady Violet, which had certainly not been merely catnapping. Why had Malinda been so stupid as to let *her* Blades walk around flaunting *other* women's blazons? He sensed her antagonism and reacted with puzzled glances. To upset her even more, Winter was now wearing a ruby on his left index finger.

She began the day by visiting Amby, provoking the usual argument between her Blades and the Guard, which was resolved as always by having three of her Blades watch from the far side of the room and one escort her to her brother's side. As always, the one who went with her was Dog, because he was Amby's favorite. The King thought Dog was a wonderful name for a man, especially one with flaxen hair like his own, and he loved his wonderful doggy noises. "Growl!" he would say and Dog would growl. "Growl again!" And again. And again. With superhuman patience, Dog could keep it up for an hour, until Malinda was driven half crazy. The King was three years old and Dog was crazy to start with.

Dog just said, "I like him. He doesn't care about other people, only himself."

"That's normal at his age."

"Then it's a good age to be." Sometimes the big oaf could make all the rest of the world seem crazy and himself the only sane man in it.

★   ★   ★

Malinda passed the rest of the morning leading some noble ladies around the park, admiring spring flowers and first blossoms. After that, even the afternoon's swearing-in ceremony promised to seem exciting. It was very close to being a coronation, with all the grand of the land present. The Lord Protector took the oath of office, followed by the members of the Council of Regency, including the new members he had nominated. Malinda had never heard of any of them before, but Arabel had told her that they were officers from his Army of Wylderland. If so, Granville had personal control of the country.

After that, the nobility swore allegiance to the new King, whether or not they had already done so. Malinda was first, Courtney second—there was a rumor that he had tried to leave town and been brought back under guard—and so on through everyone who was of any importance, down almost to the palace gardeners. It took hours. It was the first such state ceremony in almost four hundred years that did not include the Royal Guard. The only Blades present were a few private Blades, bound to officials or nobles.

When the interminable oath-taking ended, the Lord Protector made a speech. It was curt, as befitted the words of a soldier, but it said a great deal more than it seemed to. Of course he began by proclaiming that the Council's first priority would be to ensure that His Majesty grew up in peace and health and was suitably trained to rule when he reach his majority. In the meantime, the Council would govern the realm with justice to all, curb extravagance, smite the King's enemies, and foster trade. The audience applauded. The Council, Granville said, would also make thorough inquiry into the tragic death of King Ambrose IV and the disaster that had ensued. It would look into any similar or related incidents. It would take any actions necessary to prevent such tragedies happening in future. The assembly reacted with wild cheers.

The King's Blades were in serious trouble.

And so was Princess Malinda.

There was a state banquet to follow, and on the morrow court would go back into mourning. As Malinda and her train hurried to her quarters to change, she was not too surprised to be accosted by a young herald, although of course Audley intercepted him. The worry in the boy's eyes warned her of trouble before he spoke a word.

"Commander, His Excellency the Lord Protector bade me inform Her Highness that Blades will not be permitted into the hall this evening." He bowed—message delivered.

"I will so inform Her Highness," Audley snarled.

"Consider me informed," she said. "Pray convey my sincere regrets to His Excellency."

With another bow, the lad departed. She stood in the hallway
and looked around the angry faces.

"Does that mean we have to leave the Blades outside, like servants?" asked Lady Dove.

"No," said Sister Moment. "It means we all get left outside like
servants."

"No Blades, no Princess," Alys explained. "No Princess, no maids
of honor."

"With your permission . . ." Audley began, and then started again.
"I feel obliged, my lady, to institute Sian Rules immediately. Sir Dog,
Sir Winter, proceed."

Without a word, those two vanished in opposite directions.

"What," Malinda demanded, "are Sian Rules?"

"Ironhall term, Your Grace. Shall we continue?"

She set off, flanked by Audley and Abel, the women following.
"Now explain."

"Sian Rules refer to a drill devised after the arrest of Queen Sian
in 361."

Sian had been beheaded for treason after being found in bed with
Sir Wyvern, but the King's daughter had been told no details at the
time and perhaps not all of them even yet. "I don't think I know
exactly how Queen Sian was arrested."

"Sad story, my lady."

"Please tell me."

"She had four Blades."

"I know that."

"They were dropped at her feet," Audley said grimly. "On the
grass around her, all four at once—Yeoman archers, shooting from
ambush. Their error was to offer themselves as a single target."

Malinda stopped, appalled. "Oh spirits! My father ordered that?"

"Perhaps not specifically, Your Grace, but if he ordered the lady
arrested, he must have known what would be required. So Ironhall
devised Sian Rules, although I think this is the first time they have
been invoked. Now we shall never be all in one room together or
eat from the same pot."

She looked then at Abel, who was understandably not quite his
usual cheerful, cheeky self either. "You knew all this, too, of course?"

He nodded. "Standard training. And it's in the *Litany*."

She had been a blind and very selfish fool. "When I came to
Ironhall, you all knew that I might already be under suspicion because

of my father's death and the Wetshore Massacre. You guessed that I wanted Blades as a defense against arbitrary arrest?"

"We knew."

"And yet you were willing to be bound? All of you!"

Abel forced a thin smile. "Our duty, my lady."

She shivered. Lord Roland and Sir Piers had been more ruthless on her behalf than she had realized. Grand Master had tried to keep his young charges out of her clutches. Admittedly she had been going to explain and give them a chance to refuse, but then the crazy one had volunteered and they had all followed his lead, unwilling to let him shame them.

"I am very grateful to all of you," she said and set off hastily along the hallway. She should not grudge Abel and Winter their baubles. Courage must have its due. Binding was a burden and Blades deserved the privileges it brought them.

The rain had stopped. Malinda suggested brightly that *everyone* might like to go for a ride in the park. *Everyone* knew enough to agree, so a page was dispatched to alert the stables, and *everyone* went to change. The page returned to say that the stable master reported no horses currently available.

Soon after that Sir Audley took her aside and asked if she wanted him to organize an escape by river.

"Escape from what?" she demanded. "To where? It would be regarded as an admission of guilt. And I cannot desert my brother."

She went to call on Amby and was informed that no Blades other than the Royal Guard were to be admitted to the King's presence from now on, by order of the Council. No Blades, no Princess.

So she was effectively under house arrest, and during the next few days the Lord Protector steadily increased the pressure on her, simply by doing nothing. That was how she interpreted the silence, and she did not think she was suffering from delusions of persecution.

A court in mourning was as much as fun as an icehouse to start with, and many noble families were not on speaking terms with the princess who had caused the Wetshore catastrophe. Others shunned her because they sensed the way the Lord Protector wanted the wind to blow.

Her slightest requests were ignored or denied; meals were delivered late and cold; no one would come to tune the spinet; beeswax candles were replaced with common tallow. It was the death of a thousand fleabites, and even such pettiness might break anyone's nerve eventually. Ruby and Alys both found urgent reasons to visit their families and asked permission to leave her household. Malinda refused it and waited to see what would come next.

What came eventually was a summons to meet Lord Granville on the library terrace.

It was spring and there was death in the air. Sunlight shone on marigolds and butterflies; birds sang of love and treachery. Malinda walked over the mossy paving, knowing that there were almost certainly archers posted somewhere nearby—on the roof, behind the hedges, in the gazebos or summerhouses. Audley and Winter could be struck dead behind her at any minute.

Granville was waiting for her at the balustrade, his back to the river. With feet spread and hands on hips he looked astonishingly like their father—younger, fitter, harder. He was unarmed and there was no one else in sight, but that did not mean much.

A few paces away she halted. Amber eyes locked on amber eyes. He was a lord protector, not a regent. She was a princess and the heir. But he was head of state. She gave him not much of a curtsey.

He bowed not much of a bow and smiled not much of a smile. "You have grown up, Sister."

"You have risen, Brother."

"We need to talk. Your dogs stay here."

She nodded to Audley and went with Granville. "You know they can't let me out of their sight?"

"I just want them out of earshot." He walked a dozen yards and turned to lean elbows on the balustrade. "This will do."

Ships were moving upriver on the tide, but so was the sewage. The Gran always looked much better than it smelled. Beyond it lay fine houses and in the distance, green hills. Audley and Winter stood where she had left them on the flagstones, naked targets.

"What do you want?" Granville said.

"A household of my own and our brother. Let me be his governess. There is no one you can trust more."

"No, Sister. There is no one I can trust less." He was big, gruff, and overbearing, but he was not threatening yet. "You can't afford the risk either. If he died, you'd be accused of murder."

She sighed, but held his amber gaze defiantly. "I'll take that risk. I have no ambition except to see Amby come into his own."

"Nor have I. Does that surprise you?" He smiled, and if there was a hint of her father's slyness in that smile it was gone before she could be certain. "The boy is my hold on power, Malinda. Without him I am merely your humble and obedient subject. Don't you see that? Our positions would be reversed and you'd be bullying me."

He had charm when he bothered. How long would he be content to remain Lord Protector, or her humble and obedient? She scanned the terrace. The morning was nippy for Fourthmoon, but the complete absence of other people suggested hidden hands at work, armored hands. Audley and Winter were still sweating out their lonely torment.

"He's not strong," she said. "Have you heard of the inquisitors' so-called readings?"

"Father told me last year."

She stared at him in surprise. "Even then?"

"Even then. He said he didn't believe, but he was worried. That was why he made the Dierda match. He really didn't want the bother of another wife, you know; not at his age. A chambermaid and a handful of gold was more to his taste. He felt it was his duty."

"He never confided in me like that," she admitted.

"Man talk," Granville said sardonically. "So we agree, you and I? We are both utterly loyal and devoted to the kid, very touching. Now let's decide what happens when he dies."

"*If* he dies," she admonished.

"He's sickly. Can you see Courtney as king?" Granville's sudden laugh sounded like genuine amusement.

She returned it. "It boggles the imagination. We can agree on that, at least."

"You may be amazed at what you can agree to, Sister."

"Don't threaten me, Granville. It's undignified and you know our family; we get crabby when we're threatened."

"I really don't care whether you get crabby or not. The readings give the boy a year, maybe two. When he dies no one will support Courtney, so that just leaves you and me, doesn't it? 'No such daughter shall succeed who is married at that time to any man not a subject of the crown of Chivial'—remember? The easiest way to get rid of you is to marry you off to some foreign lordling."

She had been waiting for that. "And if I refuse the marriage?"

"You can be persuaded."

They studied each other for a moment like fencers. This was the man who had promised to cleanse Wylderland with fire and blood and then done exactly that. He shifted his gaze to the swordsmen.

"That was a bold move, binding those Blades. A rash move. An illegal move. The Council will have questions to put to you about that. It will also have questions about what passed between you and the King of the Baels. And Sycamore Market. Perhaps even about the death of Secretary Kromman! You may be interrogated at length."

"You're threatening again. I didn't know you were such a bully."

"Ask the Wylds." He smiled grimly and leaned back with both elbows on the balustrade to study her. "I'll make you an offer, Sister."

"It includes a husband, I presume?"

"You must have seen the Chancellor's short list. Pick any man except Hesse, and I'll—"

"Why not Prince Hesse?" He was the man with the coughing sickness, she recalled, although she had never been shown any list, long or short.

Her half brother smiled grimly. "We don't want anyone who might try to put forward his wife's claim in defiance of her father's will, now do we? Hesse might be able to raise support. And I'll exclude the Margrave of Lautenbach for the same reason. I've met him. He's an engaging young rogue, but too much of an adventurer to trust. Pick any of the others and I promise you a dowry that'll pop you into his bed before you can brush your hair."

"That's a very fair offer," she conceded. "Very reasonable. But I do not feel ready to marry anyone yet. When the stakes are so high, I dare not trust you, my lord. My marriage contract might be a death warrant for Amby."

"Your refusal will be a death warrant for four Blades." The Lord Protector's voice stayed low, but the gold eyes burned. "I have it all now, Malinda, except the title. I don't need that myself, but I want it for my son. I've fought for all of it. Everything I've ever won I've fought for. I was conceived when a fourteen-year-old royal thug got a grandmother so drunk that she didn't know what he was doing. I had to live with three older brothers who knew I came from their mother's rape. When I was seventeen he was going to let them disown me, and I faced him down. I threatened to turn his coronation into a circus. He threatened to throw me in the Bastion, but in the end he bought me off; I won an earldom. When I came here a year ago he admitted to my face that I was the only one worthy to be his heir. He promised to legitimize me as soon as I had pacified Wylderland. I sent him the Ciarán in chains, but he went back on his word and signed up the Dierda girl instead. I won't let anyone stand in my way now."

She was too furious to heed the threat to herself. "If you harm one hair of that child's head I will see you go alive to your balefire, Granville the Bastard."

"And where will you muster support? No, Sister. Women are

always vulnerable, and you've already been stupid. Tongues are wagging. Your household includes no proper matron companion, no ladies-in-waiting, just a bubbling stew of flighty girls and sex-crazy swordsmen. By the time the Council's done with you, everyone will know that Princess Malinda is a strumpet who sells her maids of honor, orgies with her Blades all night long, and buries babies at midnight. No one will take your side."

She felt her face burn up with crimson fire. "That's a lie!" she yelled. "You're not the only one who's learned to stand up to browbeating. Bring on your inquisitors. I have nothing to hide."

Granville's anger flickered past her. She glanced around and saw that Audley and Winter were coming—reluctantly, aware that they might provoke a flight of arrows, but unable to stay away when they could see her being threatened. Somehow their slow, deliberate approach made them seem all the more menacing.

"Farewell, Sister," the Lord Protector growled. "You had your chance. I'll pick your bridegroom and your Blades are hostage for your consent. I'm going to deal with all the Blades—disband the Order and put them to honest work. Parliament will insist on it anyway, after what happened at Wetshore. Their day is over." He spun on his heel and stalked away.

23

Letting an unmarried damsel bind a twenty-year-old swordsman was not merely asking for trouble, but virtually insisting on it.

LORD ROLAND,
PERSONAL COMMUNICATION TO SIR QUARREL

To Dian's astonishment, Malinda ordered a flask of spiced wine when she retired that night, although she had never indulged in solitary drinking before. Long after the palace had doused candles and closed bed curtains, she sat by the fire in her room, huddled in a sable cloak, brooding. She was obsessed by a certainty that she had missed something in that talk with Granville. Somewhere, somehow, he had trapped her, and she would not sleep until she had worked out when and how.

If she persisted in her refusal to accept a foreign marriage, she might postpone the danger to Amby, but her Blades would be in greater peril than ever. She had told them so. They had answered boldly that danger was only their duty. Even so, if Granville issued a direct order, how could she refuse it, knowing that her guards would be struck down?

She drank all the wine, she stoked up the fire, and still the answer would not come.

She should have played for time. She should have asked to see that short list Granville had mentioned. There were probably some quite acceptable potential husbands on it—better than Radgar Æleding, certainly. She would not choose the same man as Granville would. In selecting a son-in-law, her father had considered the good of the country. Granville would have only Granville's good at heart. His ideal brother-in-law would be someone like . . .

Oh, spirits! Like the Duke of Anciers?

She established that the pilaster could be moved from the far side of the secret door, and the pilaster was all that held it closed. Leaving it ajar, she went on down, one hand holding a lantern and the other clutching the soft fur of the cloak about her. She was shivering and drunk enough to wonder how drunk she was. Her slippers made little scuffing noises on stone. Without the marks she had left in the dust there, the spy hole would have been hard to find. She knelt beside the hatch, aware that she might regret her despicable voyeurism— suppose she saw her Blades engaged in a horrible mass orgy? What if her maids of honor were in there? It was her duty to protect them from evil influences, which definitely included Blades.

She slid the panel. The light was dimmer than before, there being few candles lit on the chandelier; the hearth was cold. Someone had made an effort to tidy up, removing the bottles and making the bed. The only person present was sitting on the couch with his head in his hands and his back to her. Those were certainly Dog's shoulders and tangled flaxen hair. She waited. Nothing happened; he just sat, apparently staring at the floor.

Well? demanded her conscience. *This is exactly what you were hoping to find—Dog, all by himself. Scared to go on?*

Yes, she was scared. But she closed the hatch and went on.

At the foot of the steps, she set the lantern on the steps, removed her nightcap, shook out her hair. Even then she had to take several deep breaths before she could bring herself to try the handle. The mechanism was the same as the one in her room, but very stiff, so she needed both hands to slide the fake pilaster aside. The door swung open of its own accord.

Dog was on his feet with his sword in his hand, the great steel beam not wavering a hairsbreadth as he watched her approach. Stepping around it, she went close and touched a finger to the dampness on his cheeks. He must have been weeping for some time, for his eyes were puffed and crimson. In Ironhall he had cried out in his sleep. Now he never slept—so what happened to his dreams?

"Are you expecting someone?"

He shook his head. While fighting with the door, she had let her cloak fall open. Abel had said that if any man were to be struck by lightning, it would be Dog, so here a virgin princess comes visiting in the middle of the night wearing a nightdress that would barely make a good spiderweb. She had ball gowns that revealed more of her chest than she was showing now—but not much more, and the implications were very different.

"*Were* you expecting someone?"

Another faint shake.

Relieved that she was not interfering in a lovers' quarrel, she swallowed hard and said, "I want you to do something for me. It could be quite dangerous."

He sheathed his sword. "Tell me." He had guessed, though. He was stubborn, not stupid.

"Granville's going to marry me off, to get me out of the way so that as soon as Amby dies, by whatever means, he can push Courtney aside and claim the throne, and I think . . . I don't know, but I'm almost certain . . . that he's going to give me to the Duke of Anciers, because the Duke's already been married three times and none of his wives lived very long."

Dog's gaze slid down to the lace at her throat and then back up to her face.

"You want me to kill Granville now?"

"You know I don't." She kissed his cheek. It felt more bristly than it looked. He did not flinch, did not respond at all. "That would kill me, silly man. When a Blade commits a crime, who's responsible? No."

"Then what do you want?" he growled.

"The Duke will only marry a virgin. Lots of royalty are like that— the men can do what they want, but they insist on marrying virgins.

The Duke's an extreme case. He's had other girls, they say, and they all went the same way."

"They'd strip you and look?" he demanded incredulously.

"Maybe. Not necessarily. Just ask me. Every country has inquisitor-type people to spot lies." Or clever men who could trap her into telling the truth, as Granville had on the terrace. Well, it wasn't going to be true much longer. She shivered. The room was chilly. "I want you to . . . not here, though. Upstairs. Come upstairs to bed, Dog. Please?"

Dog pouted. "You want a man with experience, like Abel. Or Audley. Wenches swarm around him."

His reluctance did not surprise her; she was perversely relieved by it. "I'm sure the ladies have taught you how it's done."

"They don't want me much. Ugly and stupid. Can't laugh, can't tell sweet lies, got no manners. Just meat, and they joke about that, too. Go ask someone else."

She was fairly sure his face was flushed, although it was hard to tell in the gloom.

"I want *you*. You won't laugh at me for being ignorant, you won't tell tales, and you will be gentle. Must I go on my knees to you?" She tried, but he caught her elbow and raised it in a way that brought her up with it. "Burn you, man! Is it what happened to Eagle that frightens you? You must have heard about Eagle! You said you'd do anything I—"

His coarse, uneven features crumpled like a child about to cry. "Not me, Princess. Never me! I'm not worthy. I'm filth."

"I don't care what you did in the past," she said. "Do you find me repugnant?"

"Repugnant? Princess . . ." She thought for a moment he was going to laugh, but Dog never laughed. His growl became harsher. "No, not that." He took a step back. "Go find a decent man, woman! Not me! Ugly, vile Dog? I'm an *animal!*"

She took his hand. She had ungainly, clumsy hands for a woman; his were twice the size, thick and calloused from wielding that broadsword. She led him over to the stairs and he followed like a child, unresisting. The stairwell was cramped for two. When he closed the door behind them, they were very close, excitingly close.

She lifted the lantern. She remembered her wager with Piers. "Can you carry me up?"

"If you want."

"I do want."

"Don't set yourself on fire." Dog swung her up as easily as he lifted Amby. He strode swiftly up the stairs, two at a time, negotiating the corners nimbly even with the great broadsword swinging fore and aft at his thigh.

He did not seem at all winded when he set her down beside her bed and took the lantern from her to lay it on the table. He threw back the bedcovers, then lifted the fur cloak from her shoulders and spread it in their place.

"May be blood the first time," he said.

She nodded. Her heart was going crazy. How drunk was she, really? He stepped close, put a hand behind her head, and gently pressed his lips to hers. His mouth tasted of apple. It was the kiss that Eagle had started and not been allowed to finish. It began tenderly, but it went on and on, progressing to one arm crushing her hard against him and a hand stroking her hips and flanks. It made the world spin, so she needed to cling to him. Then he stroked her breast; her nipples ached strangely and the blood frothed in her veins. Eventually he moved his lips back just far enough that he could look at her with eyes all black pupil.

"Any more and I won't be able to stop, Princess." He sounded even hoarser than usual. He was flushed and he could not be faking that. He was as excited as she was! He *wanted* her, and that was the most exciting thing yet.

"Don't you dare stop!"

"Take off that rag, then. Get into bed." He released her carefully, as if aware how unsteady she felt. Turning his back, he opened the lantern to blow out the flame.

Naked, she slid shivering down on the fur and pulled the covers up to her chin. She could see him faintly in the fire's glow, so she turned her head away, suddenly overcome with shame. No, not shame! And not regret. Just shyness. It was certainly too late for remorse. He scrambled in beside her, body warm against body, heavy and very solid, pressing her down with a kiss.

He was still gentle, soothing and stroking. He knew her body better than she did, for he roused it to reactions she had not foreseen and could not control. He seemed to approve, for he made encouraging noises and persisted until mutual caressing gave way to striving and straining, then tumult and struggle. He parted her legs and climbed on top of her. She felt him enter her, but it was gently done. He thrust in and out three times and climaxed with a whimper, as if he was in pain. He collapsed, gasping.

"I didn't feel anything," she said. "Isn't the first time supposed to hurt?"

He moaned. "I felt something! Oh, did I ever feel something. . . ."

She chuckled and kissed his ear. Great strong Dog was as limp as sea-

weed! She wondered if he was as happy as she was and dared not ask.
Was Dog ever happy? She ought to be thoroughly ashamed of herself
and instead she felt she had won a victory, blocking Granville's best move.
Why must men always be the conquerors and women the conquered?
Blame the wine. Blame it on the Legend—say she had been enchanted—
or say she had raped him by using his binding against him. She did not
care! Why did everyone make such a fuss about the silly business?

After a while she realized she had been dozing. His eyes were just
in front of hers, two faces on the pillow. Blades never slept. His
mouth had tasted of apple, his sweat had a pleasantly musky scent.
His arm was around her, sticky but immovable, strong enough to
crush her to paste if he tried.

"Have I been asleep long?"

"I wasn't bored."

"Are you sure you did what I asked?" she asked. It seemed like
cheating that she had not felt pain. She hadn't felt anything very much.

"Absolutely certain. It was wonderful. Being your first time
helped. That made it really exciting."

Well, if she had wanted poetry, she'd have gone after Audley.
Action mattered more than words. "Second time wouldn't be any
fun?" The Anciers theory.

"It would be more fun."

"Then perhaps you should try. Just to be sure you did what I
asked. Can you?"

"Maybe."

"How do I find out ?"

"Try a kiss. If that doesn't work, I can show you other ways."

Trail hair over their naked bodies, Dian had suggested once, but such
drastic measures were not required in this case. The kiss worked very well.

The second time went on a lot longer. She was ready for those
strange reactions, or thought she was, but they came sooner, and
stronger, and then they seemed to take over the world. Yes! Oh, yes!
This must be what Dian had meant—waves of urgency—she soared,
she squirmed in agonies of joy, thunderclaps of release, first her, then
him. A whirling descent into peace, sweat, slow thumping hearts.

She heard him say, "I must go," and jerked awake. They had
changed sides sometime in the last turmoil, so he was between her
and the wall. His head lay heavy on her breasts.

She wondered what it would be like to do this every night, and
knew that nights would never be the same again. Even when she slept
alone, she would think of what might be. She stroked the coarse,

tangled hair, the gritty-rough jaw. "Dog, will you come to me again? Tomorrow? Would you? Can you? Without anyone finding out?"

He sighed. "Are you appointing me your lover?"

"That would be wonderful. Do you want to be?"

"Woman, that is the stupidest question you ever asked anyone in your whole life."

"Thank you, Dog. Really? Every night?"

"Always. As long as you want me. No one else." He sighed again, and his huge chest could produce a very long sigh. "You're crazy," he growled. "How can a crazy woman have breasts like these?" He kissed them.

"They're too small."

"*They are absolutely perfect!* Don't like flabby fat women." He took them in his great hands, one each. "Perfect fit. You are perfect, all over. Big, strong, lusty—just what a man needs."

Disbelieving, but pleased by his brave effort to be romantic, she tousled his hair. "Thank you. You're a magnificent man. I'm very happy."

"I can't believe it." A few moments later his face returned to the pillow beside hers. "Audley must be told. He won't talk, but he has to know."

"I'll tell him." Easier said than . . . told.

"Tomorrow will have to be after midnight."

"Come then. I won't be asleep, but if I am, waken me. That's a royal command, Sir Dog."

He took his time climbing over her, but she was deliberately not making it easy.

24

Love for money is more plentiful than money for love.
PRINCE COURTNEY

Despite a desperate need to scream the blissful news from the rooftops, by morning Malinda had decided she must not share her secret with anyone except her Blades, not even Dian. If it came out, it would provoke no ordinary scandal; Granville could use it to ruin her, her lover would die. But informing Audley of Dog's new duties without also informing everyone else was going to be tricky. After breakfast she announced that she wished to visit the royal greenhouses, which had been built by Queen Haralda and in Fourthmoon would be full of summer blossoms. This prospect provoked no great enthusiasm among her ladies, but maids of honor did not argue with princesses. Making absurd small talk about pruning, bedding out, and even fertilizer, she led her parade along aisles of foliage, past master gardeners bowing low and apprentice gardeners kneeling in mud, until she found a very small greenhouse packed with roses. There was only room inside that one for her and the two Blades currently in attendance—Audley and Winter.

The first rosebuds were opening. Dog was her lover and her heart would burst with joy. Alas, a whole day and half a night until she could be with him again . . .

She admired a scarlet flower. "I have something to tell you, Commander, in confidence."

"You can trust your Guard to the death, my lady. It is unfortunate that you do not always do so."

"It concerns— *What* did you say?"

"A few days ago I heard the chambermaids twittering about the dirt on your slippers and robe—cobwebs and stuff. You went exploring the staircase, although you promised me you would not."

Oh, spirits! "I did not promise that. I just promised to keep it secret. What did you tell them? That I like to dabble at housework in the middle of the night and a housecoat makes a dandy duster?"

Audley's face flamed even redder. "I suggested the dirt came from the ten years of dust under your bed and they should clean that up. Lady Bandit added her voice to mine. Fortunately, nobody had noticed your footprints by the door; they were very faint and I wiped them away with a rug. I should have mentioned the incident to you, but I assumed that once you had satisfied your curiosity that—"

"How did you know about the bed?"

"I look under it regularly, of course." Audley had totally lost his customary respectful manner. He was young, unsure, probably struggling to remember lectures on Ward Management. "A *midden* . . . I had not ordered it cleaned up sooner because any evildoer meddling under there would have left marks. But your slippers were filthy again this morning, so obviously you went snooping again last night. Today I could do nothing but threaten the skivvies. I had to warn them that spreading rumors about Your Grace would have very serious consequences."

The robe? She had found a very tiny, inconspicuous stain on it, but then she had hung it in the wardrobe, so the chambermaids would not have seen it. She must get to it before Dian did. Just the slippers.

"I went down to call upon Sir Dog."

Her Commander's face changed comically, from furious red to ashen white. "You walked into that room without even knowing who was in there?"

She moved along to a collection of white rosebushes in pots. "No."

"But . . . Oh! *Dog?*" His rage came rushing back. "Dog left the door open for you? I shall have words with Sir Dog, Your Grace! Any agreement—"

"You do not know about the spy hole?"

Audley deflated instantly. Ironhall reflexes were superhumanly fast. "No, Your Grace. If I have given offense—"

"Not much. I suggest you explore the stairs as carefully as you peer under my bed. There was no assignation kept secret from you; indeed Sir Dog insists you be informed of what has already happened. Last night I went downstairs knowing full well that there was no one in that room except him." She bent to sniff at a blossom so her face was hidden. "I invited him upstairs. He may attend me in my chamber in future. You are now fully informed and will be kept so in future." She straightened up without meeting his eyes. Her cheeks must be redder than any rose.

"I am truly sorry to have doubted Your Grace. Or Sir Dog."

She forced herself to look at the men. Winter's eyes were very wide, but at least he wasn't smirking the way Abel would when he heard the news. Audley was hiding his wounds well. She awarded him a smile. "I owe you an apology for being so careless, though. What can we do about the servants and my slippers?"

"Buy them off or fire them."

She found another early bloom to admire. This tête-à-tête must be ended before the people outside became suspicious. "No. Ashes. Next time you see them, mention that I was complaining of scorching my shins because I went to sleep on the chair with my feet on the hearth. It's weak, but it should satisfy a bunch of chambermaids."

"Very ingenious, my lady." They studied each other across the bush, Winter listening with a worried frown.

"Until further notice," she said, "Sir Dog will share my bed. I needn't tell you that the rules for princesses are not the same as those for princes and I will be seriously damaged if this becomes known. It isn't fair, but that's the way it is. The Lord Protector will certainly use it against me if he finds out. Dog will certainly die." And so might they. "Can you keep my secret?"

"Yes, my lady, but only if you don't mind varying the hours he spends with you. Otherwise the Guard will wonder why Dog is given special treatment."

She could not hide a smile. Very special treatment! "Of course. The stairs had better be cleaned, though. I hope my Blades will not object to performing some light housework?"

A familiar twinkle returned to Audley's eye. "The honor will be Dog's."

She laughed. "Very fitting! Thank you. And thank you, Sir Winter. I am in your hands."

"You're in Dog's hands, my lady," Audley said, "and I am mad with jealousy. We both are, and I know from things he has said in the past that Sir Abel will be also."

She was too taken aback to say more than, "Thank you!" She had been promoted to woman of the world.

"If I may presume, Your Grace . . . you are aware of the ring problem, aren't you?"

Thrown off balance, she looked from one Blade to the other. "Abel's pearl was for services rendered?" She did not look to see if Winter was wearing his ruby.

"Not really." Audley was having great trouble keeping his face straight, now that he was back on the winning side of the discussion. "That pearl ring is well known around the palace. It indicates that the wearer currently belongs to Lady Violet and she will rip out the eyes of any other woman who looks his way. But it is also a conjurement. I'm sure you know, my lady, that lovers' rings normally provide protection for a year or more." She had not even known such things as lovers' rings existed, and he had guessed as much. "Before the enchantment wears off, that is. The problem is that an Ironhall binding is so potent that it deflects other conjurations, and on us the rings need to be re-ensorcelled every two or three weeks. The cost is extreme, far beyond the means of any Blade." He fished in his pouch and produced a simple gold band. "We do try, but most ladies prefer to provide their own, so that they can rely on the enchantment to perform as required."

Her blushes must be visible to the spectators outside. She had known that there were ways of avoiding unwanted pregnancies without ever realizing that the Blades' trophies served that purpose. Dian's confessions had never veered toward such sordid, unromantic matters, and she had no idea whether Dog had been wearing a ring in the night.

Nor could she even be certain that Audley was speaking the entire truth, for the Blades liked to spread legends about their prowess. She could not see why they would spread this one.

"Thank you for reminding me," she said. "You still have some crowns left in your expense purse?"

"I believe there may be enough, my lady."

"Then please give it to Sir Dog and allow him some free time this afternoon so that he can have his ring, um, recharged."

"As Your Highness commands. Sir Winter?"

"I just wanted to tell Her Grace," Winter said solemnly, "that from our point of view, her choice of a bedmate who is one of us, and therefore trustworthy, is very welcome because it makes our task of guarding her much simpler. I just wish, like you, Commander, that she had chosen the best man."

"We agree in general on that but not on the particulars."

"That will *do,* gentlemen!" Malinda moved to the door, relishing the flattery and wondering if—incredibly!—there might even be some truth in it. Dog had said she was beautiful.

She was dreading the moment when she must face him in front of witnesses, and this happened as soon as she returned to her apartment. Fortunately he threw himself on his knees, grabbed her hand to kiss, and babbled about how he wanted to die for her. He had these manic outbursts every few days and everyone just ignored them now, but it made her blushes understandable.

The complications of romance showed up again when young Sir Abel arrived to relieve Winter. All the women screamed in horror at the four raw scratches that adorned his face from left eye to jaw.

"Fencing," he explained vaguely. "Fencing lessons down at the gym."

Amid the squawks of disbelief, Dian said, "And just who is expert enough at fencing to put four *exactly parallel* scratches like that on your cheek?"

"Sir Snake," Abel said, giving Malinda a peculiar look. "Amazing for his age. Must be thirty if he's a day. Devious!"

Young Blades could be devious too. Obviously the marks were some hours old and he had made no effort to have them treated. Furthermore, he was making quite sure everyone noticed the garnet that now adorned his finger in place of the pink pearl. Lady Violet had been displaced in his affections, if they deserved the name.

Stupid kid!

Soon after that he sidled close enough to pass Malinda a note, and she withdrew to read it in private. The elaborately cursive script was so snarled that she could barely decipher it—the sign of a devious mind, no doubt.

You still have friends in high places, although they dare not show their hand at present. Do not be alarmed when the Royal Guard is removed. He may make threats, but he plans to find you a foreign husband and cannot create open scandal. Play for time, discourage any who offer to rally support for you, because they may be playing a false game. Burn this note. Trust no one except your own Blades and your friend—

Stealth

Hmm! The younger Blades often referred to their heroes by the names of their swords. Abel's hint was a strong suggestion that Stealth must be Sir Snake, and she would ask Dog later. Snake's being one of Roland's henchmen explained the reference to high places. She had seen Snake only twice since the Night of Dogs, once at her wedding. Basically the note was advising her to do what she would do anyway, but the reference to "playing for time" was worrisome. Time for what? Time for Granville to find her a husband? Or time for Amby to die?

After another ten or twenty years even that day ended and she went to bed. She still had hours to wait until midnight, of course, but she did manage to sleep—seven or eight times. She was up not long before Dog came, stoking the fire and lighting candles, but she must have dozed off again. Suddenly there he was, beside the bed, looking down at her as if he had been there for hours.

She whispered, "Darling!"

He did not move. "Why?" His growl rasped like a saw on steel.

"Why what?"

"Why me? You're a princess and I'm just dirt. Why soil your pretty body with dirt like me?"

He was in one of his difficult moods. She held out her arms, careful not to dislodge the quilt any more than necessary. "Come and dirty me, then."

He licked his lips. "Why?" he growled again. "Is it my muscles? Is that all? You just like bulgy arms?"

"I love your muscles, Dog, but that isn't why I love you. Come into bed and I'll tell you why. Hurry!"

"You want the candles snuffed?"

"No," she said, although she had never realized that there was a choice.

Dog was not in the least shy. Fascinated, she watched as he unsheathed the broadsword and laid it carefully on a chair near to hand, then shed cloak and baldric, dropping them around him on the floor, similarly jerkin, boots, and breeches. He untied the laces that fastened his hose to his doublet and took all those off, so he was left standing there in only his shirt, which barely came low enough to meet the silver fuzz that covered his legs.

She had overlooked the fact that the fox can run with the vixen—he lifted back the covers and stared down at her naked body. *Eeek!* And stared, as if he didn't believe it or was trying to memorize it. She was certain she must be blushing all over.

"You're sure?" he growled.

"Sure? I'm bursting into flames, you great ox! Bring those muscles here at once." She lurched up, grabbed him by the shirt, and hauled him down into bed. Even then, when she finally had him in there beside her and the quilts over them both, he just lay like a hot snowdrift, although she was already experienced enough to tell that his body wanted her.

He turned from her kiss. "Tell me why me."

"Because you're you, you idiot! If I wanted a pretty man, I'd seduce Audley, and he'd jump right into some other woman's bed the same night—wouldn't he? Winter's good for talking politics. If all I wanted was a quick bounce, I'd ask Abel. I wanted you because you know what pain is."

He grunted.

"I don't know your burden," she whispered, struggling to work his shirt off him in a suitably romantic way, "and I don't care. You bear it. You suffer. You understand that life is hard and cruel, and sometimes you don't think you can go on any longer, but you always do and you always will. You're strong, Dog, and I don't just mean your muscles. You're a man; those others are only boys."

"I'm five months older than—"

"You're ten years older than Audley will ever be. I need a man. Now I've got one lying naked in my bed and I have no clothes on. Do something appropriate. If you don't touch me I'll scream."

"I'm trash."

"I love you."

"Stop saying that!"

"Sh! All right, you're trash. You're shit. You're no good. You're a dog. Get out of my bed, animal, and go send me a real—"

Suddenly he was all over her—mouth, tongue, hands, body, kissing, sucking, kneading, punching, and without warning pulling her legs apart. She smothered a cry of pain as he stabbed into her and began a fury of thrusting and pumping.

It was all over in moments and he collapsed on her, gasping like a landed fish. She stroked his sweaty hair and waited. It was a while before he withdrew, but by then the hard breathing had become sobs and tears were splashing on her breasts. Life with Dog was never going to be predictable. It had been a test, she knew, but all she understood was that anger would be the wrong reaction; he probably understood even less than she did.

"I shouldn't have done that," he mumbled.

"No you shouldn't."

He tried to rise and her fingers closed in his hair.

"But you did and I didn't break and I still love you."

"I must go away. You're right—I'm an animal."

"You're staying right here. I love you."

He raised his head in alarm. "You can't love me! You mustn't!"

She licked the salty tears off his eyelids. "But I do and there's nothing you can do about it. Now you're going to make up for what you just did. I'm sore and you're going to have to go very slow, take twice as long. You can start now."

"I can't. A man needs time."

"A woman needs more. You will begin by nuzzling my right earlobe. When I'm satisfied with your performance there, I'll give you further directions."

A long time after that, when the sky was pale gray beyond the casement, she stirred and wakened, and saw Dog sitting by the light of the last guttering candle on the mantel. Despite the chill, he had no clothes on; he was reading a book, scowling with concentration, spelling out the words with a finger. Sensing her gaze on him, he dropped it and hurried across to her. Now he was eager, and visibly excited again. "Again?" He hauled off the covers.

"Spirits, man!" she said. "I'm not sure! Is it possible? You've been going all night. How many times . . . ?" But he was already in bed beside her, and she was facing a wolfish expanse of big white teeth, some broken, many missing. She realized that Dog was trying to smile. Sore or not, she could not refuse him. "All right," she said. "Begin gently."

In broad daylight, when the maids were dressing her, she saw his book still lying on the rug and asked for it. It was old, dirty, and tattered—junk picked up for a copper groat. The title was worn off the cover and the title page missing, but she recognized the *Arcane Lore* of Alberino Veriano, one of the classic spell collections. It had been written in deliberately obscure language and the formulae in it were long out of date, even those that had been of any value to start with. No one would study enchantment with this anymore. The place-marker ribbon had been inserted at a conjuration headed "Invocation of the Dead."

25

A king should be a sheepdog, not a wolf.
AMBROSE IV

Two days later, as if to prove that the mysterious Stealth was a reliable prophet, the Royal Guard disappeared. Later the *Gazette* reported that the Council of Regency had chosen the palace of Beaufort as the most suitable residence for the King's Majesty during his childhood. Where the King went his Blades went, so the familiar blue and silver liveries were gone overnight. The Princess's Guard continued to work on improving its swordsmanship with the help of the few knights and private Blades who remained in Greymere.

The first Malinda knew of the new arrangement was when Arabel arrived in distress, clamped her Princess to her copious bosom, and wept on her. Lady Cozen had been appointed His Majesty's governess and Lady Arabel's services were no longer required.

"He needs faces about him he knows!" she sobbed. "They packed him off with strangers! They could have let me go with him, at least for a few weeks."

They could also have consulted, or at least informed, the child's sister. Comforting her old friend, Malinda reflected that the faceless *they* that everyone talked about was a mask for Granville, and she now had just cause to hate the Lord Protector.

★　　★　　★

Her turn came a few days after that, when she was called before the Council. She was not caught unprepared. Almost every day one or other of her Blades would bring a verbal message from Sir Snake.

"Stealth says," Dog grumbled as he scrambled into bed, " 'Tell her the Council's going to question her. Tell her to talk freely about anything that happened before her father died and nothing after. Tell her to keep an eye on Ratface. He'll bluster, but he's really on her side.' And you've got to be specially careful when he rubs his ear."

"Who's Ratface?"

"Didn't say. That's it. Can we forget all that now?" Dog was very single-minded.

Next morning she was summoned on an hour's notice. Eight men sat behind a long table, but only three of them were members of the Council, the rest inquisitors or mere clerks. The one introduced as Sir Wrandolph was so obviously Snake's Ratface that she decided the other two would be Mouse Rampant and Pig. Pig was chairman. At first the proceedings were decorous enough, the tone respectful. She sat in the center of the room under a cloth of estate, flanked by Abel and Audley. Dian and Sister Moment shared a bench over by the fireplace.

"Will Her Highness graciously inform the Council who selected Wetshore palace as the site of her wedding?" Pens scratched as the clerks filled up tomes.

"I did."

"Will Her Highness graciously inform the Council why she made that choice?"

And so on. Some of the topics surprised her, as when she was questioned for some time about the death of Aunt Agnes. Having nothing to hide, she answered truthfully. Gradually the queries grew more pointed. Would she confirm that she had made all these plans in concert with Ambassador Reinken and the Lord Chamberlain, both of whom had died in the massacre?

"I did not see their bodies, but I was so informed. However, the deliberations were recorded, so the Chamberlain's office can confirm what I have said."

Would she specify all matters on which her stated preferences were overruled? Ratface scratched his ear.

"I can't recall in detail. Not all the final arrangements were my first choices, certainly. May we have the records brought?"

Of course not. She agreed that her father had been annoyed by her parsimony, but pointed out that he had retained personal control over the security arrangements. She reported what she recalled of the wedding itself. No, she had not been alone with Thegn Leofric at any time, even after the ceremony. She described her conversation with King Radgar.

"Will her Highness graciously inform the Council," inquired Mouse Rampant, "how much time elapsed after she disembarked from the longship before her father was shot?"

His real name was Marshal Souris and he was clever. Pig was pompous and unsure of himself; Ratface—whether because he was secretly helping her or just from incompetence—was always wandering off into irrelevancies; but little Souris with his long nose and bristling mustache was brisk, brusque, impatient, and asked the most penetrating questions.

"Just moments," she said. "I walked about half the length of the jetty . . . roughly the length of this room."

"Her Highness did not see the longbow being shot?"

"It sounded more like a crossbow. I did not see it at all."

Mouse Rampant's eyes glittered. "Will Her Highness graciously explain to the Council how she could have overlooked a crossbow, which must have already been spanned and ready to hand? In an open boat? It is not the sort of object that can be hidden in a pocket."

She awarded him a patronizing smile. "The ship was not an empty box, Marshal; it was cluttered with chests and ropes and barrels and heaps of leather covers. The bow was hidden somewhere. It was not in view, I assure you."

What happened when the first shot was fired? Soon they were approaching quicksand—Fox and Fitzroy and the Kromman vendetta—but so many people had seen her on Lord Roland's horse that she could not deny that he had been her rescuer.

"Can't we move on?" Ratface complained, digging for earwax. "Will the accused tell the court what happened when she returned to the palace with the Chancellor?"

"*Court?*" She jumped up. "*Accused?* I understood that I was assisting the Council of Regency in its inquiries, not that I was on trial. A princess can recognize only a court made up of her peers. I have been deceived. I refuse to answer any more questions."

Pig and Mouse Rampant glared at the ham-fisted Ratface.

Malinda walked out and no one tried to stop her.

The next day a troop of men-at-arms came for her. They tried to keep her Blades out of the meeting room, but wisely decided not to argue the point when shown *Evening* and *Willing,* both of which had very sharp points. Inside the chamber, respect and politeness were things of the past. The clerks and inquisitors had been relegated to the background; men-at-arms were posted at the door as if to prevent anyone leaving. She was expected to stand while the three Councillors sat on grandiose chairs like thrones—Pig and Mouse Rampant as before, but Ratface had been replaced by Fish-Eyes.

Malinda protested this insult, then refused to utter another word. Granville wanted no public scandal, Stealth had said, but she could guess that the inquiry had been told to find enough firewood to light one, so that she could be forced into a marriage. Remaining silent in the face of threats and insults was hard work. After several hours of it, when everyone was coming close to a boil, Fish-Eyes made the same sort of clumsy error Ratface had made the previous day. He uttered an outright threat to have Malinda thrown in the Bastion.

Evening flashed out of its scabbard. "Try giving that order, my lord," Audley snapped. "You won't finish it."

Pig jumped to his feet. "Guards, remove those two men!"

The guards' eyes were on Audley. Abel perhaps seemed too young to be dangerous, but it was Abel who flashed across the floor and slid *Willing* between Pig's legs.

"Please be careful, my lord," he said earnestly. "This edge is very sharp."

Pig had his throne at his back and nowhere to go. When his men-at-arms started to draw their swords he screamed at them not to move. "You won't get away with this!" His normally ruddy face was ashen, and dribbling sweat.

"On tiptoes might be safer, my lord." Abel raised the blade slightly. "Higher still? That's better. Now, I believe you were about to adjourn this inquiry? Her Highness and her escort are free to go?"

Pig nodded.

"Say it, my lord."

Pig squeaked out those instructions and watched as Malinda and her train departed. Abel stepped back, bowed, and followed them, but he kept *Willing* in his hand and used it to gesture aside the men-at-arms on the door. They let him go unimpeded. He ran after his ward, leaving the door open so they could hear his laughter.

Malinda staggered back to her rooms with a screaming headache. She needed to lie down, she said, and did so. Audley sent Dog around by the secret passage to help her. In fact Dog was not much good at just-lying-and-holding, which was what she needed, but after a while she felt restored enough to let him proceed with what he was good at, and that helped too.

As night was falling she sent him off, made herself respectable, and rang for a ladies' maid. The summons was answered by Commander Audley clutching a warrant with seal dangling. His dark eyes were grim with worry. "Decree from the Council, Your Grace. A royal residence has been set aside for your use. An escort of Household Yeoman for the journey . . . first light tomorrow."

"Where?"

"Somewhere called Ness Royal, Your Grace. Winter thinks it's on the coast, northeast. . . ."

"I know it." Strangely, the prospect of being shut up in Kingstead, that moldering pile, did not appal her. It even held a certain appeal. Her image of it was softened by the golden mists of childhood, and she was intrigued by the thought of running free with Dog there. Anywhere would be better than court now.

Meanwhile, Audley was looking very young and out of his depth. "What are your orders, my lady?"

"What are my options?"

"Submit or flee, I suppose."

Not flight, even had she anywhere to fly to. "I cannot see that I will be in any greater danger at Ness Royal than I am here. And I am certain that you will be safer."

Audley bit his lip. "If we arrive."

"Oh! I see." No wonder he was frightened. The ride north would take three or four days, some of it through very wild, open country where Sian Rules would be of little use. She might arrive with four fewer Blades than she had when she started. "I need Stealth's advice. Dog went off to do some fencing, so he may have heard from him already. If not, you'd better hunt him down."

The news set her household a-twitter. Dian said she would certainly accompany Malinda back to Ness Royal and visit her family there. Even Arabel thought she might come, although she had hated the place before. The maids of honor were unsure, and Sister Moment would need permission from the Prioress. There was a great upheaval as the packing began, with box after box being sent down to the stable to be loaded on wagons.

After that, everyone was sympathetic when Her Highness decreed an early night, even dismissing her ladies' maids, saying that Dian could give her all the help she required.

The instant the door was closed, though, Malinda drew a deep breath and said, "I have been keeping something from you."

Her friend grinned and hugged her. "If you're going to tell me you're in love, darling, that's no secret. You've had the sun in your lantern for weeks."

"Oh!" Malinda was nettled. "It is not weeks. . . ."

"You've been lighting up the world! Don't suppose other people would notice, but I know you too well. And since your Blades are not crawling around peeking under doors and through keyholes, I can guess who it is. Congratulations!"

"You can?"

"Oh yes! He's gorgeous. I'm jealous."

No one would ever describe Dog as gorgeous unless he had a sack over his head. Malinda shook her head. "Guess again!"

"Not the Commander?" Dian pouted and then smiled knowingly. "Oh, well he is very clever, and . . . Not him either? Why, that young rogue! He is reputed to be the fastest needleworker in the palace, but I'd never have guessed—"

The door opened just wide enough to admit Dog and his trusty broadsword. He closed it silently.

Dian's smile fell into ruins. "He's a striking hunk of man," she whispered gamely. Scowling at her, he stuck his big chin out, marched over to Malinda, and thrust a single red rose at her.

She said, "Thank you, darling," as if this was his usual practice, and offered her lips to be kissed. She hoped she was hiding her astonishment better than Dian was. Had the others put him up to this, or was it his own idea?

What Dian might have said next remained unknown, for Dog then proceeded to open a section of wall and admit the rest of the Princess's Guard. With them came a very surprising visitor indeed— not Stealth, as Malinda had expected, but the man whose equivalent nom de guerre would be Harvest. He had almost twenty years on everyone else in the room and his clothes were nondescript compared to his usual crimson robes, but Lord Roland was still man enough to turn Audley into just a pretty boy. He bowed low to Malinda.

She bussed his cheek. "I misjudged you for a long time, my lord. Now I appreciate your singular loyalty and I am ashamed that I ever doubted you."

"You were right to distrust me, Your Highness. My first loyalty was always to your father. Now it is to your brother—your *younger* brother." His smile was as deadly as his cat's-eye sword.

"There is no divergence between his interests and mine, and never will be."

"I was already sure of that but it gladdens my heart to hear you say so."

"Come and sit, Excellency." She led him to a chair and took one beside him. The others moved in, remaining standing. "If Granville can persuade Parliament to legitimize him, then where will your loyalties lie?"

Lord Roland looked over his audience, his gaze hesitating a moment at Dian. Even sitting, he dominated the room. "His Excellency is, of course, being encouraged to summon Parliament as soon as possible for that very purpose."

Malinda sensed evasion under the charm, like some deadly water monster lurking in a sunlit pool. "Encouraged by whom?"

"By me and many other loyal supporters," the Chancellor said blandly. "Unfortunately, your royal father bequeathed him a very full treasury. . . . I'm sure you know that no king of Chivial may collect taxes until Parliament has voted him the necessary authority, known as 'supply.' With the wealth of the elementaries in hand, the Council of Regency so far needs no supply. That situation cannot long endure, since the Baelish war has been resumed and the Lord Protector must still support both the army he left behind in Wylderland and the troops he brought south with him. He will run out of money before winter."

The Chancellor had parried her question, not answered it. "So why cannot he just suppress a few more conjuring orders?"

Lord Roland smiled. It was not the sort of smile one would like to see on an opponent. "Resume the Monster War? That would require the help of Sir Snake and his associates, or else a new band of similar daredevils. It would also require the White Sisters, and I have reason to believe that Mother Superior is proving uncooperative." He shook his head in sad disapproval. "Furthermore, the Lord Protector has refused the protection of the Royal Guard. His mercenaries are sturdy enough on a field of battle, but they may lack something in subtlety when it comes to dealing with monsters and similar treachery."

"He won't dare?"

"Let us say he should be loath, if he has any brains at all. Which he does. He is a clever man, Your Grace. He is hesitant to summon Parliament, because he knows that its moods are never predictable. Returning to your original question, why am I encouraging him to summon a Parliament? First, it is highly unlikely that a bill to legitimize him would ever pass. Consider your former betrothed, His Grace of De Mayes." Roland waited to see if she had caught up with him, which she had not. "Until he comes of age, his mother will act as regent for him. The duchy is one of the greatest landowners in the country. Although he cannot yet take his seat in the House of Lords, his mother can sway many peers who are his relatives or tenants. He controls a score of seats in the Commons. But he has two older brothers on the wrong side of the blanket—do you suppose his mother will favor legitimizing Lord Granville? Many peers have sons they would prefer not to acknowledge in daylight. I could go on, Your Highness, but you get my gist. Legitimization would create far too many precedents; it is possible but not likely."

His explanation was persuasive but not comforting. It raised more dragons than it slew.

"If this matter did come before Parliament," the Chancellor continued, "I should have to report words your honored father said to me not long before he died. Concerning Lord Granville, he said that the man was a brilliant soldier but too ruthless to be a ruler and that if his lordship were to attain supreme power he would soon start treating the Chivians as bloodily as he had treated the Wylds. I would not serve such a king, Your Highness."

She nodded her thanks for that assurance. "You think he will be content to remain Lord Protector?"

"While you remain heir, yes. The alternative is civil war to take the crown by force, and why should he risk that when he already has the power? He can eliminate you painlessly with a foreign marriage, and he expects to neutralize Prince Courtney by implicating him in his mother's mysterious death. Lord Granville is smart enough not to underestimate the Prince. He is also vain enough to believe that he can provide four or five years of competent rule without difficulty, and he may well be right. At that point, if anything were to happen to His Majesty, then Parliament would almost certainly accept a coup."

And she would be working on her fourth or fifth baby in some distant land. "How can I help Amby survive his childhood?"

Again the celebrated fencer deflected her stroke. "We must wait on Parliament, my lady, and gamble on its good intentions. My main reason for wanting to see it convene is that it may set aside your father's will and name you regent. More likely, I think it will try to restore the Council to the sort of governing body he envisaged, replacing most of the Granville toadies who now control it. I and others like me have very little influence at the moment and are at constant risk of being dismissed entirely. Parliament will certainly want to see you married to a Chivian, not sent into exile."

Malinda looked around at her companions. Lord Roland had been offering comfort to her but not to the Blades, and their faces were grim. "So we play for time—and you advise me to accept banishment to Ness Royal?"

The Chancellor sighed. "I have nothing better to suggest. Flight overseas would ruin your case and cannot be considered while the Baels maintain their blockade. If you flout that warrant, you will be arrested, which means death for your staunch defenders here." He looked around at the youngest of them. "Sir Abel, you are in grave danger of being arrested anyway, after what you did to Sir Hilaire today. I wish I had seen that! It's amazing that you got away with it."

Abel's boyish grin lit up the room. "He was afraid I *was* going to get away with it—on the end of my sword."

Roland led the laughter, but it was short-lived. Worry returned. "Obviously the journey will be dangerous. The last I heard, your escort is to comprise four Yeomen lancers and thirty mounted archers of the Black Riders, under Marshal Souris himself." He glanced interrogatively at Malinda.

"Wasn't he on the committee questioning me? Small, long nose, very fierce?" *Mouse Rampant.* "Clever, I thought."

"Yes, indeed. His Black Riders are one of the most respected mercenary units in Eurania. They learned their trade in the Fitainian Wars. In Wylderland Souris was Granville's chief lieutenant."

"The Little Butcher?" Winter wailed. "We're dead men!"

"I hope not. What I suggest is this. Nothing much is likely to happen for the first few hours, and you will have to pass close by Beaufort. If we send word to Sir Dominic, then surely he will spare an escort of a dozen or so Blades—they must be going whirly sitting around guarding a child in the middle of hay meadows. A force of, say, sixteen Blades would discourage Souris from trying anything nasty on the journey."

Malinda detected no signs of enthusiasm among her troops.

Audley said, "With respect, Excellency, the Lord Protector has vowed to disband the Guard, and he can only do that by force. Her Highness is not its primary ward. Will Leader risk dividing his forces and sending a third of his strength on so perilous a trek? That may even be the Lord Protector's intention—we four and a sizable portion of the Guard removed at a stroke. Perhaps even Her Highness, too."

Winter took the warrant from Audley's hand.

Durendal pulled a face. "I hate to think even Granville would be capable of that." But obviously he was baffled and close to admitting it. "The Black Riders are good, not superhuman. Frankly, Commander, your task is almost impossible, because four men cannot oppose the state. If your ward defies that warrant, she will be imprisoned or outlawed. Where could she flee, where would you conceal her? Unless anyone else has a better—"

"Shush!" said Dog.

It must have been many years since anyone spoke like that to Lord Roland. His eyes widened. Winter was reading the warrant by the light of a candle on the mantel shelf. When he reached the end he went back to the beginning again. He was chewing a nail, and Malinda had thought she had broken him of that habit.

The Chancellor shrugged. "I was about to say—"

"*Shush!*" Dog repeated, louder.

This time Roland's eyes narrowed. There was an embarrassed silence as everyone else tried to pretend they hadn't heard.

At last Winter turned to Malinda with a puzzled frown. "It says you have to move to Ness Royal tomorrow, my lady. That's going to be today very shortly."

"That's right."

"And an escort will be made available."

"Yes."

"It does not say you must avail yourself of that escort."

After a pregnant moment, Roland said, "I must be going senile!"

"Me too," Audley agreed, "and I'm only a year older than he is."

"I don't get it," Dog growled.

Abel thumped him on the shoulder. "Don't worry about that, Horse. When we need someone killed, we'll call you. The rest of the time, you just do whatever Her Highness tells you."

26

You condemned me to languish on this frightful, barren, ghost-ridden, uninhabitable, storm-lashed rock with a pack of subhuman, ogreish, verminous, troglodytic domestics.

LADY GODELEVA, LETTER TO KING AMBROSE IV,
THIRDMOON 354

It was the ride to Ironhall all over again, except that Ness Royal was more than twice as far away. It began like the Night of Dogs, with fugitives creeping through the secret passage to the boathouse. Sir Victor stood on the jetty with boatmen ready to take them a short way downstream, to where Snake and Bullwhip waited with horses.

As the knights' "Good chance!" rang in their ears, the fugitives clattered off along the unlit cobbled alleyways of Grandon. By the time the sun came up, they were ten miles from the city, riding north on fresh horses—one princess, one matron companion, and four swordsmen, with not a single sumpter beast. Back at the palace, Arabel and Moment would delay discovery as long as possible. It should be hours before the government learned that Malinda had run and might be days before it knew where.

Even Audley, who was required to be chief worrier, soon agreed that they had made a clean getaway. He could also concede that any group's speed was set by the pace of its slowest horse, so a small party would travel faster than a large one. The weather was fine, the roads in fair shape, and highwaymen would not meddle with a troop of four Blades. Having no need to kill themselves or their mounts with heroics, they might as well enjoy the journey.

Malinda was grievously tempted to turn aside at Beaufort to check on Amby, but she knew she would just upset him and the delay might put her at risk. Late on the first day she was similarly tempted to visit Oakendown, the famous tree city of the White Sisters, but that would require an even longer delay and her curiosity must wait for happier times.

One experience with travelers' inns had been educational, a second would be morbid folly. Toward evening she told Audley to find out the names of some local landowners, but Winter, that bottomless well of information, recalled that the castellan at the Duke of Eastfare's seat, Valglorious, was a knight in the Order. The detour required was not serious; old Sir Vincent and his gracious lady were overjoyed to have the Princess stay overnight. Next morning he provided Audley with a list of other knights residing along their route, so the second evening they found hospitality with a Sir Havoc, who had achieved every Blade's ambition by marrying an heiress both beautiful and wealthy. His home on the banks of the Knosh was not a ducal palace, but nor was it the King's Head at New Cinderwich. On the afternoon of the third day, the fugitives came to Ness Royal.

The Blades had talked of little else the whole way, demanding every scrap of information about the island that the women could muster. It was reputed to have been the birthplace of Ranulf himself, and had certainly been in his descendants' possession for centuries. For much of that time it had been a favored repository for persons of doubtful allegiance—princes and others whose suspect loyalties required sequestration without the embarrassment of actual imprisonment. Its single entrance allowed the authorities to inspect all who came and went, or, in extreme cases, to block any coming and going at all.

"Its most famous inhabitant was Queen Adela," Malinda told them. "Ever heard of her?"

Winter remembered better than the others, of course. "Chivial's first queen regnant."

"Exactly right. But within months of her father's death, her husband declared her insane and shut her up in Ness Royal. When he died, her son continued the tradition."

The Blades did not like that story. How much family history did Granville know?

"That's the Gatehouse," Malinda said, shouting over the gale. "And the lumpy bit beyond it is Ness itself. Come on!" She kicked her weary horse into a last game effort.

For an hour they had been riding across a plain of coarse grass that seemed as infinite as the wind or the pale blue sky. They were all tired—even Blades could be tired. Without warning, the trail dropped steeply away to a cluster of weathered stone buildings, beyond which the ground rose and fell in bizarre swells and hollows. The sea remained hidden from view, but its tangy scent was everywhere.

Although about two hundred men and women lived on Ness Royal, there was no harbor or farmland to provide a living and little pasture. Its only industry was making children and its only export adolescents. When the King needed servants for his great house, the inhabitants were cooks, pages, scullions, footmen, or hostlers. When the lords and ladies departed and the island sank into neglect again, they scratched out a living from garden patches and whatever thatching, carpentry, and masonry work the seneschal commissioned. Most of the money the Treasury had provided over the years for upkeep and repairs had gone straight into seneschals' pockets, of course, but the current caretaker was phenomenally honest, although not by choice.

His name was Sir Thierry. He had lost a leg as a knight banneret in the Isilond War and was now a crotchety old man, embittered by his disability, an unhappy marriage, and an infuriating inability to skim enough off the maintenance budget to fund his retirement somewhere far away. His predecessors had been ignored for years on end, but he was mobbed by auditors and deluged with acid demands for reports. He had pretty much concluded that the Greymere bureaucrats were using conjury to peer over his shoulder, but the truth of the matter

was that all his actions and inactions were reported by Dian's mother
in her letters to Dian, Dian told Malinda, and Malinda made the Lord
Chamberlain's life a misery.

She had never been interested in the condition of the Gatehouse,
though, and it had fallen into ruin—windows boarded up, a few doors
creaking eerily in the wind, weeds in the courtyard. Ness Royal stone
was a dove-colored marl, soft and drab, easily weathered. Half the
walls were ready to crumble away completely and most of the thatch
had gone.

Audley yelled, "Halt!" and everyone reined in. "They'll be refur-
bishing this place. Let's explore it while we have the chance. I want
every man ready to walk through here blindfold in pitch darkness."
He belatedly looked to Malinda for permission.

"Go ahead!" she said. "Dian and I will hold the horses for you.
Holding horses is one of the things I do best. No, I'm joking. Go."
She slipped her boots from the stirrups and uttered a plaintive,
"Ooof!" as Dog lifted her down. "Thank you, love. Without you I'd
have been stuck up there forever."

Abel, Audley, and Winter ran off. The weary horses were not
going to go anywhere and could be ignored.

"This place has shrunk! It used to be much bigger."

"Oh?" Dian was pointedly looking elsewhere.

Malinda turned as suggested and saw Dog flat on his belly in the
nettles and thistles, head on the ground. Now what? She went over
and knelt.

"Dog?"

He lifted his head, then rose slowly to his knees. His eyes, all
white in the sunlight, were wide with . . . fear? horror? She put her
arms around him, which usually felt like embracing an oak tree, but
in this instance he was trembling.

"Dog! What's wrong?"

His teeth chattered.

"Tell me!"

"Surf. I can hear surf. I didn't know there would be surf!" He
spoke in a whisper, although Dian had wandered tactfully away and
there was no one close. How could that be fear in his eyes when he
had not been afraid of a sword through his heart?

"You'll hear it everywhere on the island, all the time. It never
stops. Surf can't hurt you."

"It kills people!"

"Are you frightened it may hurt you?"

"No. I saw it . . . once . . . Once I . . ."

She hugged him tighter. "Never mind what you saw. It must have been a long time ago, and this is now. Dog, I need you. Your ward is in danger and needs you. The woman who loves you needs you to protect her. Even if you can't love her, she—"

"I *hurt!*" He gasped for breath and then said, "Not surf. Not just this place. It's been going on for days. It hurts!"

"What hurts?"

"You do!" Words came pouring out in the longest speech she had ever heard from him, his throaty growl all chewed up by gap teeth: "I want to lock you up in a cellar where no one else can ever see you or harm you. I want to kill any other man who goes near you and yet I want you to be happy and laughing all the time and I can't do both. I can't be with you all the time. I hurt terribly, more than when . . . ever known. Want to serve you every minute. Most of all want you to want me and I know not worthy to look at your shadow." His colorless eyes were wide with pain. "Is that love?"

"Yes, that's love." She assumed love might take a man that way. "And it does hurt. I would be happy in that cellar always if you were with me. I tremble at the thought that you may get hurt. I don't feel worthy of you, Dog. I worry all the time you're not with me. But it brings happiness too, doesn't it? I am so full of joy when you come to me that I think I will burst. You don't want me to send you away just because it hurts, do you?"

"No."

"This is love, Dog. I love you."

"And me you. You're crazy." He kissed her. It was a very long kiss for two people kneeling on hard ground, a highly improper performance for a princess in the middle of a courtyard, but she could feel his need and her own was no less. If Dian and the other men saw them, they tactfully did not interrupt. Gradually his trembling stopped and finally he gave her an abashed look and jumped up, lifting her with him. He growled, "Sorry!" with a suitable hangdog expression.

She clung to him. "I'm not," she told the side of his neck. "Not at all."

Dog had said he loved her! With that admission he had crossed a bridge. Soon he might trust her enough to tell her why he was haunted by dragons that sounded like surf that killed people.

"This way to the Baels' Bathtub," Dian proclaimed as they left the Gatehouse. The trail pitched down into a gully but soon opened up to become a ledge angling across a cliff that fell sheer to foam-mottled dark water. Waves surging through the canyon moved like monstrous lips over rocky teeth, chewing at the tall stacks, sucking in and out of caves. The silvery walls echoed the sea's mournful voice and the wailing birds, making the horses twitch and tremble. Ahead, and lower still, the trail ended at a rickety timber bridge that descended to a rocky, weed-circled pillar in mid-channel. A second span angled back and up to another stack, and the third rose steeply to the trail on the far side.

Malinda had told the story three times on the journey north: "There is no path down the cliffs and you can't bring a boat near them anyway, because Ness is completely surrounded by reefs. The only road in goes over a bridge across a gorge called the Baels' Bathtub. I don't know what its old name was, but about thirty years ago, in the First Baelish War, a couple of dragon ships sacked Fishport, a few miles to the north. The raiders heard about Kingstead—or perhaps spotted it from their ships, although there's very little to see—and came marching along the coast. The gatehouse was unmanned and the bridge intact, so they left guards on the landward end while the rest went across. They found the island deserted, because everyone had hidden in the caves. The caves have openings near the seaward end of the trail, and in the night the defenders came out and chopped down the bridge.

"The Baels who had stayed at the Gatehouse ran back to Fishport and brought one of the longships around at the next high tide to try a rescue. The waves smashed it to toothpicks and them to jam. The rest of the raiders collected all the rope they could find and tried to cross the channel when the tide went out. The surf got all of them, too. They say the last half dozen just jumped off the cliffs, because that was a better end than what was done to prisoners in those days. It was one of the worst Baelish defeats in the war, and it was done by a gang of footmen and gardeners with wrecking bars."

The canyon was as cold and dismal as its history. Hungry waves ran a hundred feet below the travelers; the sunlight was a hundred feet above. As the rumble of surf grew louder around them, Malinda kept careful watch on Dog. He was sickly pale, but seemed to be staying master of whatever haunted him.

Although the horses tried to balk at the first bridge, they were too tired to make a real fight of it. Audley coaxed his to go ahead, then Malinda's and the rest followed. Looking pleased with himself, he said, "There's no other way across?"

"I said there's no other *road* across," Malinda corrected him. "I also told you that there's no path down the cliffs."

He raised a shapely eyebrow at her. "So this bridge is the only way to reach or leave the island?"

She was amused, wondering whether it was him or his Blade instincts that detected her equivocation. "The south end of the Bathtub is shallow. At the time of spring tides—that's new moon or full moon, when the range is greatest—an active man can scramble across the rocks at low water, if the sea is calm. Boys do it on dares, of course, and don't always make it. The only way down to it is through the caves. Ness Royal is riddled with caves."

There was hardly a flat inch on the island. The trail led between rocky spines and grassy mounds, through twisting canyons and bowl-like hollows. Whitewashed thatched cottages crouched in sheltered nooks, showing no inclination to get together to form a village. Dry-stone walls kept cattle out of vegetable gardens and children out of sinkholes, of which there were at least a dozen. Many of those led down to water—fresh in some that served as wells, salt in others, while a few opened directly to sea caves and made good fishing holes.

The first stop had to be at Dian's mother's cottage, which was larger than most, with glazed windows and separate outbuildings for livestock. Dogs and geese put up a cacophony of warning as the visitors rode in; chickens and children screamed and fled. Widow de Fait came plodding out to investigate. Since her husband's death, she had remarried and begun rearing a second family, but in spite of all the mouths she fed with her superb cooking, the money her daughter sent from court made her the richest person on the island after the seneschal himself. She uttered an earsplitting shriek of joy at Dian's unexpected return and rushed forward, arms wide. Fortunately Dian was able to dismount in time, or her mother might have embraced the horse instead—they were a very cuddly family.

Children flocked around to squeak and squeal and jump up and down. Even Malinda had to be hugged and the Blades barely escaped. Weeping copiously, Mistress de Fait marveled at seeing the tiny princess she had once known now grown to (enormous, although she did not say so) womanhood. She seemed much shorter than she had nine years ago, grayer and more breathless, probably even fatter. Dian met her youngest brother and sister for the first time and embraced six other siblings she had not seen for years. Her stepfather appeared and was presented to Malinda, who remembered him as a gangly page. Now he was a tall man, as thin as ever but pleasant enough and still known just by the name of Pinkie. His wife seemed to have remained Widow de Fait, perhaps because she was so much older than he was.

★   ★   ★

Kingstead was a jumble of originally separate buildings now linked by covered corridors, mismatched additions, and poorly judged afterthoughts. Most of it clung like a frozen rockslide to the side of a sheltered hollow, which contained the only trees on the island, but Upper House stood on the cliff top, overlooking the sea. Although Upper House tended to be drafty, with gales wailing in chimneys and casements, Malinda had already decided that she would occupy her mother's old bedroom with the fine view of the coast to the south, even if she had to evict Sir Thierry himself to do so. That chamber had a secret door in one corner, and she had worked out how she would allocate adjoining rooms so that no one except the Blades could know if Dog came to her. At Ness Royal, without the snoopy Royal Guard around, she need not fear scandal even if he spent all night every night guarding her at the closest of close quarters.

Dian's mother had predicted that the seneschal would be indisposed by that time of day, but he was able to totter forward to greet his visitors, wobbling dangerously on his crutch. The miasma of wine around him caused Sir Audley to take a hasty step backward as soon as he had presented the Council's warrant. Sir Thierry examined it at arm's length, moving his lips. Eventually it occurred to him that no one argued with four Blades, so he mumbled a welcome to Her Grace, breathed fumes over her fingers, and told his steward to make all necessary arrangements. He asked leave to keep the warrant overnight so he could copy out the financial details, of which it contained none.

While Audley was demanding food, linen, hot water, and other comforts for Her Highness, Her Highness gazed around her with much more nostalgia than she had expected. How small and old and shabby the place seemed now! It should be filled with unhappy memories and the ghosts of pined-away ancestors, but she was glad to have arrived. Her banishment could not last long. In a month or so Granville would summon her back to court and hand her over to her future husband. Whether she submitted or resisted at that point, her love affair with Dog would inevitably end. She must snatch every moment of happiness she could find.

27

Stories are truths in party clothes.

FONATELLES

The Queen's Room had not changed. Indeed Malinda was shocked to find her mother's toiletries lying on the dresser under nine years' dust and many of her garments moldering in the clothes chest. Worse, she now realized that it was from the terrace outside this window that Godeleva had leaped to her death.

"On second thought, I know a better place," she said and stalked out. Dog and Audley followed at her heels. Dian was giving Abel and Winter a tour of the lower buildings.

Her second choice was a much smaller chamber, the one that had been hers. It was barely large enough for the bed, which would itself be extremely snug when it had Dog in it. Wind moaned through gaps in the ill-fitting windows, whose tiny panes looked out on two sides over the reefs and the coastal cliffs beyond. The walls were of solid gray marl and the door of ancient oak. She would order a fire lit right away and heated bricks to air the mattress.

"This will be my room," she announced.

Audley looked surprised and Dog pouted, even surlier than usual.

"I can post a man right outside, I suppose," Audley remarked tactfully. "The door is very visible from the stair and the passage."

"Good solid stone," Malinda said, thumping a wall and secretly teasing. "It's very secure. The only thing I must watch is that rug in front of the fireplace. If it got moved, then candlelight shining down through the cracks might be mistaken for a signal."

Dog brightened. Audley whipped back the rug and knelt to inspect the trapdoor beneath. "Wasn't there a rug like this in that room you said would be the Guard Room?"

"Very likely." She poked Dog hard in the ribs. "Why don't you ever smile?"

"Like this?" He drew back his lips to expose the awful gap and the fangs flanking it.

"It's a start," she said and took the chance to tickle him while Audley wasn't looking.

She followed the two Blades down the stone stair into chill dimness and a stale reek of rot. It was half cellar and half cave, lit by a reluctant glow trickling through slits in the foundations. Audley muttered angrily as he registered all the potential hiding places among the discarded furniture, barrels, and piled crates.

"Rats, bats, and cats!" he snarled. "Do you have to sleep in this wing, my lady? There must be somewhere easier to guard. Where do those go?" He pointed to two other staircases.

"You have nothing else to do, and you haven't seen the worst yet. One goes up to your Guard Room and the other to a nook off the Queen's Room. That one can be bolted shut, I think. Come here." She picked her way through the clutter to a masonry wall, which had been left suspiciously accessible.

Audley frowned. "What of it? Looks solid enough."

"It's not." It was, in fact, an enchanted curtain concealing a wooden door. Malinda just reached out and pulled it aside. Then she heaved the door open to reveal steps spiraling down into bedrock. A dim light from below showed chisel marks on the wall of the stairwell. "Take care," she said. "The risers are uneven."

Again Audley led the way, but his angry muttering gave way to sounds of wonder when he reached the bottom and found himself in a chamber much larger and brighter than the dingy cellar they had just left. Once it had been a natural sea cave, formed when the sea was higher or the island lower, but now a glass screen closed off the original opening in the cliff, leaving it dry and bright. Its floor had been smoothed and leveled. It was furnished with rugs, chairs, tables, and as many shelves of dusty books as any sage's study. The two Blades looked all around, gaping, and then strode together over to the great window to stare down at the rocks and foam far below. Probably no one had set foot here since the day Queen Godeleva floated past the window in her death leap.

Dog looked around angrily at Malinda. "What *is* this place?" The beat of the surf was unending, felt through the feet as much as heard, but he seemed much less distressed than before.

"My mother called it Adela's Room, but she may have invented the name." Malinda turned her back on him and pulled up a corner of the largest rug, peeling it back. "That's one of the finest libraries on conjuration in all Eurania." In her last months on Ness Royal she had purloined some of its volumes and tried to read them, but they had all been far beyond the understanding of a nine-year-old. Wrong rug—she replaced it and tried another. Dog had never commented on the Veriano volume he had left in her room. On his next visit he had removed it without a word. She knew now that he was no scholar; if the others ever saw him with a book they would guffaw and mock him. Ah! She had found what she was looking for—a series of very scuffed lines drawn on the rock floor in ochre.

"An octogram?" Audley exclaimed, coming to see what she was doing. "Could you conjure in a cave like this?"

"Of course not. Only earth elementals would answer your call, maybe some water spirits. My mother was crazy, Commander. She hoped to use enchantment to win back my father's love. She spent an enormous fortune collecting those books and trying to bribe scholars to come and aid her, but if the King had ever learned what she was up to, he would have thrown her in the Bastion or chopped off her head. So her Blades followed her around, frustrating her efforts, sending away the experts she had summoned, rubbing out her octograms, forbidding the locals to help her."

Poor, abandoned, crazy Godeleva! Malinda had never spared much sympathy for her mother before, but now she knew what exile to Ness Royal felt like. Yet she had her lover with her and was confident her term there would be short. Her mother had known she would never be allowed to leave.

Audley sighed. "Just wait until Winter sets eyes on those books!"

"Winter is interested in conjuration?" She did not look at Dog. "He'll certainly never find a more complete collection."

"Winter is interested in anything. Are there other secret passages we have to see?"

"Not near here," she said. "Some down in the lower buildings. Under one of these rugs there's a trapdoor leading down into the caves. Go down far enough and you'll come to a great sea cavern, with surf rushing in and out and sometimes seals basking on the rocks. Leave it for another day. No one's going to be coming up that way."

Audley headed for the stair. "Then let's go back in case anyone's looking for us. We'll explore this when we have more time."

Malinda and Dog followed, holding hands.

A bloated moon in an indigo sky was painting silver ladders on the sea when Malinda said good night to Dian and bolted the door. She rolled back the rug so Dog would know the coast was clear. Dropping her nightgown, she wrapped herself in an ermine cloak of her mother's that she had found in a closet—it must have survived when things of much lesser value had been stolen simply because no one on the island knew where to sell such a luxury or dared be seen with it. She continued to admire the view, listening to the soughing of the wind and the untiring boom of breakers below the cliff. Dog could move astonishingly quietly—she did not hear him open or close the trap, although she felt the floor quiver under his weight. A quick glance confirmed that it was he, and he was wearing even less than she was. Though she was sore and bone weary from the long journey, she yet felt like a coiled spring that would lash out in frenzy the moment he touched her. Love denied was torment unendurable. It had been three whole nights! She could not understand how she had ever survived without Dog in her life.

"Come and see!" She gazed again at that impossible moon. She imagined him coming to stand behind her and running his hands inside the cloak—

"No." The bed creaked as he climbed in. He pulled the quilt up to his chin.

"All right, don't." She went to join him, but there was so little Dog-free space left that she stretched out on top of him, body on body, and hauled the covers right over them both. She kissed the end of his nose. "Say those three words."

"I love you."

"Hmm. You need to practice putting passion in them. Never mind. You've told me, now show me. Begin soft as the spider spinning and work up to paroxysms of earthquake devastation."

He crushed her in his best bear hug, kissed her, stroked, kneaded. . . . She had just realized that he was faking when he tried to break free. She could not have restrained him had he used his true strength, of course, but he let her force him back down.

"Let me go. I'm no good tonight."

"I won't abandon a man who loves me."

"I'm not a man tonight. You know." In the moonlight his ugly face was distorted with shame.

"Poor darling! You've had three days on a horse, that's all." She had no idea whether that was relevant, but it sounded plausible. "Or is it the surf? I'd take you where we couldn't hear it if there were any such place on Ness Royal. Don't worry. We have all night. I'm happy like this."

"I'm not." Was he ever happy as other people were happy? Never laughing, never smiling. Now he just lay uncomplaining, neither speaking nor moving. She set to work, trying all the little wiles that she had learned to rouse him—Dian's technique with hair was normally one of the best—but tonight none of them worked. Eventually she stretched out on top of him again, resting her head on his chest, tracing fingers over the swells and hollows of his body, listening to the steady thump of his heart.

"I'll tell you a story."

"No. Let me go."

"Listen. Once there was a child who lived on an island much like this one. She was allowed to run free with her friends, exploring its hills and valleys, even its caves and secret places. She belonged to a most peculiar family, for although she had a mother of her own, she had no real father. She had been sired by a monster she was expected to remember but could not, a hateful despot. Her mother spent all her time in a cave, studying secret books, and was too busy ever to love the girl. Fortunately she had two lesser mothers and two substitute fathers, the parents of her best friends, who let her share them. One day she saw her mother fly away. She was wearing red, and when she flew from the top of the cliff, her gown flapped and fluttered like wings and her hat blew off, so that her hair streamed above her in a silver banner, but mostly it was the fluttering red wings that the girl remembered—fluttering all the way down until the woman vanished into the white surf below. And then, for a moment, the sea itself was red, like berry juice."

Dog grunted, and she laid a finger on his lips.

"Her two substitute fathers fell to fighting over who should have guarded her mother better, and they killed each other. The girl wept much harder for them than she had for her mother, so she knew she was wicked and unnatural.

"She was carted off to her monster father's lair, away from all her friends, to a hateful prison of a palace. Years later he gave her away to his worst enemy as the price of his shame—as a token that the enemy was a better fighter and could take whatever the father monster possessed, even his only daughter. The enemy laughed and spurned her as of no worth and sent her back. She had not been a prize at all, only bait in a trap, but she did not call out to warn her father, and the enemy slew him."

Again Dog drew breath to speak, and this time she kissed his lips to catch the words before they could emerge.

"Listen, it is not over! She had not mourned her mother, and she did not mourn her father, so she was doubly wicked. Just today she came and saw the place where her mother had jumped; she heard the voice of the surf that had eaten her mother; but she did not weep. She is a monster, that girl, and daughter of a monster. She does not deserve a real man to love her."

"Princess—"

"Silence!" She punched him, hard enough to hurt her knuckles on his barrel ribs. "You are not to comment on my story. It is mine. You may tell me a story instead. If you know of anyone so wicked that he should be punished by being made to love that terrible monster girl I told you of, then I will hear that story. If you do not, then you may not speak at all."

The wind wailed in the casement and chimney. Faint smoke writhed in the moonlight and she feared it was not going to work. Minutes crept by.

"Once upon a time there was a giant," Dog growled in her ear. "He was a smith. He could bend iron bars with his bare hands. He could lift his anvil off the ground, which no two other men could. He had a wife, very young, very beautiful, very dainty. He loved his wife so much that if any other man looked bad at her, he beat him almost to death with his fists. She gave him two sons. The second son killed her. He was too big and would not come out of her. She screamed for three days until she died, and then the barber was called to cut her open, because the murderer was still in there and still alive. Often the blacksmith would tell the murderer how he had killed his mother."

Malinda tried to speak and a horny hand closed over her mouth. With a huge lurch Dog rolled them both over so they were side by side.

"You don't want to hear more," he rasped. "It gets worse."

She nodded. "Mm!"

"You'll hate me and send me away."

"No."

"The murderer grew up big for his age, but his brother was bigger, and more beautiful, and more clever, and was a help to their father and had not killed their mother. One day, he and his friends went collecting birds' eggs on the cliff, like boys do, and the murderer followed them, like younger brothers do. The one place where the older boys dared not go was the cliff where the gannets nested, because gannets lay only one egg in a nest and defend it fiercely. Instead, the big boys challenged the murderer to climb up there to show he was big enough and brave enough to be their friend. So he did. It was very hard. His hands and knees and toes got cut and bloody, he slipped and scraped himself, and the gannets flew at him, screaming. But he got a gannet's egg and he brought it back down to the shelf where the other boys were and showed them his prize. Then his brother struck his hand so the egg flew up into the air and fell and broke.

"And they all laughed.

"So he jumped and pushed his brother, who was bigger but was taken by surprise and went over backward and fell, spinning and screaming all the way down into the rocks and the sea."

She was weeping now, dribbling tears on Dog's chest.

"Blubbering already? It gets worse."

"Go on." She had wanted to know, wanted him to trust her, but she had not expected anything half so terrible as this.

"The blacksmith went into red rage, because the murderer had killed both his wife and his best son. He called the murderer an *animal* and said he was not fit to live with people. He riveted an iron collar around his neck and chained him naked with the dogs and threw food on the ground for him. He beat him every night. He punched him in the face, knocking teeth out. He thrashed him and kicked him and jerked his chain until his throat swelled and he could hardly breathe. But one day the blacksmith had been drinking more than usual and passed out in the middle of the beating, so the animal was able to wrap the chain around his neck and choke him to death."

"Oh, spirits! Oh, Dog, Dog!" She tried to kiss him, to stroke him, to do anything to ease his pain, but he turned his face away.

And still the awful words spilled out. "The animal thought he would starve there, then, because he was still chained, or perhaps he would eat the blacksmith's body, and eat the dogs also and then starve, but before he got hungry enough to begin—about two days—a neighbor heard the dogs howling and came to see. He released the animal and found him clothes and told him to run away."

The wrecked voice fell silent. Only the surf and the wind . . .

"Oh, Dog, Dog . . . None of that was your fault, love!" She was almost choking. "Your father put the seed in your mother. If the baby was too big it was his fault, not yours. Your brother hit you first and what followed was an accident. Any father who would treat a son like that deserved what happened."

He knew all that, and had always known it, and it was not enough. She slid a hand down to confirm what she had just realized.

"It's back," she said. "You're a man again."

"An animal."

"A man. My man."

"You still want me?" he snarled. "After what I just told you?"

"Oh, love, more than ever!"

It was a memorable lovemaking. It was revelation, two people discovering things about love itself. On top of three days' riding it was a penance, but she would not have missed it for all the crown jewels of Skyrria.

"You not asleep *yet?*" he grumbled.

She started, because she had indeed been asleep or very close to it. Sometimes a Blade's immunity to sleep could very annoying. "No, dear. Go ahead. Do it again."

"Don't be stupid, woman."

"Just hold me, then." He had no choice, really. They were very cramped, sticky and sticking together. . . .

"You know conjury?"

Again she jerked awake. "Little, very little . . ."

"If conjurers can see the future, why can't they see the past?"

"Hmm?"

"They can talk to the dead, can't they?"

Mother, brother, father? She wanted to say, *Some claim to be able to summon the dead and make them speak—but only for a little while and never more than once. None say they bring dead back to life.* It was easier just to mumble a sort-of *Yes* sound. So sleepy . . .

His voice kept coming back and fading away. "So if they can talk to the dead, why can't they warn the dead? Seconds matter more than years do. One instant can change your whole life forever."

Hmm? "How . . . know which instant?"

"Sixthmoon 350 . . . worked it out . . . need to go back there, just minute or two . . . warn my da to keep away from my ma next month . . . just tell him no good will come of it. . . ."

No Dog would come of it, which didn't bear thinking on, but she was too much asleep to say so.

⌘═╬═⌘

28

Although time is my own dominant virtual and I have had the benefit of four years' Oakendown training, I am endlessly amazed at [Malinda's] innate mastery of that element. From the sureness of her steps in the ballroom to the unwearying patience of a hunter, her control never falters, and did not fail her even in that long, suspenseful summer of 369 . . .
SISTER MOMENT, CONFIDENTIAL REPORT TO MOTHER SUPERIOR

The next week was pure bliss. With Dog at her side Malinda explored her childhood haunts, greeting and being greeted by old friends, all very respectful now. The other Blades ran around like puppies, exploring caves and secret places, coming to understand that the inhabitants were her allies and a whole army would never find their ward in Ness Royal if she did not want to be found. She was happier than she had ever been. Dog still never laughed or smiled, but when she asked him he would say he loved her and was happy, too.

Even crabby Sir Thierry was quite cooperative. Sometime between the evening of her arrival and the following morning, which was the first time she met him sober, he had acquired an obvious terror of her Blades, especially Dog. What pressure might have been applied she preferred not to inquire, but it was not impossible that he had been required to count to forty-nine while being dangled by his ankle over a sea cliff. He did complain shrilly that he needed funds to reopen Kingstead, but she told him to apply to the Treasury and be patient. Although she had brought plenty of money with her, she was not about to subsidize Granville's government with gold Lord Roland had so kindly embezzled for her private use.

The reopening happened anyway. Rooms were cleaned and aired, bushes and trees pruned. Ness Royal unfolded like a dawn daisy, with fathers hastily teaching sons how to groom horses or wait on table, mothers showing daughters how the gentry's beds should be made— and perhaps also telling of other ways royal gold traveled during the good times. It was better not to ask too many questions.

Time was the enemy. "So brief!" Malinda whispered on her third or fourth night in that oversnug bed. "Granville will marry me off. We must net every butterfly of happiness."

"Scratch every fleabite of lust," Dog mumbled while chewing her left ear.

"Don't be horrid. Worse—how long can we trust that ring of yours? How can we get it conjured again?"

He munched her neck gently. "No need worry. Asked the Chancellor 'bout that before we left Greymere."

"You did what?" How public could a secret romance become?

"Durendal. Asked him. Said babies not good idea. Gave me bagful of them. A year's supply, he said, no matter how potent I was." Content in a Blade's certainty that no man could be potenter, Dog continued his explorations.

At the end of that first week, the Black Riders arrived and pitched tents in the remains of the Gatehouse. By then Audley had recruited a corps of sentries to give advance warning of any hostile move, but Marshal Souris seemed to have no such intentions. He sent a letter requesting an audience and accepted Audley's conditions without argument.

Malinda received him in state. The hall in Kingstead was cramped and dowdy and gloomy at the best of times, but she laid on the best show she could. A pretentiously gilded chair that had belonged to her mother was dusted off and set up at the far end from the door. Malinda herself stood in front of it, where dust-sparkled sunbeams slanting down through the highest windows would illuminate her. She was attended by Audley and Winter and half a dozen local girls dressed up as ladies-in-waiting; they stood in the shadows, where their attire would not seem too unconvincing. Dog and Abel guarded the door.

The Marshal arrived alone, as had been agreed, and was allowed to keep his sword. He clumped along the length of the hall with his helmet under his arm and his spurs jingling. He made the requisite three bows and was permitted to kiss Her Grace's fingers, all according to protocol. With his long nose and bristly mustache, the little man was still very much Mouse Rampant as he glowered at the two smirking Blades he had perhaps been ordered to kill on the road.

"The Council of Regency has instructed me to guard your person, my lady, and that means guarding your residence." Something in his manner suggested a steel-lined crypt might be a good, safe place in which to store princesses.

"I am honored to have a warrior of your reputation caring for me, Marshal. I cannot believe there is danger on the island that my Guard cannot handle, but we shall rely on you to keep the entrance secure."

His nose, she thought, twitched. His eyes certainly glittered. "On this side of the bridge you should be perfectly safe."

"Others may not be—although I do try to keep my Blades under control, of course."

"Of course, Your Grace."

"Should any matter require my presence back on the mainland, rest assured that I shall notify you well in advance, Marshal. I rely on you to keep unwanted intruders away."

He nodded and—almost—smiled. "Your Highness is most gracious."

They understood each other perfectly. Thus was a deal struck. Thus was a boundary drawn.

Three days later, Arabel arrived with Sister Moment and maids of honor Dove, Ruby, and Alys, plus about a dozen servants. The reunion of Lady Arabel and Widow de Fait was a memorable impact that should have been accompanied by peals of thunder. They had been close friends nine years ago and had a lot of catching up to do.

*　　*　　*

A man vaguely described as a distant cousin paid a brief visit to Sir Thierry, who was thereafter assumed to be a spy in the pay of the Dark Chamber. The inquisitors might be reporting to the Lord Protector or just gathering information for their own devious purposes, as they were wont to do.

The Blades had their own network. It was astonishing how swiftly news filtered north, how Kingstead so often knew things before the Gatehouse did. Cloth, nails, spices, wine . . . the list of goods the Nessians needed to acquire in Fishport was endless, so that never a day passed without some woman on a donkey or an ambling youth being sent to fetch something from the village. An elderly couple of quality had recently purchased a home there; the old gentleman still wore a cat's-eye sword.

The Duke and Duchess of Brinton lived about half a day's ride from Ness Royal, and early in Fifthmoon they came to visit. Although Malinda had always regarded him as a soporific old bore and her as a prude, she was immensely grateful for this show of support. Of course, he did have a couple of aging Blades whispering in his ears, but it was also true that prudes did not approve of bastards running countries.

"I expect the Parliamentary writ will be dropped soon," the Duke huffed. He was big, in the Ranulf fashion; his head resembled a well-weathered tombstone coated with whiskery patches of lichen. "You planning to take your seat, Cousin?"

The idea had never occurred to her. "The last time I checked, Uncle, I was a woman."

"You're the senior peer of the realm! Obviously you don't see women in the Commons." He chuckled ponderously at the thought. "But there have been some in the Lords. The Countess of Mornicade, now——"

"I don't think we need discuss *her*," his wife said sharply. She sat erect and unyielding; her face always looked starched.

"It might be interesting," Malinda said ambiguously. "The Council has ordered me to remain here. If I have the right to attend Parliament, then it probably does not have the right to keep me away." It might be an interesting challenge, and she would send word to Snake and Roland suggesting it.

"You will journey south with us," said the Duchess. "We'll call for you on the way."

"You are very kind."

The Brintons must have spread the word, because never a week went by after that without some local notables dropping in to pay their respects and check on her well-being. The upper layers of Chivian society did not like the way the Lord Protector was progressively replacing the aristocrats on the Council with his lowborn henchmen, although his shining armor still shone bright enough in commoners' eyes.

Repairs to the Gatehouse were completed. One of the apprentices employed bore a striking resemblance to Sir Abel, and this curious coincidence might help explain how Commander Audley came to own a duplicate set of all the keys.

Later in Fifthmoon came word the King's health continued to give concern, that negotiations for the Princess's marriage were advancing on several fronts (how many husbands did she need?), and that Snake's Court of Conjury had been disbanded, so the traitor enchanters had won the Monster War by default.

Sixthmoon brought summer heat but still no invitation to her own wedding—although she heard unofficially that King Radgar had offered astonishingly generous peace terms for a second chance at her. Even Granville had scorned that offer. Prince Courtney had been closely questioned by the Council and was now confined in the Bastion. Poor Courtney! All his life he had been a penniless parasite on the body politic, and when he finally received his due in titles and honors he had the misfortune to run into a human landslide like Granville. Was he just a dust bunny on the steps of the throne being swept aside, or were his problems intended as a warning to her?

Dian, who had now been a widow longer than a wife, was frequently seen in the company of Sir Winter. She claimed she had found a way to stop him biting his nails.

Malinda invited Sir Souris to dinner. Butcher he might be, but he was also amusing company. They talked of horses, harvest prospects, foreign campaigns, and other safe topics.

Seventhmoon brought bad news of Baelish raiding and several private Blades being attacked by mobs or found murdered in ditches. The Council had ordered the Royal Guard confined to Beaufort "for its own protection." It was universally agreed that Parliament, when it met, would suppress the Loyal and Ancient Order of the King's Blades completely.

A pompous Grandon merchant who was also Consul General for Dimencio came to pay his respects to the Princess, bringing an artist to sketch her. Dimencio, as he tactfully reminded Her Grace, who had never heard of it, was a minor principality in southeastern Eurania, known for its olive oil and smoked fish. His Highness the Prince had

recently been bereaved and was anxious to foster relations with Chivial, et cetera. His age? Oh, about fifty, the consul thought . . . Yes,
several children already . . .

"You may convey my deepest appreciation to His Highness,"
Malinda said, "for his interest and also convey my regrets. As heir
apparent I will neither marry nor leave Chivial without the express
permission of Parliament. Perhaps you would also be so good as to
make this decision known around the diplomatic community?"

This defense had been suggested by Durendal. It should, he had
written, knock the shoes off Granville's sneaky marriage plans.

By Eighthmoon the Baelish raiding had increased, there was unrest
in Wylderland again, and it was common knowledge that the government could not pay its bills. An election writ had been issued.

Just before dawn on the first day of Ninthmoon, Malinda was
awakened by knuckles beating on her bedroom door.

29

*Come, and if thou but canst be here by Dawn surely Nightfall will see
thee crowned Sovereign Lord; yet if thou canst not then flee now, for
by Sunset shalt thou be dubbed Traitor, felon, and all Men raised
against thee.*
DURENDAL TO RANULF, ON THE EVE OF THE BATTLE OF ARBOR

"**W**ho's there?" Dog was not, of course, because the bed was
too small for both of them. He frequently returned around dawn "to
see if there was anything she needed," but he had not done so yet.

"Dian and men. Emergency."

Malinda lurched out of bed, kicked the rug over the trapdoor,
clutched a robe around herself, and unbolted the door, all in pretty
much a single movement. In came Dian and Audley, supporting between them a slender, shabbily dressed youth. His head lolled as if he
were barely conscious, but he groaned when they laid him on the
bed. His clothes were nondescript, and it took Malinda a moment in
the dim light to notice the cat's-eye pommel on his sword and then

recognize the haggard and unshaven face of Sir Marlon, one of the Guard youngsters.

"Don't think he's wounded," Audley said, "just exhausted." Winter and Dog had arrived, Dog filling the doorway so Winter could not get past. The eastern sky was brightening over the sea. "I've never seen a horse worse used."

"Spirits!" Malinda said. "What in fire is going on?" But she knew. Of course she knew. Marlon was one of the best horsemen in the Guard. It made sense to send Marlon.

"Marlon!" Audley said, bending over the boy. "Her Highness is here. Malinda is here."

She pushed him aside and knelt. "Sir Marlon? What message did you bring me?" She remembered Lord Roland telling of her betrothal to Radgar and Dominic bringing a lethal message to her mother, here in Kingstead. Messages brought by Blades were never good news.

His eyes opened, but they wandered. "Princess?"

"I'm here. Tell me and then you can sleep—rest, I mean."

"Come," he mumbled. "Dominic . . . Roland . . ."

"The King, Marlon! What of the King?"

"King," Marlon muttered. "Kid's dying. Wants you. Gotta come." He shook himself and made an effort to focus. "Roland and Snake are in the Bastion."

Malinda convened a council in the solar soon after. Yesterday, she recalled, Dog had wakened her early and she had seen the last silver sliver of Eighthmoon above the sunrise. The spring tides were running.

The solar was a small room in the lower house and misnamed, although its windows might have seemed large when it was built, two hundred years ago. Trees and shrubs had buried it in greenery long since. It was private; she normally used it as a writing room, and it seemed as good a place as any to plan an escape, if that was what she must now do. *Amby dying! Wanting her!* To leap on a horse now might be suicidal. Could the summons be a trap? She would be defying the Council's warrant the moment she set foot on the mainland. Even if she found a way past Mouse Rampant, she could be arrested on the steps of Beaufort.

She had all four of her Guard here, plus Marlon and Dian and the diminutive Sister Moment, who looked acutely uncomfortable at being so close to so many Blades. The rest of Kingstead was still asleep.

Marlon was recovering already, although he made the room smell powerfully of horse. He had gulped down two flagons of ale and was now tearing at a meat bone like a ravenous dog. He had set out the

previous night with Oak and Fitzroy and ridden from Beaufort to
Ness Royal without a stop. All three had managed to escape through
the cordon around the palace, but he had outstripped the other two
on the road. Ominously, they had been the second team Dominic
had sent. Reynard, Fury, and Alandale had left the night before.
Where were they?

Despite Malinda's unwritten agreement with Souris that they
would each keep to their own, Audley held the bridge under constant
surveillance—a Blade by night and lesser men by day. The Riders
were known to keep watch on their side lest the prisoner try to
escape, but Abel insisted there had been no alarms before Marlon's
horse came staggering across the Bathtub. That might mean that Marshal Souris had not yet heard the news of the King's sickness, but
Granville must know of it and might be setting up ambushes even
now. Three days ago he had thrown Roland in the Bastion, with
Snake and several other Old Blades, as if laying the groundwork for
a coup.

Malinda had already discarded some of her wilder ideas. Marlon
was really Marlon—Sister Moment had been fetched out of bed to
testify that the only enchantment on him was the unmistakable taint
of an Ironhall binding.

"Give me your counsel?" Malinda said. "Dian?"

"Wait for Mother," Dian said quickly. Widow de Fait had been
summoned.

"Very well. Sister Moment?"

Moment was huddled in the corner of a divan like an errant child,
easily the smallest person present. Now she grinned and shook her
head, a move that always seemed certain to dislodge her high white
conical hat but never did. "I cannot advise you on politics, my lady,
only. . . . You have clung here like a barnacle all summer . . . do
you feel that the time is now ripe to leave?"

"Certainly I do."

"Then trust your instinct in this. May chance favor you."

"Sir Abel?"

Abel, too, grinned eagerly. "Spring tides! Let's sneak across at low
water and be gone before the Butcher even knows it."

And where would they obtain horses? "Sir Dog?"

"Marlon got in," Dog growled. "If we go now, we can get out
before they're properly awake; we can ride right past the turds and
be gone. Or fight our way through if we must."

Sweet he was, but not a great thinker. "Sir Winter?"

Winter was chewing his nails again, ignoring Dian's glares. "Sneak out, Your Highness. Forgive this, but we could make you look like a youth . . . cut your hair . . . put you on a wagon beside the driver and you'd slip out past the garrison without a second glance. They're sloppy sentries. Marlon got in."

Yes he had, and Winter ought to have seen the implications.

"Sir Audley?"

Audley looked ready to chew some fingers himself. Reluctantly he said, "Wait, Your Grace. Send a message to Brinton. If the Duke came and escorted—"

"No! My brother is dying and wants me. Delay is not an option. I just want to know how best to get past the Gatehouse alive, and with you all alive too, because I know you must come with me. Dian, I can't wait any longer for your mother." She headed over to the escritoire.

"Beg pardon, my lady," Audley said, "but why Mistress de Fait?"

"Everyone seemed to be spying on everyone else, so I thought I should fly a few birds of my own. You heard no disturbances in the night? How about the night before?" She found a piece of paper and uncapped the inkwell.

"We can't *hear* anything across the Bathtub," Audley said. "On a clear night with a moon we can see the sentries marching, that's about all." He looked to the others.

"Lights in the windows," Dog rumbled uneasily. "More than usual. Night before this one. Around midnight. Just some drunks having a party."

Or had it been Fury, Reynard, and Alandale being tortured? Dog was muscle. She was more annoyed at Winter and Audley, whom she expected to think. "You're all underestimating Marshal Souris, one of the most respected mercenary leaders in Eurania. What happened to Reynard and the others?" She paused a moment to write. "I don't think footpads or angry peasants got them. Granville may have done so, and whether he did or not, he's certainly had enough time to send orders. So Reynard and company probably tried to pass the Gatehouse and failed, in which case they're dead or chained up there. Tonight Marlon comes along half-dead of exhaustion and is let through?"

Audley barked, "Pig guts! They know?"

Other voices muttered.

"We must assume they know." She put into words what they had all been thinking: "I may be lawful queen of Chivial by now. Granville may have proclaimed himself king. Most probably he wants Souris to keep me bottled up here on Ness Royal until he's established."

"Or kill you!"

"Possibly." The most worrisome question had always been why the Lord Protector had assigned a man nicknamed the Little Butcher to guard his sister. On Ness Royal, murder had been an option many times in history and the final choice more than once.

The Blades all tried to speak at once. She dribbled wax on the paper and pressed her signet in it.

"I promised the Marshal I would not try to escape and I am a woman of my word. Sir Audley, I give you an hour at most. Souris is a mercenary. Go and buy him."

Squeak! "Go and *what?* I mean, Your High—"

She had never seen Audley lose his poise like that, but she was sending a boy to deal with a man who had been waging war since before the boy was born. She had no one else to send. She handed him the paper, on which she had written at the bottom, "Done by my hand at Ness Royal this First day of Ninthmoon, in the year 369 of the House of Ranulf," followed by her signature and seal. "Give him this. He'll be waiting for our bid. Go and top Granville. Hurry! I'll follow in half an hour."

"W-what do I offer, my lady?"

"Accept his price. If he won't name one, start at two hundred thousand crowns and an earldom and be prepared to go higher. I'll make him a duke and Earl Marshal of Chivial if he wants. *Buy him!*" she yelled. "Buy the Black Riders. This is a queen's ransom you're negotiating. You must make me more valuable to him alive than dead. He's to escort me to Beaufort and get me there by sunset tomorrow. Include any Blade prisoners in the terms. Now—"

The door swung wide to admit the ample form of Lady Arabel, gasping for breath. "Yes!" she puffed, waddling to the nearest stool. "You're right."

"Where's Mother?" Dian demanded.

"Can't come . . . baby got colic . . . but girls say they had . . . best night in months."

"Right!" Malinda barked. "Sir Audley, they're expecting you. Go! We shall follow directly."

As Audley ran through the doorway, Arabel wheezed out the rest of her report: "They were packing. Some actually said good-bye."

"What *girls?*" Sir Abel demanded uneasily.

"The ones who work the Gatehouse, of course," Malinda snapped. Dian's mother was privy to the locals' secrets and the many ways royal gold could trickle down to the natives. It was not only unmarried daughters—some husbands were not overfussy about how the family income was supplemented. Malinda's edgy temper betrayed her again. "Including, Sir Abel, at least *three* girls whom you have promised to marry. I thought Blades did not need to stoop to such deception."

Abel made choking noises.

"Go and get the horses ready. Dian, can you organize some food? We'll eat in the saddle." She had a couple of letters to write first.

"Yes, Sister?"

"Just wanted to say I'm coming with you," Moment said, with her wry little grin. "I wouldn't miss this little piece of history for an earldom and two hundred thousand crowns."

Waves rumbled through the canyon, white birds shrieking rode the damp wind overhead, hooves clattered on the stones. Malinda let her horse take its time plodding up the track toward the Gatehouse. There was no need to tire it so early, she told herself. Audley might still be negotiating. She should have told him to take along a boy who could bring back the news. The news might be Audley dead, of course. All these thoughts were just excuses to put off her arrival as long as possible. Had Mouse Rampant already received instructions from Granville? Mercenary soldiers were notoriously bribable, but suppose she had run into one who was not? She would find herself in a cell or even at the bottom of the sea; the two women and three Blades behind her would perish with her. There might be crossbows pointed at her and her companions already. Despite all her efforts to remain calm, the horse could smell her fear, for it kept flicking its ears.

No road could last forever. She turned her mount in through the arch and entered the yard—and gulped a great sigh of relief. Souris and Audley were waiting for her, both mounted and both smiling, although the Blade's smile was more believable than the mercenary's. Souris had his sword raised in salute, while behind him fifty or so armed men sat their mounts in two arrow-straight rows, easily as smart as she had ever seen the Household Yeomen. The Gatehouse itself had been transformed in the four months since she last seen it: new thatch, walls brilliant white, shutters bright, courtyard stripped of weeds. By the eight!—most welcome of all, the four men standing back against the wall were Reynard, Fury, Alandale, and Oak. Oak and Fury sported bandages and they all looked shaky, but they wore their swords, they were smiling. She hoped Fitzroy was still on his way, just *late* and not *the* late Sir Fitzroy.

Clad in shiny steel helmet and cuirass and mounted on a warhorse,

Souris seemed much less a Mouse Rampant, but he was smiling as he
sheathed his sword and rode forward with Audley.

"Good chance, Marshal," she said, reining in and offering a hand.

"And may all spirits favor Your Grace." Souris pulled up alongside
and tickled her fingers with his mustache. "It is indeed an honor to
serve Your Grace."

He told them all that.

"It is comforting to have a force of such repute at my back,
Marshal. May I ask what arrangement you reached with Commander Audley?"

The rodent features twisted into an even toothier smile. "I admire
the way Your Highness negotiates." He handed her a roll of paper.

Over her seal and signature it promised her "trusty and well-
beloved" knight, Sir Souris of Newtown, an earldom, three hundred
thousand crowns, and four baronetcies. She returned it with a nod of
consent to him and one of congratulation to Audley, who breathed a
deep sigh and lost some of his anxious look.

"Of course, a good general remembers his officers," she said. "If
the tales are true, you are worth every groat, Marshal. Now, the
sooner we can be on our way, the sooner I shall be in a position to
pay my debts."

He held his ground. "There are a couple of points to settle yet,
Your Grace. You understand that you may find it a great deal easier
to enter Beaufort than leave it? Also, it is not humanly possible for
you to reach there by sunset tomorrow. For one thing, there is no
moon just now."

"Blades can do it in that time. Suppose we rode on with no
breaks at all, except to change mounts? Could it be done then?"

The little man frowned. "Possibly."

"Then I shall determine our halts and you may add their duration
to the travel time. You should need no more rest than I do."

Souris's glance at Audley suggested they had already held this
conversation. "If the tales are true, Your Grace, I am not certain of
that. But you are talking of posting. My men own their own horses
and prize them highly. Even with each man leading a remount, we
cannot travel like the Blades."

She was annoyed that she had not foreseen that. "My quest is
urgent. Pick out a smaller escort to post and let the rest follow as best
they can."

Souris uttered a harsh guffaw, a surprising roar from one of his
size. "You should have been a man, my lady! It shall be done. These

lads are only a quarter of the Black Riders, though. The rest are billeted at Spurston. Will you require our full strength?"

His rapier stare conveyed both question and challenge, for by leaving Ness Royal and hiring personal troops, she was raising a banner of rebellion. Her promises on that scrap of paper were worthless at the moment, so Marshal Souris still held the option of reverting to his former loyalty and taking her into custody. Audley's innocent smile suggested he had not worked all that out even yet. He might shortly be very surprised to find four or five arrows imbedded in his chest. . . .

"You know the answer better than I do, Marshal," she said as icily as she could. "You are better acquainted with the Lord Protector. You say you can get me *into* Beaufort—will you need your full strength to get me out again?"

"That and then some, I should think, my lady."

With a mouth suddenly dry, she said, "Then pray have the Black Riders muster at Beaufort." She would be rebel and outlaw and very likely at Granville's mercy. "If my brother dies, I shall claim the throne. If he does not, I shall demand that Parliament set aside my father's will and name me his regent."

"As Your Grace commands," Souris said, apparently satisfied just to know that she understood the stakes. "Nothing can end before it begins, but the Black Riders would be honored if you would inspect them." He turned his horse to face the rows of statues. It was traditional to let such troops see their current employer. "Then we can be on our way directly."

"I must first thank those men for their efforts on my behalf," she said, pointing to the watching men of the Royal Guard. "After that I shall be happy to inspect my loyal and gallant force. I also have here a couple of letters I wish delivered."

The last troops she had inspected had been Baelish pirates. Would men prepared to die for the highest bidder be any more trustworthy?

30

Know when to set an anchor watch and when to ride the storm.
RADGAR ÆLEDING, *THE ART OF PIRACY*

The ensuing journey was certainly historic, as Sister Moment had been the first to suggest. It might even have been the stuff of legend, which was one of Dian's less scurrilous descriptions, but "a blur of pain" would have adequately described Malinda's recollections. She spent a few hours in a feather bed at Valglorious, but that was the only significant break she took. Dian and Moment gave up there and stayed behind when she left, as did three of her Black Rider escort. Another two disappeared somewhere en route.

It was not very long after noon when Souris called a halt to let the horses drink where the track forded a scummy stream. "We are here, Your Grace. You have outridden the Black Riders, and I thought no man could do that, let alone a woman."

Malinda blinked herself out of a stupor of exhaustion and looked over her companions—four Blades, Mouse Rampant, and only one of his men. They were all clad in the sort of anonymous, shabby leathers any traveler might wear on the king's highway; their faces were gray with dust and fatigue. Even Audley was not his usual glamorous self when his eyes were bloodshot holes in a mask of dirt. Horses snorted and jingled their harness, slurping and splashing.

The mercenary leader gestured to a cluster of tumbledown hovels on the far bank. "That is Beaufort. The palace is over there." He indicated a coronet of cypress trees and chimneys a mile or so beyond. The land was flat as spilt milk, golden with ripe grain, which the inhabitants were harvesting with scythes and sickles, carts and horses. She wondered if their backbreaking work made them any more weary at the end of the day than a princess felt after such a ride.

"Why are we stopping?"

"Tactics, my lady! From what we have heard, the palace is cordoned off by Household Yeomen and the Lord Protector's personal cavalry. You are not supposed to be here and neither am I. It will be wisest to keep our agreement out of sight for the time being."

She nodded stupidly, flogging a brain that still seemed to be cantering madly down a road, hours behind her, trying to catch up.

"Commander," Souris said, "I never appreciated you Blades before. My congratulations."

Audley managed a smile, although it seemed somewhat forced. "I don't think I did, either. And what a ward we have!"

The mercenary flashed a glance at Malinda. "Goes without saying. If you need to get word to me, Commander, send a man to the Beaufort smithy with the password 'Rainbow.' If I send to you, it will be from 'Thundershower.'"

"Argh!" Dog uttered a bestial roar and whipped out his broadsword like a rapier. "He is going to betray you!" Winter and Abel sent their mounts plunging forward to intercept him, and Malinda bellowed at him to behave himself. Reluctantly he obeyed orders and sheathed that enormous blade.

Nothing like a near murder to waken a girl up. "My apologies, Marshal. Sir Dog is motivated only by loyalty." Of course his instincts were probably accurate. It was more than likely that the mercenary had been instructed to bring his prisoner south and she had made his task easy by volunteering.

Marshal Souris smiled without taking offense. "Loyalty is a rare fault. You could use a few hundred more like him. Good chance, Your Grace." He touched his helmet in salute and rode off along the river path, followed by the one other Black Rider who had managed to escape disgrace.

A head-high stone wall enclosed the palace grounds. At the gates, the visitors were challenged by men in Granville's brown and gold livery, then waved through when Audley proclaimed the Princess. She reined in at the door and fell out of the saddle into Dog's arms. He carried her up the steps. Blades in King's livery came rushing from all directions like bluebottles, buzzing with joy that she had arrived, firing questions about the six who had defied the Lord Protector by leaving the grounds and riding north. The King lived, they clamored; he was failing, they admitted. He had been asking for her, no one else. The healers and enchanters would promise nothing. Dog carried her upstairs as he had carried her once to her deflowering.

The bed was enormous—it could have slept horses—and the wispy flaxen hair on the pillow was attached to a doll's head and body. Had he shrunk, or had her memory betrayed her? "Amby!" she said. "Oh, Amby, it's me! I'm here."

The eyes opened. Too-bright eyes, pink fever patches, a face so wasted it seemed almost transparent. So small a smile, so small a whisper . . .

"Lindy!"

She fell on the bed beside him and gathered him in her arms.

How long after that? One day or two? Day or night? She was never quite certain and it did not matter. That first night she lay back against heaped pillows on that great bed and barely moved from it. She almost never let go of Amby. He did not speak, except rarely to whisper her name, yet when the healers came to take him down to the octogram, he screamed in terror.

"There is some discomfort, Your Grace," they admitted, not meeting her eye.

"Discomfort or pain?"

They shuffled their feet . . . significant discomfort . . . necessary, of course, but at this stage . . . four times a day now . . .

"Can it lead to a cure or are you merely prolonging his suffering?"

Scuffle, mumble, fidget, mutter . . . It was illegal to imagine the King's death, but eventually they admitted that some things were inevitable. Without enchantment it would have happened months ago. With it, perhaps a week now . . . without it . . . Shrug.

No more enchantment, she decreed. The ensuing lack of argument showed that she had just made the decision nobody else had dared make. Thereupon Lady Cozen, His Majesty's sow-faced governess, stormed in and threw a carefully rehearsed tantrum. Malinda told her to go away and complain to the Lord Protector himself, which was exactly what the nasty old crone wanted to hear. Very soon after that, her carriage rumbled along the drive and disappeared to the south.

"You must try and eat, Amby." She coaxed soup into him, spoonful by reluctant spoonful.

Sometime in the night she felt sufficiently recovered to send for Sir Dominic and demand a report. She meant, "What happens when the boy dies?" but she did not need to put it in those words.

Of course Dominic must have already cross-examined Audley and learned how she had escaped Ness Royal. A couple of times he inadvertently addressed her as "Your Majesty."

"They have us cooped up," he said. "About two hundred of Lord

Granville's personal cavalry . . . more arriving . . . I worry that Marlon and the others were *allowed* to break through, my lady . . . that I have lured you into a trap. . . ."

"You did exactly right."

He drew a deep breath. "Thank you, Your Grace. There are no precedents. . . . We are down to one day's victuals and they keep us at that. . . . Lord Roland, Sir Snake, about a dozen others are in the Bastion . . . no news of how they are faring. . . ." Of course a prisoner in the Bastion might live like a lord with his own suite of rooms and servants, or be subjected to unimaginable torments in the foulest of dungeons, or anything in between. "I fear that their efforts on your behalf were the cause of their misfortune."

"I think it would have happened eventually anyway. Do you know any details of those efforts?"

"No, Your Majesty. I hoped you did."

They stared at each other woefully.

"And Prince Courtney?" So many distinguished prisoners! In all its bloody history had the Bastion ever held so many?

"The rumors are that he stands accused of murdering his mother, Your Grace, although as a prince he cannot be tried in an ordinary court. It is reported that Parliament will be asked to pass a bill of attainder against him or strip him of his titles, so that he may be convicted."

Malinda sighed. "Poor Courtney! I wonder if his peers will stand up for him? The Lords do not approve of the Lord Protector, you know. I wrote to the Dukes of Brinton and De Mayes before I left Ness Royal." But she had trusted Souris to have the letters delivered, so they might have turned into smoke. "It is only four days until Parliament assembles, so . . . No?"

"The writ dies if . . ." Dominic looked down at the child with horror in his eyes. "I mean, each new monarch must issue a new writ."

"Of course," she said. Amby's first parliament would never meet. There would be no rescue there.

Dian and Sister Moment arrived the following morning. That was nice. Malinda told them to leave while there was still time, but they refused. Thereafter Dian mothered her with hot food, bathwater, fresh clothes. Amby no longer knew she was there. He knew nothing and would not swallow. That was the end; without food or drink his hours must be few.

★   ★   ★

That night, as before, Malinda slept fully dressed on the bed. At times she would waken and listen to the rasping struggle while the doomed child fought for each next breath with all the stubborn courage of his royal forebears. Suddenly she was wondering how long Sir Audley had been standing there, holding papers, his bony face just a white blur in the candle-lit gloom.

"Message from Thundershower, Your Grace—Marshal Souris, I mean. He says that Constable Valdor is a key player in the game—his words, my lady—and is available on the same terms and conditions. He asks that you sign and return this . . . Your Grace."

She took the parchment and peered at it. Another peerage, another three hundred thousand crowns. That must be several months' income for the crown of Chivial. "Who is this man?"

"Oh, beg pardon, my lady. He was recently appointed commander of the Household Yeomen. I understand that he is a lifelong friend of Lord Granville. He has indicated to Marshal Souris that he will support Your Grace if suitably rewarded."

"Has he really? Marshal Souris is a mercenary, always available to serve the highest bidder, whereas I always understood the Constable of the Household Yeomen to be a sworn officer of the crown."

Audley sighed. "Not all men are bound like Blades, Your Grace."

"No, they are not." She realized that she no longer believed in Marshal Souris. He was another long-time friend of Granville's, and no doubt all three of them were convulsed with mirth over her efforts to subvert their little coterie. To bribe the commander of the Yeomen was treason of the first water.

She signed and gave the paper to Audley, along with her signet to seal it.

"Malinda!" said the whisper. "Lady Malinda. Your Grace?"

From the feel of the night it was close to dawn. Reluctantly she turned her head and saw the small figure standing there, white robe glimmering in the near darkness. Only her tall hat made her adult size and her face was almost as pale.

"Moment? Sister?"

"Malinda, they are gathering! I can feel them."

Understanding took an instant, then Malinda sat up with a quick shudder, as if she had wakened to find her bed full of ants. Moment was speaking of elementals, and in this instance she meant the spirits of death. Amby's breathing stopped, started . . . stopped again, every gasp like the cry of a suffering cat.

"Fetch the healers!"

"They cannot . . . Yes, Your Grace." Moment faded off into the darkness.

He lasted until daylight, never moving. His breathing became more and more erratic. One silver-bearded healer remained, frequently bending to lay an ear on the tiny form, as if the entire room could not hear that struggle. Finally even he hastened out, muttering about fetching a philter.

"Amby?" Malinda said. "Amby! *Amby!*"

A few rattling breaths . . . pause . . . a few more . . . longer, agonizing pause . . . gasp . . . more breaths . . .

"Amby!"

No answer. Wheeze, rattle . . . The room was filling up. Four green liveries close by the bed—Audley, Winter, Abel . . . *Oh, dear Dog, have I spoken a word to you since we left Ness Royal?* Beyond the four greens, the pale blues. Dozens of them tiptoeing in. The word was out; the time had come. Surely that was Oak, one arm in a sling? And Marlon? How long had she been here? Only Blades now, no one else.

She and Amby and a room full of Blades. *All* the Blades? Were they now so few?

Wheeze. Rattle. Silence. Rattle . . . Silence . . .

Dog held out a hand to help her off the bed, then put his great arms around her as they stood and watched the pathetic little body take its last few breaths. Everyone else sank down on their knees.

Staring eyes . . . *Rattle* . . . Silence . . .

Still silence.

Unbearable silence.

She reached down to close the gaping eyelids and they stayed shut.

Dog tilted his head back and bayed at the roof in a horribly discordant yell: *"Long live the Queen!"* The room exploded. With screams and tears and howls, all the Blades echoed him. They chanted it, yelled it, screamed it. *"Long live the Queen! Long live Queen Malinda!"* No one drew a sword, no one rampaged, and soon they were on their feet, hugging one another and weeping and endlessly repeating, *"Long live the Queen!"* They had exorcized their curse. They celebrated.

Malinda wept in silence on Dog's shoulder for a little space, while all around her the chant continued, echoed, repeated, spread out in circles, raced away on horseback to Grandon and all the realms of Eurania. . . .

The King is dead! Long live the—

Long live who?

31

Count your friends first.
LORD GRANVILLE

"You may continue to wear that," she said. "You have our complete confidence."

Sir Dominic was already kneeling to the new monarch with the commander's baldric draped across his hands. "Your Majesty, it is traditional. . . ." He somehow contrived to look as if he was squirming, which was a tricky feat for a man on his knees. "Yours was not the hand . . . I mean, I will gladly defend Your Grace with my life, but . . . when the king dies, my lady, the prince's . . . I mean the heir's . . . ."

Spirits! Her brother lying there with his last tear not dry, probably an army outside waiting to arrest her—and necessarily massacre all of these men in the process—but they had to have this sort of pointless argument? Audley like a schoolboy, trying very hard not to show his feelings or look in any direction at all . . .

"How many years have you served in the Guard, Sir Dominic?"

"Near eleven, Your Majesty."

"And in normal times Sir Audley would still be a candidate at Ironhall, possibly not even yet a senior."

Still he argued. "It is traditional. . . . The Changing of the Guard, Your Majesty."

"Fire and death!" she snapped, but all the dismayed faces reminded her that these men might well have to throw down their lives for her within this very hour. If they needed their precious traditions to comfort them, then she owed them that much.

"All right. Sir Audley, I appoint you Commander of the Royal Guard, but only on condition that Sir Dominic is your deputy, and that you keep him informed and heed his advice." As the worried-looking appointee knelt to kiss her hand, she added, "Sir Dominic, I charge you that if you disagree with anything Sir Audley decides or does, then you inform me without delay. Is that clear?"

Clear or not, it was enough to fill the room with grins and even some laughter as the two men rose and Dominic draped the silver ribbon across Audley's chest, being first to hail him with the revered title, Leader. "Don't forget his ball and hoop," said a gruff voice. "Must be nearly time for his nap," said another.

"Quiet! Stop that foolery! I shall be reviewing the Guard's pay, which I believe is inadequate. I also want you all in new liveries. Green, not blue, and more fashionable. Submit sketches for my approval by next week, Commander."

Still pink from the ribbing, Audley said, "Certainly, Your Majesty."

Dian and Moment were waiting for the new sovereign's attention. They curtseyed when she noticed them. She gave them each a hug, took a second look at their faces, especially Dian's, which she had known for so long, and said, "All right, tell me the worst."

"Everyone's gone! We're besieged."

"I am hardly surprised."

Blades hurriedly cleared a path as she headed over to the windows, which offered a view of lawns, flower beds, and the main drive running arrow-straight to the boundary wall. Along it scurried a few departing servants and other civilians like frightened ants, with the last of them being the white-bearded healer who had so recently left the room. The men-at-arms on the gates were letting them through; a troop of lancers was riding in and forming up on the grass. In the fields beyond, a tent city had appeared, large enough to house several thousand men.

"Has the standard been lowered to half-mast?"

Audley said. "Er, no. I'll send a man directly—"

"No! Leave it." Let the watchers wonder a little longer. "What word from Marshal Souris?"

"None, Your Grace. No one has been allowed in since noon yesterday. We are out of food."

She had already identified the liveries of Granville's own troops and the Household Yeomen, but could see no sign of the Black Riders. Was Mouse Rampant coyly keeping his change of loyalty a secret until the right time or had there been no change of loyalty? She could not rid her mind of that image of Souris amusing his longtime comrade in arms Lord Granville with the hilarious story of her clumsy efforts to suborn him and Constable Valdor.

"Lord Roland and the others are still in the Bastion?"

"The last we heard they were, my lady. There have been more arrests."

While she had been helping one brother die, the other had been preparing his coup. She had tried to bribe with paper promises, but Granville could empty the treasury to buy support and lock up those who would not be bought. No doubt he was now standing by in the capital, still tightening his grip on the government while avoiding being implicated in whatever disaster was planned for Beaufort. When word of Amby's death arrived he would have himself proclaimed king and only a civil war could oust him.

"We have a problem," she said. She had no training or experience to help her and only these forty or so Blades to back her. Granville, in contrast, had been living by his wits and his sword since before she was born, and he had had months in which to bend the government to his bidding. "Just how do you propose to get me out of here, *Leader?*"

Audley drew a deep breath. "Sir Dominic and I discussed the matter with some others, Your Majesty, and the consensus was that word should be sent to the officers in charge of those forces, summoning them to come and swear allegiance to Your Majesty."

"And if they arrest your herald?"

The boy commander shivered. "Kill him? I'll have to send a Blade and Blades can't be arrested. I think then we wait until dark, my lady, and hope to smuggle . . ." He withered under her glare.

"You think they will wait that long before they burn the place down around our ears? Queen Malinda the Brief?"

The room had fallen very still. Audley looked around despairingly and found no help. There was more to being Leader than just fighting off admiring girls. Nor was it true that bound Blades did not know fear. The room stank of it. They would do their duty, but they expected to die.

"Never!" said the Queen. "Bring three horses to the front door. I shall go out and— *Silence!* How *dare* you? Did you expect my father to explain his orders?" She glared around until the hubbub collapsed into sheepish quiet, but then she did explain, knowing that what she was asking was almost impossible for them. "A competent soldier like the Lord Protector will use archers against Blades. To usurp the throne, he must dispose of the rightful sovereign, so if you offer yourselves as a target, I shall die in the crossfire. His simplest solution is to massacre everyone presently in this house and announce to the nation that he had to suppress another Blade rampage. Sir Dominic, only you and one other will accompany me. Commander, it is your task to make sure everyone else stays out of sight until I send for you. If I am removed by force, you are to keep the Blades alive even if you must surrender your swords and swear allegiance to the usurper. That way, one day you may be able to rescue me."

She was answered by sullen silence. There was not a chance in a million that their bindings would let them obey those orders.

It was a fine late summer morning, with blue skies and a few first golden leaves speckling the grass. A good day to die. Sheep placidly grazed the lawns, caring not what name followed Ambrose V in the chronicles of Chivial. Hooves crunched gravel as she rode along the driveway with Dominic and Winter, whom she had chosen for his wits and because she knew he would obey her. They had given her a young chestnut gelding, handsome enough but skittish, as if he lacked exercise, and since she was mounted sidesaddle, she had to direct too much of her attention to controlling him when she should be studying the ominous situation ahead. Granville's lancers were lined up to the left of the gate, archers of the Household Yeomen on the right. A small conclave of officers and civilians had gathered between them; as she drew closer, three men separated from it and rode forward a little way.

"You two wait here," she said, and was astonished when Winter and Dominic both halted. She rode a dozen or so paces, then reined in.

Accepting this compromise, the three advanced to parley. They were all in battle gear, their faces shadowed under the wide brims of their helmets, but even at a distance she could identify Souris on the left by his lack of stature and Valdor on the right by the scarlet Yeoman surcoat over his steel corselet. Surprisingly, the one in the center was Granville himself. They all halted and there was an expectant pause.

If that was a test of nerve, she failed it. "The King is dead," she said. Her gelding tossed his head and tried to go sideways.

"But the King lives," said her brother.

"No, the Queen lives. We await your oath of allegiance."

Granville laughed and doffed his helmet to wipe his forehead with a sleeve. Even half armor must be unpleasantly warm on such a day. "You may grow very old doing that, Sister. On the other hand, if you do not give us yours very swiftly, you will find your liberty cruelly curtailed."

"By what right do you claim my loyalty and that of these men? My father's will names me my brother's heir."

"Only if you are not married to a foreigner." Smirking, he replaced his helmet at a rakish angle. "You were married in state to Radgar of Baelmark."

The accusation took her breath away, so that she could only gape at him in despair. It was an absurd charge, but it might be enough pretext to satisfy all those who did not want a female ruler, and she knew they would be many. Chivial's previous experiments with queens regnant had not been its happiest times. Again the gelding fussed and thumped feet on the gravel.

She found her voice. "It would take a very crooked legal mind to see that marriage as valid, my lord. Even if it were, Prince Courtney takes precedence over you."

"Baron Leandre has been stripped of his improperly acquired titles and is currently under indictment for the murder of his mother, dear Aunt Agnes." Granville sighed, obviously enjoying himself. His companions sat like statues.

"That is absolute nonsense. Supposing it were true, there is still no precedent for a bastard inheriting a title in Chivial, *Master Fitzambrose*."

He laughed. "Insults will not help you, *Mistress Æleding*."

"Are you prepared to give me your oath of allegiance as your sovereign queen?"

"I thought we had already settled that?" His yellow eyes slitted warily, but he was very, very confident. He must have good reason to feel like that. She was sure she must look very frightened in comparison, and no doubt all three of them were enjoying watching her flounder. This was where the dice must stop rolling.

"Marshal Souris?"

"Your Grace?"

Your Grace not *Your Majesty*. Granville turned his head to study the mercenary, but that ambiguous form of address did not commit the little man to either side.

"Where are the Black Riders?" she asked. Her mouth was dry, her stomach knotted with tension. Sensing her fear or anger—it was probably both—the gelding fidgeted and fussed under her.

"They are here, my lady," the Marshal said blandly. "Do you wish me to summon them?"

"If you would be so kind."

Souris raised the bugle dangling at his belt and blew three notes. The chestnut gelding was either not battle-trained or out of practice, for he shied and whinnied; he bucked halfheartedly and tried to run in circles. Malinda brought him under control while making mental promises to have his hide for shoes. He seemed to be doing everything possible to embarrass her. By the time she had regained her position—

and of course none of the other horses had been allowed to move a hoof—a column of mounted bowmen in black war gear had come trotting around the side of the main palace building. There were about thirty of them, fewer than she had seen at Ness Royal. They formed up in a line across the driveway behind her, so that now she was cut off from the Blades in the palace and effectively enclosed by three separate forces: Black Riders, Yeomen, and Granville's cavalry. She had just sprung a clever trap on herself.

She could not tell if Granville was surprised to see them, nor if Souris was prepared to betray his former superior. They might just be having fun with her. And where were the rest of the Riders? Was the Marshal trying to show her that he had tried and failed, that there had not been time to muster his entire company here?

"Take Lord Granville into custody and have him held in the Bastion on a charge of high treason."

Souris looked up at Granville, who shrugged his corselet up and down dramatically.

"With all due respect, Your Grace," the mercenary said, "I believe that task should properly be assigned to the Household Yeomen."

Granville turned his head to look inquiringly at Constable Valdor on his left. Malinda had never met him before, for he was another of the Rector's Wylderland veterans. She did not like what she could see of his features under the wide-brimmed helmet—hard, humorless, and cruel. He was scowling.

"Constable?"

"Your Grace?" His voice was the deepest she had ever heard.

"Take Lord Granville into custody and have him held in the Bastion on a charge of high treason."

"With all due respect, Your Grace," he rumbled, "I foresee a problem with the second half of your command, in that the newly appointed governor of the Bastion is Neville Fitzambrose, the accused's son."

Yes, they were all laughing at her!

"I don't believe you've ever met Neville," Granville said cheerfully, "but I am sure the lad would rather be his aunt's host than her guest."

"The Black Riders will be honored to escort Your Grace wherever she wishes to go," Souris remarked blandly.

She was clenching her teeth so hard they hurt, but those ambiguous words fanned a tiny flame of hope. After all, treachery was a dangerous business. Nobody here dared trust anyone else, which meant that Souris and Valdor, fellow conspirators though they might be, could not even trust each other. Neither dared go first.

"We shall ride to our palace of Greymere and there bestow on you the earldom we promised," she said firmly. "And you also, Constable, if you will now obey the first half of my—"

As Granville reached for his sword, the two horses flanking him crashed inward simultaneously, spoiling his draw and pinning him in place. Souris grabbed Granville's sword arm and hauled, pulling him over and off balance, vulnerable to a blow from Valdor, who struck up under the back piece of his cuirass with a dagger, probing for a kidney. Undoubtedly both armor and poniard were enchanted, because the blow was accompanied by a clap of thunder and a bright blue flash. The chestnut gelding tried to fly over the treetops and sent Malinda hurtling through the air.

32

Number 280: Sir Abel, who, on 5th Ninthmoon 369 . . .
IRONHALL, *THE LITANY OF HEROES*

She was fortunate to land on grass and not gravel, but the impact wrenched her shoulder and knocked all the wind out of her. She registered a chaos of bugle calls, screams of men and horses, the hard *thwack!* of bowstrings, and a rolling thunder of hooves as the Black Riders went past. Then screams. By the time she caught her breath and lifted her head, the Battle of Beaufort was already won. Winter and Dominic stood over her with drawn swords while the rest of the Blades came sprinting from the palace. Granville's men had either fled or thrown down their arms. Household Yeomen and at least a hundred Black Riders held the field—and might have been tempted to hold Queen Malinda also and use her to political advantage, had the Blades' arrival not closed off that option.

She let Winter help her to her feet. "Thank you," she whispered. "That was very nicely—*Ouch!* That shoulder's a little tender—nicely done. Where is Lord Granville?"

"Dead," Winter growled. "Down there." He pointed with *Fear* and then, as an afterthought, sheathed it.

The news needed time to sink in. She felt no regret for Brother Fitzambrose, she decided, but she did feel some for herself. She had caused men to die, so she had shed her innocence in the game of dynasts; a woman who took lives was no longer sacrosanct. But one monarchial candidate less meant fewer loyalty problems. Treason was defined by the winners.

The Blades tried to make the Marshal surrender his sword before he could approach the Queen to swear the oath of allegiance, but she overruled them. Indeed, she borrowed it to tap him on the shoulder and dub him Earl Souris of Beaufort right then and there. Constable Valdor arrived and him she named Earl Valdor of Thencaster—it being understood that a traitor's lands and titles were forfeit to the crown. With those two firmly nailed to her mast, she could start to worry about any other forces that might still be marching around.

"Lord Souris, what can you do with the prisoners? I shall gladly pardon all who will swear allegiance, but I don't want penniless vagrants terrorizing the countryside."

The little man's smile implied that he found this murderous warrior queen amusing. "You are both merciful and gracious, Your Majesty. I shall enlist them to my own troop for the time being, reserving the right to petition Your Majesty's treasury for reimbursement. I have your permission to threaten to hang any who refuse? I doubt many diehards will carry their loyalty so far."

"Permission granted," she said, wondering when she had become so bloodthirsty. It must be hereditary. "What of the rest of Granville's men?"

"He sent many back to Wylderland to keep order there. The others are spread about in various castles and royal strongholds, none close enough to be an immediate threat, Your Grace—except for the Bastion, of course."

"I had not forgotten it." That grim keep dominated Grandon and hence the country. In times of trouble, whoever held the Bastion usually wrote the history books. "Lord Valdor?"

The Constable rubbed his stubbly chin for a moment before he rumbled, "I think a little subterfuge should work, Your Grace. I know today's passwords, and if I take the precaution of dressing a few of my men in the traitor's livery, we should be able to gain admittance and open the gates. Do you want something fatal to happen to young Fitzambrose?"

"No. Lock him up for now. Anyone else who swears allegiance

is automatically pardoned. Pray ride with all haste." She glanced around at the Guard. The Bastion was too vital to be left in the hands of Constable Valdor, who had just demonstrated so fickle a loyalty. "Sir Piers, go with them. I hereby appoint you provisional Governor of the Bastion. Send word back to me as soon as you have secured the keep. Release Prince Courtney and Lord Roland, and any other captives they vouch for."

Piers looked stricken at the thought of abandoning his ward in such dangerous times, but he knelt to kiss her fingers. She was annoyed to detect some hastily hidden grins among the Blades. Admittedly the certain death of a few minutes ago had just become a resounding victory, but had they thought a woman could not make decisions or give orders? "Marshal, we shall follow the Yeomen to Greymere. Will there be trouble in the streets?"

"The Constable can judge that better than I," Souris said warily.

"An escort of Household Yeomen," Valdor rumbled, "would be less likely to attract unfavorable attention. Blades are very unpopular now, still being associated with the Wetshore affair. If I may presume so far, Your Majesty, Lord Granville was well liked by the masses, and many persons of quality were just waiting to see who came out on top—begging Your Grace's pardon. The Traitor had not yet sent word to Grandon to have himself proclaimed king, but the sooner Your Majesty can arrive in his stead, the better."

She could feel the Blades' angry bristling all around her. Did they think she would fall into so obvious a trap?

"I will keep the Guard under control," she said firmly. "Lord Souris, I will not enter my capital with an unnecessary display of force, but I want the Black Riders within call. Where can you bivouac?"

"Great Common has served in the past, Your Majesty."

"Then make camp there. The password for today is *Fine morning* and the rejoinder *Fair prospect.* You have your orders, my lords." She nodded to acknowledge their salutes and turned to Audley. "Commander, round up the palace staff here and put them to work. Lower the flag to half-mast; have the King's body prepared for transportation back to his capital tomorrow with full royal honors. I want the Traitor's head struck off and mounted over the Bastion gate. Send two of your best riders posthaste to the College of Heralds in Grandon to bid Griffon King of Arms have me proclaimed as rightful queen of Chivial, and tell Eagle King of Arms to assemble all available members of my father's Great Council and the recent Council of Regency to swear allegiance. Here you may gather up the weapons, obtain a body count, see the traitors' corpses are burned without ceremony. Provide horses for my lady companions and find me a better beast than that lump of dog meat—with a proper saddle; none of that sidesaddle rubbish. Be ready to ride for Grandon in fifteen minutes."

"That lot ought to keep the kid out of mischief," somebody murmured.

Audley's eyes had widened in panic. It was totally unfair, of course. Almost nothing on that list was normal Blade business, but she was a queen without a government. She had to give orders to *somebody*. He parried with Ironhall brilliance.

"See that Her Majesty's commands are carried out, Sir Dominic. I shall accompany Her Grace indoors."

That snapped the tension. The onlookers burst into yells of mirth and approval. Even Dominic laughed. Grinning like a schoolboy, Audley offered his arm to the Queen. "May I venture to advise a few minutes' rest, my lady? And something to eat before we ride."

Realizing what was probably obvious to others—that she was shaky and needed to sit down for a while—she nodded and accepted his arm. As they moved away, someone shouted a cue behind her, and the Royal Guard burst into cheers. She ignored them and kept walking.

"They all expected to die," Audley said excitedly. "You saved us. They'll run to Grandon on their knees for you now if you want."

Not trusting herself to speak, she just nodded. She was queen! That was going to take a lot of swallowing. She could do anything she liked now and fear no one. *Really?* asked a cynical little voice inside. *Announce that you're going to marry a lowborn swordsman named Dog and see what happens to your dominion.* Well, almost anything. And she had done it herself. The honor was hers. Had she delayed even a day at Ness Royal there might not have been time to bring up the Black Riders. She wanted to hug someone, to join hands and dance.

"Well you helped, Commander. Your skill at bribery should win you mention in the Litany."

"I do believe you overlooked one thing, though, Your Grace."

"And what's that?"

"When you were handing out all those grand titles? I think you should have given one to the commander of your Guard. I was hoping to be made Baron Starkmoor."

She tried to groan and laughed instead. "That one was *definitely* a capital offense. I provided the titles, so you'll have to find all that money you—"

They stopped dead, having almost walked into Dog, who stood foursquare in their path with his battered face screwed up in grief, tears pouring from his colorless eyes. In his arms he held a body clad in green.

"No!" she cried. "How?"

Audley peered closely at the corpse's jerkin. "Arrow?"

Dog just nodded, unable to speak.

"That tiny hole?" she said, disbelieving. There was no blood at all. A good seamstress could stitch that up in no time and the jerkin would be as good as new.

"It would go—" Audley's voice cracked. "Go straight through him. He was wrong. He thought *Abel* was a lucky name, but he's put it in the Litany at last."

The toll for the Battle of Beaufort was seventeen dead, twenty-four wounded, she was informed. She regretted them all, but Abel hurt more than all the rest together. Abel was a personal grief. The shaft had probably come from the Yeomen, aimed at the charging Black Riders while the Blades were running to Malinda's side. No one had seen it strike. Only Dog had realized he was missing and gone back to look for him among the flowers and low hedges. It was customary, she was informed, for a fallen Blade to be honored on the field, so she allowed them to hold their rites and return Abel's body to the elements. They did not insist on waiting until the pyre burned out, but it was past noon when the Queen and her train left Beaufort, cantering along the Grandon road.

One more name in the Litany, and yet the funereal woe soon dispersed. Soon the Blades were again fizzing with excitement and relief—joking, singing, yelling, making more noise than an army of drunks on Long Night. Every few minutes some crazy youngster would run his horse in circles. Months of house arrest had ended; the death sentence had been lifted. Abel had been honored as tradition required, and they seemed to have totally forgotten the little king for whom they would have died just a few hours ago.

Dog, Malinda noted, had been positioned well back in the column, and although she longed for his company, she knew she must avoid the taint of scandal. Audley rode at her side, as was his right. Dominic was staying close.

She was beset by the problems ahead. Lord Roland was the only possible choice for chancellor. He would know who had refused, as he had, to support the Lord Protector's coup, who had supported it, who had managed to avoid a decision. He would also know who else was competent and trustworthy, for she had an entire Privy Council to appoint, indeed a whole government, and her knowledge of the men available was limited to social gossip. Why only men? Because there were no women with experience. The previous Grand Inquisitor had been a woman; there had been a female Grand Wizard a couple of reigns back; but those had been exceptional. The Council would summon Mother Superior when it required her advice, but the old lady spent most of her time at Oakendown now, rarely coming to court.

The procession thundered through a village without slowing down. The inhabitants had been forewarned and lined up on both sides of the street to cheer. In moments Her Majesty was gone past, and the year's excitement was over.

"Who ordered that demonstration, Commander?"

"I did, Your Grace. Did I do wrong?"

"Did Sir Dominic approve?"

"He said he saw no harm in it. Said he was waiting to see if I would suggest it, my lady."

"Then you are doing well."

"Thank you, Your Grace."

"You have men out in front?"

"Yes, my lady."

"I wish to be advised at once if you intercept word from Sir Piers at the Bastion."

"Certainly. May I presume to ask a question—regarding your security, Your Grace, of course."

"That is your privilege, Commander."

"I—we—are concerned by your destination. Greymere is not readily defensible, and until we can be sure that—"

"I have no intention of going to Greymere today. If the Bastion has been secured, we go there. Otherwise we shall head for the Black Riders' camp on Great Common."

Audley nodded, then braced himself. Staring straight ahead at the rutted trail, he said, "If I may presume so far, Your Majesty, should I not have been entrusted with that information sooner?"

Of course, but she had only just worked it out herself. "You have been entrusted with it now, Commander."

"Yes, my lady."

Huge and foreboding, Grandon Bastion dominated the skyline of the city always, but it seemed especially menacing at dusk, when its black walls showed stark against the silver of the river and the last rays of evening painted blood on the roofs of its towers. So it was when Queen Malinda rode up to the gates with her escort of Blades, and the joyous tolling of the city's bells to welcome her could as easily have been a call to Amby's mourning. Constable Valdor and Sir Piers were there to welcome her, proudly offering ceremonial keys on a scarlet cushion. Screaming fanfares sent birds wheeling upward, and an honor guard of Yeomen men-at-arms lining the drawbridge pounded the butts of their pikes on the timbers in salute. Her half brother's head stared sightlessly over the scene; in the games of the mighty, one miscalculation was too many.

Already the wheels of government were starting to turn for her. She had been proclaimed throughout the capital without incident, heralds on lathered horses were bearing the word to the far corners of the realm, and Neville Fitzambrose was chained to a dungeon wall. No resistance had been reported, although that might change when outlying contingents of Granville's troops heard the news. The monarch's progress through the streets had provoked precious little cheering but no riots, and at her back, on the far side of the square, onlookers stood in respectful silence. Hundreds of curious faces peered down from windows. It seemed the citizens were reserving judgment. So the baby King was dead, the gallant Lord Granville had been put to death, and the girl claimed the throne of Ranulf? Good for the big lass! As long as she was better than Adela or Estrith . . .

Every century or so, the spirits of chance dealt out a queen regnant. Adela and Estrith, Estrith and Adela . . . Malinda had been thinking about them all day. Now, as her horse's shoes rang on the cobbles of the tunnel gateway, she thought especially of Estrith, who had been brought here to the Bastion a hundred years ago to be beheaded. The stupid woman had begun the beheading by shortening her husband, had then married a brigand baron, antagonized the great lords, tried to levy taxes without Parliament's approval, started wars, and generally made every mistake imaginable. In six short years she had earned an unquestioned reputation as the most inept ruler Chivial had ever known. Indeed, the only good thing she had done was to die of a fever two days before the date scheduled for her execution, and no one had ever much believed in that fever.

Adela, more than a century earlier still, had probably been more victim than villain. "Stay close, please," Malinda had told Moment during the ride from Beaufort. "Don't forget what happened to Adela." The little Sister had twinkled her gamin grin and said she had not forgotten Queen Adela.

But what *had* happened to Adela was something of a mystery and evermore would be. Although her reign of thirty-six years had been one of the longest, she had ruled for only the first couple of months of it before being hustled off to captivity on Ness Royal. Even her Blades had agreed by then that she was mad, yet the evidence suggested she had been sane enough at her accession. Most historians believed she had been poisoned by some foul conjuration—there had been no White Sisters in those days—and her husband was the favored suspect, since he had then claimed the crown matrimonial and reigned for twenty years in her stead.

Third time lucky?

The horses clattered through the echoing tunnel, past gates and under portcullises, into the wide expanse of the bailey, filled with tents and many people. Malinda had not been there for years and was surprised at how large it seemed when lit by fiery torches in the twilight, for the Bastion was almost a small town of its own, several minor fortresses enclosed by massively fortified outer walls. The royal apartments were located in the tallest, the Sable Tower, looming against the last ruddy glow in the west. Even at noontime this was a dismal place, a monument to inhumanity dating back a thousand years. It was grimmer still in the dusk, yet she felt a deep sense of relief at being there. She had enough Yeomen to hold this keep and enough Blades to keep the Yeomen loyal; even if Souris played false, she could withstand a long siege in the Bastion. She was queen in fact and deed now, and anyone who disagreed would have to topple her from the throne.

All around her Blades were dropping nimbly from their saddles, but a queen must maintain her dignity. She reined in her horse at the mounting block and accepted Sir Dominic's aid to descend. All her life men and women had treated her with the deference due her rank, and yet already she sensed a change, for until now there had always been a higher authority with power to overrule her whims. No more. The monarch was unique, and while she lacked the despotic power to chop off heads at will, as rulers of many other lands could, she certainly had the power to make a special hell for anyone who displeased her. With power came duty, and all day she had felt it settling on her shoulders like a winter snowfall. Privy Council, government, Parliament . . . but ultimately the responsibility was the sovereign's alone, and she might kill hundreds or thousands of her people with one ill-advised fit of pique. From now on she must weigh every decision and consider every move.

She turned to the warriors waiting, men of steel and blood. Most of them had studied her father for years and knew better than she did how a ruler ruled. "I thank you all. I am aware that I would not be here without the Blades. For your support and help I shall always be grateful. Sir Piers—I am tired and dirty and hungry, but tonight belongs to Chivial. What needs be done most urgently?"

"Why, everything, Your Majesty!" he said somberly. "But I often heard your honored father remark that a country that could not wait an hour was not much of a country. History will not censure you if take a break to freshen up, to eat and change clothes."

"Clothes?" she said disbelievingly.

"I fear that the garments I have been able to find at such short notice will not befit a queen in style or quality, but they are clean and should not be so very bad a fit. I have ordered hot water and soft towels."

Just for a moment the weight lifted and she could laugh. "You tempt me to bestow earldoms with those words, Sir Piers! Lead me to this mirage." Then she paused and studied him. His face had always been hard to read, but there was pain in those midnight eyes. "What's wrong?"

He shrugged. "Many things, Your Grace, but more things are right, and your safe arrival here is cause for great rejoicing. Let the bells ring; the rest can wait until its due season."

Dian had never visited the Bastion before, and she scowled in disbelief at the dingy rooms of the Royal Suite, their bare stone walls, worn rugs, and ancient furniture. Nevertheless a huge copper tub steamed invitingly, a fire crackled in every grate, and there was enough food piled up on a sideboard to feed the entire Royal Guard. Knowing Malinda even better than Malinda knew herself, she promptly shooed everyone else out—all but Sister Moment, who flopped down on a chair, closed her eyes, and moaned dramatically. Being much less skilled on horseback than the others, she had done very well to keep up.

"Strip!" Dian said, reaching for flannel and soap. "Reveal yourself in all your naked majesty, Your Majesty!"

Malinda began to strip. "I want you to set up a household, please, Dian. I expect we'll be staying for several days." She sank gratefully into bitingly hot water. "Don't let me fall asleep in here!"

"There's pheasant with chestnuts over there. Sturgeon and kid pie. Candied berry cake."

"Oh, all right." The Queen began sponging. "I'll stay awake for the cake. Do please see that my bed is well aired. It probably hasn't been slept in since the Fatherland Wars. I shan't be late—just long enough to accept their homage, appoint Lord Roland chancellor again and dump the country in his hands. Then back here and into bed."

"Warm bricks in it?" Dian asked, struggling with tangles in the royal hair.

"Definitely."

"And warm Dog?"

"No! Not here. Dog must remain a state secret. I don't even want the rest of the Guard to know about him!"

"Mm?" her friend said skeptically. "You think they don't? You let him hug you this morning."

"Flames, so I did!" Could forty Blades keep such a secret? What sort of jokes might they be making about her? Malinda splashed in angry silence for a while, then heaved herself reluctantly out of the bath. "The trouble isn't just scandal, you know. That's bad enough, but in my case it's also heir-to-the-throne trouble, a purity-of-the-Blood thing. And men have this stupid idea that women can't think for themselves. When I do get married, they'll expect my husband to make the decisions and me the babies."

"Stay single then." Dian enveloped her in a thick towel. "Dog's wonderful. He won't mind being kept secret. He won't expect to be made a duke just because he has such an attractive anatomy."

"I do *not* love him for his anatomy!"

"No?" Dian said. "But it helps. I saw it in the Forge, you know. Very impressive! I'm screamingly jealous."

Unsure where that line of conversation might lead, Malinda said, "Sister?"

Moment's eyes popped open. Evidently she had been meditating, not sleeping. "Your Majesty?" Without her absurd hat, she seemed no larger than a child.

"Is it not true that White Sisters can detect spoken falsehood as well as inquisitors can?"

"Some can. Never as well, probably."

"You? If anyone foreswears himself in the oath of allegiance, could you detect that?"

The Sister's eyes were very large and very blue, adding to her customary air of childlike wonder. "That would be treasonous. A lie of that magnitude should be obvious, but it will be hard here, my lady."

"Why?"

"Because lies are made of air and death. Air I can handle, it being dominant in my own makeup, but this place is saturated with death. The very stones reek of death. Death shouts at me everywhere. I will do my best, but an inquisitor would do much better."

"What inquisitor can I trust as I trust you? I will appoint no liars to my Council."

Moment was rarely solemn like that; she normally regarded the world with impish glee. "You may be trusting me beyond my abilities, Your Grace. I have told you that our skills are very personal and distinctive, which is why we like to have at least two Sisters present on any vital occasion."

"But today there is only you," Malinda said, "and me, and history rattling bones at our backs. Preserve me from conjuration and warn me of falsehood. I ask for no more than your best effort."

33

You think you can get your own way all the time.
AMBROSE IV TO HIS DAUGHTER

The Bastion's Hall of Banners had hosted many memorable quarrels, murders, and trials, but grand it was not. Its floors were rough planks, and the bare masonry walls still bore evidence of ancient fires. By day it seemed more suitable for arms drill than stately pomp; that evening it was awash in ominous shadow, its ceiling barely visible. Light from the smoky torches found no gold or jewels to sparkle on, only silken embroidery on the heralds' tabards and the steel of men-at-arms. Everyone else was kneeling as the brazen fanfare's echoes faded and the Queen entered, following Sergeant Usher of the Silver and Basilisk King of Arms and a couple of other mace-bearing worthies, followed in turn by this and that personage of enormous dignity, not to mention almost the entire Royal Guard.

Her robe was scarlet, trimmed with white fur, and must have been made for her father or some equally stalwart forebear. Fortunately, she had a page to carry the train, because the whole thing weighed as much as a horse—but at least it kept the drafts off, and it did hide her dowdy gown. On her head she wore a simple gold circlet, which could not be reconciled with any fashionable bonnet, so her hair hung unbound down her back. Queens set fashion, and that might be proper style by tomorrow.

There was no dais; an ill-shaped chair of state served as a throne, but sitting was no easy move in that cartload of robe. The page adjusted her train and then backed away, bowing. She appraised the crowd—about thirty, she estimated, with Grand Inquisitor the most conspicuous, looming over the rest. Allow two minutes apiece and in an hour she should be able to stagger off to bed and close the book on this epic day.

After another fanfare Griffon King of Arms proclaimed Her Gracious Majesty Malinda, by the spirits ordained, rightful Queen of the Realm of Chivial and Nostrimia, Prince of Nythia and so on. She had warned the heralds that she would speak then. The hall hushed for her.

"Today," she said, hearing her voice reverberate in the darkness overhead, "our dear brother died of a fever. He never ruled, but he shall be mourned as befits a king of Chivial. We claim the throne by law and custom, by our father's will, by right of the Blood. If there be any here who disputes our rule, then let him rise and speak." With three dozen Blades fiercely eyeing the audience, and about as many Yeomen, no one was stupid enough to accept her invitation.

"The former Lord Protector attempted a coup and was slain. His lands and titles are forfeit. But since he failed and the harm done was small, any who will now swear allegiance to us will be automatically pardoned for any part played in his treason or conspiracy to treason, excepting only the Traitor's son, Neville Fitzambrose, who remains in our royal mercy. This pardon will not cover any unrelated felonies or misdemeanors." She nodded to the waiting heralds. "Proceed, my lords."

The one who bowed in acknowledgment wore the tabard of Eagle King of Arms, but he was the youngster who had read out her father's will, so the spirits must have taken the old man at last. He proffered her a card on a silver plate. She raised an eyebrow.

"The enthronement oath, Your Grace!" he whispered.

She should have remembered that. She took the card and peered at a script so ornate as to be close to indecipherable in the uncertain torchlight. "I, Malinda . . ." She struggled through it, swearing to respect the ancient rights of her people, uphold their traditional liberties, protect them from perils foreign and domestic, impose justice on high and low alike, levy taxes according to law and custom, also attend to a basket of other things. Polish up the crown jewels in her spare time, maybe.

The Basilisk herald besought her most gracious permission for the courtiers to sit. She so granted and they rose to take their places on the benches with a rustle like wind in a forest.

The first to kneel at her feet was Commander Audley in green livery and silver baldric, exercising a traditional precedence on behalf of the entire Royal Guard, although Blades' bindings made the oath superfluous. As he rose he caught her eye and winked. She sneaked a smile in return. Neither of them would ever forget this day of sorrow and triumph.

The courtiers would now swear allegiance in order of rank. . . . Overhearing whispered exchanges including the name "Courtney," she realized that dictates of protocol had put Sister Moment far away, out of reach. Worse, she was in among a cluster of Blades. Blades were human blizzards, Moment claimed, hailstorms of every element at once numbing her.

"Wait!" Malinda said. "Begin with Grand Inquisitor."

"That would be completely out of order!" Then Griffon King of Arms's jaw dropped as he realized what he had said and to whom. He gabbled apologies. Heralds hastily conferred with heads bent, papers ashuffle. Apparently the councillors were listed by name, not by office, and no one knew which name belonged to Grand Inquisitor. Malinda certainly did not. Eventually a decision was reached and Basilisk King of Arms bellowed in a voice like a bugle: "Master Horatio Lambskin!"

Amid a general muttering of surprise and outrage, the gaunt old man rose to his astonishing height and worked his way along the row to the aisle. Even when he sank down on the cushion before her, he seemed tall. A herald handed him a copy of the oath, and he read it out in his creaking voice.

"We would have the benefit of your wisdom in our Privy Council, Grand Inquisitor, " Malinda said, still practicing the royal plural, "as did my, er, our, father."

He favored her with his fish-cold stare. "I can imagine no greater honor, Majesty."

"Meanwhile, stand here, by us. If your skills detect any falsehood or reservation, then speak up according to your oath. Proceed, Lord Herald."

"His Highness Prince Courtney, Duke of Mayshire!"

After some hasty whispering and rushing around, Courtney was located on the wrong bench. He had apparently been dozing. Whatever clothes he had worn in his cell would now be fit only for burning, and there had been no time to fetch any garments of his own, so he had been dressed in whatever could be found to enclose his short-legged tubbiness. The result was a bizarre distribution of colors and wrinkles. Courtney himself was in no better shape than his outfit. Too much celebration of his release from imprisonment had turned his usual delicate mincing gait to a stagger, his prissy little smile to a bewildered leer. Senior heralds tried to intercept him as he reached Malinda's chair, but too late. He managed a slurred mumble of, "Lindy! You skewered the . . . bastard! Flaming good . . . good . . ." and then his legs began to fold. Eagle, Basilisk, and Griffon all leaped forward to catch him, but in the resulting melee, the Prince escaped them all and collapsed in a snoring heap.

"Put him back in his cell to sober up!" Malinda commanded, biting the words. She sat on the throne of Ranulf and steamed, while her errant cousin was removed. How dare he! To think that disgusting drunken lecher was her heir! If anything happened to her, Courtney would inherit Chivial. This was unthinkable; she must produce an heir, a legitimate heir, and as soon as possible. *Oh, Dog, Dog!* She would have to marry someone—male presumably, aristocrat certainly. Biddable . . . Parliament would insist on a Chivian. But never Dog.

When the proceedings were resumed, the next man forward was, surprisingly, the ponderous, platitudinous Duke of Brinton, who must have rushed south as soon as he received her appeal for help. She smiled at him, said a few polite words, and made a mental note to send him a suitable gift. A spare castle, perhaps.

And so it continued, all the great ones of the kingdom whom the heralds had been able to locate. Many of her father's old councillors were there—Lord High Admiral, Baron Dechaise of the Treasury, Mother Superior of the White Sisters—and also many of Granville's men, including those she had named Pig, Ratface, and Fish-Eyes.

But not . . .

Eagle King of Arms bowed. "All persons summoned having sworn true fealty to Your Majesty, this audience now awaits Your Majesty's pleasure." It was over, in other words.

"Where," she said quietly, "is Lord Roland?"

Eagle looked at Griffon; Griffon glanced at Basilisk; Basilisk considered Sir Dominic. Sir Dominic was staring up at Grand Inquisitor with hatred almost palpable. She realized that everyone near her knew something that she did not, something that must have been whispered around during the ceremony, while she was accepting the oaths. She remembered the strange shadows in Piers's eyes.

"If we may withdraw to the robing room, Your Grace," Dominic muttered thickly, "we have some tragic news to impart. I suggest you bring Grand Inquisitor along—for his own safety."

* * *

By the time Malinda reached the cramped little robing room it was packed so full of Blades that they even blocked the doorway, although she had no idea how they had managed to get there before she did. She dropped the massive robe off her shoulders into the arms of the page, who staggered under the load, and by then Dominic and Audley were clearing a way in.

She registered sounds of heartbroken sobbing, a sickening stench of sewer, a pervading emotional tension as intense as physical pain. The crowd squeezed back to reveal two people embracing on a sofa. One of them was a dainty woman of around thirty—exquisitely dressed and with a striking beauty that her terrible pallor failed to mar. She did not rise, just turned her head to stare accusingly up at Malinda. She was not the one sobbing. She was comforting the man in her arms, but she herself looked as if she would never feel any emotion again.

Malinda trawled her memory for the correct name. "Countess Kate!"

The woman nodded and turned her attention back to the man she held. Malinda knew who it was, of course, but she had to force herself to look directly at him. He was the source of the foul odor and the weeping. His clothes were disgusting rags. Huddled in his wife's embrace, he kept his face down and sobbed. Sobbed, sobbed, sobbed.

All the Blades in the room had turned to stare at the Queen, waiting for her to do something, say something. Kill somebody. All she could think of were her shattered plans to put the government back in this man's hands. What in the name of death had they done to him? And why was he being tortured with this public shame?

"I am waiting for an explanation. Sir Dominic?"

"They put him to the Question."

She spun around to Grand Inquisitor. "Is this true?"

His face was an expressionless skull. He nodded, shrugged.

Malinda's hand struck his cheek with a crack like an ax; with all her strength behind it, the blow made him stagger. *"Kneel when I address you!"*

Ancient knees crackled as he went down, but he still seemed to find the fuss unnecessary. "Yes, Your Majesty. He was arrested nine days ago on a charge of high treason. When interrogated, he refused to answer questions."

"Interrogated by inquisitors, of course?"

"Of course." The old man must be finding it very odd to be looking *up* at a woman, or indeed at anyone. His gaze glided from face to face as if he were calculating his chance of leaving the room alive. All these young swordsmen had worshiped Lord Roland since their boyhood. This black-robed serpent had destroyed their hero.

"It was all legal, Your Grace," the inquisitor protested. "The law allows no exceptions in cases of treason. Suspects failing to testify fully and truthfully shall be put to the Question." The marks of his queen's hand glowed red on his cheek.

"*Treason?* You thought the Lord Chancellor was guilty of *treason?*"

"But I was!" Lord Roland cried. Gasping for breath between sobs, he said, "I revealed state secrets! I embezzled money. I conspired—"

His wife clapped a hand over his mouth to hush him. He did not resist, just stopped talking and sobbed harder, tears streaming from blood-rimmed eyes.

"He did this to aid me!" Malinda shouted. "That was not treason! He was trying to block treason, block a conspiracy to dispossess the rightful heir!"

Silence, deadly silence. Knuckles were white on sword hilts all around the room. Grand Inquisitor's life hung by its fingertips.

"You may well approve of his intent, Your Grace," the old man protested shakily, "but the fact remains that what he was doing was in violation of his Privy Councillor's oath, and once enchanted he confessed to numerous breaches of trust. He is consequently under sentence of death. It is as blatant a case as I have ever—"

"Silence! Countess, I cannot begin to convey my horror and sorrow. Whatever treatment is required will—"

"There is no treatment!" the little woman said harshly. "He can never be a real man again. Can you?" She removed her hand. "Tell them."

Lord Roland groaned. "Never. I must tell the truth always, the complete truth. I must confess everything, however trivial, volunteer anything relevant, answer any question." He was quite conscious, aware of his shame, his eyes wide with horror. "The tears I shed are of remorse. Even now I am compelled to say, Your Grace, that I considered you a spoiled and willful, impetuous, oversexed—" His wife's hand slid over his mouth again. He choked a couple of times, then buried his face in her shoulder to weep more.

Nothing was more dangerous than truth.

Well, Queen Malinda? Everyone else was looking to her. The monarch makes the decisions, doesn't she? She wanted to scream. She could do nothing for Lord Roland and one careless word from her would make Grand Inquisitor a colander. She would shed no tears over that bloodless reptile, but his murder would be a crime to doom her reign before it had even begun. What could she possibly say? "Countess, I am truly heartbroken. I needed him as much as you do. And as your children do." There were two children, she recalled, a boy of eleven or twelve, a girl about half that. "Chivial needed him. Whatever can be done . . . ask and I shall order it."

"Carry out the sentence!"

"What!?"

"You heard me—*Your Majesty!*" The little countess had an astonishingly piercing voice when she wanted to use it. "You think the Durendal we all know wants to live like this? Being this blathering, halfwit horror evermore? Seeing pity in every eye? Spewing secrets with every breath? Sign the warrant, Queen Malinda. Get it over with. Don't make him suffer longer!"

Silence. The pain was unbearable, nobody looking at anyone.

"Sir Piers," Malinda said, "have Lord Roland and his lady escorted to the best available rooms and provide anything they require or request. We shall discuss this matter in council as soon as possible." She looked down at Grand Inquisitor, whose unwinking eyes stared up at her like holes. Shuddering, she looked away to locate the bone-white face of Audley.

"Commander, this has been a day of great sorrows, but none worse than this."

"Yes, Your Grace."

"Unfortunately, we cannot punish the man responsible, because he is already dead. Those who put Lord Roland to the Question were doing no more than their duty under the law." She heard a few Blade growls and looked around to locate their source, but naturally failed to do so. "We will not start our reign with a lynching or vendetta, is that quite clear? Pray inform every Blade—and I mean *every* Blade, every Blade in the entire Order, not just the Royal Guard—that the inquisitors are covered by our royal pardon and there is to be no private vengeance for what was done to Durendal. Is that understood?"

Audley's eyes glanced around uneasily, looking for guidance. "I think so, Your Grace."

"Deputy?"

Dominic sighed. "Yes, Your Grace. The Blades are aware that they owe their continued existence to your efforts, my lady, and they will not mar the beginning of your reign with a crime for which you will undoubtedly be blamed. *There must be no vengeance!*"

The Guard moaned. The real Leader had spoken. They would

obey Dominic as they would not have obeyed Audley, whoever might be wearing the baldric. Fingers opened, releasing hilts.

She could relax a little then. "You have our permission to withdraw, Grand Inquisitor. The Commander will find some Yeomen to escort you home."

Shaking, she turned and swept from the room.

Blades conducted her to the royal suite. Dian was waiting. . . . It was all a blur. None of it mattered. Roland was useless, as good as dead. Who was going to be her chancellor? She had absolutely no second choice in mind. Her father had gone through four chancellors, learning from the one he had inherited from his father, Lord Bluefield, and subsequently training Bluefield's successors. Roland, she had heard him say several times, was the best of them all by far. Rookie monarch and rookie chancellor together were a recipe for disaster.

She pulled arms out, pushed hands in, sat for hair brushing, went through all the standard motions of preparing for bed, and her mind danced like a moth elsewhere. Whom could she find to be chancellor? Some halfwit noble who would create a dog's vomit of her government? An upstart lowborn clerk who would rile the aristocracy and antagonize the Commons? She knew no one. Her father had been a superb judge of men, at least by the time she knew him—he had made his share of mistakes in his youth—but she had no experience. The most important decision she would make in the next five years, she was going to be making blind. Roll dice? Draw lots? Write the names of all the men in Chivial and throw them into a hat . . .

Some hat.

"All done," Dian said, giving her a hug. "I'll leave this candle burning. There are eight Blades standing guard outside the door. Dog's there . . . ?"

"Not tonight."

"I'll tell him. I think you'll find the bed warm enough. Try to get some sleep."

Some hope.

"Tell Audley that I'll need a secretary and—"

"You need sleep," Dian said firmly. "Get into bed, Queen!"

So ended the first day of her reign.

34

She summoned the raven and the lion and all the mice of the field.
THE LEGEND OF ELBERTHA

The room was small and stark and furnished with only a table and a single chair, as she had commanded, but someone had thoughtfully kept a fire burning overnight to warm the ancient masonry. The chair was almost a throne, a pretentious thing of carved oak with a cloth of estate over it, which she hoped she would not need to bolster her authority. Like her father, she preferred to conduct business standing. She was better dressed this morning, in a queenly gown Dian had miraculously produced, and she had decided to stay with the gold circlet and unbound hair—they made her look like pictures of her ferocious and notorious great-grandmother, Queen Charis.

Now she placed herself comfortably near the fire with the light from the narrow window at her back, then scowled bleakly at Sir Fitzroy, one of the two Blades present. He was standing against the wall as if he were painted there.

"Standard procedure, my lady," he said stubbornly.

Her father had done nothing without a Blade present, even bathe. She had established already that she would not tolerate that level of supervision, but she strongly suspected that an attempt to evict Fitzroy now would not succeed. She would just have to get used to life with Blades everywhere. At least Fitzroy was among the oldest of the current Guard, an ancient of more than thirty. He would not babble if she made a fool of herself today.

The other was Winter, whom Audley had appointed as her secretary—a wise choice, because most of the Guard would have hated the task. He had an excellent memory and typically had brought no papers with him, just fingers to chew.

"Well, Sir Winter? Who wants to see me? I rely on you to rank them in some sort of priority."

He took his hand away from his mouth. "Then, Sir Piers first,

252

Your Grace. Seven former privy councillors and eleven peers, all wanting to swear allegiance. You want their names?"

"Written, please."

"Yes, my lady. Constable Valdor to report on unrest, except there isn't any." He paused just long enough for a hasty gnaw at his right thumbnail. "Marshal Souris with a list of Granville garrisons that should be called on to surrender. Two senior clerks from Treasury in a panic because they have no money to pay bills. The Lord Mayor of Grandon and alderman with a loyal address. Eagle King of Arms about your late brother's funeral . . ."

"I'll see Piers first, then the herald, and send for Sir Snake. The Lord Mayor mustn't be kept waiting very long. Most of all I want to talk with Mother Superior. I expect she's at Greymere."

"I'm not sure . . . believe she stayed here overnight, my lady. I'll see. . . ." Winter bowed and withdrew to send in Piers.

Malinda had guessed the news Piers would bring and the look in his eyes confirmed it before he opened his mouth. With deep regret he must inform Her Majesty that Lord Roland had died suddenly in the night. She turned and pretended to stare out the window, although its little bottle-glass panes distorted the view to a blur. Sudden tears did not help, either. "Of the same infection that struck down Secretary Kromman last spring, I presume." Had they drawn lots again? The Dark Chamber could probably ferret out which one had actually done the deed, but to order such an investigation would turn the entire Guard against her. It was done and fury would not undo it. "His wife?"

"She went home to her children last night, my lady."

Kate had asked for this mercy, but it must have been Durendal's own idea. He would have known that the Blades would grant his wish. The Queen had not granted it! Nor had she forbidden it. She had forbidden revenge, not mercy. They would not have obeyed her if she had. It had been an internal Guard matter. So last night the Rolands had said good-bye and Kate had left. . . .

Malinda turned, struggling to keep her voice calm. "I think you should deliver the news to his widow yourself, Sir Piers, since you are in charge of this fortress and the royal hospitality extended to its guests."

He winced at the jab. "As Your Grace commands."

"I do not know her financial circumstances, but you may inform her that she and her children will not want. Now listen to me. You will go at once to Dominic and tell him to pass the word throughout the Order that I will tolerate no more action of this kind—none whatsoever, *under any circumstances!* I must summon a parliament right away and I will have to fight tooth and claw to stop it from dissolving your Order outright. My case will be hopeless if rumor of this crime gets out. The Blades will be finished, utterly! *Now get out of here!"* Her sudden roar sent him leaping for the door handle. She even tried a glare at Fitzroy, but Fitzroy was technically not there, neither hearing nor seeing, and in this case he definitely did not allow himself to see the glare.

Next came the new Eagle King of Arms to discuss Amby's funeral. She accepted that the arrangements would require at least two days. "Include whatever seems fitting. All the bands you can find. He loved bands."

The herald nodded, but it was a deep enough nod to be classed as a small bow. "Eulogies, Your Grace?"

"I shall say a few words, very few. Anything more would be hypocrisy. Nobody else really knew him. No banquet."

"May I include some additional fireworks, then? Did he enjoy fireworks?"

She liked the herald's terse style. He was a bookish-seeming man of around thirty; it was his grotesque tabard that made him seem young, because she was accustomed to think of heralds as old.

"Fireworks startled him. But include them by all means. The public likes them."

Nod again. "Thank you, my lady. I also brought sketches for your great seal. This is a matter of some urgency, because all official business . . ." He was already spreading drawings on the table. She glanced briefly at the designs. They were all much like her father's seal with a token addition of a rose, a symbol from her mother's family. "That one."

He gathered his papers. "There are many other matters, Your Grace, but none that cannot wait a few days."

She smiled. "One won't. You may be able to help me. I need a private secretary, someone who is industrious, efficient, and circumspect. I could not entirely trust a Blade"—that was for Fitzroy's benefit—"nor an inquisitor like Master Kromman. I wonder . . . can you think of some promising clerk in the College who may be willing to take on a regiment's work, at least for a few months?"

Eagle King of Arms turned geranium pink, drew himself up stiffly in his fancy tabard, and gulped twice. "If Your Majesty would consider me . . ."

She had thought that one of the senior heralds of the kingdom would greatly outrank a mere secretary, but a few questions revealed her error. There would be more money, more respect, and vastly more interesting work. There would also be considerable opportunity for taking bribes, but he did not mention that. He was the Honorable Robert Kinwinkle, eleventh child of a baron noted more for physical prowess than fiscal prudence. As a herald he was still, just barely, a gentleman, but even his recent promotion to a King of Arms had brought him only enough income to stay lean, never enough to grow fat or support a family. He claimed he knew as much about the workings of the government as anyone. He would work himself to death for the honor of being Her Majesty's secretary.

"You are appointed, Master Kinwinkle! You will not be required to work yourself to death very often. Can you start now?"

He went down on one knee to kiss her hand. "This instant, Your Majesty!" He thereupon repeated the entire oath of allegiance without a single hesitation.

She dared hope that she had struck lucky. "Pray inform Sir Winter that he is relieved as soon as he has brought you up to date. Make your own decisions about priorities, but I want to see Mother Superior when she arrives."

As Kinwinkle went out she caught Fitzroy's eye and this time it was being allowed to convey amusement. She repeated her earlier glare and it went blank again.

The next caller was Sir Snake, who had been among the ex-councillors swearing allegiance the previous evening. He bowed with both verve and style. In the small hours of the night she had considered him for chancellor, but he was not another Roland. He was too slapdash, a daredevil, cynical—he would make enemies for her. Besides, he had other uses.

"You do not appear to have grown fat in the dungeons, Sir Snake."

"Nay, Your Grace. Another month and I could have slipped out through the bars."

He showed no signs of his ordeal, although he must have escaped the same fate as Durendal by no more than the width of his arrogant string mustache. They chatted for a moment without mentioning the late Lord Roland. She wondered whether the knights had been invited to join in the Guard's murderous lottery and if Snake would have been capable of putting his old mentor out of such misery. His face maintained its usual supercilious smile, revealing nothing. She went to business.

"First, my thanks for all your efforts when you were Stealth. Your service will be acknowledged in the first Honors List of my reign."

"My sword is always at Your Majesty's service." He bowed again.

"I hope so, because our treasury is empty. It will take time to summon another parliament and persuade it to vote supply. I want to resume the Monster War."

His eyes lit up. "The Old Blades are ready!"

"I saw enough of the evil," she said, "to want it stamped out even if I did not need the money. How soon can you move?"

"I have to muster the lads, of course. Most of them are down at Ironhall."

"Yes, Sir Dominic told me. I am impressed and touched by the way your Order continues to serve the best interests of the crown, Sir Snake." When Granville had disbanded the Court of Conjury, Durendal and Snake had secretly sent the knights off to Ironhall to help train more swordsmen. She had not inquired how the school had been financed during the protectorate.

"Happy to serve, Your Grace. I can have them back here in three or four days. There are nests right here in Grandon that need to be smoked out. May I borrow some of those troops on Great Common?"

That took some discussion of terms of payment and granting of authority, but it was not long before a grinning Snake went striding out to prepare a detailed plan. This time Malinda smiled sweetly at Fitzroy, who looked sick to his stomach. She was going to resume the Monster War with the Guard down to less than forty?

Master Kinwinkle delivered a scroll bearing some fifty names of persons anxious to wait upon Her Majesty. He also announced Mother Superior.

The old woman who entered, ducking her tall hennin under the lintel, was a national monument, tall, gaunt, white-draped; she had been at court when Malinda was a child, seeming no less ancient then than she did now. Her eyes were awls and her nose could have served to fashion dugout canoes; the wimple framing her face hid what the years had done to her neck, but her back was as straight as a pikestaff. It was true she treated Malinda as an errant nine-year-old, but she treated everyone as an errant nine-year-old. She curtseyed stiffly, waited to hear what her sovereign required of her and somehow conveying disapproval in advance.

"You have heard the tragic news about Lord Roland?"

Mother Superior's thin lips grew even thinner. "Absolutely disgusting!" She did not explain whether that comment referred to Lambskin's Question or the Blades' reaction.

"Certainly. I often heard my father say Lord Roland was the finest chancellor he had ever had, and I fully intended to confirm him in that post. Now I must find a replacement without delay. It occurred to me that you have been a privy councillor for many years, Mother."

Wrinkles deepened in a frown. "True, my lady, but I rarely attended meetings until your father began what is now known as the Monster War."

"But you have seen men come and—"

The frown became a satisfied smile. "And you wish me to recommend possible chancellors? Well, Baron Dechaise must be the longest serving . . . reliable and honest, but anxious to retire, I suspect. Some of Lord Granville's appointments were doing very well, although whether or not Your Grace is prepared to trust . . ."

Malinda was shaking her head. "This was not why I summoned you, Mother."

"Oh." The old lady did not like finding herself in the wrong. "Then how may I serve Your Majesty?"

"As my chancellor."

It must have been a long time since Mother Superior's jaw dropped like that.

"You have experience on the Council itself," Malinda said. "And you have run the White Sisters for . . . how many years?"

"Thirty-two."

"It is without doubt the most efficiently run organization in Chivial. You have no political enemies, so far as I have ever heard, which is important. And," she added mischievously, "you fear neither man nor beast."

"I don't know about that . . ." The old lady looked ready to pinch herself. "Your Grace, this is a totally unexpected honor and a very daunting . . . overwhelmed . . . need time to . . . You do realize that the hairier half of your subjects will have enough trouble accepting even a female ruler? To offer them a female first minister at the same time—is this wise, Your Grace?"

Perhaps not. Malinda was determined not to look directly, but she was fairly sure that Sir Fitzroy was white with shock. "I am not *offering* anyone anything. I am appointing you. If you wish to regard the post as temporary, we may reconsider our decision in a few months. Meanwhile, you are now the Chancellor of Chivial." She held out her fingers to be kissed. "You may call yourself Lord Chancellor, or Lady Chancellor, whichever you prefer, but of course there

is always at least an earldom to go with the position. Countess—"
She laughed. "I don't know your name!"

"Few remember these days." A notable glitter in the old lady's
eyes suggested she was already starting to see humor in the situation.
"It is Burningstar, Your Grace." However odd White Sisters' names
often were, they always seemed to suit their owners.

"Excellent!" Malinda said. "Lend me your sword, Sir Fitzroy.
Kneel, please, Mother. Arise Countess Burningstar of Oakendown.
Thank you, Sir Fitzroy. Now, Chancellor, the government is destitute
and there are some Treasury bead pushers waiting outside to tell me
so. Master Kinwinkle will point them out to you. Find out from them
what we shall need for the next week. Then embrace the Lord Mayor
fondly, inform him that he will be invited to a formal levee in a few
days so he may pay his respects, and send him off to raise a loan to
us for whatever the amount is."

"One week?" said the new Chancellor disbelievingly.

"That should do. Between you and me and Sir Snake, I am about
to resume the Monster War. I expect to confiscate some valuable real
estate that can be sold or used as collateral, and possibly the odd hoard
of ill-gotten bullion, too."

The old lady shook her head. "I really don't think I am competent
for all this, Your Grace."

Malinda eased her gently toward the door. "I am sure you are
more competent than I am, my lady, and I am doing quite well so
far. If mere men can do it, then government cannot be too difficult,
can it? After you have thrown out the Lord Mayor and alderman,
pray draw up a list of potential privy councillors that we can discuss
over lunch. I want to have the government up and running by sunset."

"This may kill me, you know!" the new Chancellor said sharply.

"I'll give you a state funeral," the Queen promised.

Some matters she must now defer to Burningstar, lest the two of
them snarl things up between them. Others fell squarely within the
royal prerogative, and one of those was Cousin Courtney, Prince of
the Realm, Duke of Mayshire, Baron Leandre, drunken lecher, per-
sona non grata.

When he was shown in, Malinda was seated on the throne. He
was better dressed than he had been the previous night, but a faint
odor of dungeon still hung around him. He advanced, bowed, and
smiled sheepishly.

"Congratulations, Your darling Majesty. A *classic* countercoup, I understand. Historians will love it. I never *really* doubted you, but I confess I was starting to get a *teeny* bit worried."

She continued to project her best House-of-Ranulf glare. He was going to kneel to her if she had to call in the Household Yeomen to cut off his shins.

Courtney pulled a puzzled little frown and turned to regard the Blade. "Do we need old Sir Fitz, here, darling? This is just a family chat, after all, isn't it?"

"No. It isn't. Had you done to my father what you did to me last night, he would have thrown you back in that dungeon and left you there for years. He would probably have had you flogged. I still may."

Courtney pulled himself up to his full shoulder-high height. "I think you are displaying a *cruel* lack of sensitivity, my dear! Do you know how many weeks I *languished* in that *sewer*? Never in my *life* had I slept on anything except the *best* quality silk, and down there even the *straw* was damp and unacceptable. The food . . . oh, *spirits!* . . . the food . . . You *cannot* imagine! Day after day, night after night, dreading the torments! Hearing the screams of the tortured! The rats! Hoping always for the tyrant's downfall, the triumph of my *dear* cousin Malinda. Of course I had a nervous reaction! You are being un*necess*arily cruel even to mention it."

"Just how many people were tortured within your hearing?"

"Several . . . I kept no exact count. Although I assure you they suffered no more than I did this morning. My head—"

"Bah!" Malinda said, steeling herself. "The way you behaved last night would shame a swineherd in his wallow, let alone a—"

"Careful!" Courtney raised a hand. "Say nothing you may regret, darling. Consider our future."

"Future? *Our* future, did you say?"

"What else? You know how Chivians feel about queens regnant, dearest. I certainly grant that you are the legitimate heir, princess of the Blood, first in line, but you have Estrith and Adela around your neck. You also wear some very curious whispers about Blades and orgies and such. You have put a national hero to death, and there are still lurking questions about your part in Ambrose's murder—what you said to King Radgar and what he said to you . . ." He preened, showing bad teeth. "Now I, dearest, am your Heir Presumptive. The law says so. Your father's will says so. I admit that I am ten or twelve years older than you are, but—"

"Almost twenty-four years older."

"Spirits! Is it that long? It feels like yesterday. The fact remains,

Cousin, that the country does not *savor* the idea of a juvenile *female* autocrat, but when you marry me and we rule jointly, the Commons will be joyous, the Lords mollified, the—"

"Stop!" she roared, making him wince. "I wouldn't marry you if my only alternative was being burned at the stake. You won't slip any sleazy potions to me, Courtney."

"Your Grace speaks in riddles."

"Love potions. I know now how you cheated in affairs of the heart. The White Sisters have always known. Father knew, but preferred to avoid the scandal of charging you. Well, I have no such scruples. Go back to your lair in Mayshire, you debauched horror. Stay there until you are thickly coated in moss or I will have you indicted on charges of multiple rape."

Courtney swelled up as if about to argue, but Sir Fitzroy's hand gripped his collar and spun him around. He was thrust roughly out the door, and the door was slammed behind him.

Malinda said, "Thank you!" breathlessly and leaned back on the throne until her heart stopped thundering. *Marry Courtney? Ridiculous!*

It was only later, during lunch with Chancellor Burningstar, that she realized Cousin Courtney had still not knelt to her.

So the day went.

The afternoon light was fading when she sent for Neville Fitzambrose, the Traitor's son—her nephew, about the same age as herself, whom she had never met.

Although he had been imprisoned little more than a day, his clothes were already fetid rags and he brought a stench of dungeon that fouled the room. He was delivered in his chains, clanking and stumbling, yet six Blades came with him, led by Sir Dominic himself. They hurled the prisoner to his knees before the throne. Having his hands manacled behind his back, he pitched forward helplessly onto his face, so they hauled him up again by his iron collar.

"That will do!" Malinda said angrily. "Control yourselves!" This was the way prisoners were always treated, of course—any man who found himself in such a predicament must have done something to deserve it—but she hated to see the Blades indulging in wanton cruelty.

Neville's face was filthy, unshaven, recently bruised. His hair—dark and thick—kept falling over his eyes, and his efforts to shake it away scraped his neck against the rusty collar. Height was hard to judge when he was down on the floor, but he was certainly well built. Under normal circumstance he would probably appear quite handsome. He scowled up at her defiantly.

"How much have they told you?" she asked.

"The brat is dead and you killed my father. *Bitch!*"

"No!" she yelled, just in time to save him from a boot in the kidneys. If Neville guessed what he had escaped, he gave no sign.

"I will tell you the real facts. If you wish, I will summon an inquisitor who can testify that I have spoken only the truth. Do you want that?"

He sneered. "Why bother? You think I'd believe one of your inquisitors more than I believe you?"

"You should," she said. "However, here is the truth. My brother died yesterday morning. By law and right, I was then queen. Your father refused to swear allegiance, tried to resist arrest, and was slain in the resulting struggle. So were several innocent men."

His surly expression remained unchanged. "What man is innocent?" A Blade fist slammed into his ear, almost knocking him over.

"Stop that!" Malinda shouted. "Dominic, if you maltreat this prisoner again, I will dismiss you from the Guard and have you expelled from the Order. The same goes for all of you. Bring him a chair and a glass of wine and release his hands. Now!"

She sat in angry silence until her nephew was seated on a chair facing her. He took the proffered goblet in both hands and drank greedily. Then he glowered at his young aunt as if ashamed of having revealed weakness. His glower was nothing compared to the detestation on the faces of the Blades behind him.

"Your father was not innocent," Malinda said. "He knowingly rebelled against the law."

"He was the eldest son! He should have been king!"

"Then why did he ever acknowledge Amby?"

The prisoner had probably not thought of that argument. "He was fit to be king!" he said sulkily. "He would have made a great king!"

"Would he?" She tried to sound reasonable, not gloating. "I'm sure he told you so, and your loyalty is understandable, but look at the facts. He had an army, the treasury, and complete control of the government for half a year. All I had was right on my side and a few men willing to die for me. Our contest lasted all of ten minutes. Does that sound as if Granville Fitzambrose was kingly material? But he served the realm well until then, and I am truly sorry. Now I must decide what to do about you."

"Go ahead and chop my head off!" Neville's blustering made him seem very immature, but he was probably terrified beyond endurance, desperately trying to hang on to his self-control.

"I'd rather not. I bear you no grudge. Your father made you governor of the Bastion."

"That was his right!"

She smiled. "Yes, because he was Lord Protector. It was a legal appointment, although it may not have been a wise one. You were outwitted and overpowered quite easily. But you have done nothing I can see as treasonous."

Neville tried to hold his scowl, but hope had widened his eyes. They were brown eyes, not amber.

Quite attractive eyes. He was her half nephew. Under the laws of consanguinity that was still too close for marriage, but sovereigns could decree themselves exemptions. If some sort of dynastic marriage was inevitable, Neville would be a much less abhorrent choice than Courtney. Best not to leave him lying around as a temptation to Parliament.

"As I understand your situation," she said, "you have no other family. Your father's lands and titles are forfeit. You know no trade or craft except that of soldier. Constable Valdor describes you as a handy man with a halberd. He is willing to enlist you as man-at-arms in the Household Yeomen."

The prisoner raised the goblet to his lips. His throat showed no signs of swallowing, so he was merely concealing his face while he thought. Had he really expected her to chop his head off?

"My, you must have been thirsty," Malinda said. He lowered the goblet and she smiled again. "It's a fair offer. You swear allegiance, the Constable gives you employment so you can eat, and I promise that if you behave yourself, in three years or less I will find you more honorable estate, befitting your blood and name."

The boy sulked for a moment longer, shame wrestling with fear. "That's all? Swear allegiance?"

"That is quite a lot. Read him the oath, Commander."

"Your *Majesty!* He—"

"Silence!" she yelled. "Did you question my father's commands? I will not hear another word. Do you have a copy of the oath?"

Dominic did have a copy of the oath in his pouch, it being much in demand today. Glowering, he read it out.

Neville shrugged. "I so swear."

Malinda relaxed with sigh. "No, you have to say the words. But I am glad, Nephew. Perhaps one day we can get to know each other and be friends. Our family isn't very good at that. Carry on, Commander. Administer the oath, clean him up, clothe him, release him. Absolutely no maltreatment!" She rose. *"And no arguments!"*

"Deliver him to the Constable, you mean, my lady?"

She paused at the door. "No. He's a big boy and we trust him. Let him walk." She did not expect to see Neville again.

She ended the day with a family dinner party, entertaining the Duke and Duchess of Brinton and a trio of assorted Candlefens. Not Courtney. It was a dull affair, not helped by the dismal Bastion food, which arrived cold from some incredibly remote kitchen. The Queen withdrew as soon as she reasonably could—and monarchs need not be excessively polite to anyone. She went off to bed.

"So how do you like it?" Dian asked when the last lady's maid had withdrawn and they were alone in the firelight with the customary hairbrush.

"Like what?" Malinda asked contentedly.

"Being a despot. You've had two whole days of it. Your hair is much easier to handle than usual."

"I may leave it like that always and set a new style. Despotism is fun. I had no idea it was so easy. I enjoy it tremendously. Is Dog out in the antechamber?"

"Dog and seven others."

"Never mind the seven others," said the Queen. "Just send in Dog. I feel a need to rape somebody."

35

I had no idea it was so easy.

QUEEN MALINDA

The state funeral was poorly attended. Amby would not have cared about that, and he would certainly have enjoyed all the bands the efficient Master Kinwinkle had managed to collect—almost two dozen of them, from great military companies down to the squeaky but enthusiastic marching band of the Worshipful Brotherhood of Silk

Washers. He would probably have liked the fireworks, too, and the great pyre brightening the night sky.

Although official mourning lasted for months and a new reign began officially at the moment of the previous ruler's death, in practical terms it was often the funeral that marked the change of leadership. With the capital peaceful, she had decreed that the following morning—her fifth day as queen—court would move from the Bastion to Greymere. There she would preside over the first formal session of her Privy Council. She would start to rule.

The move was a chance for the people to view and greet their queen. She had dressed with care, in a purple gown and a jeweled coronet, and had ordered a large escort of Yeomen and mounted Blades to conduct her coach through the streets. She expected at least some cheers, but her passage was marked by sullen silence at best and frequently by boos. She arrived at the palace in a very grim mood, heading straight to the Royal Suite to change her clothes and calm her anger. The first was easy, but the booing was still rankling when she went down to join the Council.

The council chamber was an ugly, squarish room, paneled with dark wood. Even at noon its mullioned windows failed to let in enough light; the white marble fireplaces were unlit. Audley entered first and then stepped aside to take up his position beside the door. Malinda was greeted by a dozen bobbing hats as their wearers bowed or curtseyed. Although the big table in the center was already well littered with papers, she was pleased to see that none of the chairs lining the walls had been moved. When the door had closed behind her, she realized that she faced an assembly ominously divided into three distinct groups.

On her right stood old-timers from her father's day: the monotonous Duke of Brinton to supply all the clichés and platitudes required; Grand Inquisitor like a gallows wrapped in crepe; breezy Lord High Admiral, whom Ambrose had valued mostly as a drinking partner; the fusspot Grand Wizard beside the fireplace; mousy Baron Dechaise, First Lord of the Treasury, who had begged in vain to be allowed to retire; and Sir Snake.

Facing her with their backs to the windows, were the newcomers. Chancellor Burningstar had replaced the white robes and hennin of her Sisterhood with a dove gray gown and a conservative bonnet, and thus seemed shorter but still intimidating. Beside her was the horse-faced Dowager Duchess of De Mayes. As Lord Roland had once remarked, Ansel's mother would wield enormous power in Chivial during her son's minority; that had been enough excuse for Malinda to appoint her to the council. She was a massive woman and just as stubborn as she looked, notorious for speaking her mind. She was usually loud, too. Master Kinwinkle stood at a writing desk, fighting yawns and ready to fall asleep on his feet.

By the other fireplace, to Malinda's left, were the three Granville men she had reappointed: Constable Valdor, Marshal Souris, and Lord Wrandolph. Wrandolph was the one Snake had called Ratface, Granville's master of commissariat and later Lord Chamberlain. Although he had not taken up arms against the Lord Protector as the other two had, he had turned traitor even earlier, supporting Malinda's cause at her interrogation. She wanted to keep all three of them under her eye—visible but also vulnerable, because members of the Privy Council were notoriously susceptible to trumped-up charges of treason and the fatal results thereof. It was a small council, in need of being fleshed out with a few more senior aristocrats and officers of the crown. Meantime she must try to blend the separate groups into one efficient body.

She did not invite anyone to sit. "My lords and ladies, I repeat now what I have said already to most of you individually. I require from you honesty, diligence, and loyalty, but most of all I bid you give me true counsel, without fear or favor, being mindful of my needs, not my feelings. I shall chop off no heads in fits of pique, I assure you." That won not a single smile. "Let us begin with a sensitive topic. New monarchs are normally cheered, but on my way here I was booed. Can any of you explain this?"

A lack of surprise suggested that the information had already been reported and discussed.

"We think we should make inquiries," the Chancellor said.

"That is what I am doing."

A sepulchral rumble from Constable Valdor: "The riffraff were undoubtedly just booing the Blades, Your Grace. Wetshore left a bad taste. . . . Sycamore Square, also. Just the Blades. Next time you have occasion to ride out, try dressing them up as Yeomen and I'm sure you'll have no trouble."

No trouble except a Blade rebellion. She saw Snake's eyebrows shoot up.

The Duke huffed. "It only takes one bad apple to spoil a barrel. There's always a few malcontents about."

"I should like to believe you." She waited to see if there were any more original suggestions, but how could these hidebound aristocrats possibly know what the people in the streets were thinking? Then her eye caught a vague and deniable fidget from Kinwinkle.

"Yes, Master Secretary? You have our leave to speak in these meetings."

"I am honored, Your Grace. Um, it was common knowledge for some time that the young king was dying. The Lord Protector was generally expected to succeed him, Your Grace. He was a popular warrior hero. He *looked* like a king, if you'll forgive . . . a younger version of your respected father, my lady. He spent a lot of time riding around with his son beside him, and the people—I mean . . ."

"They wanted a king, and one with a grown son would be even better. They hate the very thought of a queen regnant or of a disputed succession?"

"Er, some think that way."

And then the hero's head was on a spike. Noticing the Duke opening his mouth again, Malinda said quickly, "Thank you, Master Secretary. I believe you have defined the problem exactly. Can anyone suggest any solution?"

Burningstar said, "Time, patience, and good government."

"Well said! Well, let us practice some good government. What urgent business do you have for me?"

"Finance, my lady! Money!"

All eyes turned to the wizened little Baron Dechaise. He donned a pair of spectacles—with a mutter of apology—and limped closer to the table so he could shuffle papers, although that must be only habit, for he did not look at them. "The situation is not good, Your Grace. Most government employees have not been paid in weeks. The Treasury is empty. It is fortunate that your household is in large part supplied directly from the royal estates, else there would be nothing to eat in the palace. Tradesmen are reluctant to deliver. The problem, my lady, is that the crown has had no revenue since your father died and has sold off or mortgaged everything marketable. Lord Granville waited far too long to summon Parliament. Then, of course, the writ died with your brother."

"We must issue another immediately, surely?"

"Harvest time!" Brinton growled. "Serious labor shortage just now, you know. Bad time to give the men a day off for yet another election."

"A worse time for the government to go broke, I'd think," Malinda said crossly. "We need a loan from the bankers, then? You spoke to the Lord Mayor, Chancellor?"

"I did. We did." With a look of extreme distaste, Burningstar passed the question on to Dechaise, who took off his spectacles and breathed on them. "The burgesses' terms are impossible, Your Grace.

Twenty percent a week is the lowest they will even consider, and that is for very limited—indeed I must say in my experience, entirely inadequate—amounts and duration."

"They don't think much of their new monarch, you mean?"

"Bankers hate anything unusual," remarked the Duke.

The Dowager Duchess's voice entered the conversation like a charging bull. "It would help if you had been crowned. A fine display of pomp and ceremony will win the city over and establish you as monarch beyond dispute! And I do believe the Chancellor was saying earlier that foreign governments are reluctant to recognize Your Majesty until you have been properly crowned. It is rather like a wedding, where—"

"How much does a coronation cost?" Malinda inquired.

The little baron ignored the question. He could be very deaf when he wanted. "The burgesses are well aware that the crown is deeply in debt and has no real source of revenue. We must hope that Parliament will vote supply when it meets, but traditionally the crown's income is heavily reliant on customs duties and with the Baelish blockade reimposed we can anticipate very little real revenue until a peace treaty has been signed."

Malinda turned to eye Snake. "How soon can you confiscate some elementaries for us?"

Even his cynical aplomb seemed a little frayed. "Don't know, Your Grace. I did have a list ready, but I am finding that many targets have moved, and others have cleaned up their bill of fare. I'm sure you can still buy a sex slave or a love potion somewhere, or have the evil eye clapped on your mother-in-law, but the seamy side of the conjuring business is not readily *visible* anymore. The protectorate gave the enchanters a six-month respite, and they've used it to go underground. Your Commissioners need to start from scratch, and it may take much longer to win convictions now. I'm sure we can help Your Grace, but we can't do it very soon."

In the gloomy silence that followed, the Duke exercised his battle-ax tact again. "What's her debt to the Constable, mm, Baron? And the Marshal here? Did you include those in the tally, eh?" The mood of the room soured abruptly at the thought of paying off the turncoats.

"No," Dechaise said. "Such amounts are not normally listed in the state rolls. How would they be categorized?"

"As the price of justice!" Malinda snapped. "My lords Beaufort and Thencaster—I trust you two gentlemen appreciate that payment will have to be delayed until the current crisis is resolved?"

"Of course," Mouse Rampant said briskly. "The Constable and I quite understand. We shall try to explain to our men, who are, for the most part, uneducated, rather simple fellows. None of them have been paid in months. It was their disaffection that persuaded us to support the rightful claimant in the recent dynastic dispute." His beady little eyes gleamed with amusement, but the threat was blatant: their steel and muscle had put her on the throne and they could whisk it out from under her just as easily.

Had Granville been such a bonehead as to go to Beaufort and put himself at the mercy of two military leaders whose pay he had let fall into arrears? Or was the little mercenary spinning yarns now, inventing a claim against the crown?

"We thank you, Lord Beaufort. We appreciate your loyal support," Malinda said carefully. *We would appreciate it if we believed in it.* Mention of his new title had sparked a little mental tinder—"As for the recompense we owe you, perhaps part of your eponymous honor of Beaufort might constitute your settlement. Since our dear brother died there, it has little sentimental value for us, and I am sure that fine edifice must be worth far more than the trifling sum we owe you."

"Actually, no, Your Grace, it isn't." Souris sighed deeply. "I presumed to inquire and discovered that the hideous place has been mortgaged all the way to bedrock. Isn't that right, Baron?"

Dechaise shuffled papers and this time kept his eyes down. "I have not yet compiled a complete list of properties pledged by the, er, Traitor . . . if such a list is even available."

The meeting was rapidly turning into one of those nightmares where a new horror sprang up every time one turned around. The lack of revenue she had expected, but not this talk of staggering debts. She must appear unsurprised and confident before her advisors.

"Glamorous warrior hero he may have been, dear Granville seems to have made a thorough botch of governing my brother's kingdom. What did he *do* with all that money?"

After a perceptible pause, it was Souris who answered. "He fortified coastal points, my lady, and raised garrisons to man them. He was determined to make Chivial impregnable to Baelish raiders . . . so he said."

Dangerous implications rumbled like thunder in the hills.

"How many strongholds? How many men?"

"I was not privy to the complete list," the Marshal said evasively. "Constable?"

"Nor I, my lady. At least a score of fortresses and walled towns, perhaps twice that many. As for men . . . His Grace here was remarking about the labor shortage only a few minutes ago."

More thunder, closer this time. Malinda's countercoup had perhaps not been so adroit as she had believed. If Granville had enlisted his own army and neglected to pay the Yeomen and Black Riders—perhaps even threatened to disband them—then the traitors' dramatic switch of allegiance became easier to understand.

Needing time to think it through, she said, "The crown simply must find some money. Has anyone any clever suggestions?" Oh, why was Lord Roland not here when Chivial needed him?

After a sullen pause, Constable Valdor rumbled, "If the merchants will not provide, then Your Majesty will have to ask the rich landowners for loans."

"The Black Riders will be happy to assist in collecting," Souris suggested.

The Duke of Brinton and the Dowager Duchess of De Mayes collided head-on, at least verbally, each shouting so loud that neither could be understood. Chancellor Burningstar bellowed for order, and then everyone seemed to join in. The Council split, aristocrats screaming that they saw no reason why they should be beggared to pay bribes to traitors; the military responding with insulting comments on useless, bloated parasites; and the others shouting at cross-purposes.

Malinda stood and glared at any eye she could catch until the racket finally subsided into embarrassed silence.

"This is a council, not a school yard," she said icily. "We had established that the Lord Protector tried to fight Baelish pirates with castles, cavalry, and foot soldiers. Is that right? Did he actually kill any Baels? Didn't he understand that the blockade was the real problem? Was he completely crazy?" Her grandfather had discovered that forts and fortified towns were useless when longships could be beached almost anywhere along the coast. Building a fleet was equally futile, because nobody could beat the Baels on water. The only defense that had met with even limited success was a mobile mounted militia maintained by the local sheriffs. Even those rarely managed to do more than chase the raiders back to their boats after the damage was done.

Souris shrugged. "He was a foot soldier himself. He thought that way."

"Well!" she said angrily. "His estates were forfeit to the crown. If they were mortgaged too, that's bad luck for someone else. We must seize them right away. I trust you have had the necessary proclamations prepared, Chancellor?"

"There has not been time to—"

"They are here, Your Excellency," Kinwinkle murmured, passing papers to the Chancellor.

Malinda flashed him a grateful smile. Her secretary was the greatest success of her reign so far. "How much are the Granville lands worth, does anyone know?"

"A pretty penny, I'd say," mumbled the Duke.

"Probably a sizable amount," Constable Valdor agreed in his deep rumble. "But only when you are in a position to make your claim good, Your Grace. Thencaster's up north, near the Wylderland border. We haven't heard from there yet."

Suddenly nobody was meeting the Queen's eye. Could so disastrous a meeting actually get *worse?*

"What have you heard from?"

"Tharburgh," the Chancellor said, taking up a list from the table, "Fullers Knob, Horselea, Pompifarth—"

Now the thunder was right overhead, rolling on and on.

"Those are some of the places Granville fortified? And garrisoned?"

Burningstar nodded sadly, as if wondering how she had deserved this terrible job. "Not one of them has yet submitted to Your Majesty."

The ensuing silence was very long and very weighty, and yet when Malinda spoke her voice seemed unnaturally small. "Are you telling me that I have a civil war on my hands?"

No one wanted to answer that question.

"But what do they expect to gain?"

"Bah!" the Duke mumbled. "Not civil war, just local rebellions. Armed rabble wanting to be paid off and sent home."

"They do not wish to be summarily disbanded," the Chancellor agreed. "And their pay is in arrears. I do think we should give them time, Your Grace. Let them come to terms with Lord Granville's death."

"The Black Riders are experienced in siege craft," the Marshal volunteered, but even he was wary now.

At least a score of hostile strongholds within her realm and she lacked the funds either to buy them out or pay troops to take them?

The Duke cleared his throat. "As long as they have no banner and no leader they're no danger. But, by the cold hands of death, Your Grace, it's a good job you've got the Traitor's son safely under lock and key, what?" He laughed.

Chancellor Burningstar said, "Is something the matter, Your Majesty?"

36

It is not true that calamities come only in threes. They often come in sixes or nines.

ANON.

After that, the day could get no worse, but it certainly did not improve, at least not until close to midnight, when Malinda was able to cuddle into Dog's embrace and weep all over his fuzzy chest. The wonder was probably that her Council had not just resigned en masse and left her to her fate. Why appoint a Council and then make crazy decisions like that without consulting it?

"So why did you?" Dog growled.

The Queen sniffled in very unregal fashion. "I was being kind! Neville had done nothing wrong. Stupid, stupid, stupid! Dominic tried to tell me and I shouted at him! I didn't see that Neville had inherited his father's claim and would be just as dangerous or even worse, because he was born in wedlock, which will carry weight with the snootier nobles. Even if he would have a baton sinister on his arms, plenty of them do. He can turn Granville into a martyr."

"He swore allegiance?"

"He can always claim he did it under duress."

"I'll kill him for you. Where is he?"

"We don't know! I sent him to Constable Valdor, who says he never showed up—but he may be lying, playing on both teams. Grand Inquisitor says the Dark Chamber has a sniffer spell it could use to track him if we had a suitable key—meaning something closely identified with him, that he'd owned for a long time. Which we don't. He's almost certainly far away by now. . . . Oh, Dog, I feel such a fool!"

Her father would never have made that mistake. Ambrose would have let Neville molder in a dungeon for years, just in case. If she ever did get to sleep tonight she was going to have nightmares of her own head on a spike alongside Granville's.

★   ★   ★

Nobody had been so disrespectful as to call the Queen an idiot, but the Duke and Chancellor together then took over the proceedings and abandoned any pretense of being mere advisors. They arranged everyone in chairs around the table and kept the meeting going until sundown.

The Council agreed that nothing could be done about Neville unless and until he showed up, and nothing should be done about the holdout garrisons at present. The Council summoned Parliament for the fifth day of Tenthmoon. The Council decided it needed more members and discussed names; Malinda humbly agreed to appoint the half dozen selected. The Council even found some money, or Master Kinwinkle did, when he pointed out that a tax known as "relief" must be paid whenever a vassal of the crown died. The Treasury and the College of Heralds, he said, had been working all summer, calculating the relief due for the nobles who had died in the Wetshore Massacre, and most of it had not yet been collected. With ill grace, the Dowager Duchess confirmed that the De Mayes relief was still owing; Baron Dechaise was ordered to raise ready cash by mortgaging these prospects.

The Council even had the audacity to start discussing possible royal husbands. Then Malinda slammed her fist on the table and shouted that when she wanted advice on that matter she would ask for it. The Chancellor frowned at her as if she were still only nine years old and changed the subject, but the implication remained that the sooner they found a man to take the stupid girl in hand the better.

"So what can you do?" Dog growled.

"Just this." She kissed him. He needed no more encouragement than that, having managed to lie still in uneventful embrace while she recounted her woes. The resulting frenzy drove her worries away, for a while.

They returned later, when she had her breath back. "It isn't fair. A man makes mistakes and he needs experience. A woman makes them and she needs a husband!"

"You've got a man already." The turmoil had left them turned over so that Dog's head lay on her breast.

"And a wonderful one, the only man in the kingdom who isn't seeking preferment." The Council meeting had been followed by a long audience and even longer dinner, honoring the nobility flocking to court to pay its respects to the new Queen. "They all want appointments or settlements or their daughters made maids of honor or grants of this or that. You don't expect me to dress you up in jewels and make you a marquis . . . do you?" The thought of the Council's reaction made her mind boggle.

Dog just snorted.

"You never ask me for anything," she whispered. "What do you want?"

He took a while to answer. "To be your man always. To have you as my woman." He nuzzled her breast.

She stroked the massive muscles of his arm. "All the Guard knows you're my lover, so I don't suppose it will stay a secret much longer."

"What the Guard knows Ironhall knows. Heard you're going there to harvest more Blades."

"That's a state secret. Nobody's supposed to know that, except Audley and Dominic and Chancellor Burningstar."

"Probably just someone's lucky guess, then. Makes sense. I heard Grand Master has a dozen ripe ones for you to pick."

"So did I," she said, annoyed. "Why can't men keep secrets? I expect you're the subject of political classes. You suppose they're holding you up to the juniors as Royal Gigolo, an example of rewards available to the diligent student. You want that?"

"No."

He moved his tongue and lips to her other breast, making it even harder to concentrate on other matters. They were experienced lovers now, knowing every pore of each other's bodies, every secret whim, every unspoken thought—and also every evasion.

"You haven't told me what else you want. Crave a boon, Trusty and Well-Beloved Subject. Anything."

"Send me back to Sixthmoon of 350 to tell my pa not to kill my ma by making me."

She shivered and stroked his hair. There was no arguing with him on this. No such enchantment existed or could exist, she was certain, for it would create an impossible paradox. He wanted to cancel out his own existence, but if he did not exist he could not do that, so he would exist after all and could do it, and so on, round and round forever. Conjuration could do many things, but that was not one of them.

"Then you will never meet me and become my man."

He did not answer. He could not accept that his desires were contradictory, let alone impossible. Crushed by guilt for deeds that were not his fault, Dog was not always entirely rational.

"Listen, love," she said. "As queen, I can give you a letter to Grand Wizard ordering him to find you the spell you want or make it up. If he says it's impossible, will you believe him?"

Dog stopped his foreplay. "I won't understand his talk. Can I take Winter with me?"

"Yes, love, you can take Winter with you."

They lay in close and sticky silence for a while, then she said, "Aren't you going to finish what you were doing?"

"You go ahead," Dog said. "I'll catch up."

On the twelfth day of her reign, Queen Malinda rode off to Ironhall, escorted by the entire Royal Guard. Her purpose was not only to raise the strength of the Guard by adding a dozen recruits; she had also summoned a general assembly of the Order. She left by moonlight and did not travel the most direct road—precautions her father had taken during the Monster War, and which seemed only sensible now, when a dozen garrisons scattered around the coasts had either declared for King Neville or refused to declare allegiance at all.

Circumstances had changed since her first visit to Starkmoor. The presumptuous princess had become queen, overturning a revolution while losing only a single Blade. The entire school was assembled at the main door to cheer her arrival, and Grand Master had become a model of cooperation. Hammered by the Old Blades and forged in the fires of necessity, he declared, a dozen sharp and shining youngsters were ready to serve Her Majesty; indeed he would now venture beyond his written reports and release fourteen. Starting with Prime and Second, they were summoned in groups and asked in turn if they were willing to serve. Each declared his readiness and knelt to kiss the royal hand. With a couple of exceptions, they all looked absurdly young, but of course she did not say that; she reminded them instead that they were special, because they were the first to be bound by a reigning queen in almost a hundred years. She did not mention that they might be the last Blades ever bound, if Parliament proved as antagonistic as she expected.

The following day she had no trouble finding food for thought during the hours of meditation that must precede a binding. On her first visit she had spoken with the candidates out of boredom, this time she did so to take her mind off her troubles. Hunter and Crenshaw she recognized, but there were another dozen names to memorize: Lindore with the smile, Vere the tall one, Mathew the freckled one, Loring the gorgeous, Terrible the fidget . . . all eager, all scared. They all had their sword names ready: *Avenger, Glitter, Lady, Gadfly,* and so on.

Several times Sir Lothaire, the Master of Rituals, came around in his fussy, absentminded fashion. Uncertain how to address his sovereign when she was sitting on the floor leaning back against the side of a raised hearth, he tried to bow while kneeling, which was not a success. And once, after a fatuous query about her preference in wine for the banquet, he said brightly, "Sir Dog is performing satisfactorily?"

Anything the Guard knew, Ironhall knew. Malinda turned to him in shock. Did he not realize she could have his head for that remark? His eyes were hidden by the reflection of firelight on his glasses, but the inane grin on his mouth seemed innocent enough. Giving him the benefit of the doubt, she decided that the school bookworm was unaware of the gossip. The onlookers were not—fourteen young faces around the octogram struggling very hard not to leer. Her cheeks were probably as red as the coals in the grates.

"Of course. He wields a mighty sword," she said.

Vere and Terrible developed coughing fits, confirming her suspicions.

Lothaire was still not flying with the flock. "Ah. I am pleased to hear that. It is wonderful how the binding solves problems, sometimes." There must have been some other purpose behind his question. Here it came—"I was just talking with Sir Jongleur . . . old classmates . . . both here and later at the College. He mentioned that Sir Dog came to see him, posing a problem in conjuration. Apparently—"

"Sir Jongleur is here?" She had given Dog the letter to Grand Wizard, but he had not taken Winter with him when he went to the College—probably because he still could not bring himself to reveal his secret past to a friend. Grand Wizard had referred the question to another conjurer. Dog had refused to say much about their discussion, meaning he had not understood a word of it.

"He's come for the assembly. Lots of knights—"

"Go and fetch him," the Queen said. *"Now!"*

As Lothaire scrambled to his feet and scurried away, she glanced around the circle. Twenty-eight eyes avoided hers. She was almost as angry at herself for being embarrassed as she was with the conjurers for discussing Dog's private problems. She rose in silence and headed for the stair.

The door led out to a grassy space between the gym and the perimeter wall at the northeast corner of the complex, not overlooked by anyone. She was standing there, studying cloud shadows on the sunlit tors, when Lothaire came hurrying back with another sword-bearing knight. He was in his forties, with a belly and jowls, which were unusual on any member of the Order. His beard was streaked with gray and hung halfway down his chest, but he bowed nimbly enough. Lothaire fidgeted, uncertain whether to go or stay.

Malinda ignored him, concentrating on the conjurer. "Last week we sent Sir Dog to see Grand Wizard. He told us later that he had been sent to you."

Jongleur chuckled lightly. "Blades in the raw unnerve the old gaffer, so he always refers them to me. Sir Dog is a deeply troubled young man, as I am sure Her Majesty is aware."

Her Majesty was mainly aware of hunger and worries and shortness of temper. "Then why do you breach professional ethics by discussing his case with an outsider?"

His eyes narrowed. "I am sure Sir Lothaire will be discreet."

"Why should he be, when you are not? Furthermore, the letter Dog brought bore our seal. That made it crown business. You have violated your oath of allegiance."

He fell on his knees and bowed his head. He said nothing, which was his wisest option. Malinda looked at Master of Rituals, who promptly dropped beside his friend. She let them shiver for a moment before she spoke.

"Taking the inquiry on that basis, what answer did you give our messenger?"

"What he wanted would not have worked, Your Grace," Jongleur told her shoes. "It would violate the laws of conjury." He was almost as pompous as the Duke of Brinton.

"What *laws of conjury?*"

"Well, to start with, Damiano's Axiom and the Prohibitions of Veriano, my lady."

"I am aware of Damiano's Axiom: 'Action prescribed without available resolution will dissipate the assemblage.' Alberino Veriano's Prohibitions are merely a list of things that he considered conjuration could not achieve, many of which have been accomplished since his day. Be more specific." Malinda had put her mother's library to use during the summer, seeking either a solution to Dog's problem or proof that it had none. She had found neither.

The men looked up in surprise. Sunlight flashed on Master of Ritual's spectacles; Jongleur tugged nervously at his beard.

"Your Majesty shames me. . . . The principle of superposition."

"Continue."

He gulped, worried now. "To assemble elementals and command them to perform an impossibility is extremely dangerous, leading to uncontrolled release of spiritual power. It is impossible for one thing to be in two places at once, which rules out traveling in time—even conjury will not let you go back and strangle yourself. Nor can you exist when you do not exist, that being another forbidden outcome. Sir Dog's desire to visit his childhood cannot be satisfied by any means known to modern spiritualism."

"And did you explain that to him in words he could understand, or did you amuse yourself by confusing him with technical jargon and overblown vocabulary?"

Jongleur hung his head. "I did not understand that he was acting on Your Majesty's behalf."

"Well you do now. You will go and find him at once and explain the problem in detail, until he is completely satisfied. Do you understand? Furthermore, since my request was directed to Grand Wizard, I shall expect a written reply from him to be delivered to my secretary, Master Kinwinkle, *before I return to Grandon.* Otherwise you may see the inside of the Bastion." She turned her glare on Lothaire. "And you, Master, will remember that Sir Dog's past is none of your business. Nor his future, either."

She stalked back into the Forge, leaving them on their knees. The whispering there stopped abruptly when she entered.

Now she had something else to worry about. She should *not* have lost her temper! Dog was her weak point. Enemies could strike at her through him. She did not have time to work up a good fret over this, though, before Audley came trotting down the steps and presented her with a dispatch just in from Chancellor Burningstar.

The ports of Horselea and Tharburgh had declared for Fitzambrose. Neville himself had been reported in Pompifarth, claiming royal honors and issuing a summons for Parliament to meet there, instead of in Grandon.

Members of Your Grace's Council, the letter concluded, *respectfully recommend that Your Grace consider declaring Pompifarth to be in a state of insurrection and in breach of the Queen's Peace; and that Your Grace may wish to charge the Black Riders with freeing its loyal inhabitants from the traitors who have deflected them from their true allegiance and to bring all contumacious subjects under the royal mercy; but the Council will of course loyally wait upon Your Grace's instructions.* The Council, in short, was not going to start a civil war without the Queen's command but was protecting itself in case things got worse before she returned.

The Queen was in no mood to start a war, civil or uncivil, but as she rammed swords through fourteen young hearts that night, she found herself wishing that one of them belonged to Neville Fitzambrose. That one, she would cheerfully chop in slices.

★   ★   ★

She still had to preside over the general assembly before she could leave Ironhall and race back to the capital. Knights and some private Blades had been flocking in ever since she arrived; and on the morning after the binding the Loyal and Ancient Order of the Queen's Blades assembled for the first time since 361, when Sir Saxon had been elected Grand Master. Master of Archives, that professional pedant, muttered that there was no record of a general meeting of the *Queen's* Blades, not ever. Now there was, for the Head of the Order, seated below the broken sword of Durendal, was Queen Malinda the First, bejeweled and wearing a crown.

More than six hundred men had gathered in the hall. The entire Royal Guard was present, still in the old blue liveries, alas, because the Queen could not afford to outfit them with new. Snake and his Old Blades were there in force, as were knights so ancient that they could remember Ambrose II and would insist on doing so if given the slightest encouragement. Every private Blade in the land had begged and bullied his ward to attend, and many had consented. These non–Blades were shunted off to a safe, quiet corner to dispose of a butt of fine wine from the royal cellar, but no other strangers were present.

The ceremony was brief and matter-of-fact, yet many an eye blinked tears. Grand Master read out a blood-chilling list of additions to the Litany, including a "Sir Wolfbiter, slain in a far country" and ending with Sir Abel. But the main business of the meeting concerned the three Blades who had been crippled at Wetshore: Sir Bellamy had lost a leg, Sir Glanvil the use of an arm, and Sir Dorret had been both blinded and horribly mutilated by a kick from a horse. For half a year they had lived in torment, driven by their bindings to defend their ward and balked by physical inability.

The conjuration to release them could hardly have been simpler, yet only the sovereign could perform it, and Amby had not been capable. Each in turn knelt before the Queen with bared shoulders, and she dubbed him knight, touching his flesh with the sword that had bound him. Right after that, as Snake cheerfully remarked, they could go off and get roaring drunk for the first time in their lives.

Commander Audley floated in bliss, ever at the Queen's side, being *Leader* before the entire Order, the youngest ever recorded. No other man had ever gone from Prime to Leader in just half a year, either. Much drollery was being lobbed around just behind his ears, on the lines of "do-you-suppose-his-fencing-will-improve-when-his-balls-drop," but he could pretend not to hear that. He was not allowed to hear the praise, of which there was considerably more; the Guard had developed an affectionate respect for its mascot commander. He had made no mistakes, and that was a talent swordsmen valued highly.

Malinda, for her part, could breathe more easily. As long as she had the power to release Blades, she was sovereign. They recognized her, their bindings recognized her, and no one could deny her.

That situation might change very rapidly, though, and her intention was to leave as soon as possible. If she went by midday she could reach Bondhill by sunset and be home before noon tomorrow. She would find more trouble waiting there, she had no doubt. So she fretted through the ceremonial meal—which was barely appetizing, because Ironhall was neither staffed nor equipped to create banquets—and through some very windy speeches after it. She cut her own remarks to a barely decent brevity and departed, knowing the knights would now indulge in a memorable orgy of drinking at her expense. Companions were kept sober by their bindings.

Even in Ironhall she went nowhere without an escort, and she was dogged upstairs by fourteen young men who could hardly endure to let her out of their sight. She went straight to the royal chamber, a solitary oasis of luxury in Ironhall's stony austerity, furnished with her father's taste for overstuffed, overcrowded mishmash. There she found Dian laying out her riding clothes, but she also found Winter.

"What are you two getting up to?" she said cheerfully, then saw that he had more on his mind than Dian. She dropped the smile. "Spit it out! And I don't mean your thumbnail."

"Your Grace . . . I've been talking to knights." Winter was rarely so hesitant. Either he had not finished solving his problem or he could not convince himself of the answer he had found. "There are knights from all over Chivial here."

"And?"

"There's something strange going on just west of here." He pulled his hat off and scratched his hair. "At Lomouth, Waterby, Ashter . . . all around Westerth, southern Nythia . . . Mayshire."

She waited, knowing that interruptions would only slow him down. Hunter and Vere were quietly inspecting the room for hidden assassins, while the rest of the fourteen had packed up in the doorway and corridor behind her, reluctant to push past their sovereign.

"Lots of knights," Winter mumbled. "Sir Florian from Waterby mentioned it first, then Sir Warren, who's running a private fencing school near Buran. . . . They're good men, my lady! So then I started asking, and hunting out others to ask, and I got eight or nine certains and a couple of probables. . . ."

"Tell her!" Dian snapped.

"Please do," Malinda said.

"Hiring swordsmen, Your Grace! And men-at-arms. And even farmhands. Strong arms and weak heads, if you know the expression. Several hundred, at least. I think someone's building a private army out in the west, here, Your Grace." He stared nervously at Malinda, like a child expecting a scolding.

She was training herself to take time to think. So she took time to think. Her first conclusions remained unchanged. In troubled times, men of property naturally wanted protectors, no matter what the law said about private armies. Half a dozen bullyboys to guard a mill or dockyard were of no account. A thousand or two with weapons and veterans to train them would be something else entirely. But who could find the money to do that? She couldn't!

"Is it only hereabouts? Have you asked?"

Winter nodded vigorously. "There's some of it going on all over, yes. Fitzambrose is openly hiring in the north. Farmers everywhere are screaming about a shortage of hands to bring in the harvest. But it does seem a lot just west of here, Your Grace."

What else was bothering him? "Any idea who's behind it?"

"Mayshire seems to be the center, Your Grace." Winter drew a deep breath. "Several people mentioned your cousin, Prince Courtney." He waited anxiously to see how Her Majesty liked hearing her heir being accused of treason.

⊙══✦══⊙

37

Until death do us part.
CHIVIAN MARRIAGE CONTRACT

The members of the Council rose when their sovereign entered— three women and sixteen men around a paper-littered table. She and her Guard had spent the night at Bondhill and been on the road again before dawn, pounding along in a blustery wind that threw rain and sleet by turns. At Abshurst she had told Audley to send his best two horsemen on ahead to warn Chancellor Burningstar to call the Council into immediate session. She stalked in with Audley and Winter, all three of them soaked, windswept, and muddy.

"Please be seated, Excellency, my lords and ladies." Malinda squelched down on her chair at the head, facing down the length of the table to Chancellor Burningstar.

Everyone had noted Her Majesty's evident displeasure and was trying to appear noncommittal, with varying degrees of success. The new Mother Superior, especially, tended to simper or chew her lip as conditions warranted. She was a pale little spider of a woman; it seemed she and her predecessor belonged to different factions of the Sisters, because they obviously detested each other. Today lip biting was in vogue. The Dowager Duchess of De Mayes was doing it too. None of them could come close to Grand Inquisitor's graven inscrutability. Master Kinwinkle remained standing at his writing desk.

Malinda chose to give the suspect a chance to redeem himself. "What bad news do you have this fine day, before I tell you mine?"

The Chancellor peered over the eyeglasses she had recently adopted. "The members of your Privy Council are, as always, deeply honored to have you join their deliberations, Your Majesty. We were considering a map Master Kinwinkle has prepared, showing the insurgent garrisons."

A paper was hastily passed along and spread out before the Queen. She frowned at the red names disfiguring the outlines of her realm like festering pox. The north was especially bad, for Neville's supporters were concentrated near the Wylderland border, but there were pustules less than a day's ride from Grandon itself. The absence of trouble spots in the southwest now seemed ominous.

"None of this is especially new. Can we continue to deny that we have a revolution on our hands?"

"Local unrest," grumbled the Duke of Brinton. "Horse of a different color. These towns are being held against the Queen's Majesty by armed bands of malcontents. The inhabitants in general are, we can be certain, loyal subjects of the crown."

"Is that true, Grand Inquisitor?" Malinda asked.

Lambskin spread his hands. "We have conflicting information, Your Grace. In some case yes, in others no."

"So you see no imminent armed rebellion springing up?"

"Certainly not imminently, no."

He had been given his chance. He had failed.

"Setting Fitzambrose aside for a moment, I believe the Council should hear certain information we obtained at Ironhall. Sir Winter?"

Winter stepped forward and began to recite. He was more confident now, having had time to prepare, and he spouted a damning stream of names and places. The last name, of course, was that of Prince Courtney.

"Have the honorable members any questions to put to the guardsman?" Malinda inquired sweetly. Most of the honorable members were staring hard at Grand Inquisitor. *It isn't just me,* she thought. *They all suspect him. They don't think it's just age and incompetence.*

The old man glanced calmly around the table, waiting for others to speak first.

Burningstar, who detested him, said, "Grand Inquisitor?" Her cheeks bore little red rosebuds of anger.

"It is an impressive indictment," he said. "All hearsay, of course, but still disturbing. If I may presume, without prejudice to your royal cousin's loyalty, Your Grace, would it not be advisable, in these uncertain times, to summon His Highness to court to explain what, if anything, may lie behind these rumors?"

"What can, other than treason?"

Lambskin cracked his knuckles. "Defense. Baelish ships have been seen skulking in the Westuary several times in the last few months. The locals fear a major Baelish raid, which is something we have all dreaded since the collapse of the treaty last spring. Before Your Grace was born, King Æled scored the greatest triumph of his bloody career by seizing, looting, and razing Lomouth. While still not what it was, the city is now prosperous enough to repay another rape. Since his son has never touched it, Lomouth would not be an unlikely target for him to choose now." He scanned the company again, as if assessing reaction. "Your boy may merely have stumbled on traces of many landowners looking to their own protection. To assume that His Highness the Duke of Mayshire is behind *all* the recruiting is to jump to unwarranted conclusions."

Butter should be so smooth. Malinda kept tight hold of her temper. "We fully intend to summon him before this Council. Would you care to explain why we learned of the situation at a drinking party, instead of from our Office of General Inquiry?"

He shook his mummy head sadly. "Overtaxed resources, mainly, Majesty. The inquisitors have been concentrating on Fitzambrose. I did withdraw five agents from the north last week and dispatch them to the west country to investigate why our permanent personnel in the Prince's household had fallen behind in their reports."

"What in flaming britches do you mean by, 'permanent personnel,' eh?" the Duke demanded, suddenly scowling. "You dare to plant spies on a prince of the realm, the Heir Presumptive?"

Grand Master's glassy stare avoided him, wandering around the rest of the company instead. "Her Majesty's Office of General Inquiry keeps watch on anyone who might present a threat to the Queen's Grace."

Brinton spluttered. "You implying the Dark Chamber spies on *me* too?"

"Such matters should be discussed in private, Your Grace."

"I take the matter extremely seriously," Malinda said. "I am more concerned about Courtney than I am about Fitzambrose." To back Neville would be open rebellion—and there had been few signs of general support for him as yet—but many people who would draw back from that grim plunge into rebellion might see little wrong in forcing a juvenile queen into marrying a mature prince who was her heir and next of kin anyway. Even, perhaps, some of this very Council. Like grim old Horatio Gallows, there. *Never treason! Oh no, just rationalizing the lines of command. . . .* How many of the other councillors were in his power?

"Is it agreed that we summon Prince Courtney?" she said harshly and watched the heads nod. "Then, if there is no new business, we can adjourn. Perhaps you would bring me the warrant to sign in an hour or so, Chancellor?"

It was the twentieth day of her reign. Already she had defeated one rebellion, and now she faced two more.

The Queen's Chamber was the largest and finest room in the Royal Suite at Greymere, large, and commanding a fine view above huddled city rooftops to the hills of Great Common. It was renowned for its framed Duville tapestries, whose improbable shepherd youths and maidens frolicked in an idyllic landscape and a much warmer climate than Chivial's. Queen Haralda had often threatened to hang smocks on some of them.

As a child Malinda had wondered why her father did not claim the best room as his own, but she had guessed the reason after the Night of Dogs; and when she returned to Greymere as queen she made the Guard show her the secret door and the spyholes concealed by the famous tapestries. They posed no real problem, though, because they led through to a bedchamber in the attendants' wing, and the door to that was fitted with a lock and a strong bolt. That was how Dog came calling after curfew.

She had bathed, dressed in a comfortable gown, and was nibbling a snack of fruit and cheese when Chancellor Burningstar was shown in. As soon as her guest was seated and had accepted a glass of cordial, she went straight to what they both knew was the main reason for the meeting.

"Is Lambskin playing me false?"

Burningstar sighed. "I honestly do not know, Your Grace. I personally despise the man, but I feel that way about all inquisitors. To most White Sisters, a Blade smells like hot iron and an inquisitor of rot and decay. He reeks stronger than any. If your cousin is gathering and training an army, as you obviously fear, then you certainly have cause to dismiss your chief of security for not warning you of the danger."

"The next question is: Can I do it?"

"Indeed it is! Who defends the hunter from his dogs? Your father always appointed elderly persons to head the Dark Chamber, on the theory that none of them could ever be trusted for long, and it was much safer to let them die off than to try and remove them."

Lambskin had not been many years in his post. Malinda could remember his predecessor, a huge and sinister woman, dramatically dropping dead at a concert.

"Forgive my asking, but you are worth a hundred Lambskins to me. If he has any hold over you, I will sign a pardon for it, no matter what it involves."

Burningstar smiled, obviously pleased by the compliment. "I have nothing on my conscience except maybe some sarcastic comments when Your Grace was much younger. I fear that others on your council are more vulnerable. Your honored uncle, for example."

"Brinton?" Malinda said incredulously. "How can anyone blackmail a duke? Dukes can get away with anything." Perhaps not murder or treason, but she could not conceive of the bovine Brinton murdering anyone. Boring them to death, maybe.

"Well . . ." said the first minister of her government, "it is old gossip, and I swear I have never repeated it to anyone before. . . ."

Malinda grinned and leaned closer. "But when it is a matter of fealty to the crown . . . ?"

"Exactly. Do you know why he's never fathered any children?"

"Um, no. Do tell."

"When he was about ten," the old lady said in a conspiratorial whisper, "he watched a mountebank juggling axes. He was so impressed that he went off behind the barn and tried it himself."

The Queen guffawed, much to her shame. "I can see why he would not want the tale told, but I don't think he would let it trap him into open treason."

"It might sway his judgment if there were doubts. Add a few

more cases like it, and your Council may have trouble supporting you against Grand Inquisitor."

"I don't need its support in a case of treason," Malinda said grimly. "And this time I would not make the mistake of emptying my dungeons too quickly. But we have no proof yet. Let us see how Courtney responds to the warrant, and then decide."

She read over the summons to her cousin, which the Chancellor had brought, then moved some plates to make a space for signing it. When she looked up, she caught Burningstar staring at the tapestries.

"My great-grandmother's choice. I like the lad with the drinking horn. Impressive, isn't he?"

"Oh, I beg pardon, Your—"

"Don't apologize. Everyone reacts that way at first. For sheer beef, perhaps the one with the plow, and I don't mean the ox in front." For sheer beef, Dog put them all to shame. "I doubt if Prince Courtney will look much like that with his clothes off, but I know of course the Council wants me married, so—"

"Not at all, Your Majesty! Far from it! You don't think we're enjoying ourselves? No, most of your Council . . . if you will pardon my presumption, Your Grace . . . we really think you are doing very well, and with a little more experience . . . and when we ourselves have more . . . I doubt if any of us wants to see Prince Courtney wearing the crown matrimonial. Most detest him."

"Thank you for this assurance. I am less worried by Fitzambrose's threats of armed rebellion than I am by an insidious campaign to pressure me into marrying my cousin."

"Ah," the Chancellor said sadly. "That wasn't quite what I said. If Lambskin has sold out to him . . . The Prince has been around court all his life and may be as well equipped to apply blackmail as Grand Inquisitor is. Together they would be formidable indeed."

"I wonder why everyone claims to despise Courtney and yet he always rises to the top?"

"Scum always does," said the Lady Chancellor. "Begging Your Grace's pardon."

"Pardon granted. What about *that?*" Malinda pointed out at the view of Great Common, still disfigured by rows of tents, a deliberate threat to the city. "I don't want the Black Riders there when Parliament meets."

"Your Council recommends sending them to Pompifarth."

"So you said in your letter. But to turn mercenaries loose on my own people! That is abhorrent! And *unpaid* mercenaries, at that. I wish I could pay them off and ship them overseas." She had been glad of their help three weeks ago, but drawing a sword was always easier than sheathing it again.

"We do not propose storming the town, Majesty!" the Chancellor said, looking shocked. "We merely want to invest it, to block Neville's call for an anti-Parliament to meet there. We expect very few lords or elected commons to attend, probably none, but he may claim that they have. If he puts on a puppet show, people may be hoodwinked."

"Starve him out, you mean?"

"Not even that. Pompifarth is a major port, which we cannot hope to blockade without attracting the attention of the Baels, who would love to feast on your troubles. We propose throwing a cordon of Black Riders around the walls and declaring a siege. The inhabitants will not starve. I doubt very much that Neville himself is even there."

Malinda scowled at the window. The rain had started again, blocking out the view of Great Common. "Let us discuss it at a full meeting of the Council tomorrow," she said reluctantly. She could not hold back forever; she must do something about Neville.

Continuing rain ruined the roads and threatened the harvest. With Parliament due to convene in another four days, members were still struggling toward the capital, and messengers returning from Mayshire were long in coming. Prince Courtney's reply to the warrant was a curt note pleading indisposition.

By the time the Council assembled to discuss this defiance, Malinda was so furious that she could not bring herself to take her seat. The weather was murky outside and the mood inside even grimmer. Only the lashing of rain against the windows disturbed the silence as she paced back and forth on the rug; her ministers stood around the table and watched her. All except one.

"Where is Grand Inquisitor? By the eight, if he does not appear in five minutes, I will send the Royal Guard to fetch him! What news from Pompifarth, Chancellor?"

"No change, Your Grace. The town is sealed off from the land, but boats continue to enter and leave the harbor. There has been no fighting."

"And no news from Mayshire?"

"Nothing official . . . rely on Grand Inquisitor . . . more rumors, of course."

Rumors, indeed! Lord Candlefen, Malinda's squirrel-brained cousin, had arrived from Westerth that very morning with a whole cartload of rumors. He had been more interested in describing the hardships of his journey, but when pressed he had passed on stories of Prince Courtney raising an army with the help of Isilondian military advisors.

"Where is he getting the money?" she demanded, still pacing. "Constable, how much has he spent already?"

"Depends how many men he has hired, Your Grace," Valdor rumbled. Before she could call him an idiot, he added, "Warm bodies come cheap, but assume at least one crown per man so far, including board and shelter. The problem will be weapons. Even a pike needs first-quality steel. Ash poles are cheap enough by the dozen, but just try to collect a thousand! Shields and arrows and helmets—all very specialized artifacts. Strong boots, warm bedding. Horses and oxen and carts. But weapons first. A good sword, even, can cost more than a matched team of horses; the Lord Protector stripped the country to arm his garrisons."

"So Neville Fitzambrose has them all now? Very comforting!" Still no sign of Horatio Lambskin . . . Had he fled to join his master, Courtney? "Commander Audley, since Grand Inquisitor has refused our summons to this—"

There was a knock on the door.

Audley, whose brows had risen very high at the thought of arresting the head of the Dark Chamber, said quickly, "By your leave, Your Grace . . ." and opened the door a crack. And then wider, to admit the gaunt, gibbet form of the missing inquisitor, who entered clutching a bulky mass of papers under his arm.

He bowed to the Queen. She sat down and gestured for everyone else to do the same, leaving Lambskin still on his feet, heading for his usual seat.

"We are not accustomed to being kept waiting."

He looked at her reproachfully, making her wonder if he had deliberately staged this entrance.

"I humbly crave Your Grace's pardon. I tarried to finish gathering some savory tidings, and I trust that they will compensate for my tardiness."

"My cousin is *not* raising an illegal army?"

Shaking his head sadly, Grand Inquisitor laid the papers on the table. "Indeed he is, Your Grace. About a thousand men, as near as my office can calculate. Abandoning subterfuge, he has now concentrated them in a camp just outside Lomouth."

"So we face two armed insurrections!" Malinda looked around at the shocked faces of her Privy Councillors and wondered which rats would start launching lifeboats first. "I thought you said you brought *good* news?"

She had never seen Grand Inquisitor actually smile before. She hoped she never would again.

"It seems very good news to me, Your Grace. Two nights ago, the Baels landed in force near Lomouth and attempted to seize the city. As I said, the Prince had just established his camp there. He organized resistance and sent out a sortie that engaged the Baels in battle and routed them. They withdrew to their fleet and attempted to depart, but another contingent of the Prince's forces had so damaged the longships on the beach that a great many of them sank when they were launched. Hundreds or thousands of the invaders were drowned. At latest word the survivors were being hunted down in—"

The room exploded. Even the Chancellor was on her feet shouting, waving her arms overhead, looking ready to start dancing. Never in the long and blood-soaked struggle had the Chivians ever managed to bring any significant Baelish force to battle. There was no precedent for even a real fight, let alone a victory. That *Courtney* should be able to claim credit! Among all the tumult of joy, Malinda sat in silence, wondering why the spirits of chance were being so kind to her cousin and so unfair to her.

No, this could never be coincidence! She had feared all along that Courtney was being backed by Baelish gold, because Radgar Æleding had more money than anyone. Must she believe that the invincible Bael had blundered so badly?

When the pandemonium faded enough for her to be heard, she said, "Are you quite certain this battle was genuine, Grand Inquisitor? Is there a reliable body count? Can we really believe such an improbable story?"

The room fell silent, and the councillors sheepishly resumed their seats. This time Grand Inquisitor sat down, too.

"I believe it, my lady. There are some questions still unanswered, yes. The messenger arrived just after dawn, exhausted, having ridden all night. He was still being interrogated when I came away to attend this meeting. I left instructions that I was to be informed at once if deeper probing revealed any inconsistencies in his story."

Malinda shuddered. "What does 'deeper probing' mean? You put your own agents to the Question?"

"Oh no, nothing so severe, just a mild conjuration to search out details or omissions. The subjects rarely show much permanent impairment. The man is merely a part-time agent, you see. A trained inquisitor can be emptied like a bottle."

"It is not like the Baels to leave their ships vulnerable," Constable Valdor rumbled.

Grand Inquisitor favored him with a snakelike stare. "I hear of hundreds of dead and a large number of prisoners. Including one whom Her Majesty may wish to identify personally." He paused to let the implications penetrate, eyes to widen. "Radgar Æleding."

Amid the renewed tumult his words had caused, ancient Horatio Lambskin sat in brooding stillness like a reef in surf, but his gaze was restless, assessing everyone's reaction. Malinda was doing the same. The Chancellor had smiled at first, but now she was frowning. Master Kinwinkle was another who had seen that this seeming triumph held dangerous implications.

"Military protocol is not my speciality," Burningstar said when order returned. "Am I correct in thinking that a royal prisoner automatically belongs to the monarch?"

Several men spoke up in agreement, including Valdor and even Kinwinkle, the former herald.

"Whistle for him right away!" the Duke boomed. "Have him brought to Grandon posthaste. Bird in the hand, what? A king ought to be worth a king's ransom."

"Not in this case," said Grand Inquisitor. "Granted he is rich beyond measure, he has no close family to ransom him, while he certainly has many rivals who would seek to block such a move. And his person is of no value, since kings of Baelmark are elected by the moot. The moment his capture becomes known, the earls will assemble to elect another. After that he will be just another pirate."

"He may be willing to ransom himself," Chancellor Burningstar said. "I agree with the Duke's suggestion that a troop of lancers be dispatched to Lomouth to remove the royal prisoner here. We should not give him time to buy his way out of jail."

"Not unless he pays the rent to Her Majesty!" Brinton said, much taken with his own wit.

Malinda sprang to her feet in fury. "I remind you, Cousin, that Radgar Æleding murdered my father and broke a formal treaty to do it. All he will buy from me is a stroke of the headsman's ax and for that I will not charge him one copper mite. Constable? Go and get him!"

The Trial,
Day Three

◦━◆━◦

"**Y**ou killed him," the chairman rasped. "The moment you heard that the King of Baelmark had been taken prisoner, you dispatched a troop of lancers posthaste to Lomouth with a royal warrant to seize him and bring him back to Grandon. Is that not correct?"

"Yes," Malinda said wearily. It had been a hard day, the third of three hard days. Dusk was settling on Grandon and its Bastion. Workers must now be heading home to their families, wives preparing the evening meal, footsore horses munching oats in warm stalls. On the river ships rode at anchor. In the Hall of Banners flunkies were setting out candelabra so the commissioners could see the witness and clerks record proceedings.

The farce was almost over. She had almost ceased to care. Her first brave illusion of something approaching a fair trial had been as ephemeral as a rainbow. With distortions, half truths, browbeating, and his own lies, Horatio Lambskin had served her up to his master like a trussed calf. He had also intimidated the commissioners until they had abandoned any pretense of having authority. They asked no questions now. She was obviously guilty and they would vote as instructed.

"So, without even an attempt at a trial, you struck off his head and stuck it on a spike. You put your husband's head alongside your brother's?"

Some faint remnant of the famous royal temper stirred—"If Radgar was my husband, then my claim to the throne was invalid, so why did you pledge allegiance to me right here in this hall, Master Lambskin?"

"The inquiry will take note that the witness refused to answer."

"The answer is simple—I followed the advice of my Privy Council, to which you belonged. It was you who instructed us, Chancellor. If we wanted to execute the King of Baelmark, you said, we must do so quickly, before he could be demoted."

"But did I not argue that so important a prisoner should first be put to the Question, or at least thoroughly interrogated?"

"I do not recall." She half expected the inquisitor jailers standing alongside her to call her a liar, but she spoke the truth and they remained silent. "He had been thoroughly interrogated, in Lomouth, before my men even reached him. Interrogated most horribly! I did not see him myself, but I was told that, as Lord of the Fire Lands, he bore some sort of conjuration that made him immune to fire. Flame would hurt him but not burn him. He had already been tortured out of his wits.

"Besides, I saw what the Question did to Lord Roland and I vowed I would never treat any man so, no matter how evil he was. Am I charged with being too soft-hearted? The Council agreed to Radgar Æleding's execution and you were present at the meeting." She could not remember which way he had voted in the end, though. She certainly remembered the Radgar she had met briefly on the longship at Wetshore, and her conviction then that he was not the monster of his reputation. She remembered her revulsion at the thought of turning such a man into a gibbering rabbit.

The chairman peered along the table, first left, then right. "The honored commissioners may well wonder whether the Bael's hasty execution was designed to suppress his version of what exactly passed between the two of them before her father was assassinated. A transcript of the testimony he gave in Lomouth will be placed before the commissioners in due course."

"Testimony given under torture?" Malinda shouted. "Or did you write it yourself this morning?"

"The witness will speak only when addressed. But let us by all means discuss Lord Roland, since you mention him." The chairman bared yellow stumps of teeth. "The traitor Roland. Now that one *was* put to the Question, whereupon he confessed to treason against the Council of Regency, the supreme authority in the land. Before he could make a full and detailed statement, your agents took over the Bastion and you ordered the prisoner released from his cell."

"I did. I still have nightmares about what you had made of him. How do you manage to sleep at all, Chancellor?"

"You ordered the prisoner moved to—"

"He was not a prisoner then."

"Be that as it may, that night he was murdered. Who killed him?"

"I do not know." The Blades, of course, but she did not know which.

"Who do you think killed him?"

"My suspicions are not evidence."

"The inquiry takes note that the witness refuses to answer. Was he not murdered so he would not testify to your part in his foul treason?"

"I do not know why he was killed."

"The witness is lying!" barked one of the guards alongside her chair.

"All right, he was murdered out of pity! Murdered by one of his best friends—and I do not know which—because your horrible conjurations had turned him into—"

"Silence! The witness will speak only to answer a question." The chairman sighed. "Radgar, Roland—I am sure the honorable commissioners have noted that witnesses to your crimes had very brief lives. Now let us consider Pompifarth. You sent the mercenary troops known as the Black—"

"You were at that meeting! You know how I fought to have the terms of engagement restricted! You know—"

"If you persist in interrupting the court," the chairman said hoarsely, "then I will have the guards gag you and allow you to testify only by gestures. Your seal was on the warrant by which those mercenary brutes sacked Pompifarth. Those violent men were ragged and hungry, yet you sent them to storm a city you claimed to rule. The killing, rapine, and looting were done in your name and by your authority."

"Is that a statement or a question? In either case it is a lie. Souris was strictly forbidden to enter any part of the city other than the fortress that abuts it on the north. The massacre was ordered by—"

The chairman nodded and a hard, rough-skinned hand clapped over Malinda's mouth, banging her head back against the wood of the chair. Other hands grabbed her arms, immobilizing her.

"This is your last warning. The next time you speak unbidden, you will be gagged and bound." The chairman glanced to left and right. "At this hour we usually adjourn for the day. Howsoever, I do believe that we can wind up this tedious business fairly rapidly now. May I suggest that the honored commissioners take a brief break to partake of some of Governor Churle's splendid hospitality and then reassemble in about an hour? At that time we can question the witness about the last and perhaps most terrible of her crimes, the murder she committed with her own already blood-soaked hands."

38

We see most clearly out of the backs of our heads.
FONATELLES

News of the Pompifarth disaster reached Grandon early on the fourth of Tenthmoon. Malinda's first notice of it came while her maids were dressing her—Chancellor Burningstar was in the anteroom, begging an audience at Her Majesty's earliest convenience. She called for a robe and the visitor and shooed the girls away.

Burningstar came hurrying in, her flustered manner utterly out of character. She bobbed a small curtsey at the door, came close, and then lowered herself unsteadily all the way to her knees.

"Something is wrong," Malinda said, offering a hand. "And that is not a good position for clear thinking. Here, let me help you up."

"But I am tendering my resignation, Your Majesty. I have failed most—"

"Your resignation is refused. Come and sit here." Rejecting protests, she led the old lady over to the chairs by the fire, and only when they were both seated would she listen. "Bad news, obviously." *Was there any other kind?*

Out it came: Pompifarth, sack, murder, looting, mass rape . . . Within minutes Burningstar was close to tears, and the redness of her eyes said she had wept hard and long already. "Even the Baels are never that bad!" she finished. "They leave the towns standing so the people can generate more wealth to be looted the next time. This was total destruction. I cannot continue as Your Majesty's—"

"You will continue." Malinda felt no desire to weep. She wanted to kill someone. "I think you have been doing amazingly well, and you know I speak the truth. Did I fall into the same pit as Granville, trusting unpaid mercenaries? Souris has switched sides again, obviously. Who put him up to this?"

"Fitzambrose himself, of course! The fake call for an Anti-Parliament . . . it was a trap and I led you into it. His men opened the gates for the killers, I'll swear! Look at the timing—Parliament meets tomorrow and now everyone thinks you made an example of the city."

Malinda sighed. "You are right, I fear. Well, write the truth into my speech and let's hope they believe me." She looked at the Chancellor's careworn expression. "There is more?"

A nod. "A letter from Prince Courtney. I beg your pardon, my lady, but I forgot to bring it. If I may send—"

"Just tell me. I think I can guess."

"He wants . . . he *demands* that you marry him, my lady. He wants the crown matrimonial."

Malinda sat in silence for a while. It was a month since Amby died. They had not given her much of a chance to show how a queen would rule.

The next day, she addressed Parliament.

Although she had never met one before, Malinda had enough experience in public speaking to recognize a hostile audience. As she paraded after the sergeants-at-arms with their maces and Blades with drawn swords, down the aisle between the kneeling Lords and Commons assembled, she could smell hatred in the air. When she sat enthroned, with Audley standing beside her holding *Evening,* she looked out over an ocean of angry stares. The Lords were splendid as kingfishers, robed in scarlet and ermine, crowned with coronets—a real crown was a horrible thing, and she was going to have a deathly sore neck by the time this nonsense ended—but in back of them the Commons were a flock of drab sparrows, two knights from every shire and two burgesses from every town.

She swore the enthronement oath again. The ancient promises flew away like bats into the sullen silence. She read her speech. No one was rash enough to boo a monarch, but several times she sensed a low rumble of disapproval—notably when she mentioned her renewal of the campaign against evil enchantment. Only her account of the capture and execution of Radgar Æleding won a cheer, but everyone knew that Courtney deserved the credit. They even knew that

Courtney had been industriously torturing the monster until the Queen's men stole him away; they thought that a much better idea than just chopping off his head.

Courtney was not present. Courtney had not resisted when her Yeomen seized the captive Baelish king, but his refusal to appear before the Privy Council and now his absence from Parliament were acts of rebellion. How could she denounce him when chance had made him the greatest hero in the land? She could condemn Neville, of course, and did so. She laid the blame for the Pompifarth massacre on him, but who believed her?

When she spoke at last of the crown's desperate need for money, she thought she heard knives being whetted, but perhaps it was only teeth grinding. Parliament traditionally demanded redress of its grievances before voting supply, and this Parliament was going to pile corpses at her door—Granville, Pompifarth, the carnage at Wetshore, Sycamore Square. Parliaments impeached chancellors quite regularly, but none had ever tried to depose the monarch. That record might be about to change. Her Heir Presumptive was the new national hero, Prince Courtney.

Dog came to her that night as soon as Dian had left, and their lovemaking was even more urgent and passionate than usual. Either he took his cue from her or he had worked out the situation for himself. Later, in the lull after the storm, she broke the news. "It is nearly over, love. We have very few nights left."

He just grunted. He rarely spoke much, and it was almost impossible to make him speak of bad things.

"We always knew it could not last. We have enjoyed much longer than I expected."

"I have brought shame upon you," he said bitterly. "You heard what they were shouting at you in the streets. They know you have a lover named Dog."

"Perhaps just coincidence," she said, but not believing that. "Not the scandal . . . Parliament will force me to marry Courtney so it can make him King. No, don't offer to kill him for me. I know you would if I said please, but that would probably mean Neville succeeding, so killing Courtney would only make things worse."

"How can they force a queen?"

"By refusing me money." She sniffed away a tear. "He's a lot older than I am. I'll outlive him, I swear! I'll be older then, and have some experience, and . . . Oh, Dog!" She started to wail, so he kissed her and went on kissing her. It wasn't possible to kiss and blubber at the same time. After that he would not let her speak about the future at all.

The following morning Parliament set to work. At first there was only angry talk, but soon resolutions were being moved, bills read, committees formed, petitions introduced, questions asked. A motion declaring a female chancellor a breach of parliamentary privilege was defeated, but narrowly. The crown's appeal for supply was ignored.

Day by day Burningstar's reports to the Queen grew grimmer, until, at the end of a turbulent week, the first bill cleared both houses and arrived at the palace for the Queen's signature. It was very brief and unambiguous, and exactly what she had feared it would be.

That evening she held a private party in the quarters she had occupied before her departure for Ness Royal, and the participants were those who had shared them with her—Ruby, Dove, Alys, and Sister Moment. Laraine had vanished into matrimony, but Lady Arabel had just returned from Ness Royal plumper than ever; and naturally the three surviving Blades of the Princess's Guard were there. The night twinkled with music and dancing and brave efforts to be merry.

Next morning, Malinda addressed the Guard—not all of them, but the dozen or so who were then attending her, for they comprised a fair sampling, from Fitzroy, the eldest, down to Vere and Terrible, the most junior.

"You have heard, I am sure," she said, "that Parliament has sent me a bill dissolving the Order. This is a foggy area of law, because ever since Ranulf, the Blades have been regarded as being within the royal prerogative. Ironhall is paid for out of the privy purse. On the other hand, Parliament does vote taxes to cover the cost of the Royal Guard, and it did approve the Charter, which exempts bound Blades from criminal penalties and so on. I do not intend to sign this bill."

They waited in silence. They were bright young men; they knew the relevant law and history, but they also knew that when Parliament clashed with the sovereign, although it might not get all it wanted, it rarely came away empty-handed. The most affected were the young-sters, who had been sure of many years' employment in the Guard, whereas the seniors would have already been looking forward to re-lease and private life. Eventually Winter took his finger from his teeth just long enough to say, "The Commons will withhold supply."

"You are right," Malinda admitted, "up to a point. Since this is the first bill they have passed, it obviously lies near to the members' hearts. They will bluster and blather; they will pass bills, motions, and resolutions galore, but eventually Parliament and I must come to agreement. The country is close to civil war; the burgesses know that and do not want it. In the end I must grant redress, they must vote supply. If they will not see reason, then I will dissolve Parliament and run the government on funds gained by suppressing evil elementaries." Snake had not clinked any gold into her hands yet, though.

"But—" Winter thought better of what he had been about to say and went back to nibbling.

"But," she said, "Parliament does not want me to do that, and knows I would not dare challenge the enchanters without you to protect me. There are many layers to this. I assure you that if this matter has priority with the members, it certainly does with me. I am as bound to the Blades as you are to me."

Fitzroy thanked Her Majesty for her gracious words. She did not think she had convinced her troops.

Everything fell apart very rapidly after that. The Commons began debating the Queen's marriage. Malinda summoned the ringleaders, including the Speaker, Alfred Kildare. She left them on their knees while she roasted them with a tirade on the royal prerogative. She warned them that any further discussion of that subject would see them all in the Bastion. Her father had done it and she would. She used words she had overheard in stables.

At the next meeting of the Privy Council, Constable Valdor gave a review of the military situation in his bone-grinding bass. "Fitzambrose is definitely on the march," he said. "He's bringing all his father's troops south from Wylderland, pulling in the garrisons that support him. I expect the Black Riders will join him. If he meets no resistance, he should be here in nine or ten days."

Studying those coarse and ruthless features, Malinda wondered whether Valdor himself would stay loyal that long. "How many men?"

"Probably less than three thousand in total, Your Grace, but at least three quarters of them are battle-hardened professionals. The rest have been intensively trained over the last few months."

"And Courtney?"

"He hasn't moved yet, that we know of."

No doubt he was too busy showering the nobility with blackmail notes. Courtney would always prefer subversion to overt military action, in spite of his stunning victory over the Baels—or even *because* of it. Malinda was convinced that the true story of that engagement had yet to be told.

"We estimate the Prince has five or six thousand men at his disposal," Valdor growled.

"Not close," Grand Inquisitor snapped with the delicacy of a falling tree. "Less than half that, and most of them untrained, unequipped farm boys."

"How sure are you?" the Queen asked. She no longer believed much of what he told her, but she dared not beard the lion until Burningstar found a replacement lion. Even the Blades might not be able to defend her if Lambskin's Dark Chamber supporters chose to retaliate.

"Courtney had about a thousand when he attacked the Baels—he only won because he took them by surprise and caught them with their force divided. They lost far more men to drowning than—"

"And the bodies were washed out to sea, of course?"

"Some of them, Your Grace. Some were washed up on the beach. A victorious commander never has trouble recruiting, but most of those who have gathered under his banner since then are untrained and armed with pitchforks." Lambskin's insistence on downgrading the Courtney threat did not necessarily mean he was not corresponding with Neville as well, of course.

"Constable?" Malinda said.

Valdor growled. "I agree that he needs weapons. The drowned Baels took theirs to the bottom with them. You can't buy a good armorer now for his weight in rubies. Arms are the biggest bottleneck."

Malinda had always understood that the problem bottlenecks were the small ones. Which side was Valdor on? Having killed Granville, he ought to fear Granville's son, although Souris seemed to have made the reverse switch easily enough.

"We cannot assume," the Chancellor said, "that they will kill each other off and leave the realm at peace. Is it not time and past time, for Her Majesty to call up the levies?"

The bitter truth was that the Chivian crown had no permanent army, other than the Household Yeomen and the mercenary forces in Wylderland that were now supporting Neville. To go to war, Malinda must call on the peers to muster and arm their tenants; cities would supply money or raise regiments. She had wide estates of her own, of course, but Granville had drained them of men to garrison his strongholds.

Valdor shrugged. "But how do you arm them? You have the same problem as the Prince. Will you fight a civil war with fists and pitchforks?"

"The lords are already arming," Burningstar said bitterly. "Half of them have left town. Spirits know which side they'll be on in the end."

"I suspect most of them will lean toward Prince Courtney," Malinda said. "Does anyone disagree with that? No? So the plan, I suppose, is that I am expected to appeal to my cousin for help against my nephew, and the price of his help will be the crown matrimonial." She looked around the table, searching for dissent. "I do not—"

The door flew open. Audley jumped like a cricket and came down with sword drawn, but the intruder was only Sir Piers—hatless, hair in wild disarray, doublet hanging open, and half-unlaced shirt exposing an extremely furry chest. He stopped just inside the doorway, seeming quite unaware of *Evening*'s razor edge almost touching his throat.

"Ironhall!" he howled. "Your Majesty, they have sacked Ironhall!" By then the Council was on its feet, everyone shouting at once, so the rest of his announcement was barely audible. He rattled off unfamiliar names . . . "rode all night . . . drove them into the moors . . . burned . . . dead . . ." He belatedly went down on one knee, and tugged his doublet closed. Audley slammed the massive door in the faces of the Blades gawking outside.

Malinda alone had remained seated. Again a Blade had brought her a fateful message. How many times had that happened in her life? Dominic bringing her summons to court and thereby provoking Godeleva's suicide. Lord Roland telling her of her betrothal to Radgar. Marlon's frantic ride to Ness Royal to warn of Amby's imminent death. Now Piers. She waited until the others sat down again, abashed.

Piers said, "I most humbly beg Your Majesty's—"

"Repeat your report. Who did this?"

Courtney's men, of course.

When he had finished, Malinda said, "Thank you. You may withdraw. I will address the entire Guard in the Rose Hall, right after this meeting. Bring as many private Blades as you can find, even if you have to drag them there. First I want to speak with Sir Dog."

As the door closed behind the Blade, she surveyed the shocked faces of her Privy Council.

"Absolute idiocy!" Constable Valdor growled. "What sort of military objective was Ironhall? A few boys and old men? If that's the best his Isilondian advisors can do, the Prince is no threat to her Grace."

"Parliament will be pleased," the Chancellor muttered hoarsely. "That finishes the Blades. Popular move."

"I doubt if that was the main reason," Malinda said. "Now you know how to arm an army of farm boys, Constable—there were five thousand swords just hanging there for the taking. However, it is an act of overt rebellion against the crown. Chancellor, summon Parliament into joint session. Announce the news and ask for a loyal address attainting Courtney a traitor. Better prepare a writ of dissolution for my seal and take it with you, to be used if necessary, at your own discretion. If they get the bit between their teeth, send them home."

"And call out the levies?"

Malinda thought of men slain, men crippled and mutilated, perhaps towns burned, women raped . . . just so she could choose who would lie in her bed? She sighed. "No. I think they would simply join one rebel or the other, not me. I am not going to throw the land into worse turmoil than it is in already. Does anyone have any better ideas?"

No. Heads shook in morose silence.

They all knew that it was over.

When everyone had left, they sent in Dog. He glanced curiously around the Council Chamber, strode purposefully across to where Malinda was standing, crushed her into his arms, and kissed her. She had not expected that, but she cooperated.

Then they looked at each other, still embracing.

"I want you to go first, love," she whispered. "They know what you mean to me, so it will help the others. Can you do that?"

His ugly face twisted in pain. "Must this be?"

She nodded. "I'll explain to them. And then I want you to do something. This is just as hard for me . . . I'm going to send Winter and Dian back to Ness Royal. I want you to go with them, see they arrive safely. Wait there. If I need a place to hide, that's best."

"And who gets you there safely?"

"I'll set up something with Snake. Promise me!"

Dog argued, of course. He couldn't help but argue. She won his promise eventually, but she could not be sure that it would last long enough.

As she entered the Rose Hall, the waiting Blades sank to their knees, which was a breach of normal procedure, a unique tribute. It brought tears to her eyes. It would not make things easier. She went to stand behind the red cushion that lay on the edge of the dais. She looked over the assembled Order—Snake and some other knights in the background . . . half a dozen private Blades also. She gestured for them to rise.

"Ever since Durendal and Ranulf," she said, "your Order has

been the bulwark of my house, an unfailing source of honor and duty, of courage and dedication. More than once it saved the dynasty. Now, alas, times have changed. The *Litany* itself has perished in flames. The sky of swords has fallen."

She located Dog, at the back. She could not read his expression.

"Worst of all, I must tell you that, through no fault of yours, you have become a liability. If you insist on remaining to guard me, I shall be in greater danger than if you disperse. Your predecessors protected my ancestors from death, but the rebels who destroyed Ironhall and now march on Grandon are intent on marrying me off, not beheading me." Courtney, yes, but Neville might prefer to avenge his father. "Forced marriage is a peril of queens, not kings. From choice I would not wed either my royal cousin or my nephew, but unwelcome marriage is a common fate for women and we survive it. I will still be Queen of Chivial. On the other hand, if you stand in the rebels' way, they will slay you to the last man. It will be a bloody battle, and I will be blamed for the slaughter. I may even perish in it, so you serve me best now by disbanding. I ask you all to make this sacrifice. Companion Dog?"

Would he? Could he?

For a long moment she held her breath. Perhaps she had been wrong to ask him. All Blades resisted release, although they were usually very glad of it afterward. She was counting on Dog's love to overcome the conjured reluctance, but perhaps it would make the struggle harder for him.

Then he shouldered Fury and Winter aside and strode forward to the cushion. A sigh seemed to fill the whole hall. He hesitated again, staring at her in puzzled agony, before he drew his broadsword and offered it, hilt first. She had forgotten how much that great slab of steel weighed. He had refused to name it when he was bound, but one night at Ness Royal she had teased him that it must be called "Sword," and later he had shown her that word clumsily scratched on the blade near the hilt. She saw it again now: *Sword*.

Dog never did things by half measures. Instead of fumbling to unlace jerkin, doublet, and shirt, he just put both hands to his neck and ripped, hauling the remains down to his elbows. Shoulders bare, he knelt for the dubbing.

"Arise, Sir Dog."

She returned *Sword* to him. As he backed away, rubbing his eyes, Audley turned to face the throng. "Companion Dominic!"

Dominic hesitated, face twisted in horror. Bloodfang shoved him and he stumbled forward.

"Arise, Sir Dominic . . ."

"Companion Oak!"

Dog took Oak by the elbow and delivered him to the cushion as surely as a team of horses would have done.

"Arise, Sir Oak."

Dominic brought the one after, and then the pattern was set. A few wept, but none of the Guard made a serious attempt to resist.

Sir Reynard . . . Sir Brock . . . Sir Crenshaw . . .

Most of the private Blades had to be dragged forward, although not one drew his sword or tried to flee. Normally only the death of his ward could release a private Blade, but in this dissolution of the entire Order, the effort was worth making. It might work for some of them.

And last of all: "Arise Sir Audley . . .

"I thank you all from the bottom of my heart," Malinda said, "and wish you long life and happiness. The Treasury will distribute some funds . . . not nearly what you have earned, but all I can spare. I hope some of you will write a proper history of the Blades to replace the archives lost in the destruction."

She stepped down and Dog offered his arm to lead her out. The knights bent their knees to her as she went by them, but no one could manage to raise a cheer. After nearly four centuries, the Blades were finished. Radgar Æleding, once himself a candidate in the Order, had destroyed it with a single bolt. It was small consolation that his head now adorned a spike in Grandon.

<hr />

39

I will be your friend, the lion told the antelope. The antelope replied, Then I shall not fear my enemies.

FONATELLES

On the twentieth of Tenthmoon, Courtney's army pitched camp on the outskirts of Grandon, having marched from Ironhall without meeting resistance. Grand Inquisitor reported that Neville's forces were scattering and retreating northward. Parliament had adjourned, with many members hurrying away to join the triumphant Prince, and most of the Privy Council had gone with them. Even the Queen's ladies-in-waiting had headed home to visit their families, just in case.

The palace seemed deserted. As the sun was setting, Malinda sat in her private withdrawing room with Burningstar and Secretary Kinwinkle. They were eating sweet cakes and sipping dry mead. There was nothing more to be done.

"How early it is getting dark now," the Chancellor remarked.

"Very symbolic," Malinda said. "Tell me, both of you, what did I do wrong? If I ever write my memoirs, what lessons should I pass on to the next queen regnant, if there ever is one?"

Burningstar displayed one of her grim little smiles. "You first, Master Secretary."

Kinwinkle looked stricken at the thought of criticizing a monarch, but he plunged bravely ahead. "I think you did very little wrong, my lady, nothing to be ashamed of. The dice were loaded against you right from the start. Lord Granville ruled badly and waited far too long to face Parliament, so you inherited a bankrupt realm. The manner of your father's death . . . if you will forgive me, there is still some lingering doubt about your part in that. And the Blades' rampage alienated everyone, so perhaps you should have disowned them instead of supporting them." He stopped, watching nervously to see how she reacted.

"Thank you." *Disown the Blades after three hundred years?* Malinda looked to the Chancellor, who sniffed.

"I blame your father. He should have either named Lord Granville as his heir or left him out entirely, certainly never made him Lord Protector. Your claim was left foggy. It was a miracle that you managed to win the throne at all, Your Grace."

"And you are too kind to tell me I was too kind to keep it?"

Burningstar took a sip of mead in ladylike fashion. "Perhaps. You should certainly have left Prince Courtney and Master Fitzambrose in the Bastion until you had established your rule. Your leniency was an error, although one that does you credit. Apart from that, you made no real mistakes. Your father certainly blundered more than that in his youth, before he learned that kings must listen to their councillors and take time to weigh their actions. Courtney's capture of the Bael was a drastic interference by the spirits of chance, against which no mortal can stand. Without that, we might have Neville at the gates instead of him."

That was no figure of speech; Malinda thought she could hear cheering in the distance.

"I am too softhearted. I did not want even Granville to die as he did. As one of my Blades did . . . and other men . . . I did not want to cause *any* man's death."

The Chancellor emptied her goblet in one swallow and clinked it down on the table. "If I may say so, Your Grace, you may still have time to redeem your final mistake." Her eyes drilled holes in Malinda. "You admit that you do not wish to marry your cousin."

"I always found Courtney amusing, but as far as being married to him . . . I hope he still uses love potions."

"With respect, my lady, I have met your nephew only briefly, but he seemed a pleasant enough young man, quite ordinary. He ought to be a lot more malleable than your cousin. If you really want my opinion, I still believe you should have headed north to join him—yes, married him and made him King Consort! That debauched butter churn of a Courtney will be a hopeless disaster. There is probably still time."

"Unlikely, I'd say." Malinda sighed. The cheering was growing louder. "I have thought much on this, these last few days. Neville seemed like a strapping stripling, I grant you, but he thinks I killed his father. He broke his oath to me. If I flee to him, I shall be throwing myself on his mercy and will end up a prisoner, not a wife or co-ruler." She, too, drained her goblet. "It would still cause civil war. I do not want innocent people to die because of me!"

After a moment she added, "Love potions or not, I can outlive Courtney."

The door swung open. Lady Burningstar and Master Kinwinkle rose. Two burly men-at-arms entered, Grand Inquisitor peered over their heads, and then all three went out again. Courtney came mincing in, resplendent in gold and scarlet, the feather in his hat as long as a scythe. He paused to consider Burningstar, who was halfway to the door already. She offered him a barely visible curtsey.

He pouted. "You should have stayed with the wimple, darling. That neck is an eyesore. I'll take the chain now." He held out a finely manicured hand.

She straightened so she could look down at him from as high as possible. "Her Majesty gave me this chain and until Her Majesty—"

"Let him have it, Chancellor," Malinda said. "He's spiteful. And thank you again for all you have done."

Burningstar angrily lifted the golden chain over her bonnet and relinquished it.

"If you are wise, lady, you will now return to Oakendown and stay there." Courtney turned away from her and frowned thoughtfully at Master Kinwinkle, who wilted.

"Footman? Gardener? Night soil attendant? No . . . You were the herald who read out Uncle's will so badly. Well, run along and find something useful to do."

Dismissing them with a flick of his fingers, Courtney pranced the rest of the way to Malinda, bringing a powerful odor of cloves. The door closed, leaving them alone.

"I did warn you, darling." He helped himself to a chair and held the flask of mead up to the light to see how much remained.

"You have still not sworn allegiance. I should not have let you get away with that."

"No, you shouldn't." He filled Burningstar's discarded goblet. "But you did. And now you are going to be swearing wedding vows. I did warn you." He sipped. "Mm? Too dry for my palate. We are currently preparing a brief ceremony, at which you will sign and seal a few simple documents: our betrothal, a proclamation announcing it and setting the date for our wedding, a bill granting me the crown matrimonial—and precedence—and letters patent appointing me regent in the meantime with plenipotentiary powers to stamp out the current unrest." Removing his hat briefly, he looped the gold chain over his head.

She did not bother to hide her contempt. His face was freshly powdered, the rich red velvet of his jerkin displayed not one speck of dust, and his fingers glittered with gems. He smirked like a satisfied child and took up his goblet again.

"Can't you at least say you are glad to see me? Even relatively speaking? Would you rather have that ghastly Fitzambrose boy sitting here? A marriage knot is preferable to a hangman's. He has sworn to post your head next to King Radgar's."

"He's no threat now," she said. "He must be scampering back over the Wylderland border about now."

Courtney smirked. "Um . . . no, darling. You have been misinformed. He's south of Pompifarth, heading this way. But I am advised that we can meet him and wipe him out before he disturbs the peace around here. That's assuming he turns down my final offer, which he probably won't—it's very generous. He will live in luxury for the rest of his days, few though those will undoubtedly be. Forget him, beloved, and think only of our future together. Tomorrow we shall hold the formal betrothal ceremony for the peers and diplomatic corps and so on. Then I will go off and deal with the Fitzambrose pest. You will stay here to bake the wedding cake."

"You must be the only general in history to lead his army in a coach and four."

He winced. "Dearest! You are not suggesting I should ride a *horse* are you? I leave all the nasty sweaty, smelly rough stuff to underlings. Except for breeding heirs, of course. I'll attend to that in person."

"And if I refuse this romantic proposal you ply me with love potions as you did all those other women?"

Courtney chuckled, laid down the goblet, and rose to his feet. He came close, and she instinctively leaned away from him. She had never cared for cloves.

"Daaaarling!" he said, smiling down at her. "Do you know the nicest part of having an army at your back? You don't have to keep being nice to people all the time! It did get to be wearing sometimes. No, my love, no potions. Have you ever heard of the Quiet Pool?"

Something unpleasant was coming. "No."

"Well, you know those elementaries your father suppressed so energetically? All their books of evil enchantments were supposed to be destroyed, yes? Well, they weren't. Very few, in fact. The College managed to get their palsied hands on some, but the Dark Chamber collected most. The Quiet Pool is a conjuration that used to be especially popular with henpecked husbands and bullied wives." He chuckled again, studying her with bloodshot eyes.

"You wouldn't dare!" she said, her mouth suddenly dry with fear.

Grinning inanely, he nodded and chucked her under the chin. "Oh, yes I would, kitten! Let's settle it right now. Which is it to be? Will you be a good, obedient, and passionate wife, or do I have Grand Inquisitor turn you into royal jelly?"

"He wouldn't dare!"

"No? He drools at the thought. You really should not have struck him that night in the Bastion, my sweet. He even dreams of being Chancellor—we'll let him dream a little longer. Now, beloved, will you marry me?"

That it had come to this! She wondered how bad Radgar Æleding would have been, really.

"Yes, I will marry you. I have no choice."

"With passion and babies and all the naked-body-in-bed stuff?"

"I will provide the body, as required. You'll have to supply the passion."

He lifted her hand and kissed it. "Tonight, beloved, I will test your commitment. Until then, keep me in your heart."

She had always suspected that Courtney's cynical mask hid a wounded, sensitive soul. Now she knew that the inside was much nastier than the outside.

He paused on his way to the door. "I'll have you fetched when we're ready for the signing ceremony. Meanwhile, stay here, out of trouble."

The Trial,
Day Three
(CONCLUDED)

The Governor's hospitality must have been even more splendid than the chairman had predicted, because Malinda was left to her own devices for several hours. She paced her cell frantically, planning what she would say in her defense. "I know he's vindictive," she told Winter, "but even Horatio Lambskin will have to allow me a chance to speak. He must! Briefly, maybe, but he must let me make a statement and have an inquisitor tell them I am speaking the truth. Even in treason trials, they all get that grace. So what do I deny first?"

Winter did not answer. Nor did Horatio, and poor little Moment down on the floor had been washed away by the fish soup Malinda had dropped two days ago, or had fled from it. Malinda had looked everywhere for her.

Eventually she realized that she was staggering with exhaustion, weakened by the ordeal of the last three days on top of the months of physical and mental inaction. She fumbled in the dark to find her chair and flopped down on it. She had waited too long. It seemed only a few minutes before a chink of light crept in under the door, the lock clattered, hinges creaked. In came Nightmare, holding a lantern.

Pestilence followed her and headed straight to Malinda, reaching for her, one-handed. Malinda leaped up and backed away, but there was nowhere to go. She was slammed back against the masonry with fingers at her throat choking her. A fist pounded into her chest—once, twice.

She croaked, trying to protest. Her head was ground against the stonework. She knew better now than to struggle or fight back. That brought much worse hurt and humiliation.

"This is a warning," Pestilence snarled. Her breath was rank. "Tonight you behave yourself, or tomorrow we put the men to work on you. You think this hurts?"

A foot stamped on her instep. Malinda squealed.

"That was nothing, nothing at all. Now go!" The jailer hurled her across the room in the general direction of the door.

Obediently, the prisoner limped down the gloomy, twisted stairs, with Pestilence and Nightmare and the lantern at her back, giant shadows swimming on the stonework ahead. At the bottom the usual squad of men-at-arms waited to escort her along tunnel-like corridors, back to Great Hall and her solitary chair in the center.

Two of the commissioners already had their heads on the table. Another three arrived late, weaving along the walls in efforts to make inconspicuous entrances. Several of the foreign observers came with them, in a similar unsteady state.

"The inquiry will come to order," the chairman said, folding his snaky hands. He frowned to right and left, until the sleeping commissioners had been prodded awake by their neighbors. "We must now consider the last and perhaps the most despicable of this woman's crimes. She will describe to the honorable commissioners her actions on the night of the twentieth of Tenthmoon."

Malinda gathered her wits for the battle. "I went to bed. I had instructed my ladies not to open the outer door of the suite to anyone or for any reason short of the palace being on fire. I bolted myself in, lay down, and went to sleep."

"There were how many doors to your chamber?"

She was not going to let Dog be dragged into this. She had sent him away days before, and by that night he should have already been safe in Ness Royal. She hoped desperately that he was still safe, not caught up in the web of the Usurper's vengeance.

"Officially one. There was also a secret door known only to me, the sovereign, and senior members of my Royal Guard. The Guard had by then been disbanded and—"

"A secret door to a lady's bedchamber would be for purposes of illicit fornication?"

"If you say so, Chancellor. It dates from long before my time."

"But you had a lover who used it?"

Malinda stayed silent. She was *not* going to implicate Dog in this, no matter what. She had nightmares of him already chained up in a dungeon, tortured or mutilated. They might even try to shock her into some dangerous admission by producing him here.

The clerks' pens had stopped scratching.

"The inquiry will note that the witness refused to answer."

"Was that a question?" she said. "It sounded like a statement."

"How many lovers came to your bed?"

She thought she detected a shimmer of disapproval among the commissioners, although none protested. "That question is indecent and irrelevant, and I demand that it be withdrawn."

"It is not irrelevant, as we shall see. So there was a second door. Did you also bolt that or leave it unbarred for your paramours?"

"The secret door led through to another room and I made certain that the outer door to that was firmly bolted also."

"You claim you slept. When did you awaken?"

"Around dawn."

"Who or what roused you?"

The commissioners had come alert, all of them, and she suspected that all the foreign observers had, too. This was the story they had been waiting for, the mysterious palace murder that must have been the talk of all Eurania for months.

"A very bad smell."

"And the cause of that smell?"

"A corpse on the floor beside my bed." Yes, she agreed, it was— or had been—her cousin, Prince Courtney. Yes, he was naked, and yes he had been run through by a sword. How long he had been dead she did not know, but of course death had loosed his sphincters. In his final appearance onstage, Courtney had not smelled of cloves or roses or lavender.

Being unfamiliar with sword wounds, she did not know whether he had been impaled from front to back or back to front, but the chairman was careful not to ask her that. He and other inquisitors had arrived at the scene within minutes and had questioned her then; he knew that her statements had been truthful and her bewilderment genuine. Wanting now to brand her a murderer, he must allow her no saving denials.

"What did you do?"

"I screamed for help. For all I knew the killer was still there." It was a lame excuse; in fact the scream had been sheer reflex. "I unbolted the door to let my ladies in. Then they screamed, too."

"The secret door?"

"Was closed."

"And the outer door to the other room?"

"I was informed later that it had been found bolted on the inside."

"This was a few hours after your betrothal was announced?"

"It was."

"Had you agreed to receive your fiancé in bed that night?"

"He had implied he was planning to drop in. That was why I had made sure both doors were bolted."

There was a pause, as if the chairman was mapping out his route very carefully. He risked another question. "You honestly expect the honorable commissioners to believe that both the Prince and an assassin entered through a bolted door and then the killer went out again, bolting the door on the inside?"

"No."

"Inform the commissioners of the names of the lovers who regularly came to you by the secret door."

"Again I protest that question."

"Again I insist that it is relevant and your refusal to answer is to be taken as admission of guilt. However, I can inform the commissioners that the testimony of several former members of the notorious and disbanded Royal Guard will be placed before them tomorrow and—"

"What did you do to them?" Malinda screamed. "Produce the men themselves and let the commissioners see what—"

"Silence! One more unauthorized remark and you will be charged with contempt of Parliament." In the murky candlelight and under the brim of his hat, the chairman's face looked even more like a skull than usual, and the shadowed eye sockets directed their ghoulish stare at Malinda in warning. He meant contempt of Pestilence and Nightmare, of course: *behave or suffer.*

Why did it really matter if he painted her an assassin when he had hung enough other crimes around her neck to sink her without a trace? Why was he risking so much on this last accusation? Because in the eyes of the other ruling houses of Eurania, assassination was the great unforgivable, the supreme villainy, worse even than the trumped up charges of treason—all dynasties were rooted in treason if one looked back far enough. It was the false friend and poisoned kiss that kings really feared. If she could clear herself of this taint, then there might still be enough foreign outcry to save her neck from the block. It was a long shot, but the alternative was certain death.

"The witnesses affirm," Lambskin said, "that the accused accepted at least one guardsman into her bed every night. She herself has testified that only members of the royal family and swordsmen of the Royal Guard knew of the secret door. So now, mistress, will you admit that the most logical explanation of your cousin's murder is that either you murdered the Prince personally or one of your lovers did and you bolted the door again after he left?"

"That is not the most logical explanation."

The inquisitors flanking her chair did not accuse her of falsehood. The commissioners stirred and exchanged glances. She had won a point! Now the chairman would have to ask her to elaborate. However much he could and would make her suffer for it later, tonight she could clear herself of this, the most dangerous charge.

He chuckled mockingly. "I doubt that the commissioners agree with your peculiar personal logic." His rasping voice was hoarser than ever after three day's haranguing and badgering. "However the hour is late, and we are all anxious to adjourn. Guards, you may remove—"

"Wait!" said a shrill voice. All eyes swung to the Honorable Alfred Kildare, Speaker of the Commons, four seats to the chairman's right. "I wish to hear the witness's explanation."

The chairman scowled. Whether his feelings had for once escaped his control or whether he sought to intimidate the Speaker, he scowled most horribly. "I repeat, the hour is late."

"A few more minutes will not hurt." Kildare had withstood King Ambrose in full roar; compared to him, Horatio Lambskin was an ill-tempered butterfly. The last time Malinda had seen the Speaker she had called him a lowborn meddling upstart and worse; she had threatened to throw him in a dungeon in the Bastion. But today he was the only one of them with the manhood to do his duty. Good chance to him!

The chairman conceded defeat. "Very well. Witness, you will be brief. What in your view would be a more logical explanation?"

Malinda drew a deep breath and began to gabble as fast as she could. "First, my ladies found no weapon in the room, so I could not have been the murderer." It must have been a rapier or a stiletto. Dog's *Sword* would not drill a hole through an opponent, it would chop him in half. "Second, I am a light sleeper and would certainly have heard a struggle or a body falling, so the corpse was brought in already dead and placed where I would fall over it; furthermore it was lying on its back and there were blood smears on its chest, so it had been stripped after death—my cousin was killed with his clothes *on*. As for the locked door, it is common knowledge that the Dark Chamber has a device called a Golden Key that will open any door; whether it will draw a bolt closed also is something the chairman can discuss better than I."

As Lambskin opened his mouth, she rushed on. "There is no need to invoke conjuration, though. Prince Courtney may very well have known of the secret doors—he had been snooping around court for forty years—but it is absolutely certain that the Dark Chamber did, because its records go back before the palace was built, and therefore the most logical explanation of the paradox is that there is another secret way into one of those two rooms."

The chairman said, "That is the most absurd—"

"Let her finish!" Kildare squealed.

"Thank you, Mr. Speaker," she said. "I am grateful for a little courtesy. As a final fact to be weighed, I remind you of the legal maxim: Who benefits? What good came to me from that bizarre crime? Within an hour my own Grand Inquisitor returned with a squad of men-at-arms and carried me off, prisoner, here to the Bastion. The case against me is ridiculous, but the case against Horatio Lambskin, who was then Grand—"

"The witness is lying!" one of the inquisitors shouted at her ear.

"The witness is raving!" the chairman snapped. "Guards, remove—"

"Wait!" shouted several of the commissioners in tumult. Truly, it was a night of miracles, for the spokesman who emerged from the hubbub was the chinless Lord Candlefen, on his feet, flushed and squeaking with rage.

"Your evident bias is unbecoming, Lord Chancellor. I am quite put off by it, I must say. You have accused the witness of innumerable rather unspeakable crimes; it is only fair that she be allowed to, er . . . register a few remarks. . . ."

"Thank you, Cousin," Malinda said as his outrage dwindled. She could hardly breathe for the pounding of her heart; sweat ran into her eyes, making her blink. "You all know that Lambskin here was my Grand Inquisitor, a sworn member of my Privy Council. He betrayed his oath by plying me with false information on the strengths and whereabouts of both rebel armies, and probably in many other ways. He was eating out of all three bowls, and when Prince Courtney reneged on the promise of the golden chain, Lambskin had him slain and his body left in my bedroom to dispose of me also. He then claimed the chancellorship as his reward from his other traitor master—"

"Silence!" The chairman slammed his fist on the table. "The witness may denigrate me, but this inquiry will not hear sedition against our Sovereign Lord King Neville! I trust that none of the noble lords or honorable members supports such treasonous remarks?"

He glared to left and right, and the commissioners subsided into tremulous silence. The penalties for treason would cow anyone.

"I have not finished!" Malinda shouted. "I claim the right to make a statement in my defense."

"This is not a trial," the terrible old man said sourly, "so there is no such right. However, the witness will be provided with pen and paper and allowed to submit a written statement to the inquiry.

"Silence, mistress! One more word and you will be removed.

"Honorable commissioners, over the last three days you have heard the witness confess that even as a child she was in frequent rebellion against her father and liege lord, King Ambrose IV; that she gave her aunt, Princess Agnes, a conjuration that caused her death; that she connived at a massive deception to conceal the true facts of that murder; that she and the traitor Roland between them arranged for her father to be at Wetshore at a time known to his sworn enemy, the Baelish King; that she spoke with the Bael on his ship and obtained promises from him, and that he, having allowed her to disembark, then slew her father, the said King Ambrose of Chivial; that when Master Secretary Kromman was murdered shortly thereafter, she was cognizant of the killers' identity and failed to report it to the authorities; that she proceeded to Ironhall and bound a troop of half-trained swordsmen as her personal Blades upon improper authority; that while under her direction these killers caused the deaths of fifteen innocent people in Sycamore Square the following day; that she conspired with the traitor Roland, accepting money she knew to be embezzled; that she suborned the servants of the crown in raising a private force, although she was aware that this was a treasonous act; that she flouted a lawful command of the Council of Regency by leaving the place where she had been confined for her protection and coming into the presence of the King's Majesty, namely her brother, the late Ambrose V; that she deliberately shortened the child's life by withholding spiritual treatment from him in his sickness; that he died very soon after she had fed him his last meal with her own hand; that she then conspired with others to slay her brother, Lord Granville, and did claim the throne of Chivial although she was excluded from the succession by reason of her marriage to Radgar Æleding; that the confessed traitor Roland was treacherously assassinated here in the Bastion while her guest, but that she passed off his death as natural and failed to initiate a proper inquiry or hunt for the murderers; that in her unlawful position as ruler of the land, she committed divers acts, including the improper execution of her husband, the said Radgar Æleding, in a hasty and illegal manner before he could be properly questioned about the conspiracy in which they had joined; that it was by her warrant that mercenary troops sacked the town of Pompifarth, causing the death of hundreds of people and widespread loss of property." The chairman paused, and for a moment even he displayed normal human weariness. Then he rallied in a final burst of venom. "You have also just heard her peculiar explanation of how unknown malicious persons disfigured her bedchamber floor by leaving upon it the naked body of her cousin, Prince Courtney.

"Guards, remove the prisoner. The inquiry is adjourned."

40

I told you so.

SIR DOG

Back up the twisted stairway she went, back to her cold, cramped, and lonely little cell. The men-at-arms thumped the door closed behind her, clattered the lock shut, and doubtless then marched away. There was no sign of Pestilence or Nightmare, but a stub of candle stood upon her chair, flickering a tiny flame in the windy darkness, and beside it an inkwell, a quill, and a single sheet of paper. Exhausted, the Queen flopped down on the pallet and huddled herself up small to stare at this wonder.

The Chancellor had kept his word! She could write out her defense. She had only one page and perhaps one hour left on that candle; no doubt the paper would be removed at dawn, ready or not. She wondered whether it was Lambskin or his master who was so spiteful—whether she was being punished for slighting the grim old man or for the death of Granville. Neville might not be the master in that team, only the puppet. After so long in her solitude, she could not even guess.

The lock clattered again, hinges squeaked, and she cringed, fearing it would be Pestilence and Nightmare coming to carry out the Chancellor's threat to hand her over to "the men." They had not specified whether they meant the Bastion's professional torturers or miscellaneous ruffians. She had gambled that their intimidation was only bluff. They would gain nothing by maltreating her now. All the same she

was relieved when a single man-at-arms entered and closed the door
quietly behind him. He seemed no threat so she ignored him.

After three days she still did not know what the trial had signified.
That brief intervention by Mister Speaker—may the spirits favor him
forever!—suggested that Parliament was not totally under the Usurper's
heel yet. Alas, the powers of the crown in dealing with treason were
almost unlimited. More than likely the inquiry would wind up its
parody hearings tomorrow . . . approve a report the day after . . .
allow one day for each house to debate. . . . Probably they would
move right after that, before foreign governments could lodge protests.

"Five days!" she told Winter. "In five more days they'll come for
me and cut off my head!"

"Over my dead body," Dog said.

She hit the far door with a bruising crash and turned around to
scream at the apparition—not madness! Not that! *She was not going to
go crazy like her mother—*

He caught her in his arms and ended the scream before it properly
got started. He had sounded like Dog. His kiss tasted like Dog's. He
hugged like Dog. He smelled like Dog. He was much lumpier than
she remembered Dog; under his peculiarly flimsy cloak he seemed to
be studded with a variety of odd packages and hung about with a coil
of rope—but he was Dog.

Eventually they came apart one finger width. "You're all bones!"
he growled.

"You're all sharp edges." They kissed again.

"You're trembling."

"You're real! It's really you. Not a prisoner too?"

"Hope not. Brought you this." He fumbled under his cloak and
pulled out something that had once been a flower. It was badly man-
gled and smelled more of him than of rose; she could not see it in
the dark, but she did not need to. She choked on tears. "Oh, Dog,
Dog, Dog darling! No one has ever given me anything more
welcome."

"Better go now. Finish this later. What's outside?"

"Just a walkway."

He grunted. "How far are we from Rivergate?"

"Right above it. The walkway is, I mean."

He made a pleased sound. "Couldn't be better. Let's try that."

"But—"

He eased her aside, although she wanted to cling to him like ivy.
He did something to the lock, and it clicked.

"Golden Key?" Her voice was lost in the squeak of the hinges.

Of course there had to be enchantment involved when a rescuer appeared like this. *It was not illusion! It was really Dog!* "They have White Sisters!" That use of spiritual power might have been detected.

"Didn't meet any." Dog strode out and stopped to survey the iron bars overhead. Even as he did so, the moon fled behind a silver-edged cloud, leaving him in starlight. The wind ruffled his cloak, his hair shone like milk. "Was afraid . . . might have to kill some. Where does that other door lead?"

"Don't know." She was staying very close, unable to keep her hands off him. "The Rivergate's just below us." And if that conjurement he had just used had been detected, then the Yeomen would be on their way already. Tower windows overlooked this walkway.

He pulled off the lumpy cloak and the coil of rope he wore over his shoulder, dropping them both. He jumped, caught hold, went up, swinging his boots up to hook in the bars farther along. He clung there like a bat, face up and back down, with *Sword* dangling below him like an icicle. He grunted, came down again. "Any of these bars loose? Rusted? Need to move two, maybe three."

Her mind was muddled by shock. She could think of nothing except *DogDogDog* . . . loose, rusted? "Along here," she said, and took his hand—that big, hard, familiar hand—to lead him to the far end, where water dripped off the other tower and moss had crumbled the mortar. "Try here. I'll get the chair."

The moon peered out cautiously, just enough to give her a shadow as she ran to her cell and hurried back with the chair. Dog stood on it, peered, fingered. Then he said, "Stand clear!" and went up again. The moon vanished as if it disapproved, leaving him only a dark shape against the shining clouds. He grunted. She realized he was trying to pry bars loose, pulling with hands, pushing with feet. In a moment he came down and rubbed his hands, muttering angrily under his breath.

"It can't be done!" she said. "We'll have to leave the way you came. Let's go, love! Let's hurry, not waste time here."

"I would if I thought you could use the cloak. Here." He lifted his baldric over his head and handed her *Sword* in its scabbard. "Keep this handy." He went up again to try another place. "Must have been given these muscles for a reason . . . ah!" Something scraped, metal on stone.

She hugged herself, shivering, wishing she had her blanket but terrified to go and leave him again in case he vanished like a bubble. Besides, she was guarding *Sword*. Somewhere in the distance men's voices spoke loudly in the still of the night. Not shouting, not raising an alarm. Probably just changing the guard. Another bar scraped . . .

Escape, escape, escape . . . It might have taken half an hour. It felt like years. At the end of it, Dog stood upright to catch his breath, rubbing one bleeding hand on his cloak and hugging her to him with his other arm. He had pulled two bars completely out, but they were not adjacent. He had loosened several others at one end only and bent them down, but he had not yet made a hole large enough for an escape.

"Need more light," he muttered, and kissed her again. "They've been starving you," he mumbled when they broke loose.

"Not really. How did you get here?"

"Walked in the gate. Followed them when they took you back to your cell. We weren't certain where you were being held, see?"

"This is conjuration!"

"The cloak is. It's a Dark Chamber secret, but the College has copied it. . . . Lothaire stole one for us . . . not really invisibility, just unimportance. You knew I was there and paid no attention."

"I was sure I was seeing a man-at-arms."

"It does that." He hugged her tighter. "I'd put it on you and send you out, but it doesn't work for smart people. Ah!"

The light was brightening as the moon headed bravely for a wide expanse of black sea between cloud islands. Dog knelt to fumble through the cloak.

"Got more tricks in here . . . You're sure we're right over the Rivergate?"

She nodded, then said, "Yes."

"Going to send a signal . . . Got a boat standing by, but the Yeomen may get here first. I'll lower you on the rope to the dock. Do whatever I say, no arguing. Ready?"

"Yes. Oh, I love you!" She kissed him, but he cut it off.

"And me you." He stepped up on the chair and reached out through the bars. He must have thrown something down to the dock, because a moment later a brilliant flash lit the towers overhead. A ball of white fire sailed up from the landing into the sky, brightening the entire Bastion before it faded and disappeared.

Dog grabbed *Sword* from her hands, unsheathed it, and repeated, "Stand back!" Then he swung it against one of the bars he had bent down. *Clang! Clang!* Like a woodsman loping branches, he chopped iron, abusing that magnificent weapon, treating it like an ax. *Clang! Clang! Clang!* After the third blow there was a quieter ring as the bar broke off and hit the flagstones. But the racket must have been audible all over Grandon; and voices were raised now, candles flickering in windows, sounds of men running. Then a drum, rousing the Watch. *Clang! Clang! Ring.* Another bar fell.

"There!" Panting, Dog dropped *Sword* and grabbed Malinda in both hands. He almost threw her up through the gap he had made. Voices high overhead showed they had been seen. She felt her dress tear on a jagged end, found a purchase, doubled over on the ladder to haul herself up, and Dog transferred his grip to her feet, pushing her. She scrambled onto the bars and rolled to the flat top of the outer wall, which was four or five feet thick. She turned to help Dog and a coil of rope was thrust in her face. Then *Sword* in its scabbard. Then Dog himself, who did not need help. Voices were shouting all around, the drum beating. She heard the hard *thwack!* of a crossbow, but could not tell where the quarrel went.

"They're coming!" Dog said. "There, see?"

Moonlight glimmered on a sail. Heeled over by the wind, a boat sped toward the landing stage, and it was the most beautiful thing she had ever seen. *Thwack!* again and now the *clink!* of the quarrel bouncing off stonework, much too close.

"They're shooting at us!"

"Let them," Dog said, looping rope around her, under her arms, knotting it. "Lucky to hit a tower in this light. Got you. Go!"

Trusting him, she stepped backward off the edge and began walking down the wall. The rope cut into her ribs. It was hard to keep herself away from the rugged, abrasive stonework—she had not realized how weak she was. Unexpectedly her feet met air and she swung free, striking her shins against the capstone of the Rivergate arch. Then she spun, banging a shoulder against iron-studded timbers as Dog lowered her the rest of the way. She landed in a heap at the base of the gate. The rope went slack. She freed herself and jumped up.

The landing stage was a stone shelf along the base of the wall. It was closed off at the ends by the protruding towers and could be reached only from the Rivergate or the river itself. The tide was in, so waves slapped foul-smelling spray up onto the paving.

Time had stopped. The boat was coming, but painfully slowly. It had seemed much closer when viewed from above. She could see faces, though, and light flashing off steel.

Dog was visible against the clouds, climbing over the top of the wall, starting to work his way down the rope. Crossbows sang their death song, *thwack! thwack!* and the quarrels replied from the stones: *clang! clang!* Fortunately crossbows took time to reload. The archers were up in the towers, shooting, she supposed, at Dog. The great

Rivergate itself was still closed but even as she stood up, a smaller postern beside it swung open and a Yeoman ducked through and straightened up. Moonlight flashed on the spike and blade of his pike. She turned to flee on legs that suddenly felt like reeds. A quarrel rang off flags at her feet.

She came to the end of the quay, right under her cell, and there was nowhere left to go. She turned at bay. A dozen Yeomen had emerged now, and the leaders were on her already. A hand grabbed her arm. She tried to claw at the man's face and that wrist was seized, also, and twisted up behind her back.

"Take the bitch back to her kennel!"

They pushed her forward so she almost fell. That seemed like a good idea, so she let herself go limp, and as a result dropped to her knees. She screamed and went on screaming. She tried to kick, without much success.

"Behave, bitch!" one said. The rest of the troop arrived and got in the way. The two holding her hauled her upright, took her by the arms, and began to run her back toward the gate. She screamed, yelled, tried in vain to struggle, but they kept her moving. Despite all her efforts, she was too weak even to slow them down.

The boat caught an eddy of wind off the Bastion. The sail went limp, then rippled. Voices cursed. It rolled, momentarily helpless. Slowly it regained way, but it was not coming fast enough for the men on board to save her. Once she was through the postern, she would be lost. She was too weak; they were too many. They were at the gate. Feet stumbled on the unneeded coils of rope.

She looked up. Dog had stopped halfway and had somehow turned over, so that he was looking down at her and the Yeomen. He had his feet against the wall and the rope over one shoulder; he was stretched out from the stonework like some bizarre gargoyle. As the two men holding her were about to push her in through the postern, he howled at the top of his lungs and let go. It was deliberate—he threw himself down on them. Several of the men were hurled to the ground, including one who was gripping her. She went with them in a tangle of limbs and bodies and pikes. A couple were flung into the river. There was shouting, screaming, confusion. As the boat swept in, a dozen swordsmen leapt across the gap, some falling on the stones, two in the water, the rest landing on their feet. Battle was joined—but briefly, because a Yeoman against a Blade was a very unequal struggle and the newcomers had the advantage of numbers.

Malinda was not interested. She was on the ground, tending to

Dog. Blood was jetting from his chest, a black fountain in the moonlight. His eyes were wide, stark white.

"They're here!" she said. "You've saved me . . . Dog? *Dog?*"

He tried to speak and made horrible grating noises.

"What?"

It sounded like, "Told you . . ." but more blood gushed from his mouth and the sentence was never finished. It was probably, "Told you I would die for you."

"Come quickly, my lady!" Audley shouted. "Oak, Fury, get him aboard—"

"No!" Malinda screamed. "No! I will not allow this."

41

The invoked are in no wise to be trusted and assuredly will seek to bend the vaticinators to their purpose, for they hold firm to the desires they held at their dissolution, yet know not the gentler prospects of the living, viz., not pity, love, nor hope.

ALBERINO VERIANO, *INVOCATION OF THE DEAD*

Judging by its smell, the boat's normal business was something involving fish. Caught in the lee of the Bastion walls, crammed to the gunwales with the living and the dead, it responded reluctantly to its rudder, tipped dangerously as it scraped along the tower's masonry, and took several more hits from quarrels before it broke free to open water. After that it was out of danger.

Shivering, Malinda crouched on the boards with Dog a dead weight in her arms and his lifeblood cold all over her. No tears, not yet. Perhaps never. This could not be true. He must not be dead. It was some horrible illusion, some torture Horatio Lambskin had dreamed up.

"We must go to an elementary quickly," she said. "Dog needs healing."

Audley beside her: "He's dead, my lady."

"He must not be!"

"He fell on *pikes,* Your Grace! It was quick. But he is dead."

"No!"

He sighed and looked up at the faces gathered around. "What's the tally, other than Dog?"

Men's voices answered from the dark.

"Bullwhip."

"Reynard."

"Victor's missing. Could he swim?"

"Lothaire took a bolt through the gut, needs healing soon."

"Brock?" Audley said. "You bring those conjured bandages?"

"Be all right," said a shaky whisper.

"Mercadier and Alandale need healing too."

"Piers has concussion, can't be sure how bad."

"Jongleur's wrist is broken."

"Just sprained," said another voice nearby. "Nothing serious."

Then others still: "And a dozen Yeomen!"

"I only counted eight."

"Not enough of the bastards, anyway!"

More chorused agreement.

The words were slow to line up and make sense to her. So many men dead or injured. Just to rescue her. And many of the enemy, who had only been obeying orders. She struggled to free herself of Dog's dead weight; willing hands helped her. They sat her on a thwart, wrapped her in two blankets, and gave her a flask of strong wine to drink. The boat rocked on over the dark waves. The moon had gone, but the helmsman seemed to know where he was headed.

"Thank you." It was hard to talk, her teeth kept wanting to chatter. "I am very, very grateful to you all. I am heartsick at the losses. It may not be so bad, if we get them to an octogram right away."

Audley said, "They all knew the risks. They all came freely, unbound."

"How did you do it? I know Dog had a conjured cloak." Why had they sent *Dog* into the worst danger?

They were huddled around her, anonymous shapes in the dark, about a dozen of them. Some of the names she'd already heard were of much older men than Audley, yet he still seemed to be Leader.

"We knew we couldn't do it without spiritual help," he said. "Lothaire . . . you remember Master of Rituals? He'd gone back to the College. We got his help, and Sir Jongleur's. You may not know him . . . older knight, senior conjurer—"

"Yes, I know him." A pompous graybeard, and she had left him on his knees in the mud.

"Well," Audley said, "between them they provided us with all sorts of gadgets, mostly inquisitors' tricks, like that light and the cloak. Trouble with the cloaks is that they're pissy hard to use. Most people never get the hang of them. Dog did it first try."

"Why?" Why must chance be so cruel? Why Dog of all of them? Why couldn't she *think*? Her mind was a tub of slop.

"It needs a special sort of courage, Your Grace," Jongleur said. "The cloaks require total concentration, so any hint of fear in the wearers disables them. Sir Dog didn't seem to fear anything. We had him walk right in the Bastion gate and out again in broad daylight and the guards never batted a lash."

"Explains a lot," someone murmured.

She would never forget him on the anvil, calmly waiting for her to put *Sword* through his heart. Even their first kiss had taken courage after what had happened to Eagle. "Tell me about Chivial. I know absolutely nothing since I was put in that cell. Neville took the throne—I know that much, but that's all."

"Winter?"

"Smaile put him on it," Winter said. "*Lord* Smaile, the former Lambskin, who was your Grand Inquisitor. Suddenly Courtney was dead, Smaile locked you up for murdering him, and Neville was the only candidate left. Lambskin put Neville on the throne; Neville made Lambskin an earl and chancellor, and now he's running everything."

"Is he doing a good job?"

"No!" voices shouted.

Audley said. "There's a lot of unrest, Your Grace. They deal with it roughly—bloodshed, torture, mock trials, executions. Lot of peers are in the Bastion and others have fled overseas. Of course, you're the rightful queen, so nobody could do much while they had you in their clutches, but Blades are being hunted down—Snake, Grand Master, Felix. . . . Half of Parliament seems to have gone into hiding."

She recalled how easily Lambskin-Smaile had cowed the commissioners at her trial. "Has Eurania acknowledged Neville?"

The boat was into the Pool, now, where the oceangoing ships anchored. The helmsman changed course through the swaying forest of rigging; spray whipped over the boat. Lights twinkled and flickered.

"Some countries have. Isilond, for one. Some are still considering. Baelmark . . . They did end the Baelish War, but that was the new king in Baelmark, mostly. Now you're safe, we expect people to start declaring for you."

Civil war? There had to be a better way out of this. She thought she knew what it was. Whether she could persuade anyone to try it was another matter altogether.

"Where are we going?"

"To a ship. Thergian. *Seahorse*. You have a friend."

Even from the lowly aspect of the approaching fishing boat, *Seahorse* did not seem much of a step up. Winter said, "In Thergy they call this a *staten jacht*, Your Grace, a sort of dispatch boat. Also used by important people in a hurry." It was single-masted and sat low enough in the water to be boarded without the need for unpleasant rope ladders. A sailor on board dropped a set of steps, and Audley handed the Queen up to the deck in her regalia of two very smelly blankets.

A man bowed to her. "Welcome aboard *Seahorse*, Your Majesty. You do us honor."

"I am infinitely more pleased to be aboard than you can possibly be to welcome me."

"Sir Audley? You were not followed. I hope?"

"Not that we could tell," Audley said warily. "This is Sir Wasp, Your Grace."

"I should prefer to sail at once, if that be possible," Malinda said.

The Blades at her back were passing up the bodies. The crew was a vague group of shapes in the background, watching and waiting to see what decision was reached.

"Your Majesty will understand," Wasp said, "that navigating a winding river like the Gran at night in a half gale without a local pilot would be a somewhat desperate endeavor. We are showing no lights and you left no footsteps. Here, in a crowded anchorage, we should be safe from detection."

"No," she said, nettled. Did he think she was some halfwit female scared without reason? "The Dark Chamber has a conjuration called a sniffer. I have slept for the last six months on the same straw mattress. It should bear enough imprint of me for spirits to track me down."

"Your pardon, my lady. I was not aware . . ." He spoke in a tongue she supposed was Thergian and one of the sailors replied at length. "Captain Klerk says we can ride the tide and carry only enough canvas to maintain steering way, but we still risk running aground, and then we shall be in the pillory when the sun rises."

And then there would be more deaths. Too confused to make the decision, she said, "Leader?" desperately.

Audley said, "I think the Usurper will go to any lengths to recapture Her Grace. We must get our injured to an elementary soon and nowhere near here will be safe. Weigh anchor, if you please, Sir Wasp."

The man sighed and spoke again to the captain.

Malinda said, "You are still Leader, Sir Audley? This does you great honor."

"Indeed it does, my lady, but they are loyal to your cause, not to me. We are pitifully few now, the last of the Blades. We call ourselves the Queen's Men."

Wasp said, "This way, if it please Your Majesty . . ." He led the way aft—only a few paces—then rapped on a door. After a moment it opened and he stood aside to let her enter.

She stepped into darkness with Wasp and Audley at her heels. After the door closed someone unshuttered a lantern, then another and another. She screwed up her eyes against the golden glory. The cabin was no larger than her cell in the Bastion, yet it must occupy the rear third of the ship. After the night outside it seemed numbingly warm and bright with soft rugs, gleaming brass, fine paintings on the walls, furnishings of bright leather and polished wood. The benches would make into bunks; they concealed chests and cupboards. Important people were rich people, of course, and this was real luxury, all the more imposing after half a year in a stone box. Clearly the whole purpose of *Seahorse* was to move this cabin and its occupants wherever they wished to go. So into this sumptuous place came a deposed queen wrapped in bloodstained rags and stinking blankets, with her hair in rattails and a reek of wine on her breath.

The woman curtseying to her was Chancellor Burningstar in robes of sapphire blue. She rose with fury in her eyes and surged forward to clasp the visitor in a very informal embrace. "How *dare* they! Come and sit here, Your Grace. How *dare* they treat you so? I am overjoyed to see you free again. *You are hurt?*"

Malinda shook her head. Feeling dizzy, she sank gratefully on the bench and huddled herself in her blankets. Voices shouted outside in a language not Chivian, feet pounded on the ceiling, the anchor chain clanked.

"Then whose blood is that?"

"Sir Dog's," Audley said. "We also lost Reynard, Bullwhip, probably Victor. Lothaire took a bad one. A couple of others hurt a bit, but the rest of us came back still breathing. I won our bet, Your Excellency."

"You think I care about losing?" the old lady snapped. "I never thought they'd get Your Majesty out at all. Wine, Your Grace? Food?"

Malinda shivered. "Not wine." She hoped that they were taking proper care of Dog.

"Wash that blood off? Clothes? We have some garments, better at least than those."

"Not yet. Soon."

"Then what? Sir Wasp can produce any miracle you want on this boat of his."

"Ship!" he said sharply. He was around thirty, with lines starting to show in his face. Short and trim, he had the rapier look of a Blade, yet he did not wear a sword. What he was wearing was obviously worth a tidy sum, and she would not have expected any man less than a duke to own a vessel like this. Just the emerald at his throat would buy a coach and four.

"Ship then."

"If you can manage some hot soup," Malinda said, "I will believe in miracles."

"That one's easy." He blew into a speaking tube, listened for acknowledgment. "A jug of hot soup right away." He replaced the tube on its hook.

"Majesty," Burningstar said, "may I have the honor of presenting Sir Wasp? He owns this floating palace. He claims to be Your Grace's loyal servant and I can detect no falsehood in him."

"I am greatly in your debt, Sir Wasp."

He bowed low. "Nay, Your Majesty, I owe you great redress, whatever I can ever do to make amends." He took a quick step to catch his balance as the ship heeled.

"Please be seated, all of you," she said. "Sir Wasp, you are a Blade?" Why would a Blade have trouble with balance?

All three of them settled on the bench opposite her.

"I was, Your Grace. I would still be a companion in good standing if the Order had not been dissolved." He shot a smile at Audley. "I am honored to be included in the Queen's Men."

"I am grateful to them all. Where will you take me?"

"Drachveld, by your leave. Queen Regent Martha promises Your Grace asylum with full royal honors. You can be Queen in Exile while your supporters prepare to wrest your crown from the Usurper."

Again the awful prospect of civil war loomed. No, she would not go to Thergy. The answer lay at Ironhall. Could she hope to convince them of the truth she had worked out over the long dark months? Would she even have the courage to face it herself if Dog were here with her now? And who was this cryptic ex-Blade who wallowed in such wealth?

"Who was your ward, Sir Wasp?"

"Radgar Æleding, Your Grace."

They all watched for her reaction.

"Sir Piers told me that my father had not only allowed the Baelish heir to slip out of his fingers but also had deeded him a Blade. It was fear of ridicule, I am sure, that made him insist on keeping the matter so secret." Even male monarchs could make mistakes. She glanced around her other companions, especially looking at Burningstar, who claimed to find no untruth in the man, but who still seemed unworried. "You know it was my signature that bereft you of your ward, Sir Wasp."

"Not so, Your Majesty. I was released from my binding many years ago, under very unusual circumstances, but Radgar and I remained close friends. Until a year ago." The ship heeled, Wasp shifted position, and Malinda saw that there was something wrong with his left arm. He was not using it, and that doubtless explained the awkwardness she had noted earlier.

"Two years ago, my lady, when I was Baelmark's consul general in Drachveld, Lord Roland came calling with a proposal to end the war by a marriage between you and King Radgar. I took that proposal to Baelmark and talked Radgar into it. I *thought* I had talked him into it. When the day came, you know what he did." Wasp sighed. "Believe me, Your Grace, I was appalled! I had no inkling that this was what he intended. I would almost swear he did not know it himself. Even the earls and thegns were horrified at the breach of faith, and it takes a lot to scandalize Baels. For the first time in his long reign, his hold on the throne was put in doubt. If it please you, you may suppose that his treachery destroyed him, for I strongly suspect that his attack on Lomouth was betrayed."

"I am certain of it. Someone provided my cousin with money and information. The quarry was not I, but Radgar."

Wasp nodded grimly, accepting that theory. "I had always known he could be a hard man, brutal if necessary, but in all the years of our friendship I had never appreciated the depth of his bitterness against your father, whom he blamed for his own father's murder. You know the story, I am sure, so I need not tell it again. He was obsessed by that foul act. Yet one treason does not justify another. I broke with him over it, Your Grace. I took my wife and children and walked out of my fine house in Drachveld and went to serve another master. I told Radgar to—"

"What other master?"

A flicker of a smile lightened Wasp's somber mood. "The King of Thergy. We had a longstanding rivalry to see who could drink whom under the table. He usually won. I lost two royal friends in short order last year." Another sigh, a shrug. "So my sacrifice was not as dramatic as I made it sound. And Radgar never gave in easily. He sent me the deeds to the house and its contents, the papers of this ship, everything. I sent them all back to him. He sent them back to me. And so on. When he died, they were in my hands, so chance decreed that I kept the ill-gotten gains of my friendship. When I heard of your misfortune, I resolved to see what I could do to make amends, because much of the blame rests on my shoulders. I misjudged Radgar."

Malinda sat for a while, struggling to think her way through a thicket of weariness and sorrow and confusion. Likely she would trust this Wasp even without Burningstar's endorsement. He had an air of competence and frankness, of simplicity even, and yet there were depths to him. No lightweight, certainly, this friend of kings.

"You admit you were Radgar's friend, yet I cut off his head."

The former swordsman met her gaze steadily. "Should I seek revenge for that, Your Grace? From what I heard I had rather be grateful to you for ending his suffering. If I did want vengeance, would I not leave you where you were an hour ago?"

She nodded dumbly. "Then I gladly accept you as one of the Queen's Men and I am grateful to you for your service this night, as I am grateful to the others. But I will not go to Drachveld, much as I appreciate the Queen Regent's kindness in her own sorrows."

The other three exchanged worried glances, perhaps wondering what her captivity might have done to her thinking. They would have much more to worry about soon.

"Then where would you have us go, my lady?" Audley demanded.

Not yet. She must be certain. "First let me speak with Sir Winter and Sir Jongleur."

The lanterns had to be shuttered before the door could be opened, and it was several minutes before the cabin was bright again. By then the others had arrived and Malinda was sipping a mug of meaty soup, which seemed to boil all the way down her throat and burn through every vein. Sir Wasp had a skillful cook, although anything would have tasted good after prison fare. The cabin was crowded; she had moved to the chair and left the benches for Burningstar and the four men.

Winter's fingernails had grown in and his chin had sprouted a whimsical little beard, so being an ex-Blade must agree with him. He beamed when asked about Dian. "Safe in Ness Royal, Your Grace. The gatehouse is unmanned and there is not even a seneschal just now." He grinned bashfully. "She is counting the days until Ninthmoon!"

"Congratulations! I am sure Dian will be a wonderful mother. That is wonderful news." It was terrible, horrible news. It was going to make things much harder. "Sir Jongleur? Considering my intemperate language to you the first time we met, I am doubly in your debt for your gallant service tonight."

"Your remonstrance on that occasion was well deserved, Your Majesty. I am glad to have had the chance to redeem myself." Jongleur's beard seemed grayer than she remembered, and his left arm was in a sling, but he was as pompous as ever.

"You do recall the subject of our discussion upon that occasion?"

"The query posed in your letter?" he said cautiously. "Yes, of course."

"Six months in the Bastion have provided me with unlimited time to think over what you said then."

He paused a moment as if to plan his words. "I shall never again make the mistake of underestimating Your Grace's learning in the spiritual arts."

"I am only an amateur, but perhaps my lack of formal training allows me to see paths that have never been adequately mapped. And in my dungeon, I was free to let my mind roam, if you understand that expression."

He nodded warily. "Of course."

"A certain inquisitor once revealed to me that the Dark Chamber obtains prophecies, which it refers to as *readings,* by a sort of inverted necromancy. It summons the spirits of the dead from the future instead of the past."

"That is a gross simplification of . . . Your Grace has stated a very generalized view of a very complex process, which rarely works as well in practice as it does in theory. Few authorities would place as much faith in the procedure as the Office of General Inquiry seems to."

"But the point I wish to make is that spirits, unlike material objects, *can* be in two places at once! Minds *can* roam! Don't you agree? Please do not digress into the distinction between spirit and mind."

"We can agree that both may wander freely in space and time, certainly."

"So why is the translation Dog wanted not possible?" Alas, Dog's spirit was gone, disassembled, returned to the elements.

Jongleur seemed as genuinely puzzled as the others were. "You are talking now only of the *mind* going back to a specific date and time in the past, not a corporeal body?"

"A mind—a word—an idea." Malinda resisted the temptation to grab the man's broken wrist and twist. The ship was winding and turning as it edged its way down the river, but Captain Klerk was probably having much less trouble than she was trying to extract a straight answer from this pompous oaf. "Do go on, Sir Jongleur."

"The hypothesis would seem to have some theoretical merit, but I still believe that such a conjuration is impossible in practice."

"Why?"

Jongleur stared very hard at her for a moment. "You are still speaking of the dead boy, Your Majesty? You are not contemplating essaying this for yourself?"

"Just list the difficulties."

"There is a saying, my lady, that a little knowledge is a danger-ous thing."

"I could hardly have any less knowledge than I have managed to drag out of you so far. Are you loyal to me or the Usurper?"

Jongleur's plump face turned very red. "I am Your Majesty's man."

"Then answer my questions. Is what Sir Dog wanted possible or not?"

Audley looked completely lost. Winter was frowning, hanging on every word. Burningstar was probably keeping up also, for although the White Sisters' knowledge of enchantment was more empirical and empathic than theoretical, the former Mother Superior was a very bright lady.

"Even if it were," Jongleur protested, "it would be futile. When the subject went back in time, he would be faced with the same situation he had met before, so he would act in the same way as before, and nothing would change. Unless, of course, he was possessed of the experience and memories he had gained in the future. Since he has not yet lived that future, that cannot be. You create a logical circularity, and the Prohibitions of Veriano still apply."

Malinda said, "Are you familiar with Hoffman's Uncertainty Prin-ciple?" She saw Winter jump and raised an eyebrow to invite him into the conversation. "You are?"

" 'Chance is elemental,' my lady?"

"Meaning?"

He put a finger to his mouth and hastily removed it. "It's why no conjuration works perfectly every time. The Destroyer General doesn't always hit the target. Ironhall bindings can kill."

"But in this case, the uncertainty is an advantage. Right, Sir Jongleur?"

Hating to admit anything, he muttered, "Possibly . . . You imply that translation might not be instantaneous. True, there could be a slight overlap, a few seconds or minutes when the subject should be regarded as existing in both times. If so, he would carry a transitory memory of the future and of his reasons for making the translation. Do I correctly comprehend Your Grace's hypothesis?"

"Those few moments might be enough for his purpose."

"Perhaps so," the conjurer agreed, adding with a sour hint of triumph, "however—with all due respect, Your Majesty—the same uncertainty must apply to the overall translation, and on a larger scale. Even if we could invoke time elementals to carry us back, we cannot hope to aim them like crossbows. The boy would have had to revisit one exact instant in his past, because an hour too late or too early would make the exercise futile. Going back many years, as he wished, might introduce an error of weeks. Chance wins again. He presented an intriguing problem, but not one with any practical applications."

"That is the only objection you can raise?"

"It is enough, my lady."

Winter had turned as white as snow. He had seen the next step in the path.

"You have a suggestion?" she asked.

He gulped. "Necromancy?"

Sir Jongleur sat bolt upright, Burningstar muttered, "Oh, no!" and everyone stared in horror.

"The moment of death," Malinda said. "The deaths of many men occurring very close together. Instead of invoking elementals to *send* you back, Sir Jongleur, consider invoking compound spirits, the souls of the dead, to *pull* you back to that climactic moment. And, yes, you could trust their aid in this instance, because what you want for them is what they want—*a chance to live again!*"

Pompous or not, Jongleur must be clever to have won admittance to the College after a career as a swordsman. His eyes glazed as he weighed the possibilities. "You mean Wetshore, of course . . . But the risk, Your Grace! Invocation of the dead is the only conjuration I know where the enchanters stand *outside* the octogram. For what you propose, the—subject? the traveler?—would have to be *inside* with the reassembled souls. The danger of death or madness . . ."

"I am on intimate terms with danger. What other objections can you raise?"

"One spirit likely would not be enough . . . as you infer, you would have to invoke several, but those men did not all die at the same instant. You might be scattered. . . . Then there is the problem of a key, or bait, as it is vulgarly called. Some object the soul can recognize and crystallize around, something long familiar to—"

"Their swords?" Winter wailed. "It would have to be their swords. But Ironhall was sacked, Your Grace! All the swords are gone."

"I doubt if the swords of the Wetshore dead were ever hung in the sky of swords. Sir Lothaire will know. Assuming we can find them, *would it work?* I never loved my father, but he was a strong and capable ruler. Chivial has suffered greatly since he died and seems doomed to suffer more. If—and this is what I need to know—*if* the souls of the lost Blades can call me back . . . all I need is a minute! Just one minute! If I can be returned to the moment when I left the longship and walked along the jetty; if instead I can *run* along the jetty shouting a warning to the Guard . . . Surely if I just cry, *"Crossbow!"* to them they will bury my father under a mountain of flesh and Radgar will lose that easy shot. *All* our troubles come from my father's death. *One word of warning*—"

She had grown too emphatic.

"More soup, Your Majesty?" Burningstar said, reaching for the jug. "This is a fascinating concept you spring on us. Don't you agree, Sir Wasp?"

Winter and Jongleur were staring hard at each other. Then the older man turned again to Malinda, but now he spoke without patronizing.

"It is a terrifying concept! I need to think about this."

She found no satisfaction in being right, having had so long to work it out. "Time may be something we do not have! Lambskin— or Smaile or whatever his name is now—will be searching for me already. If his spies and arts gain him one whisper of what we plan, then he can block us utterly." Every day they delayed was one more day when Dog was dead. "The answer lies at Ironhall. When *Seahorse* has cleared the river, Sir Wasp, pray set course for Ironhall."

Into the frigid silence stepped Countess Burningstar. "Your Grace, you have just emerged from a terrible ordeal. A few days' rest to regain your strength will—"

"No!"

"Sir Lothaire is in grave need of an elementary," Audley said.

"We did bring conjured bandages, but he is still in great pain. And we have funerals to arrange."

"No!"

"Your Majesty," Jongleur protested, "you are proposing a major innovation in conjuration. I would expect to take *months* to finalize the invocations and revocations required, and many trials before it would work."

"You can have all night. Get to work."

Worried glances were passed around. Sir Wasp tried next.

"We lack adequate supplies for that voyage, even if we do not expect to return. Furthermore, although *Seahorse* is very close-winded, we should have to tack off an unknown coast, lacking both charts and pilot."

"Stop making excuses!"

Winter said, "If Lambskin has spirits seeking you, then you must not head for Ironhall. A day or two in Thergy will put him off the scent."

Malinda turned away from the look of horror on his face and felt her resolution deflate like a pricked bubble. "I suppose I am being hasty. To Drachveld then, Sir Wasp, if you please."

⌁

42

I just wish his wife wasn't quite so crazy about seahorses.
RADGAR ÆLEDING

Drachveld, the capital of Thergy, was laid out on a perfectly flat surface with the precision of a formal table setting. *Seahorse* sailed right through the city on a busy canal and continued a mile or so inland, to Sir Wasp's desirable waterfront residence; there she tied up at the edge of the rose garden. His house was smaller than a royal palace but few dukes would have spurned it. The designers' flair was evident everywhere from the water lilies by the dock to golden cupolas on the roof—wealth and good taste in perfect unison. Even a queen could be impressed, and an escaped prisoner who had spent half a year in jail was overwhelmed. Had she been compelled to find fault, Malinda would most likely have criticized an excessive use of seahorses as a motif. The gateposts were marble seahorses of more than human height; lesser seahorses appeared on china, towels, and cushions; in mosaic, fresco, and tapestry; as doorknobs and bedposts.

Lady Wasp, who greeted her guests at the front door, combined the beauty of a porcelain figurine with the sparkle of diamonds. Her earrings were jade seahorses.

Sir Lothaire and the other wounded were rushed to an elementary for healing. The other Blades set to the sad task of acquiring lumber and building a funeral pyre for the dead. Burningstar made repeated attempts to tuck Malinda into bed, but Malinda refused to be tucked. She greeted other members of the Queen's Men—Fox, Jarvis, and several she knew less well. Informed that certain other exiles driven from Chival by the Usurper dwelt in the city, she insisted on summoning them. She tried to help with the funeral preparations or at least assist Sir Jongleur with the incantations he was outlining. By the time she had been persuaded that her help was actually a hindrance, the pyres were ready, the wounded had returned healed, and the funeral could proceed. They let her light the balefire.

It took several hours to burn out, but she stood watch there with the swordsmen. Many of them wept, but she shed not a single tear. She could not regard Dog's death as permanent—she was resolved to go to Ironhall and revise the course of events. He would live again; they would all live again. When at last the evening shadows lengthened, Burningstar managed to drag her indoors and feed her. She still refused to go upstairs, or even sit down for more than a few moments at a time. She wanted to talk politics with Winter, inspect the conjurers' work, see to the outfitting of *Seahorse*—anything at all except rest.

It was then that Queen Regent Martha arrived, coming incognito and without ceremony. The two queens were left alone to talk and Malinda found herself talking—as she never had before, even to Dian—about the man she had loved and had now lost. The storm broke. She fell into Martha's arms and wept inconsolably until the recently widowed queen joined and wept with her.

She barely remembered being led upstairs and put to bed.

It was about noon the next day when she met with her council-in-exile: Burningstar, Audley, Wasp, Jongleur, and Lothaire, who was now healed but obviously still shaky. They were all grim-faced. Yes, the conjurers admitted, what she proposed seemed possible.

"The risks of outright failure," Sir Lothaire put in, "are less than the risks of disaster—death or madness. With respect, my lady, you would be utterly crazy to stand within that octogram."

"If I am already crazy, that halves the risk." Dog had gone into danger to rescue her; could she do less for him?

Jongleur had been up all night and was having trouble smothering yawns. "But we must have the swords and we don't know where they went."

"I am sure they were returned to Ironhall," Lothaire said. "The law required that. I don't remember them being mentioned. What happened to them would be up to Grand Master. He was hanged a month ago, so we can't ask him. Master of Rituals or Master Armorer would know, but where they are . . ." He shrugged. "Seventy swords? Even if they hung them in the sky without a ceremony, I'm sure I would have noticed. Most likely they were taken to the Forge and disassembled, blades and hilts melted down separately, cat's-eyes put in storage. . . ."

"The blades alone might suffice," Jongleur said without much confidence, "but the rebels may have taken them also."

"I know where they are," Malinda said. "When can we leave?"

Before she could be questioned, Audley intervened. "As soon as possible! If you are adamant that you must try this, Your Grace, then we must move as fast as we can. Sir Wasp, can we sail tonight?"

Wasp shook his head in disbelief. "Captain Klerk has not stopped gibbering after that trip down the Gran. . . . Yes, if we must, but why?"

Audley stared glumly at the floor, meeting no one's eye. "Because we have almost certainly been betrayed."

"Winter?" Malinda asked quietly.

"He or others. Jarvis and Mercadier disappeared right after the funeral. They may or may not have learned what Your Majesty proposes. But Winter certainly knew, and he has gone."

No one spoke for a long, hurtful moment. She had started with four Blades, and those four had seemed special even after she inherited the rest. But Abel had gone very quickly, then Dog, and now Winter. "I cannot blame him. He knows that if I succeed, Bandit will not have died, so Dian would not be a widow and the child she is now carrying will never be. If I can undo disaster for myself and my country and for the Blades, then I must undo good fortune for others. How will he try to block us?"

"Chivial has a consulate here," Burningstar said. "The Dark Chamber will have agents watching this house and your supporters in general. His hardest job will be to make them believe his story. Once he does that, then they must send word to Grandon and Grandon must dispatch troops to Ironhall."

"We can be there before them?"

Wasp sighed. "Depends how much start . . . But the wind is fair. Yes."

"Can we muster enough men?"

"Yes," Audley said, "but only just."

"Have you completed your rituals, conjurers?"

Jongleur tried to speak and was caught by a yawn. Lothaire nodded.

"Then let us sail tonight, and go to Ironhall."

43

Home is where journeys end.
FONATELLES

Newtor, the nearest port to Ironhall, comprised a dozen cottages around a fair natural harbor. It was much too small a place to support a livery stable, but it had always had one, secretly subsidized by the Order and run by a knight who was thus well placed to send advance warning of visitors arriving by sea. Ancient Sir Cedric, the last incumbent, had never had cause to do so. Now, with the Order dissolved and Ironhall itself in ruins, he had resigned himself to never setting eyes on another Blade. Common sense dictated that he should close down the business, sell off his few remaining nags, and go to live with his daughter in Prail, but either sentiment or inertia had so far stayed his hand. Hence his joy, that early morning in Fifthmoon, when a young man sporting a cat's-eye sword turned up on his doorstep demanding his nine best horses and no questions asked. As luck would have it, his nine best were also his nine worst, that being the exact number he had in the meadow, but he parted with them all most cheerfully and was almost reluctant to accept the gold coins proffered in payment. He took them, though. Later he noticed a small craft of unfamiliar lines heading out to sea and a line of riders heading off over the moor; he wondered what strange nostalgia drove them.

★   ★   ★

Much the same question spun in Malinda's mind. These men were not being moved by loyalty to obey her commands—she was certain they considered her crazier than Queen Adela had ever been. Rather, they must feel a desperate yearning for the Blades themselves, the old Order, the ideal that had shattered so horribly at Wetshore. If her mad plan succeeded, she might save them from that. If it failed, they would have lost very little. She, of course . . . but she would not think about that.

The Queen's Men, last of the Blades. They were down to eight on this final outing. The conjurers, Jongleur and Lothaire, were both in their forties, but the rest were youngsters, with Oak the oldest, at about thirty. Audley was not quite nineteen yet, although he tried to keep this shameful fact a secret; Savary, Charente, Fury, and Alandale fell somewhere between. Wasp had very much wanted to come, but the conjurers had forbidden it. He was too closely associated with Radgar, they said, and his presence would enrage the invoked spirits. While it was unlikely that they could escape the octogram to attack him, they might well vent their fury on Malinda.

The mood was somber as the nine rode up the gentle rise above Newtor, but once the sea was out of sight and sunlit moorland lay all around, Audley increased the pace and a mood of brittle humor began to show. Savary started a song that would not normally be heard in the presence of royal ladies, and some of the others joined in. Malinda wondered if they would sing on the way back tomorrow, if there was a tomorrow. It all depended on the swords. Had they been stolen or melted down or what? This whole expedition would be a futile waste of time unless they could find the swords.

Or it might be a trap. When they came within sight of Ironhall, Audley called a halt and sent Fury forward alone to scout. Malinda thought he was being absurdly cautious. Even if Winter had betrayed them, the government could not possibly have reacted quickly enough to have troops there already—governments never did. Even so, it was a relief when a chastened-looking Fury returned to report that the coast seemed clear. They rode back with him in silence. From a distance the complex seemed much as it always had, and only when the pilgrims drew close did their eyes start to pick out missing roofs and daylight showing through windows. Then an eddy in the wind brought a rank stench of disaster. All burned buildings smelled bad, and Ironhall had been so meticulously burned that many buildings had collapsed. Even the moorland sheep and ponies seemed to shun it, for weeds already grew in the courtyard.

Without a word spoken, the Queen's Men dismounted. Audley handed Malinda down. In silence the group walked up the littered steps and into Main House until their way was blocked by piles of ashes and fallen masonry. From there they could just see into the open court that had once been the Great Hall. Half-melted fragments of chain still hung from the blackened walls, but any swords that had been overlooked by the looters were certainly buried deep under the ruins.

"Come!" Jongleur growled. "Let's try the Forge."

The Forge was in better shape, because it contained nothing flammable except stacks of charcoal for the hearths, and those had not been touched. The tools had been stolen and windows smashed, but the gloomy crypt itself was little changed. Water still welled up in the stone troughs, overflowing into gutters, and finally trickling down the drain. The heaps of ingots and scrap metal were scattered as if someone had picked through them; they certainly did not contain seventy-two ownerless swords. The very few blades the visitors could find were obviously unfinished blanks or discarded failures.

"The spirits are still present?" Oak demanded suddenly, his voice echoing.

Fury, Savary, and the two conjurers were shivering as if about to freeze to death. No one bothered to answer. Instead, everyone gathered around the hole where the gutters ended as if to listen to its monotonous song.

"Surely not!" Savary said. "They wouldn't do that, would they?"

"If someone thought it up three centuries ago, they'd still be doing it last year," Lothaire answered, reasonably enough.

"It's what Durendal told me," Malinda said. "And he would know." But he had only been talking of one instance, Eagle. *They struck him off the rolls, dropped his sword down the drain, and impressed him as a deckhand on a square-rigger trading to the Fever Shores.*

Now she must gamble everything on that chance remark. Roland might have meant some other drain, real or figurative. Or that ultimate disgrace might be reserved for those who betrayed their loyalty—as, for example, by kissing their ward's daughter. Perhaps the Blades who rampaged and died at Wetshore had been seen as less despicable and their swords had been hung in the hall for Courtney's army to steal. She remembered the hole in the floor as being covered by a bronze grating, but that had gone. The hole itself was barely a foot across, too regular to be entirely natural, not regular enough to be completely artificial. What lay below? Did it twist down into the earth as a bottomless crevasse, or did it widen into a cavern?

If, if, if . . . If she succeeded, Dog would not be dead.

Charente said, "I'll get the chains." He trotted out and Alandale followed. Audley sent Savary after them, to stand first watch.

Charente and Alandale returned, weighted down with saddlebags that clinked as they were dropped. From them came long lengths of fine brass chain and a selection of hooks.

"Who's the best angler?" Alandale said cheerily. No one answered. It was Charente who lowered the first hook down the hole, and all the rest stood around him, listening. *Clatter, clatter*—no *clink, clink*. The hole swallowed it all. Oak went to help him. They attached the second chain to the first and began to feed that down also.

"Fasten something to the other end," Jongleur suggested. "We don't want to see the whole contraption disappear."

Lothaire fetched one of the unfinished sword blanks, knotted the chain around it, then stood on it.

"Anyone hear something?"

The running water sang its own song and no one would admit to hearing anything else. Soon there was almost none of the second chain left in view. The chasm seemed to be bottomless.

"Know something?" Oak said, puffing. "This isn't getting any heavier! It's piling up on something down there."

"Go to the end anyway," Audley said. "Then haul it back up."

"Your lead, Leader!"

With good grace Audley stripped off his cloak and jerkin. Alandale copied him and the two of them began to haul the chains back in. They retrieved the second chain, then about half the first.

"Listen!"

Under the chattering of the water, something rattled, clanged, and faded away. . . . When the hook came into sight, it was empty.

Jongleur stated the obvious: "You caught something and dropped it! Try again."

On the second try they failed to gain even that much satisfaction. By the third try, the chain was allowed to feed itself into the ground, which it did with great speed. It came out no faster, of course, but this time the hook emerged from the waterfall with a catch. Many hands grabbed for it—a rapier, snagged by its finger ring. The superb Ironhall steel was as shiny as new and a cat's-eye still gleamed on the pommel.

Fury ran it over to the nearest window for light.

"Suasion!" he read out, and the Forge rang with cheers and

whoops of triumph. Where Bandit's sword lay, so would all the others. Surely it was an omen that Leader's sword had come first? Audley so far forgot himself as to grab his Queen and hug her.

Her heart fluttered with sudden terror. She had been proven right, so now she would have to go through with this.

Necromancy must be performed at night. Audley ordered Savary off to Blackwater to alert the Order's agent there, if he was still at his post.

It took the rest of the day to retrieve enough swords. The conjurers said they wanted eight and then slyly withdrew to a quiet place to go over their rituals once again. The five younger men stripped off jerkins and doublets and took turns at the backbreaking work. Most casts came up empty, but not all, and each time another sword was recovered its name was read out and identified in a bittersweet mixture of sorrow and joy by those who had been friends with its owner.

Farewell? "That was Fairtrue's!"

Justice? "That was young Orvil's, wasn't it?"

Inkling? "Herrick's!"

Gnat? No one was familiar with Gnat. It might belong to some other century. It was laid aside. *Doom* the same . . . Malinda hoped that they would not find *Stoop,* which had been Eagle's. It was in there somewhere.

Lightning? "Falcon's."

"I'd rather not use that one." Malinda had killed Falcon with that sword, but they would not believe her if she said so. She ignored the puzzled glances.

They laid *Lightning* aside also.

And *Finesse,* too, because no one could identify its owner.

It was Malinda who attributed *Master* to Sir Chandos. Dian had told her.

Savary returned to report that old Sir Crystal was now keeping watch on the Blackwater road; he claimed his grandson could outride anything that ate grass and would bring word of any suspicious travelers heading west.

As the light began to fade, the swords stopped coming. Then Screwsley's *Leech* broke the drought. That made six in all. After that, again nothing. . . . The men took turns eating while others kept the hunt going. The two conjurers were shamed into helping. Malinda made herself useful with the tinderbox, building charcoal fires in the hearths, adding scrap wood and brush to give light.

They tried casting only halfway down; they tried different hooks, singly or clustered, but it seemed that the rest of the swords must lie either deeper than they could reach or around bends where their chain would not go. The men's hands were swollen by the icy water and cut by the chain; midnight was fast approaching, the best time for necromancy.

"It's useless." Jongleur said. "Six? Or seven?"

"Seven," Malinda agreed. She would have to risk Falcon. "Let's give it one more try!" She picked up the hook and kissed it. "Please," she said. "Go find me a man."

The weary men all chuckled, as she had hoped they would. She tossed the hook into the hole and watched the chain pour after it until stopped by the bar at the end. She even tried to start the pulling and was appalled by the effort required. Audley and Fury eased her aside and took over, but even they ran into trouble. The chain had jammed. More men went to help and managed to pull it free. Three times the same thing happened, and when the hook finally came into view, it was holding two swords—Mallory's *Sorrow* and Stalwart's *Sleight*. They had eight without a need to invoke Falcon.

"I suggest we take a brief break," Jongleur said. "We suspect that closer to dawn might be advisable in this instance. And we all need to rehearse our—"

Oak was on watch and now he came clattering down the steps; his voice reverberated through the crypt. "The boy's here! Says they're coming . . . about fifty Yeomen, right on his heels."

44

Seconds matter more than years do. One instant can change your whole life forever.

SIR DOG

"We must leave!" Malinda said. "We have the swords. Any octogram will do."

"Not as well!" the two conjurers said in unison.

"Not nearly as well," Lothaire added. "They will answer a call from here when they might not—"

"Besides," said Jongleur, "other people handling the swords will weaken the personality imprints."

"Then start!" Audley shouted. "No arguments!" That command was directed at Malinda.

It was crazy. The lancers might arrive before they had finished their first attempt, and a new invocation almost never worked on the first try. The Queen's Men would be trapped; she would be taken prisoner again or just quietly murdered. Flight was the only sane course. But Audley rushed her over to the center, where Savary and Charente were busily wrapping rope around the great anvil. She sat on it, then changed her mind and knelt instead. The conjurers wanted the swords upright; and as it was obviously not possible to plant them in the ground when the floor was solid rock, they set them in the rope binding. She sat back on her heels within a wall of steel: *Sleight, Sorrow, Suasion, Leech, Farewell, Justice, Master, Inkling.* She thought of *Sword,* which had been lost in the confusion and was probably somewhere at the bottom of the Gran. The men lined up as they had been rehearsed, one at each point; outside the octogram they should be relatively safe. Lothaire handed out the scripts. There was some cursing as the men peered at them in the uncertain, flickering light. For some clandestine reason, sorcerers always wrote spells on scrolls, which tended to roll up at inconvenient moments.

"I will summon Bandit to *Suasion,*" Jongleur said. "Please read off the names you are assigned."

"Sir Chandos to *Master* . . ."

"Sir Stalwart to *Sleight* . . ."

And so on around the octogram.

"Thank you. Face toward me, if you please, Your Grace. This is death point. You have your lines ready?"

She nodded. "Even if this doesn't work—and even more if it does . . . Thank you all."

"It is for us to thank you, Your Majesty," Audley said. "We—"

Jongleur cut him off, bellowing in a highly discordant voice. The séance had begun.

Malinda had nothing to do until—unless—the dead appeared. Not being sensitive to spirits, she might have very little warning. The Forge was cold. Its bizarre acoustics sometimes made the eight voices reverberate and echo, and at others swallowed them like a winter's night. The men invoked time, revoked death. They summoned the dead by name, each in turn. They revoked death again, invoked air and fire to reassemble the souls. On and on, singly or in unison, back and forth across the octogram.

She had memorized her invocation; it was very simple, little more than a plea to be taken back to the moment before the rampage began, before Radgar squeezed the trigger on the crossbow. That scene was burned into her memory—the Blades clustered around her father at the top of the steps, making him an impossible target, and then opening a way for her, exposing him. No one had thought of archery, Radgar had cleverly distracted all of them, as Durendal had pointed out.

He had been a despot, King Ambrose, but Chivial had needed him, his iron will, his supple hand, his very devious mind. One word from her would save him and see Radgar sail away frustrated. Princess Dierda would become Queen Dierda and produce countless litters of princes to secure the succession, while she, the disgraced Malinda, rejected by a common pirate . . . well she must just face a furious father and be married off to some other horror—not that Radgar had impressed her as a horror at all in the few minutes they had spoken. Queen Regent Martha had spoken very highly of him.

The fires were dwindling. The Forge was growing darker and colder, very much colder. Goose bumps marched on her skin.

The voices seemed locked in endless wheels of invocation, repeating and repeating the names: Chandos, come! Screwsley, come! Stalwart, come! Time had been revoked; perhaps it would never return. Heat had been revoked; she was freezing.

The chanting had faded into the distance and the trickle of water had stopped. The glow of the fires had faded away, and yet the Forge was not dark, rather it seemed . . . foggy? Was this what it was like to be blind? Even to recognize darkness must be a kind of seeing. Everything seemed hidden behind smoked glass, as if the very air were becoming opaque. She could not see the chanters, only . . . only eyes looking down at her. Disembodied. A pair of eyes, a faint outline of a hand resting on *Suasion*'s hilt . . . More eyes, to right and left. Behind her? Yes, some there, also, staring down at her.

Her mind went blank. She fumbled with the scroll with her invocation on it. Inevitably it rolled itself up; she unrolled it, and an icy breeze lifted it from her hand.

Traitor! The voice was no more than a thought in her mind.

"No!" she cried, struggling to remember what she must say. "Blades, you must save your ward—"

This is the traitor.

She betrayed us, said another.

They were faint, insubstantial, no more than reflections on water, clustered menacingly all around her, hands on swords.

Kill her. Take her mind. Twist, rend, scatter . . .

Icy touches, wind or fingers . . .

"No!" she screamed. "Save the King! Save your ward! There was a massacre. You died. Hundreds died." She had forgotten her text. She gabbled. "The baby prince died later and I was dispossessed." She wondered why the chanters were still wailing away in the distance. Could they not hear her screaming at the ghosts? "Take me back with you! Back to that moment and before. When I was walking back along the jetty—I will shout—"

Traitor, traitor!

Make her plead.

Make her scream.

She slew our ward. . . .

"I did not! I want to save him now, save you, all of you. Start again. I will shout a warning. You cannot shout, but I can. Take me back—"

Make her suffer, suffer, suffer. . . .

"Sir Bandit!" she yelled. "Dian was left a widow. She wept for you, but she married another man."

Dian? Must I remember Dian? That silent thought was Bandit's voice, all that was left of a fine man.

"Take me back to the jetty! I will save you all."

Ghostly anger.

Brothers, she also was our ward, our ward's heir. That was Bandit. *We swore, brothers. Let us trust her a little. If she fails us, we can still twist and rend.*

Ghostly murmurs of complaint . . .

"Yes, yes, please!" she shouted. "Quickly! To the jetty. The Usurper's men are coming."

She betrayed Eagle! That was Chandos.

"I didn't! Aid me and you will live again, the Blades will live again."

Let us do what Leader says, brothers. . . . That was young Stalwart. *Remember our oaths.*

A surge of giddiness, of nausea . . . Light? The fog brightened. A scent of water, the sea. A faint memory of rain. Grass under her feet.

And screams, screaming people, screaming horses.

"No!" she yelled. "This is too late. This is when you were dying."

Ghostly moans and wails of despair: *See, we fall! Madness! Shame!* The eight wraiths were still with her, figures of mist around her, and apparently too engrossed in viewing their own deaths to heed her pleas.

"*Take me back! Back farther, before my father died. Back, farther back . . .*"

Somewhere a new voice shouted, "Surrender in the name of King Neville!" and the distant chanting became shouting and clashing swords. The Yeomen had arrived at the Forge. More blood, more death. Malinda was in two places at once, two times at once. She was going to go mad. The conjurers had warned her. . . .

"*Quickly!*" she cried. "*Spirits! Save the King! These are the last of your Order, save them. Take me back to give the warning!*"

Brothers, we must help her! Again, that was Bandit, and then she felt Chandos add his silent voice. And again Stalwart: *She can save us.*

Another surge of giddiness, the anvil rocking, the grass moving under her feet, a misty rain in her face . . . A smell of the sea filled her nostrils, and she stared up at two brilliantly green eyes.

"How kind of him!" Radgar said angrily. "Such was not his opinion when we met twelve years ago. It seems he came very close to lying to you about our acquaintance. Would you agree that he was trying to deceive you?"

Too soon! The spirits had placed her back on the longship as it still drifted aimlessly on the rain-speckled water. The crew sat in silence, watching their king interview his new bride. The oars were spread out like wings, motionless. She could not disembark yet.

"An honest answer, my lady! Did your father deliberately hide from you the fact that he and I know each other personally?"

She heard her own voice reply. "Perhaps he forgot—" In some far corner of her mind she could still register the screams and swords, back in . . . in the Forge! Hard to relate to that and to this other place. Two places at once. Must not forget why she had come back. Soon she would disembark and warn her father that this green-eyed pirate was a monster. Must remember.

The eight shades would be no further help—*Killer! Monster! Oath breaker! Murderer!* They were still there, but now their attention was all on the hated King of Baelmark. *Liar! Deceiver!* They flitted and flickered around him in frustrated, transparent fury, slashing at him with ghostly swords. *Traitor! Traitor!* Obviously neither Radgar himself nor any of the crew could see or hear them as Malinda could. Her mind was being ripped in pieces.

"I am sure he did not!" Radgar snapped. "What other tricks did he use on you? What threats did he make to force you into this marriage?"

Again her voice spoke for her—the other Malinda spoke for her. "Your Majesty, I wrote to you! I testified before the—"

"Yes, you did, because I would not sign the treaty until I was given assurances that you were not being forced into a union you found distasteful. I must still hear it from your own lips."

Thwack! Clang! Those were the terrible sound of crossbows. The Yeomen were shooting through the windows at the men trapped in the Forge and at Malinda herself. The quarrels rang from the stones. She was going to die there. The last of the Queen's Men were going to be picked off like fish in a barrel, dying around her corpse.

"Your Grace . . ." The multitude onshore had fallen silent, staring at the longship. They did not know what was going to happen, which was, er . . . which was a murder. Someone, yes, her father . . .

"Why did you not wait for your two ladies to board?"

"My lord husband, why don't we sail?"

"Later!" he said angrily. "Because you knew they did not want to come? Because they had been forced into accompanying you? So what about you? You are happy at the prospect of spending the rest of your life in Baelmark bearing my children?"

"I am honored to wed so fine a king!" Could this man really be as bad as he was painted? Yes, yes! That was why she had come back! Back from where? Remember! She was fading. The real Malinda was driving out the wraith from the octogram. She seemed to be losing power. She wanted to scream. Perhaps she was dead. Was that Audley screaming?

"Oh, rubbish!" Radgar said. "You may be terrified or disgusted or shivering with excitement. You cannot possibly feel *honored*. I'm a slaver and a killer of thousands. But my mother was forced into her marriage, and I will not take you as my wife unless I am convinced that you are truly happy at the prospect. I think you were bludgeoned into it. Speak! Persuade me otherwise."

He was bullying her, just like her father. *"You call me a liar?"* Without thinking, she swung. Her hand struck his cheek with a crack like an ax; with all her strength behind it, the blow made him stagger.

The crew whooped and roared approval. The crowd ashore rumbled. She gasped with horror at her folly.

The wraiths had gone.

Radgar straightened up, rubbing his face, which was already turning pink. His eyes were wide with astonishment, and yet they shone with devilment. "Do that again!"

The eight had gone; the chaos in the Forge continued. Yes, Audley screaming, and Lothaire . . . and Malinda. *Pain!* . . . More dead. And all of this was ultimately Radgar's fault—

"Your Grace, I beg your—I can't imagine what—"

"Do it again!" he said. "Go on, I dare you!" He offered his face.

Dare her? How *dare* he dare her? *Crack!* Right hand last time, left hand this time.

The sounds of the Forge stopped instantly, and she had a sudden vision of History like a huge rambunctious scroll breaking loose and rolling itself up. . . .

Radgar had been expecting the slap, but she was still fast enough to connect. He reeled back against the side of the ship. Her hand stung. Spirits! What would he do to her?

The pirates cheered, howled, stamped feet, and shouted obviously lewd suggestions. The King reached out and gripped Malinda's shoulders. The marks of her fingers were clearly visible on his face, yet he was grinning widely, like a boy. "You have convinced me! No one bullies you into anything. Make a wake, helmsman! I have a bride to take home."

Leofric yelled, "Yea, lord!" and something else in Baelish. His mallet hit the rail, the oars dipped and bit. The ship leaped forward. Malinda staggered. Radgar folded her into an embrace and kissed her. He was not Dog.

The scroll, rolling faster, ever faster, ever shorter . . .

But the ship was moving! She had not done what she intended, but she had done enough. Radgar had discarded his planned assassination. SHE HAD WON! It was enough. Ambrose would live. There would be no Wetshore Massacre. The eight wraiths would live again. All of them would live. Dian would stay married to Bandit. There would be no massacre at Sycamore Square. Granville would never rule. Horrible Lambskin would never rise above Grand Inquisitor. Courtney would rot away in Mayshire. Neville would never rule. Malinda would never rule, but she had *beaten them all in the end!* TRIUMPH! Ambrose might go on for years. Dog would live again— she would never meet him and even if they did meet, they would mean nothing to each other, but he would not die for her. *Take back your life, darling, and find happiness. . . .* The man kissing her was not Dog, but it was with a sense of farewell that she returned his embrace, putting fervor and her heart into it. *Good-bye . . .*

Click! The scroll closed.

Radgar released her, eyes like green fire. "My lady, you honor me!"

"Your Grace, I am so ashamed!" Surely ladies did not behave like that when they were being kissed? What an astonishing slobbery business! And her fingers digging into him like that! What must he think of her? "I swear I will never—"

He misunderstood. "Don't swear! Any time you think I deserve a good whack, whack away! Always, always tell me when I am wrong, because that is what I need more than anything. Even the friends of my boyhood will not tell me what they really think now, because they all have too much to lose. Be my conscience, Malinda." He released her, but carefully, for the ship was pitching as it cleaved the swell in the open river, heading toward its two sisters. "Such fire can only be honored with fire." From a pocket he pulled a rope of rubies like a snake of flame. "I am sure these were stolen from somewhere, but they have been in my family longer than the crown of Chivial has been in yours."

"Oh, they are magnificent!" she said, completely bewildered by this extraordinary man and also annoyed that there was something niggling at the back of her mind that she could not quite put a finger on . . . something she must at all costs remember. . . . But whatever it was, it was good. Mostly good.

He hung the rubies around her neck and kissed her again. Evidently he wanted more of the tongue contact and hands-on-the-back procedure, so she cooperated hungrily. The crew cheered even louder.

Radgar paused in his wooing to glance back at the vanishing shore. "If you want to wave good-bye, Wife, you had better do it now."

"No! If you will grant me a single wish in all our marriage, Husband, it is that I need never more have anything to do with Ambrose of Chivial. I have paid any debt I owed him a thousand times. I despise him!"

"Well, that's certainly something we have in common," the pirate said cheerfully. "But you don't need my permission for that, my lady. Short of bearing children for the wrong man—and even that can be negotiated sometimes—a Baelish wife can do pretty much anything she pleases. I have far more important worries than making my wife answer her father's letters."

He hugged her to him and beamed at her. He was taller, but not by much, just right. A powerful man. "There's a wind coming, or I'm a Thergian. I have a carousel standing by off the mouth. We can transfer to it for the trip home."

"I don't mind a longship!" she said bravely, although the prospect was more daunting when seen firsthand.

Radgar chuckled. "I do! I was conceived in one, but I don't intend to subject you to that." He regarded her quizzically. "There is an alternative. If the weather does as I expect, we can be in Thergy before midnight."

"Yes?"

"Then . . ." He laughed and shook his head as if changing the subject. "Taking a girl home? You know, you make me feel like a boy again, my Malinda? *Mæl-lind*! You shall be my *Mæl-lind*!"

"Meaning?"

"*Mæl* is 'time' and *lind* 'a shield.' You will keep me young."

He was certainly not acting as if old age was a problem yet.

"What were you going to say about Thergy?"

"Ah. My consul in Drachveld has built himself an emperor's palace there—at my expense, of course, but he did a fine job of it."

"Seahorses!"

The coppery eyebrows shot up. "What about seahorses?"

"I don't know," she said, confused. "I must have dreamed about . . . It's nothing. It's gone. Carry on." It had felt like *relief,* so perhaps it was just the knowledge that this bridegroom she had been dreading for so many months was turning out to be a very pleasant surprise.

"As it happens, I just wish his wife wasn't quite so crazy about seahorses, but it's fit enough for a royal honeymoon. We could spend a week or two there—incognito, of course." His tone was wistful, almost pleading. His arms were iron bands around her. "Let you learn to be a wife before you have to practice being a queen as well. Drachveld's a fair enough town, a bit dull, but we could have a few days there to get to know each other and then perhaps have a proper wedding, with both of us present. King Johan and Queen Martha are wonderful people; I'm sure they'd love to be witnesses."

She studied his angular face for a moment, that juvenile gleam. She recalled Dian saying that eagerness never failed, and no one was going to question his virility. Built like an oak keel, her father had said. He *felt* like an oak keel.

"I thought we were married this morning," she said. "Do we have to waste time going through it all again?"

That was definitely the right answer.

"Helmsman!" Radgar roared. "Can't you move this bathtub any faster?" He kissed his bride again, even more thoroughly than before.

Yes, she could probably learn to enjoy this. Tonight she would find out what all the rest of the fuss was about.

Aftermath

The reading is that you will be Queen of Chivial, Your Grace, although not for very long.

IVYN KROMMAN, PERSONAL COMMUNICATION TO
PRINCESS MALINDA

It was a fairly typical Firstmoon day in Baelmark, which meant that the sleet moved horizontally, stung like needles, and tasted salt even far inland. The Queen's route home led her right into the teeth of it, so she could barely see the front of her horse.

Hatburna was set high on the slopes of Cwicnoll—a good summer home, but not the most comfortable place in midwinter. The family celebrated Long Night there only because it was more intimate than any of the formal palaces. This year, the weather had been so excessively horrible that they had lingered longer than usual, no one wanting to face the ride back to Catterstow. So why was she out in it now? Probably just because it made coming home feel so good. A plunge in the hot spring would definitely be in order, followed by a toasting at the fire, a steaming mug of hot mead and honey, and then perhaps roast boar with apple sauce.

She was returning from visiting Fosterhof, mother house of the many Queen's Orphanages she had established throughout the archipelago. She sometimes complained to Radgar that she had a thousand children to worry about. He usually replied that he found their own three more than enough and she shouldn't try to solve everybody's problems. But he never stinted when she asked for money for any of her causes.

Hands came running to take her horse as she slid from her saddle in the stable yard. She splashed over to the door, stamped in the porch, shook herself like a wet dog—of which half a dozen were presently trying to paw and lick her dry. Usually a servant would be there to take her cloak, but not today.

"Here you are, Mother," proclaimed a husky treble. "Hot mead and honey, just the way you like it. I put cinnamon on top—that's

351

right, isn't it?" Sigfrith thrust a steaming mug at her. Atheling Sigfrith was her youngest, five feet of juvenile cunning clad in armor of pure charm—red–gold curls, huge eyes of emerald green, a million freckles.

"Well, thank you!" Malinda accepted the drink; it was much too hot to sip at, but the pottery warmed her hands nicely. "You think I will feel better able to cope with your confession after I drink this?" Why was the young rascal wearing a leather rain cloak that showed no signs of wet? Why had he chased all the servants away?

"Confession, Mother? *Me?*"

"Well, I admit that you usually manage to make it seem someone else's fault, but I really would prefer to be sober when you tell me. You wouldn't want me to fly into a murderous drunken rage, would you?"

"Would you?" he asked with interest. Innocence shone in the jewel eyes. Maybe it *was* someone else's fault this time, whatever it was.

"Probably not. Where are we going?"

He pouted at being outguessed. "Over to the Old House. Would you like me to carry your drink for you, Mother?"

"Yes, please. We old folk are so clumsy." She resigned herself to postponing that appointment with the hot spring. "Let's go. I am getting more worried by the minute."

The Old House was officially used for servants' quarters, although it frequently became infested by the ragamuffin poets, artists, and musicians who swarmed around the throne. As she followed her hurrying guide through the storm, Malinda realized that it would also make a very good hideaway for a young atheling wishing to get up to mischief without his parents' knowledge. Fortunately, Sigfrith was too young to be molesting the servant girls. She thought he was. She certainly hoped he was. His brothers were quite bad enough.

The building seemed deserted, as it should at that time of day. By the time she had struggled out of her cloak and hat and boots, he was offering her the mead again and her favorite slippers, too, which normally remained in her bedroom. This was becoming serious!

The great hall there had never been very great, and after New House was built, it had been mostly hacked up into sleeping cubicles. All that remained was an artists' studio with a gigantic hearth and some large, glass windows providing a spectacular view of the volcano. Spectacular on good days. Today the prospect was of fog and a few misty pine trees. She could smell linseed oil, although she was not aware of any painters battening on the royal hospitality at present. She had certainly not authorized the enormous and extravagant fire in the great hearth. There was a painting on an easel.

"Like it?" her youngest son said gleefully. It was a portrait of Sigfrith himself, curled up small in a chair with two puppies and a kitten. "Surprised?"

"Astonished! It's superb. I don't recognize the artist."

"Thomas of Flaskbury."

She had never heard of the man and felt warning prickles on the back of her neck. There was more than a boyish prank involved in this.

"It drowns me in cute. Who planned the composition?"

"I did," Sigfrith said proudly. "We all did. See over here?"

He led her to two more easels, and predictably they bore portraits of Æthelgar and Fyrbeorn. Someone had gone to considerable trouble and expense. Æthelgar had the money, but only Radgar himself was capable of pulling this off without her finding out. This was not just a belated Long Night gift for her.

"They chose their own designs, too, did they?" she asked while her mind raced. She took a sip of the scalding mead.

"Oh, yes," Sigfrith said eagerly, too young to catch all the implications. "Master Thomas said he wanted to make us look just the way we wanted to look. He *is* good, isn't he!"

Obviously. Sigfrith and his kitten—Radgar always said that their youngest would never make a pirate because he would only have to ask for loot and his victims would give him everything they owned.

The pirate was their middle son, Fyrbeorn, shown in full war regalia on the deck of a dragon ship. At sixteen he was already taller and wider than his father, and the artist had made him look even larger. The pink fuzz on his chin had become a bristling copper beard; his muscles bulged. This was Fyrbeorn as the throwback warrior he dreamed of being, sword drawn, steel helmet, fearful green stare, the terror of all the oceans. With brawn like that, brains were redundant. Piracy was out of fashion these days, but he and a crew of young terrors were planning to sail off to ravage the coast of Skyrria and get themselves blooded as soon as the weather turned.

Æthelgar, the eldest, had chosen to be shown with a falcon on his wrist, standing beside his favorite horse and hound. In reality his hair was redder than that diplomatic auburn and his eyes not so yellow and he rarely chose to dress in such grandeur. To the best of her knowledge he owned no garments like that cloak, jerkin, doublet, ruffled shirt. . . . The artist had caught the inscrutable smile perfectly, though. Clever—or even sly . . . Fyrbeorn would take anything he fancied by brute force, Radgar said, and Sigfrith by charm, but Æthelgar would just prove to you he had been its legal owner all along. The sword at his side was a gentleman's rapier, a *Chivian* gentleman's rapier.

So why was their mother being let into this secret now? She skewered her last-born with a menacing royal glare. "Your father put you up to this!"

Sigfrith Radgaring was innocence personified. "Up to what, Mother? Don't you like the pictures?"

She eyed the gaping door to the sleeping quarters. "Radgar!"

He emerged smiling. There were depths to that smile. He came to her as if intending to embrace her, and she backed away a step.

"Explain!"

He shrugged, discarding most of the smile. "They were made for your father."

There were depths to that sentence, too—Firstmoon was churning the ocean like a cauldron. So why now?

"Shouldn't I have been consulted?"

"Twenty years ago you told me you wanted to have nothing more to do with him."

Had it been *that* long? Close enough. Those years had been kind to Radgar Æleding. There were few threads of silver in his beard; he was almost fifty, but a stranger would have guessed ten years short. In all history no man had reigned in Baelmark half as long as he, and even the fire-breathing terrors of Æthelgar's set were still loath to challenge the Ironhall-trained king. The moot always voted him a champion to fight in his stead, but he preferred to do his own dirty work—and the last contender had lost his right thumb in less than a minute.

Radgar shrugged. "I never promised that I wouldn't, though, did I? I have to keep up with what's going on in Chivial."

She shivered and moved closer to the fire. "What is?"

Of course she had not been able to remain totally ignorant. Dian wrote regularly—Baroness Dian since Bandit became Sheriff of Waterby—still popping out children with no sign of even wanting to slow down. Little Amby had died only a few months after her marriage and Queen Dierda about five years ago, still childless. Ambrose would be over seventy now . . . in poor health, the last she had heard. Things must have gone beyond that.

Radgar shrugged. "He wanted to see his grandsons. Durendal sent an artist."

"And a good one," she admitted. "That slime bucket is still around is he?"

"Roland? Still chancellor . . . well, he was."

"Why did you say *wanted,* not *wants?*"

Radgar hesitated long enough to convey the news without words. He did not say he was sorry. "About a week ago. He'd been failing for some time, but the end seems to have been . . . peculiar. Worth looking into."

She turned and walked over to the window to study the fog. She could not mourn Ambrose. After so long she could no longer find it in her heart even to hate him. She had done so once, but mainly for forcing her into marrying Radgar, who had turned out to be the finest man she knew. She could not imagine what her life would have been without him. He was ruthless to his enemies, yes, but infinitely generous to friends; a doting father and husband, yet so astonishingly self-disciplined in his own life that he often seemed indolent or uncaring. When the time came, he acted as required, berserk or icily rational.

However sordid her father's motives might have been, to bear a grudge for her marriage would be impossibly petty. He had let another man break the news to her, and that she would not forgive. Probing her feelings, she realized that what hurt most at the moment was purely selfish—her life had passed a milestone. She was next up. She had become the old generation and her sons the new. She resented that.

"Peculiar how?"

Radgar was right at her back. She had not heard him approach. "According to present information, Durendal murdered him. I find that a little hard to swallow."

"And who succeeds?" she asked, knowing the answer.

"You know who."

No! Ambrose was trying to mess up her life again, just by dying, and she would not allow it. "Chivial won't accept a queen regnant. It tried two and they were both miserable failures."

"You'll be different."

"In what way?"

"First, he's left you a land prosperous and at peace. Second, you're supremely well qualified. You've had practice. The witan say the country's much better run when I leave you in charge than when I'm around to do it myself."

"That's nonsense!"

"And third," Radgar continued, unruffled, "the House of Ranulf has fallen on hard times. There really isn't anyone else. Everyone expects you. They're reconciled to it."

"You put it nicely." But she knew Radgar always had his own

sources of information and drew his own conclusions. He would have made it his business to keep track of Chivian affairs. "And if I refuse?"

"No one seems to know. More women, I think. I may even be the closest male. I suppose the real answer is 'civil war.'"

She spun around to face him. "No! Baelmark is my home now. I am *not* qualified. I have a family to care for here, quite apart from the orphanages, the hospices, arts schools, and a dozen other important projects that will all crash into immobility if I take my eyes off them."

Radgar grinned. She had not presented a very convincing argument.

"Oh, they may put the crown on me," she said, "but there'll be all sorts of people lurking around trying to take it away from me."

Radgar laughed aloud.

"What is so fiery funny?" she barked.

"I know you too well, Malinda! If they try that sort of game with you, you'll turn the world upside down and shake them off before you admit defeat."

"Burn you!" she said. And burn that old blackguard Ambrose for dying at such an inconvenient time. A couple of years from now, when . . . *Ha!* She was overlooking something and apparently Radgar was, too. He had been hiding over there. . . . She turned more toward the draperies on the other side. "I shall refuse the throne on behalf of myself and my descendants forever!"

Young Sigfrith's eyes stretched wide with astonishment, but she saw movement in the shadows. Sure enough, Æthelgar stepped forth—slim, subtle, and sardonic.

"My sympathies on your bereavement, Mother."

Radgar scowled, but he should have guessed that their eldest son would know what was going on. Eels were brambles compared to Æthelgar. On the other hand, there was no use shouting for Fyrbeorn—he would be off fighting, hunting, or seducing; politics were not his sport. To Æthelgar there could be no other sport. As a child he had ruled the rat pack of Catterstow. He had thought to have himself painted as a Chivian gentleman, expecting that King Ambrose would see those portraits and perhaps display them to Parliament.

"Have you something to contribute to this discussion?" Malinda demanded.

He displayed the cryptic, conspiratorial smile that Thomas of Flaskbury had captured so surely. "I'm a thegn now. I won't be bound by your renunciation."

"And I'm still king," his father growled. "You'll be bound what I tell you to be bound by."

They scratched like blade and grindstone, those two. Malinda intervened.

"All right, Radgar Æleding! What solution will you impose?"

"I impose nothing on you," Radgar said softly, "as you very well know, my lady. But I have always believed that royal blood brought royal duty. Can you in good conscience let your homeland collapse into chaos just because you're too busy to bother?"

She shrugged angrily. "I have enough to do here."

For the first time a ripple of worry disturbed Æthelgar's serene confidence. "Any sword-wielding thug can make a try for the throne of Baelmark, Mother, but Chivial goes by primogeniture. Even if you bar me from putting in my claim now, my sons and sons' sons will always be a threat to them." He had worked that out years ago.

So had Radgar. He sighed. "I'm afraid he's right. Spirits help Chivial! If you turn it down, love, then we'll have to send them Snakeblood."

But Snakeblood wasn't old enough yet. Æthelgar was about the age she had been at her marriage, a brash but inexperienced child; like her then, he thought he knew everything. Burn Ambrose for dying just now!

"You won't consider abdicating and coming with me?"

Radgar laughed. "With my past? My existence will be extremely brief if I ever show my face in Chivial. Besides, I do want to put Fyrbeorn up here, and he isn't quite ready yet. You see that painting? You'd think we whittled him out of oak just to be King of Baelmark." A very fond, very stupid smirk disfigured his face. He actually kept the Baelish thegns on very tight reins these days, but Fyrbeorn inspired brainless attacks of piratical nostalgia in his father.

In Malinda's opinion, while that big lunk looked the part, he lacked the wits to rule Baelmark for long. Radgar's sons had shared out his talents between them, and she often wished she had borne more of them, just to see how many varied chips the old block could produce. None of the three could match him for versatility yet. Perhaps when they were older . . .

"What about Sigfrith?"

Radgar chuckled. "This one? This one with the big ears flapping? He'll get whatever he wants out of life and let the other two do all the work."

Sigfrith squealed with laughter and hurled himself into his father's arms, which was perfectly typical.

Radgar spun his youngest son upside down and deposited him gently on the floor. He turned to embrace his wife instead. "You don't think I want to lose you, do you, love? I'd come if I could."

"What do you suggest?"

"Give it two years. You go home to Chivial now; take Æthelgar with you and set him up as Crown Prince. They'll love him, may the spirits have pity on them. In two years he'll have the whole kingdom marching to the beat of his drum. Fyrbeorn will be ready to take over here. We'll retire together and live happily ever after."

She laid her head on his shoulder while she thought about it. Queen Malinda the Brief? Malinda the Unwilling?

"You promise?"

"I promise. Do you?"

"I'll have to think about it for a day or two."

"Can I come with you, Mom?" Sigfrith asked excitedly. "Can I?"

"In the spring, maybe. The sea's too dangerous just now. How did you hear?" she asked Radgar's collarbone.

"Durendal warned me months ago it was coming. I posted Ealda-beard in Lomouth with a fast ship. This morning he unloaded Commander Dragon of the Royal Guard on the beach at Catterstow, breathing and rational, if only just."

Malinda chuckled to herself at the thought of a Chivian crossing the ocean in midwinter in a longship. Even a Blade would not come through that ordeal unscathed. And she remembered that twice before in her life she had received bad news from Blades—from Dominic at Ness Royal when she was a child, and when Durendal came to tell her of her betrothal to Radgar. Well, she had *thought* it was bad news, and both times things had turned out well in the end.

"I might add," Radgar said acidly, "that if Sir Dragon is the best your father could find to be Leader, then either the Blades have slipped a long way from my day, or else it was past time the old man moved on."

"That makes you sound old yourself." She straightened up, kissing his cheek in passing. "Where's he now—Dragon?"

"Over at New House, eating the furniture until you return from your outing to unknown parts."

"And *Durendal* killed my father?"

"So he says."

Malinda sighed. "I suppose if anyone could outwit the Royal Guard it would be that one. Well, I'll think about it."

She was fairly sure she would agree, though. She could stand anything for two years, even the agony of being separated from Radgar. And she had a score to settle with Sir Durendal.

Note: The ensuing encounter between Queen Malinda and Lord Roland is recounted in the closing pages of The Gilded Chain.